Red Heaven

Nicolas Rothwell is the author of *Quicksilver*, which won a Prime Minister's Literary Award, *Belomor*, and five other books. He lives in northern Australia.

Red Heaven

Nicolas Rothwell

A Fiction

TEXT PUBLISHING MELBOURNE AUSTRALIA

The Text Publishing Company acknowledges the Traditional Owners of the country on which we work, the Wurundjeri people of the Kulin Nation, and pays respect to their Elders past and present.

textpublishing.com.au

The Text Publishing Company
Wurundjeri Country, Level 6, Royal Bank Chambers, 287 Collins Street, Melbourne, Victoria 3000 Australia

Published by The Text Publishing Company, 2021
Reprinted 2021

Cover design by Chong W. H.
Cover photo © David Pu'u / Getty Images
Page design by Text Publishing
Typeset by Typography Studio

Printed and bound in Australia by Griffin Press, part of Ovato, an accredited ISO/ NZS 14001:2004 Environmental Management System printer.

ISBN: 9781922458049 (paperback)
ISBN: 9781922459343 (ebook)

A catalogue record for this book is available from the National Library of Australia.

In memory of NS, brother spirit

'The morning cometh, and also the night:
if ye will inquire, inquire ye: return, come.'

I

Overture: Mont Ventoux

IT WAS LONG ago that I first heard old tales and romantic stories, on the drowsy afternoons of summer holidays, when my great-aunt Serghiana used to read to me, translating, explaining, interspersing her own brisk, judgemental comments—and though Serghiana is dead now, and the world she knew has long since vanished, the sound of her voice is still in my ear, and the books she most loved, their narratives invariably bleak, are still clear in my memory. She was a distinctly eastern figure, an exotic, the air of the faraway clung to her, even then I knew somehow she had spent her early life in Soviet Russia, a realm that seemed, in those days, quite beyond the pale—but the books she chose for us to read were invariably western, and she was convinced literature should be the school of life.

How majestic she seemed to me: all-knowing, self-possessed, at once charming and intimidating, swift in conversation, precise in thought. Her tastes in books and writers were eclectic in the extreme, her enthusiasms firm. She was fond of ancient histories, the darker the better, she tolerated memoirs if they were uplifting, but most often she preferred to read to me from her anthology of French mediaeval tales, which she regarded as eminently suitable for children, and to begin at the opening page, with the verse romance she prized above all others, the 'Châtelaine de Vergi'. The progress of this story is a familiar one: desire, deception, fatal end. The poem as a whole, though, is cast as an exercise in moral demonstration, a lesson made manifest by words. Why speak, it seems to say, why tell any story, why confess one's inmost feelings, when silence alone can keep them pure, and save them from betrayal in the bright parade of life?

The plot is quickly sketched. The central character, the Châtelaine, is the niece of the Duke of Burgundy. She loves a brave knight, the favourite of the court. He returns her love. In deepest secret, the two conduct an affair. She calls him to come to her chamber by means of an innocuous signal: she sends her little lapdog to play in an orchard. If the knight sees the little dog, the coast is clear. But the Duke's wife has conceived a fondness of her own for the knight. She approaches him. 'Really, truly, don't you know that I have given you my love?' The knight professes his devotion to the Duke, and turns away. The Duchess tells her husband that same evening that his special favourite is disloyal. 'My Lord, he begs me for my affection!' The Duke believes her, and is incensed. Interrogation follows. The knight can only avoid banishment by confessing the truth that lies buried in his heart, the secret he is sworn not to tell—his love for the Châtelaine. The Duke, astonished at this disclosure, demands proof. He must see with his own eyes. And so he too goes to the orchard, and hides, and waits. He too sees the lapdog; he sees the knight go to the chamber of the Châtelaine. 'And what then,' I would always ask: 'What happens next?' And Serghiana, depending on her mood, and the prevailing undercurrent of her thoughts, would make some quick answer, in sardonic fashion: 'Well, the human heart is made to break,' she might say, or, perhaps, 'Secrets always take wing, my child,' then sweep on with the story, the details that fulfil the plot: how the Duke betrays the secret stratagem, how the Duchess lets slip in cruel fashion that she too knows the secret, how the Châtelaine retreats to her chamber, where she believes herself to be alone. At which point this courtly romance, so similar in style and pace and setting to scores of others, departs from the formula, and takes on an urgent, impassioned tone. The heroine laments her plight out loud, and explores its bitter depths. All, she believes, has become plain to her. The knight has betrayed her; the secret he alone knew is on everyone's lips. 'Sweet God,' Serghiana would read on, speaking as the stricken Châtelaine, bending close towards me, her voice falling low: 'Sweet God, I loved him as deeply as anyone could love, I could think of no other, by day or night. He was my joy, he was my pleasure, he was my happiness and my delight. If God had offered me the whole world, and even heaven and paradise, I would not have taken it if I had to lose my love as the price—lose my treasure, my most beloved, my life!' By this stage, I could hear Serghiana faltering, struggling to pronounce each word. Eventually, she would break off. 'Now this is literature,' she would say: 'When feeling becomes form—this is art and truth, not artifice,' and shake her head, then begin her recitation of the Châtelaine's speech once more, her voice darkening, becoming resigned and solemn: 'God pity me and send me death—that death will itself be dear to me, since it comes to me from my love, so there is no sadness in my dying for him.' Serghiana, by now almost unable to speak, would put the book down in dramatic fashion, pause, and look up: 'You know the story's end already, don't you? She dies of her grief, the knight dies by his own hand, the Duke discovers everything. With a single sword stroke he kills his wife, he leaves behind all his wealth and the splendours of his kingdom, he becomes a knight templar, he sets off on a crusade, and travels far beyond the sea.'

And as I already knew the story well, from the earlier reading afternoons that summer, I would nod in assent, still unsure exactly what a crusade was, disappointed that the performance was coming to its close, awed by the intensity in Serghiana's recitation, and uncertain just what its cause might be. This was her cue. 'Let's join the others,' she would say, always with a pained expression, as if renouncing a special, private pleasure we two alone were fit to share: 'It's time. They must be wondering what it is that's kept us quiet over here so long.'

One afternoon, though, even as she was saying these words, she stopped mid-syllable, and looked at me again. It was a sceptical, assessing stare, and I can see her still in that moment: her angular, expressive features, her pensive frown, her smile, which was kind and mocking at once. Above all, though, I picture her eyes—hawklike, undying in their strength, dark, deep-set eyes that could convey any register she wished to express: amusement, indignation, world-weary wistfulness, a languid irony, contempt.

'How old are you now, in fact?' she asked me: 'You're growing up so fast.'

'Eight and a half,' I said: 'Nearly nine.'

'Is that so, really? A very cinematic age! I can still picture when you were just a little boy, in Arosa, or when we all spent the summer together in Tarasp. It doesn't seem so long ago. Do you remember any of that? The hotel, and the gardens, and the bridge beside the river rapids where we used to walk? I'll take you there again one day.'

'You're very kind to me, Great-Aunt Serghiana,' I said.

'Don't call me that,' she snapped: 'Why do you keep doing it? It gets on my nerves.'

'The grown-ups call you that.'

'I'm sure they do,' said Serghiana, grimly, 'and other names as well.'

'I meant it as a good name—someone better than a relative—closer than a friend.'

'Well! In that sense, then, perhaps'—she paused, and pondered—'perhaps I am. Perhaps I am something like a great-aunt to you, though I certainly don't think of myself as old enough to be one. But why not? As long as we're agreed it's an affinity, not a genetic tie.'

And she laughed, and tilted her head to one side a little, as if to get used to the idea.

'Yes, why not? I want to shape you, after all. Read to you, explain the words to you, give them breath and motion. How else can one live truly in the world, if not by offering the gifts of life to the young?'

'Gifts of life?'

'Books, of course. And this is what we should read next. It leads from the "Châtelaine", it leads on perfectly. We'll take a step ahead; we'll read a novel. I think the time has come.'

With a flourish, she reached into her handbag and produced a small, red leather-bound book and held it up before my eyes. I could just make out the lettering on the spine.

'La-fayette,' I said, carefully: 'Like the park in front of the White House.'

'How American of you! A different Lafayette: Madame de Lafayette, the first great novelist of French literature. I studied her when I was your age, and so shall you! Come closer.'

I perched beside her so I could see the first page.

'You start,' she said: 'Begin.'

I did as she instructed—and the book we began reading that afternoon has stayed with me as a companion ever since, appearing in a new light with each passing stage of life. The *Princesse de Clèves*, sole work of substance from the pen of Madame de Lafayette, is at once a graceful, well-turned romance and a study in psychological analysis. It is famous and much admired, it stands at the fountainhead of modern fiction, it pursues its themes of enrapturement and obligation in cool, almost glacial prose, the tale is simply told, with swift momentum, yet there is an enigma at its heart, a mystifying decision, a refusal that shapes everything—and when, in our reading of the book, we reached its central passages, and I felt Serghiana listening to me intently, eyes wide and solemn, I wondered what their special significance for her might be.

'At no time in France,' I read out loud, 'were splendour and refinement so brilliantly displayed as in the last years of the reign of Henri II. The monarch was courteous, handsome, and fervent in love...'

I looked up.

'Is it a sad story or a happy one?'

'All true stories are sad,' said Serghiana.

'And is this one true?'

'You could say that. Aren't there two kinds of truth? The story's set in history, it all happens a hundred years before Madame de Lafayette's own time, the plot turns on events that actually took place, everything in the background of the book is real—it's in the arms of reality, but all imagined.'

'So none of it's true?'

'It's all true if you believe it: let's go on.'

At least in its initial unfolding, the tale is simplicity itself. The heroine of the title, a sixteen-year-old heiress of great beauty and pleasing character, sincere, intuitive and modest, is given in arranged marriage to a distinguished husband whom she respects, but does not love. He loves her; her restraint and coolness inflames this love, and turns it into a passion, he is at his wife's feet, he adores her 'as if she were his mistress'. In due course the young Princess makes her first appearance at court, and is soon enmeshed in the play of factions and interests gathered round the throne. One evening, at a banquet in the great hall of the Louvre Palace, the King himself calls on her to dance with a majestic newcomer she has never met before. This is the drama's second principal, the Duc de Nemours. The scene that follows has the bright-lit quality of a dream or fairytale. Even before the pair are introduced to each other, they dance together, and 'a soft murmur of admiration' fills the air. Nemours easily guesses the identity of the Princess; she pretends not to know who he is. The stage is set for all that follows. The two meet often in company at court, they are drawn to each other, their feelings sweep them up in turmoil. At last, Nemours comes upon the Princess alone and is able, in coded, cryptic fashion, to confess his love. The Princess is overwhelmed. Fear takes hold of her. She is determined to remain loyal to the precepts of her upbringing, to be true to her husband and give Nemours no sign of her emotions. But her feelings master her—she feels herself on the verge of losing her self-control. She decides her only hope is to flee from court. Complex episodes soon ensnare her further: Nemours is injured in a jousting contest with the King and the distress she feels is visible; a misplaced letter she reads seems proof that Nemours loves another woman; subterfuges and deceptions and parallel plots multiply in dizzying style. Dark thoughts take hold of the Princess: she reasons with herself out loud. It is almost impossible, she believes, for her to find fulfilment in the love of Nemours. 'But even if I could,' she says, 'what do I want to do with that love? Do I want to allow it? Respond to it? Do I wish to enter into an affair? Betray my husband? Betray myself? Open myself up to the bitter reproaches and mortal pain that love always brings? I am vanquished by an inclination that drags me off despite myself.'

Several days after we had begun reading together, I reached this passage, and read it out as best I could to Serghiana. She listened, took the book, and read it back to me in a monotone, her voice very low.

'You see how trapped she is?'

'How does she escape?'

'She doesn't. She comes to realise that she herself is the trap. Her nature is the trap. Her longing, her love. Can you guess what happens next?'

The story has been presented, until this point, as a spectacle of secrets in plain view, a sequence of disguised episodes, of schemes and intrigues, played out in court galleries and royal apartments: looks and blushes, snatched words, brief whispers. Now, for the novel's best known scene and abrupt climax, the setting chosen is quite different. The lovelorn Nemours pursues the Princess into the countryside, towards her country house at Coulommiers. He loses his way in a forest. By chance, he comes upon the chateau, and sees the Prince and Princess walking towards a nearby pavilion. He hides himself, and overhears their conversation. The Prince is demanding to know why his wife refuses to return to town. She makes excuses, he presses her, she begs him not to force her to speak, he insists, she at last, in a few words, oblique and poignant as they are strong and candid, reveals to him that she cannot trust herself. 'I am going to tell you something no woman has ever told her husband—but the innocence of my intentions, and my conduct, give me the strength. It is true that I have my reasons for staying away from court, and that I want to avoid the perils that sometimes lie in wait there for young women of my age.' A thousand pardons if she has feelings that are displeasing to him; at least she will never displease him through her actions. 'Guide me,' she pleads with him: 'Have pity on me, and still love me if you can.'

Despite its brevity, the carefully preserved anonymity of its author and its refusal of romantic outcome, the *Princesse de Clèves* was a wild success when first published, largely because of the controversy this scene aroused. Would a woman ever tell such things to her husband?

Should the Princess be seen as a fool or as a saintly, moral creature? The dispute over her veiled confession divides readers to this day. The words she speaks in the quiet of the pavilion have swift and lasting consequences. The Prince, driven to distraction, presses her for details. In his hiding place, Nemours hears everything, and feels he has proof, at last, of her love for him. He is both devastated and lifted up by happiness. In guarded terms, he proceeds to tell his closest friend at court what he has witnessed. The story spreads. Soon it reaches the ears of the Princess. No one, she thinks, but her husband could have betrayed her confidence. She accuses him. He is aghast. Believing in his turn that she must be to blame, he 'sees nothing but precipices and chasms on every side'. Torn by jealousy and mounting suspicion of Nemours, the Prince decides to have him followed. Nemours makes lovelorn visits to Coulommiers, but is unable to speak to the Princess on his own. The spy returns with ambiguous reports, the Prince persuades himself that his darkest fears are true, he collapses into illness and dies. With that, the tale's final act, brief, and harsh, begins. Months pass with the Princess in deep mourning. At long last Nemours, through subterfuge, contrives a meeting with her. The two of them are alone. It is a time for plain speaking: she confesses the strength of the love she feels for him. She knows very well that both she and Nemours are free. Nothing except her enduring sense of duty to her late husband can prevent them from finding happiness, but still she turns away. She chooses solitude. She dismisses Nemours, with instructions not to seek her out, removes herself from court, travels to her distant estates, and enters a house of religion: in the novel's brusque final sentence, the reader learns that the span of life remaining to the Princess proved 'quite short'.

Serghiana closed the book. She placed it on the table before us, and clasped her hands together. Slowly I surfaced from the story, and became aware of the humming of bees from the flowerbeds behind us and voices nearby. Footsteps were echoing from the covered walkways; distant, muffled sounds of traffic came from the streets below.

'I feel a sadness when I come to the end of a book like this one,' she said: 'A dreadful, emptied sadness.'

'Why?'

'I don't know if I'll ever read it again, or in what place, leading what kind of life—or it may be that I remember the places where I read it before, in earlier days. And the summer's almost gone now—we're at the end of our time together.'

'What about next year?'

'Next year, of course, yes—but the future's hidden. We never know what lies ahead.'

'Why do you think that? Don't you mean to come back—next year, and the year after, and the year after?'

'Of course I do, but the years that lie before us aren't ours by right. If you knew my life, you'd see why I feel this way.'

'I only know the things you've told me while we've been reading.'

'What is the past of a life anyway?' she said, her voice gentler: 'Just a collection of events that don't quite hold together, and glancing incidents that don't make any sense. Lives have a shape in books. That's why we read them: that's their charm.'

'Doesn't your life have a shape?'

'My God, what a question! Who are you to ask me that—the confessor of my soul? You should be asking me about the life of the Princess. Why she acts as she acts. Why she fails to do as the storyline demands. To have any sense of what the answer might be, you'd need to examine her character, and remember everything the book tells you about her experiences, just as if you were trying to read the mind of a man or woman standing here in front of you.'

'Like a detective?'

'In a sense, yes—and there are clues to her decision. They're in the details of her life. Does she think back to the days of her marriage, and find she loves her husband more acutely in his death than his life? Does she feel her fate is somehow already decided, and there's a path marked out she has to follow? Or is she ashamed, because she looks back, and knows she fell prey to a forbidden love? Is that what makes her hesitate and tremble on the brink of fulfilment?'

'Maybe she didn't want to cause a scandal,' I said.

'But don't you see? That's the heart of everything. It's a freedom story. Freedom as threat. During all those months of grieving, while the Princess is on her own, she has the chance to change her life. How rarely that's given to a heroine: almost never. It's the whole point of the book. Everything else is just the build-up. She has no husband anymore, she has no family—there's no role left for her to play. She's in complete seclusion: she only has her own ideas and feelings for company. I see her as if she was standing on a stage, in a bright spotlight, able for the first time in her life to express herself—and she finds there's no desire she can give herself to, nothing she wants that she trusts to be true. But she wishes very much to be a true, sincere person. It's love that has bent her out of shape, and all she sees around her is the disasters love brings. I've thought about her and her decision and wondered about what lies behind it— many times. What about you? Don't you have a first impression? We've been pressed up against her and her story for days on end, as if she were a real person and we were staring at her through a window, spying on her, like all the characters in the book who spy constantly on each other. Aren't you curious? Why do you think she did what she did?'

'Sometimes,' I said, 'I don't even know why I do things—at least not exactly.'

Serghiana fell silent, looked at me in astonishment for a few moments, then shook her head.

'My poor child,' she said: 'When you're young you really should believe self-knowledge is the path to wisdom. Don't you think, in fact, the situation's quite strange? This is a clear book, a transparent book—and a famous one, as well. There was a time, not so long ago, when everybody knew it, everybody could discuss it. It's a treasure, it's still taught in schools, it's even been made into a film by Cocteau, God defend us—but none of the scholars who study it and write about it seem to understand the secret feelings in the heroine's heart.'

'And do you?'

'At first, of course,' she said, in a very serious tone, 'I was quite sure, just like every reader who picks up the novel and glides through it once, and finds it elegant, and full of grace, and admires the music of the words, and falls in love with it. I believed we should see the Princess as a noble creature, loyal to her vows and principles, and the book tells us that, several times, too many times, actually, as if Madame de Lafayette was trying to persuade herself. How strongly the weight of all that's right and fitting seems to be pressing down on the Princess! How caught she is—by position, by youth, by her sense of propriety. She can't free herself, she has to obey the codes, she has to stay within accepted bounds. But if that were all true, what would the story be? Just a social note. It's not, though. It's a deep, private tragedy. Two people, thwarted love. Love that can't escape to find its fulfilment in another. Surely that came through to you?'

I made a little gesture to show agreement. She swept on.

'All this only became plain to me when I was older, when I'd taken my first steps in life, when I could think for myself. I reread the book with more attention. I suppose I still believed it was just a sweet, romantic tale. I reached the scene near the end, in the townhouse in Paris, when the Princess sees Nemours for the last time. She says to him—it's just once, she tells the truth just once, for a second—I fear you will not love me always, I fear the certainty that one day the love you feel for me will die. Do you remember? Just those few words, and nothing more.'

'And that's the part that matters most?'

'Of course. It's the key to everything: it explains much more than her decision—her refusal. What she's describing in those words is her fear of life itself. She prefers imagination, and dreams, and the romantic books and tales she knew from childhood: art, form, elegance, not the murky, messy business of life as it's actually lived. The whole rich world of hope and promise is stretched out before her, an endless vista, a landscape of depths, of shafts of light and unknown shadows, like some receding picture background from the renaissance: beauty, mystery—and she flinches—she can't bear the idea. For her, love is a fatal weakness, a breach in the castle walls of her own perfection, love is a source of change and chaos and disorder, not joy or strength. And this is the lesson the book holds for us.'

Serghiana was speaking intently: her eyes stared into mine so keenly it was impossible to look away: 'It tells us that there's a secret in the hearts of men and women: a dreadful, crushing, all-consuming fear—fear of the world, a fear that's permanently present, permanently keeping us in check. Look around you. All these people in their summer finery, strolling so easily along, or taking their tea, waited on hand and foot. They look like the class of rulers and masters, don't they? They aren't. They're haunted by the same fear. They want stillness, they want comfort and safety. That's why they're here, cocooned in a resort—they're afraid of all the energies and the discords of life. And that's why we've been reading this book together, and not some undemanding book for imaginative children—so you can keep this in your mind, and never forget it.'

'The Princess wasn't brave, then? She wasn't a heroine at all?'

'The Princess was like everyone else, the same anguish was in her as in everyone; you see her fighting constantly against her instincts, until she doesn't know what she wishes for—and the turmoil masters her, it makes her recoil in the face of happiness, and she herself, by the story's end, has devastated everyone and everything she loves. Fear wins out— her fear of life.'

And is it so very fearful, I wanted to say—should I fear life as well—but I hesitated before Serghiana's watchful eyes.

'What made the writer think that way?' was what I asked: 'Was it her story as well?'

Serghiana handed the book to me, with a formal flourish, as though dealing a card from a deck.

'It's for you, to keep,' she said. 'To find the answer to your question, you would have to know Madame de Lafayette's life, as well as her book—and perhaps, one day, you will.'

*

Marie-Madeleine Pioche de la Vergne was born in 1634 in Paris, into a family of the provincial nobility. Much like her fictional heroine, she was brought up in seclusion until she reached the age of sixteen, when she made her first appearance at court and was promptly appointed lady-in-waiting to the Queen Regent of France. The circles of royal power were also the circles of learning—she came into contact with the scholar Ménage, who tutored her in Latin, Greek and Italian, developed a lasting fondness for her, and introduced her to the literary fashions of the day. This was a brief idyll. Once she had passed her twentieth birthday she was married off to the Comte de Lafayette, a widower almost twice her age. She followed her impecunious husband to his estates in the Auvergne, bore him children, advised him on his finances and mouldered away. During this rural exile she struck up the friendship that renders her life and character visible to later times: her connection with the French seventeenth century's best known letter writer, that artless, engaging *graphomane* the Marquise de Sévigné. Only four years into their marriage, Madame de Lafayette and her lacklustre husband discreetly parted ways. She returned to Paris, set up house in her old family home in the Rue de Vaugirard and established a fledgling literary salon there. Clerics, classicists and poets were among her regulars. Their recollections and surviving correspondence record the milieu and the time; they pay tribute to their hostess, and provide examples of her brilliance and wit. She had transformed herself into a woman of letters, alert to the nuances of every written or spoken word. She was prominent once more in court circles, she befriended Racine and Molière, she became a close companion of the King's sister-in-law. Then, at the exact midpoint of her life, her thirtieth year, a shadow, cast by a book, fell across her path.

The first edition of *Reflections; or Sentences and Moral Maxims* was closely read on its first appearance, and much discussed, not because of its content but because of its authorship: François, the sixth Duc de La Rochefoucauld, had been a celebrated military commander, a courtier, an intriguer, and one of the leaders of a great rebellion against the crown. His book, a slender volume, no more than a collection of sentences, dry, indeed arid, rather than epigrammatic, outlines a theory of human nature quite at odds with the spirit of his luxuriant age. It borrows elements from stoic and cynic philosophy, its conception of the world is openly materialist, the map it sets out of human motivations is virtually Freudian in its insistence on hidden depths: above all, though, its propositions are a species of dark poetry, the fruit of a sceptical, disabused intellect, a mind resolved to strip bare the pretences of civility, to seek out the essence of life's theatre, to follow its own intuitions no matter where they might lead, and chase them down to the bitter end. For all this, La Rochefoucauld's portrait of the shared life men and women move through is a subtle, graduated one: nothing in our world is simple, nothing is pure, not virtue, not vice either. Good and bad are so intermingled that fine, discriminating judgement is necessary to discern the forces that compel us to reflect and act as we do. The mind, in his conception, is an ingenious machine, a device to conceal man's nature from himself, and render existence bearable by a system of deceits. Self-interest drives us on, yet we regard ourselves as benign and generous. Self-regard blinds us to our true character, while self-preservation leads us to cast a veil over our eventual fate. There is something of the cartographer about La Rochefoucauld, and something of the dualist. 'Whatever discovery we might have made in the land of egotism,' he writes, 'There still remain many unknown territories.' His prose is sharp and crystalline: through its sheer transparency it reveals the ambiguities that our experience of life presents. Neither the sun nor death may be looked at steadily, he concludes—yet his *Maxims* close with a lengthy reflection on the end of life, and how best to meet it. It is almost the only extended passage in the book, and it reads very much as the author's bid to defy his own system. Reason as a trap, love as a lure, God as a nothing—the universe La Rochefoucauld paints is geometric in its elegance, and almost starved of light and hope. Such was the 'portrait of the heart of man' that fell from the presses in 1665, and caused a stir of thrilled excitement in the literary salons of Paris. Madame de Lafayette was careful to advertise her horror upon an initial reading: 'What corruption one must have in mind and heart to be able to imagine all that!' Privately, she was fascinated, and took steps to secure the company of La Rochefoucauld. So began one of the most poignant and unusual liaisons in literary history. Madame de Lafayette was a fledgling novelist with a decided fondness for romantic plotlines: even in her early writings love is a fierce, implacable force that holds sway over its victims; it shapes lives, accounts for actions, fills up the void in every human being. La Rochefoucauld's professed view of affection was very different. He was in his early fifties when the *Maxims* appeared. He was no longer the graceful, flawless man of fashion shown in the paintings and engravings of his youth. He had been gravely wounded in battle, a musket shot to the face had left his eyesight impaired, he was afflicted by gout, he had removed himself from the limelight of court politics to restore his shattered estates. By chance a detailed, closely observed description of La Rochefoucauld's character exists. It is a candid portrait: it is from his own hand. 'I have studied myself enough to know myself well,' he declares. He is of melancholy disposition, he is sometimes thought to be proud, but this is not so, he is merely reserved: he has principles, he controls his passions, he feels no ambition, has no fear of death: he is overly critical, he regards himself as circumspect, a secret-keeper, true to his word, a loyal friend. He has certain gifts in addition to his intellect and wit: 'I write well in prose and verse and if I were receptive to the glory that comes from writing I believe that with some work I could gain a reputation.' It is the sketch of a chilly, self-contained individual, a man who values accuracy above sentiment. There is, though, one soft note in the composition. He admits to feeling a reverence for women, he prefers the conversation of a gifted woman to that of men. 'They have a gentleness that is lacking in men, they express themselves with more clarity, and they give a more agreeable turn to the things they say.' As for love: fine passions, he feels, for all their disruptive impact, are not incompatible with a virtuous austerity of outlook; in fact, they can indicate a greatness of soul—and it is a source of regret for La Rochefoucauld that he, who knows so much about what is delicate and strong in the transports of love, does not believe this knowledge will ever pass from his mind to his heart.

This self-depiction made a strong case for its author to Madame de Lafayette. The two crossed paths in Paris salons. They began to spend their days together: a bond was formed between them—and the influence of La Rochefoucauld is evident all through the unfolding narrative of the *Princesse de Clèves*. Many of the book's early readers believed him to be its co-author, at the very least, but his impact on the thought and writing of the true author was both more subtle and more profound. He is very plainly there, as hero: the Nemours who makes his dramatic entry at the Louvre Palace banquet in the novel's early pages is a figure drawn in the image of La Rochefoucauld: high-born, dazzling, debonair, a man of presence, central to the schemes and intrigues of the court. Nemours is portrayed as reflective, his cast of mind is analytical, but it is his own condition that he most often probes and calls in question. He is proud, and somewhat aloof. He has been a seducer, his reputation as a lover of noble women is well established, yet he has no experience of the torments of true love that lie in wait for him as the plot unfolds. Like La Rochefoucauld, the Nemours of the book is skilled in arms and diplomacy, he is repeatedly dispatched on important foreign missions, he is a close confidant of the crown. The episode of the misplaced letter the Princess reads is based on a scandal La Rochefoucauld witnessed and describes in detail in the memoir he devoted to his early life.

Far more telling than these appropriations, though, is the influence on Madame de Lafayette of La Rochefoucauld's system—his ideas, the flavour of his thought. The *Princesse de Clèves* swiftly reveals itself as the product of two outlooks colliding, interpenetrating. It begins as a conventional story of romance, it is engineered with care to yield this outcome, the characters are stock figures, they seem at first like beings in a tapestry, surrounded by the raiment and the splendour of the court. But another pattern, darker, harsher, emerges: the narration is cool, and cooler still when the emotions are hot. Even as the Princess is plunged into the cauldron of her love for Nemours, she struggles to observe and gauge her feelings, to understand them and master them through force of will—and the watching author casts her own dispassionate gaze on both heroine and hero, recording their manoeuvres as they seek an escape from the trap she herself has set. Just as in the *Maxims* nothing is wholly pure or polluted and every human quality partakes of intermingled opposites, so too in the novel characters find themselves assailed by competing impulses and by emotions they recognise as inconsistent. Here is the Princess, on hearing the first declaration of love from Nemours, in words obliquely coded but clear at once to her: 'She felt she should respond and not let those words go unchallenged; at the same time she felt she should not listen or give any sign she took them to refer to her. She felt she should speak; she felt she should stay silent. What Nemours had said pleased her and offended her almost equally.' Here, too, is her husband, the Prince, consumed by contradictory feelings and confessing his predicament to the wife he loves: 'I have fallen prey to violent, shifting emotions which I cannot master. I no longer see myself as worthy of you, you no longer seem worthy of me; I adore you, I hate you; I offend you, I beg for your forgiveness; I admire you, I am ashamed of my admiration. Within me there remains no trace of reason or tranquillity.' It is La Rochefoucauld's version of the human heart—utterly divided. In the slow transformation of the two chief characters over the novel's course, the dance of opposing outlooks is just as clear. The Princess embarks on her life in court as a child bride, at the mercy of her feelings. By the end of the story she has felt love's destructive force, her reason has prevailed, she sees love as temptation, a mirage, she has freed herself from its sway and brought down the curtain on her life. Nemours, whose worldly glamour and self-mastery are apparent as the novel opens, becomes progressively more enslaved by his emotions—his love devours him, he loses his purchase on himself, no hope remains to animate him, he is a wraith-like figure by the story's end. And in this way a sombre tale is fashioned, a work of balance, a keepsake that serves as memorial to the tie between La Rochefoucauld and Madame de Lafayette. Her view of him is in her book; his of her lies in a brief word portrait, anonymous, but ascribed to La Rochefoucauld: its poised style makes the attribution sure. Few love letters are as devoted, or as restrained. How to describe her? Her manner is at once noble, modest, natural and self-possessed. Her blue eyes are calm and lovely, but that calm is the calm of a composed and independent being. By temperament she is melancholy, she prefers to be alone, she is bored by banquets and grand assemblies, books are her favourite province, yet there is no one more charming once in company, no one more able to accommodate herself to those she meets. Swift in understanding, free in imagination, a writer by nature, not through art and effort, she would be flawless, were it not for one strange attribute: she has an invincible aversion to anyone who likes or cares for her—there is in her a hatred of being loved.

For several years the two lived in discreet association. Mentions of La Rochefoucauld in the surviving letters of their circle are rare. His core was reticence and privacy; her special style was a brilliance of surface that masked her depths. She said that he had brought her intellect, and she had reformed his heart. In his correspondence he chose a single word to portray her character: it was true. Truth, discretion, intellect— pure ideals in a world of artifice and show. Events provided a stern test for La Rochefoucauld's philosophy. On June the fourteenth, 1672, death's solar flare blazed for all in their social circle to see. Madame de Sévigné was present at the Lafayette salon when word reached Paris of the French army's crossing of the Rhine. There had been heavy losses, among them two of La Rochefoucauld's sons. 'That hail-storm's blows struck him in my presence,' wrote Sévigné to her daughter: 'The tears flowed in his heart, but his strength and courage kept them from his eyes.' His own death, when it came, was equally in character: a new version of the last of his maxims, austere, correct. The literary-minded Bishop Bossuet was summoned to provide extreme unction, though nothing in La Rochefoucauld's works suggests the slightest interest in religion or belief in an afterlife. He refused to let Madame de Lafayette see him as he neared his end. With him gone, she fell into a despair that her nature only magnified. Her grief was very much like that of the Princess in her novel: it consumed her, it fed on itself, its unusual quality struck even Madame de Sévigné: 'She has descended from the clouds, she never forgets for a moment what a loss she has suffered; she no longer knows what to do with herself, indeed she is no longer the same person, but completely changed, she thinks only of removing all thought from her mind. Time, which is so kind to others, only increases, as it will continue to increase, her sadness until the end.'

Such was the life of the writer whose book Serghiana and I had read through in the mountains with so much attention and care.

*

Years went by before memories of those days of summer came back to me. I was far from the Swiss Alps by then: I had been sent to a New Hampshire boarding school. One weekend afternoon I was in the Founder's Library, alone. The shelves were full of newly published titles, all untouched. There were serious-looking novels, and thick biographies, there were dictionaries, atlases and encyclopaedias: nothing familiar, though, nothing vivid or appealing at all. Eventually my eyes fell on an old paperback, lying off to one side: it was a Signet Classic, worn and scuffed. The cover illustration showed a young woman with flame-red hair, wearing a ruff-collared dress of mist-grey: her hands were crossed protectively before her, her face was turned to one side, her eyes were shut. Behind her, half in shadow, stood an unsmiling figure, more assassin than admiring suitor: there was a gold chain on his black doublet, he had a Jacobean beard and moustache, his expression was hard and cold. I looked more closely, and saw the author's name in faded type on the cover: Madame de Lafayette. It was a translation of the *Princesse de Clèves*. I took it and started to leaf through it: the spine promptly broke in two. I glanced down at the pages opened for me in this unusual fashion, and began to read. 'While they were out stag

21

hunting, Nemours became lost in the forest.' It was the scene in which Nemours finds his way, almost by accident, to the country house in Coulommiers, and overhears the Princess making her veiled confession to her husband. I read on for several pages, and my thoughts flew back to my first encounter with the book, and to Serghiana, who had loomed so large in my life in those years of childhood. She had receded from my world: she moved in different circles now; I saw her name from time to time in newspaper reports from overseas. How determined she had been that I should remember the *Princesse de Clèves*, and Madame de Lafayette, and pay attention to the lessons buried in the work! I smiled at the idea, and at the insistent way things we leave behind come back to us unbidden. Everything I read in those pages seemed suddenly familiar: the jousting tournament, the king's death, the ensuing coronation ceremony, the sense of devastation and exhaustion at the story's end.

I was lounging in the cushioned window bay when the library door opened. One of the junior masters, a young man who taught me, and whose lessons I greatly looked forward to, swept in and flung himself down in an armchair. He saw me, and twisted round.

'Oh, it's you,' he said: 'Hi, guy.'

'Hello, sir,' I said, carefully.

'Well, hello to you, too.'

He came over, a friendly expression on his face.

'What are you doing here?' he said. 'I'm surprised to find anyone—the whole place is deserted. The long weekend. Don't you have a home to go to? What are you reading, anyhow?'

He reached down, and prised the paperback from me, and smiled, with a little nod, rather like a doctor noticing the first symptoms of an infectious disease.

'French classic literature. Wow! But that's right, you come from over there, don't you, from France?'

'Not exactly,' I said: 'More Central Europe.'

'Well, it's all the same cultural continuum, isn't it? At least that's what we tell everyone: cathedrals, good food, cobbled streets.'

The food's actually not that good where I come from, I was going to say, but I stopped, unsure where would be my point of origin from a strictly gastronomic perspective, and feeling that it would be disloyal to air this view. He thumbed through the book, which was in grave danger of shedding some of its pages, and brandished it before me.

'Pretty antique, isn't it?'

'In several senses of the word,' I said.

'I'd never have read something like this myself, of course, at least not for pleasure, maybe for some godforsaken college paper or exam—and certainly not now.'

'What would you read?' I asked, dropping the honorific, and he glanced at me for a second, and ignored this little liberty.

'How old are you, anyway?'

I told him, and countered: 'And how old are you?'

'I'm twenty-eight,' he said: 'More than twice you! But you're old enough to read responsibly—constructively—to build yourself by reading, aren't you? Although I have to say every time I reread something I read before when I was much younger I realise very quickly that I just didn't understand it at all.'

'That's what you find? Every time?'

'Absolutely—yes!'

This with great emphasis, as though the business of ageing and the passage of time had brought him a series of shocking revelations. He shook his head.

'Youthful ignorance,' he went on: 'Youthful presumption—they're worth outgrowing.'

'And do you think that goes on happening all through your life, so even when you're eighty-eight years old you'll keep realising how wrong you were before?'

He laughed. 'It's possible.'

'So what would you recommend? You know, to point me in the right direction.'

'That's a big question to lay on me! You moved over here not so long ago, didn't you? And you're going to stay here now? All the way through to college?'

'I guess.'

He frowned, and assumed the look of someone consulting a vast storehouse of knowledge.

'Perhaps some Pynchon. I'd be careful to start off with *The Crying of Lot 49*, though. Or Brautigan, or Barth. Steinbeck, too, for someone your age, and a bit of Faulkner to liven things up.'

He handed me the paperback.

'You should probably stay away from books like this, though. Why entrench old ideas? We're not living in the seventeenth century, are we?'

He shook his finger at me, in genial fashion: 'Don't let me catch you again.'

'Of course not, sir,' I said, and allowed this rebuke to sink in.

He left; I nursed the paperback, and tried to fit its damaged halves together. Over the next few afternoons, in a quiet corner of the school grounds, away from everyone, I made my way through the book again, increasingly caught up by its story. The remoteness of its setting and its refusal to grant its characters the faintest hint of happiness resonated with me: Nemours stupefied by his despair, the Prince destroyed by his growing knowledge of his plight, the Princess herself, drowning in love, deprived of warmth—these were fates that seemed in tune with what I knew of life. Other novels and stories were full of dramas and adventures, sudden reversals of fortune, last-minute deluges of fulfilment. The slow journey of Madame de Lafayette's characters to their appointed ends seemed dignified and beautiful to me.

This time the book remained with me after my reading, I had a fixed impression of it, I dwelt on its story—its scenes, its exchanges, its understated narrative, its silences. Gradually, by a process that was only half-conscious, it became transformed, it turned into a secret treasure, a closed world I could explore in safe passage, something no one else shared or knew. I kept it in the background of my thoughts; I even had a way of assessing events and people in its light: the various schools and colleges I passed through were much like the courts of intrigue Madame de Lafayette had described; the students and instructors there were like her characters as well. I became fond for a while of this game of comparisons—and so, long after I had first been led through its pages, the book at last left its trace inside me, and in this oblique fashion Serghiana's wish from years before came true.

*

All that had vanished, though, and many other new books and enthusiasms had replaced the *Princesse de Clèves* and been replaced in their turn by the time I took my first steps into adulthood, and began a life of foreign corresponding, country to country, new faces, new languages—and the constant sluicing of images and printed columns through my mind soon made every tale and story I had known seem equivalent. Memoirs, histories, tragic dramas, romances, science-fiction novels—they all shared the same structures and principles, they had their well-signalled plots, their heroes, their predictable, inevitable denouements. More and more the threads of different books and films and works of art were weaving into each other inside me, contending with each other, annulling each other, submerging every detail in a sea of associations—and almost the only respite I found from this tide of words and images came when I was sent on reporting trips into the Soviet Union or the satellite dictatorships of Eastern Europe, where the flow of new information stopped dead. All would be still there, of a sudden, and the mind set free: the silence of an empty night-time street or a sparsely furnished room became something very like a blessing. Even after the end of the Eastern empire and the demise of the Soviet Union, these destinations remained for several years havens of relative tranquillity, with the result that Moscow, once the most forbidding of capitals, became one of my favourite ports of call. And so it was that, midway through 1996, a year of upheavals in Russian politics, I arrived at Sheremetyevo airport, ready for the presidential election campaign, and with elaborate plans already drawn up for the weeks ahead. I would base myself in the city, but leave time free for other projects, among them one that had beguiled me ever since I first read the brief memoir of the revolutionary leader Bukharin's widow, Anna Larina. In its pages she sets out her happy recollections of childhood, when she lived with her father in an apartment near Bukharin's in the Metropol Hotel. Larina mentions Bukharin's fondness for animals: he loved hedgehogs, and gave several of these delicate and graceful creatures to Stalin as gifts of friendship; he turned a disused ornamental fountain outside his front door at the Metropol into a private menagerie—it housed in turn a marmoset, an eagle, a bear cub and a hawk with a broken wing. Eventually Bukharin was obliged to move to the Kremlin, where he kept a pet fox in his quarters. Soon after his arrival there he became an overt target of Stalin's hostility. He was charged with attempting to overthrow the Soviet state, tried, and executed. Larina vanished for two decades into the Gulag, where, deprived of books and pen and paper, she became adept at memorising verses and stories. The fox remained at large in the Kremlin grounds for several years, running here and there and searching vainly for visitors with whom to play hide-and-seek. I found this saga of Bukharin's animals particularly touching, a tale to tell. I had reserved a quiet room at the Metropol for the length of the presidential campaign. I settled in.

One morning I went down very early to the hotel's breakfast salon. It was a vast gallery, marble columned, with a wide, curved roof of decorated glass and high lunettes in frescoed Jugendstil. The tables were all set, as if for a banquet. Towering beside each one was an ornamental urn filled with an arrangement of lush flowers, peonies, tiger lilies, cattleya orchid blossoms, bright, strong-scented, their fronds hanging low. Jets of water played in the fountain at the centre of the gallery; soft violin music came from above. The space was empty, except for a lone waiter, a young man, sitting slouched beside the buffet table, reading. He looked up, saw me, rose to his feet and stuffed the book in his jacket pocket, an anxious expression on his face. After a few moments he came over to me, weaving his way between the tables and the banks of flowers. He glanced around, and made a little bow of greeting.

'*Gospodin*,' he said: 'Sir—can I perhaps interest you in one of the many delicacies on our breakfast menu?'

'What did you have in mind?' I said.

He clasped his hands behind his back and began reciting: 'Compote of tropical fruits, cloudberry muffins, caviar—Oscietra, from the best merchants—or a special omelette fines herbes, made from Siberian duck eggs.'

'Wow, Siberian duck eggs!' I said: 'It's too early in the morning for that!'

'I can personally recommend them,' he countered.

I looked at him more attentively. He was tall, and thin, with lanky hair. There was a faint tinge of defiance about him.

'How come?' I asked.

'I grew up in Khabarovsk. It's on the Amur River, close to the Chinese border, in the Far East.'

'I know where it is,' I said: 'I've been there.'

He raised his eyebrows on hearing this piece of information.

'You're a long way from home,' I said.

'It wasn't home. It's just the place where I spent my childhood.'

'And why were your family living there? Were they nomenklatura? Or internal exiles?'

'A little of both, perhaps,' he said: 'Those weren't really exclusive categories, you know, in the old Soviet Union.'

'And what are you doing here, now, in Moscow—besides being a waiter?'

'I'm a student, of course.'

'Of what?'

'Literature. French literature. I mean to go to Paris to complete my studies.'

'I don't mean to be discouraging,' I said, 'but I'm not sure that Paris is really the same kind of city today as it was in the days of Turgenev.'

'I'm not interested in Russian books and Russian writers,' he said: 'Only French. Only literature of the highest civilisational value. That's why I immerse myself in works like this.'

He pulled from his jacket the leather-bound book he had been reading and waved it in front of me.

'What is it?'

'It's the Pléiade of Madame de Lafayette, the author of the *Princesse de Clèves*, most perfect of all novels!'

I nodded, and fell silent. I felt the great gears of pattern and coincidence grinding within me. How arcane and full of depth life seemed to me as I listened, and let his words sink in.

'Are you familiar with it?' asked the waiter, in an insistent voice.

'In a sense,' I said, a touch reluctantly.

He smiled in triumph. 'You see! How little you know! It's a perfect illustration for me. Life has set a trap for us. Life, and politics.'

'For us?'

'People my age here had hopes. We thought we would have fine, free, western lives. Lives like yours. But we can already see the fate that's been prepared for us.'

I looked up at him. 'What fate is that?'

'More joke than fate, in fact. Isn't it clear enough to you? We love the West, we steep ourselves in your traditions, they seem like life and light for us, and they mean nothing anymore in your world—but it's you who will shape our future.'

'Yes,' I said. 'That's probably true. How come you're so interested in this book, though, and that period? There isn't any obvious connection to life out in the wilds of the Trans-Siberian line.'

He bridled, took a step back and began to turn. 'I don't think my story from so far away would be of any interest to you,' he said in a bitter voice.

'Go on,' I said: 'Try me.'

A handful of other hotel guests had come in, and were gathered round the buffet, talking, and casting odd glances in our direction.

'I'll tell you, then,' the waiter said, almost hissing at me, his voice dropping low: 'I'll tell you. A little anecdote: mine—my story. It could almost be from Chekhov's pen. There was one person who showed me all these things: my grandmother—and if I'm anything at all today, I owe that to her, only her. She was a scholar: she came from Petersburg. In her heart she was a true European, and she wanted me to be one, too. Even on the banks of the Amur and Ussuri rivers! Can you imagine? She loved me very much: she used to take me out, when I was a boy, every afternoon in the summertime, once school was over. We would walk from our apartment all the way to the arboretum, and sit together there, for hours on end, underneath the magnolia vines and walnut trees, reading—reading to each other, making our own world of books between us. That's how things were for me, then, in that wild east you like to talk about, with the wolves and savages. What do you make of that?'

More than you might imagine, I wanted to say in answer; I formed the words inside me, I was about to speak them—but he had turned his back, he wheeled away from me and headed to the tables full of other guests.

Weeks went by. I travelled further, then left the East and drifted into other tasks, but I found my thoughts returning to this brief exchange at the Metropol; to the tall student and his scornful eyes and hurt expression; to the book, also, and its reappearance in my life after so long—and the idea came to me that I could measure out the chapters of my existence, which seemed to be blurring almost indistinguishably into each other, by means of my successive encounters with the *Princesse de Clèves*. So I was struck, when I came back to my apartment early one morning a few months later, and saw the usual pile of magazines and periodicals just inside the door. I picked up the one on top: it was the new issue of a journal I always read through at that time in reverential fashion, as though its pages were a point of entry to worlds of seriousness and enlightenment far beyond my reach. There, prominently displayed, was a long article devoted to

Madame de Lafayette. It was by the critic Roger Shattuck, whose ideas were invariably cast in crystalline and balanced prose. He was an author I admired, and always followed, in great part because of the calm and distanced manner of his writing—and it seems very likely that this perspective mirrored, somehow, one of the formative experiences of his early years. As a young military cargo pilot in the closing days of World War II, he made an overflight of the destroyed city of Nagasaki, passing low over the wreckage and the ruined dwellings, little of which remained beyond ghostly outlines imprinted on the scorched surface of the land below. All through his life he tried to set down his impressions of that day, in vain, the words would never come to him—but the tone of clarity and warmth that suffused his later writings may have been that mission's truest legacy. The piece of his that I had lighted on was called 'The Pleasures of Abstinence'. Disregarding the title, I read straight through it there and then, bleary-eyed and jet-lagged in the hallway, surrounded by my cases and equipment, and grasping not so much the essay's argument as the scale and grandeur of its central thesis, which was sketched out, at first, in the most glancing, allusive fashion, only to be illustrated and amplified in a set of fine-grained readings from the novel's text.

We must beware standard accounts, says Shattuck—it is his opening salvo—and the version of the Princess he proceeds to give is anything but conventional. On the surface, the book is a familiar kind of love story—fierce emotions, self-dissolution in the transports of the heart—but as it unfolds, the Princess moves from indecisiveness to insight, she finds resolve, she is no longer merely an object of desire, she makes herself into a heroine. From the outset she has been wary of the force of love, which lures its victims from their proper and contracted role in life. She feels its strength: it tempts her, she trembles before it, she is on the verge of being swept away—then a still moment comes. The Princess looks inward. She sees herself: she is astonished at what she has done. At that moment she breaks from the storyline: she is no longer a character in a plot controlled by others. She is aware; she is alone. She decides both to honour the memory of her dead husband, who truly loved her, and to preserve her own love for Nemours, to keep it safe 'in the amber of the past'.

In this reading of the book, the Princess does not act: her act lies in reflection. She stands for something rare, both in life and the dream of life one finds in novels—passion joined with lucidity. It is a clean precis: the heart's disorder redeemed by the descriptive art. How simple that schema seemed to me then, how persuasive. I read on, until it dawned on me that the essay's true heroine was not the Princess, but the author of her story. Madame de Lafayette performs a renunciation of her own in the pages of her narrative. When the final set-piece scenes draw near, the degree of resolution in her storytelling shifts. All has been precision; suddenly, all is vague. Shattuck explains: 'A confident author knows when to renounce the lifeblood of narrative: words.' And so it is: once the Princess has turned away from Nemours, and has fixed on her course, she looks into her heart again, and all is murk and chaos there: not only do her emotions fight each other, they cannot be described. Madame de Lafayette has withdrawn from her story. At this juncture, her style is to suggest, rather than to tell: to renounce her own art, to be discreet, to fall silent, to stand aside.

And with this, Shattuck's task is nearly done: he has redefined a book and outlined a new theory of the imagination; he closes with a few sentences that point far forward in time, to the Cubists, and the Impressionists, and the world of modern literature—to a world of art in fragments. His ideas remain in my thoughts to this day: a faded photocopy of his final page has travelled with me from continent to continent, I have pored over it in times of happiness and sadness, and its words still seem fresh: 'Someone told me as a child how to see a star at night,' he says: 'Don't look directly at it; look slightly to one side of it'—and it often seems to me that this indirection works, in life as much as in art or astronomy. I think back to the time when I set out on my own version of the trail he first blazed for me, a trail which led him, in his search for literary parallels, from seventeenth-century France to nineteenth-century Massachusetts, and on; and I wonder if, unknowingly, I have pursued something very like his method—for as the years passed, I became increasingly convinced that the way to know writers is not to immerse oneself in their works, or even in their hesitations and their silences, but to read swiftly, then glance away, and seek to know them further through the texture of their lives: to follow in their footsteps, to move through their landscapes, to look out onto the sights they once saw. Often this is a simple enough undertaking: authors have their shrines and memorials, and the country of their fiction, they have their house museums, they have their well-marked burial sites. With Madame de Lafayette things are different: scarcely any traces of her world are left today. Her husband's family mansion in the Auvergne is dedicated to the memory of the revolutionary Lafayette, not to her; the gilded salon she presided over in the Rue de Vaugirard in Paris has long since disappeared. How, then, to find her? Where?

For some while I felt the best plan would be to get my bearings through the record of her friendship with Madame de Sévigné, almost every day of whose adulthood is documented in punctilious detail: and there are Sévigné monuments aplenty strewn through France; in Paris, where the Musée Carnavalet shows her quarters and makes much of her Chinese lacquer writing desk; at the Château des Rochers near Vitré in Brittany; at the pavilion in Vichy which bears her name; at Grignan, her daughter's palace high above the valley of the Rhône— but many of these places are little more than facades, sites of nostalgia, rebuilt, refashioned in recent times to conform with our prevailing image of the past. The realm of Madame de Lafayette's writings is also hard to reach, though the *Princesse de Clèves* is as fixed and grounded in place and time as any novel: almost every scene and every conversation unfolds in a precise setting; the particular passageway or gallery or stairwell is routinely specified by the careful author—to no avail. We cannot follow. The ballroom in the old Louvre Palace where the Princess and Nemours first encounter each other has been rebuilt, the royal castles of Saint-Maur and Meudon are long gone. As for the country retreat of Coulommiers, a house so lovely it was called the castle of enchantment, nothing but a ruined portico remains. The pavilion where the Princess makes her confession to her husband, the formal avenues and gardens, the river promenade—all have vanished into the realm of fiction, they endure only in words. Almost the only backdrop still intact is the most overwhelming of them all, the royal palace at Chambord in the Loire Valley, which has just been completed at the midpoint of the novel, when the young King ascends to his throne: here Nemours forms his plan to track down the Princess; here the Prince suffers in his suspicions, and sends out a trusted servant on his rival's trail; here fever takes hold of him and his life ebbs away. Chambord is also the preferred location for cinematic treatments of the novel, indeed it is the visual emblem of the French Renaissance—and the building has a great deal in common with a stage-set to this day, so much so that it seemed the natural choice of destination for a journey when the *Princesse de Clèves* came into my thoughts again.

It was already autumn when at last I had a chance to drive out. It was early in the morning, there were mists along the river, the day was cool and damp. By the time I reached Saint-Dyé on the Loire, the preoccupations that were with me when I first turned off the Périphérique had all vanished, the world seemed very clear around me, and that clarity was matched by my state of mind, I was both alert and calm, I felt poised and balanced in myself. As I drove, stray snatches of memory would surface inside me, only to be replaced by fresh impressions and images, by views from far away and long ago: I had the sense of hearing words and phrases I barely recognised, exchanges from old encounters and half-completed conversations; trivial things, the hum and rustle of the self at rest. How strange our condition is, I thought, caught as we are, captive to a flux of internal sounds and signals that murmur to us constantly, while we believe ourselves to be masters, in full control of our ideas, and pay no heed to this dark, tumultuous, all-inundating tide. In front of me at last I could make out the gateway to the Chambord parklands, but as I drew near, and saw the long tailback of tour buses, the prospect of a slow trudge through a touristic mausoleum seemed suddenly unbearable: I turned back, at speed, reached the autoroute again and headed west, thinking I would fare much better somewhere quiet. The exit signs came flashing by—Amboise, the suburbs of Tours, the city itself, Montjoyeux, Chambray—then, just as I was accelerating past a long flotilla of slow-moving trucks, I caught sight of another turn-off marker, the sign for Chinon and Azay-le-Rideau. I spun the wheel, and forced my way into the line of traffic, and through, onto the slip road, narrowly avoiding a police patrol car, sure at last where I was going: Azay, the dream castle that I had seen in childhood, and would now see again. The road ahead had narrowed; it ran straight as far as the horizon line. I drove on, feeling solemn and uplifted, as though it was a question of a romantic rendezvous, and I was bound for revelations, great truths about the past. The fog had lifted from the river, there was pale sunshine, a strong wind was blowing, whipping the clouds across the sky. Here was Azay-le-Rideau: the marketplace, the pathway through the wooded gardens, the bridge across the river leading to the chateau. Leaves were tumbling from the treetops in cascades—copper-coloured, russet, mottled greenish-brown, dark burnt-red—they pirouetted in the wind as they fell. And here was the entrance, the door ajar. I went inside. There was gentle lighting in the hallway. The ticket counter was unattended. I could hear no voices, no sound at all. I waited for a few minutes, listening. I paced through the rooms on the main floor, tentatively, looking for signs of life. I climbed the great staircase, vaguely wondering if I had any recollection of having seen it before—but what distinguishes one stone ornamental staircase from another? The silence, in such a setting, was oppressive; it made it hard to look. I forced myself to concentrate: on the tapestries, the portraits in their rows, the coffered ceilings, the furnishings of each room in turn, the recessed windows with their view onto the lake—I was studying everything intently: so intently I failed to notice a young woman standing in the doorway behind me, watching me. She made a slight noise. I turned.

'Is this the library?' she said, a doubtful expression on her face.

'Maybe,' I said: 'It looks like one, with all these shelves and cabinets.'

'Are you from the management?'

'Do I look as though I might be?'

'No,' she said: 'To be truthful, you don't. You look like a fairly standard kind of European visitor, just passing through.'

I felt it might be best to ignore this judgement. 'So where is everyone?' I said.

'Perhaps they decided to take the day off,' she said, and laughed a little. 'It's not exactly peak season. What brings you here?'

'It's a complicated story.'

I felt a little adrift in the conversation. The woman was elegantly dressed: her manner was quite sharp.

'Well—are you in a hurry for some reason? Tell me. I'd like to hear.'

'I'd rather not,' I said.

'Go on. Don't you like telling stories, just for the pleasure of it? There's no danger you'll be betraying any secrets. We won't ever meet again, you can be sure of that.'

And she gave a smile to indicate the astronomical remoteness of such a possibility.

'Please,' she finished—this with an encouraging gesture of the hands.

I reached for an explanation, and realised how strange and flimsy the chains of cause and connection that had brought me there would sound; how what I would be describing was a thread of my life.

'It has to do with a book,' I said: 'I came across it when I was quite young. Do you know it? The *Princesse de Clèves*—by Madame de Lafayette.'

'Of course I know it! I don't think there's a single woman of a certain social standing or educational attainment in the whole of France who wouldn't be familiar with it! We used to study it in school. We had to learn the speeches of the Princess off by heart.'

'And they were useful, in adult life?'

'Very!'

She began reciting from the speech the Princess makes, proclaiming her innocence to her husband, and laughed again at this little flight of rhetoric, and broke off.

'I loved that book too, when I was a young girl,' she said, with sudden fervour: 'It's full of air, and grace, and movement—like a ballet, like a figure in a dance. It gave us an image, an ideal to live by. Literature is much more beautiful than life, isn't it?'

'Some people would say the idea was for literature to mirror life,' I said.

She raised her eyebrows, and frowned a little.

'Realism!' she said: 'In Azay-le-Rideau, of all places. God save us! Although I suppose Balzac did like it here, when he made his visits. Come downstairs with me: I want to show you something.'

I followed. She led the way to one of the main salons, and stood in front of the marble fireplace.

'Do you know what happened here—right here?' she asked.

'Many things, I imagine.'

'I'll tell you. It's not just a pleasure palace. It's had a history. In the war of 1870 the Prussian Second Army made this the headquarters for their Loire campaign: Prince Friedrich Karl was stationed here. He was a gifted field commander, he was the victor of Königgrätz and Spicheren, he had just triumphed at the siege of Metz. But of course he was a German, he had an instinct for destroying things of beauty— I'm sorry: you're not German, are you?'

I shook my head.

'I didn't really think so. In any case, Friedrich Karl was dining in this very room with his staff officers one night when the chandelier from the ceiling above them fell onto the table!' She clapped her hands for effect. 'It was a dreadful crash. He was quite convinced there had been an attempt on his life. He told his men to set fire to the chateau. They barely managed to persuade him that it was an accident. Can you imagine?'

'Easily enough,' I said.

'And have you found something of what you were looking for? Did you really think you'd find the Princess here—or Madame de Lafayette?'

'In a way,' I said.

I tried to explain. I told her my idea, but in the explanation it made no sense: the past as active, as present all around us, if only we could turn our minds towards it; if only for a few moments we could slip through some side gate beyond the well-defended fortress of our selves. She listened for a while, then clasped her hands together in dramatic fashion.

'Astonishing! You're not a realist. You're a true romantic. Time has no meaning for you; death's not real!'

'I was talking about memory,' I said: 'That's all. Not time, not death. We remember what's gone. Aren't books a way of remembering, too? Don't they keep impressions for us of the past? And maybe places are like that as well, and they preserve the imprint of what's happened, and we can sense what they know.'

'So—if there's a book that you love, or a time you love, you can bring it to life if you long for it enough, if you pick over its bones and traces enough. Why, you could almost meet Molière, or Racine, or even Madame de Lafayette along the way! That's the most ridiculous thing I've ever heard. You really have some ideas, don't you! Too much imagination!'

'You say that rather mockingly.'

'But not unkindly. After all, why not start off by seeking clues to life in literature and art? I used to live through books myself, I was always reading, studying.'

'And now?'

'Less so. I grew out of historical romances: I grew up, of course. All that purity and renunciation and turning away from life—it began to seem inhuman to me. I wanted to have feelings that came welling up from my own experiences, not just be constantly trying to imitate some pale heroine. I didn't want to be afraid of the wildness of the world; I didn't want to have some fixed idea of perfection borrowed from another century guiding everything I thought.'

'And that shift was productive?'

'You can't hide from your own time. You have to embrace what's all around you. Otherwise you're not living—you're just in a dream.'

'You don't think there's something quite dreamlike about our lives today?' I said: 'Images everywhere, a flood of them, all second-hand, all repeating—and never for a moment stillness, never any peace.'

'Absolutely, yes, we're all part of it,' she said, in distracted fashion: 'Dreams in a dream—so much that there's no chance of escape—no chance. Anyhow—time for us to go.'

'Us?'

She turned, put one hand to her lips and made a soft calling noise, much like the sound of a dove calling from the branches of a forest tree. A small boy who had been lying curled up on a couch in a dark corner of the entrance hall and whose presence I had completely failed to register now stirred, stretched, stood up and came toward us. He took the woman's hand, and leaned against her, rubbing his eyes.

'You fell asleep, my little one?' she asked, and he nodded.

'I should go, too,' I said, 'and leave you with your son.'

'Who said anything about him being my son?' she said: 'You love jumping to conclusions, don't you? I look after him from time to time, I take him out from school: we look after each other, in fact—we go on excursions, like this one. I even read to him, sometimes—only from the classics, though, you'll be relieved to hear—just the way I was read to when I was a child.'

'Is that right?' I said, and stray thoughts ran through me.

'Yes—that's the order of life: things repeat, the generations come and go, one after the next, like falling leaves.'

'Of course,' I said: 'I understand that very well.'

'So why that look? What are you smiling at?'

'Nothing,' I said. 'I was remembering something. I was thinking about the first time I heard stories being read to me—stories from an old book, in another country, half a lifetime ago—and I can still hear the sound of those words in my mind today.'

II

Fil de Cassons

THE MONTH WAS August, high summer, bright and clear. Sunlight was streaming into my room. It woke me: I was late. I got up, looked out for a moment at the view across the valley, then ran downstairs to the breakfast room, almost losing my balance, taking the steps two at a time. I stopped: from the landing I could see Serghiana. She was seated at the centre of the long table in the hotel lobby, surrounded by a group of men and women with serious expressions on their faces: they were hunched over, all of them, listening intently, and leaning towards her from both sides. Before her on the table was a small square radio with coloured dials, its antenna set at a rakish angle. To her left was a handsome man I had never seen before; he was frowning and toying with one of the cufflinks on his shirt; a young woman was beside him, clutching at his arm. A couple in tennis clothes stood close behind this pair, craning their necks to hear; next to them was a waiter and beside him the hotel's manager, both with their heads bowed. By Serghiana's other shoulder, resting one elbow on the table, was Mr Balzer, the concierge, a figure of great distinction, the gold buttons gleaming on his uniform. At the far end of the table was the newspaper cartoonist Egon, whom I knew well from previous years, and this was surprising—there was a coldness between him and Serghiana that was plain even to me. These figures seemed frozen in place: they looked like the carved wood effigies on a mediaeval altar, bent over in the performance of their devotions. I went across to them. I could hear the radio now. There was a whine of electronic interference, and a newscast, a man's voice.

'To recap, once more—late last night troops from the Soviet Union and Warsaw Pact countries crossed international borders into Czecho-slovakia. Prague airport has been closed to commercial flights; a military airlift is underway. Moscow claims to have received an urgent request for assistance from Czechoslovak leaders; the whereabouts of Communist Party First Secretary Alexander Dubček remains unknown.'

'Maybe we should tune to Radio Moscow instead to find out,' said the handsome man, lightly.

'Is that an attempt at humour?' said Serghiana.

'Or Czech Radio, perhaps. Isn't it traditional on occasions like this to play martial music—or Bach?'

'What a tragedy,' said Serghiana, pressing one hand to her forehead: 'An utterly predictable tragedy.'

She looked up, and noticed me. I could see that the couple in tennis clothes were crying, and wiping away their tears.

'Serghiana Ismailovna, you would surely have welcomed this once,' said Egon from the end of the table.

'Your trouble, Egon,' said Serghiana, sharply, 'is that you forget nothing, you forgive nothing—in fact, you understand nothing!'

She fixed him with a brutal stare, then turned away.

'And you, Stephane,' she went on: 'What would you counsel?'

'I'm not a military attaché,' said the handsome man.

'But what?'

'A peace conference must be held, of course—in Geneva, by preference.'

'Naturally—because past conferences in Geneva have all been so successful!'

'And what good would that do?' said one of the others round the table.

'Do you see,' said the handsome man, disengaging his arm from the woman at his side, and adopting a professional tone: 'By definition, this move—everything that's happened overnight, all this creates an imbalance, an instability'—he held his hands before him, palms upwards, and raised then lowered each one in turn. 'The gravitational relationships between great powers are disturbed; there are reverberations; they die away—then comes the time for diplomacy.'

'My child, welcome,' said Serghiana, and beckoned to me: 'Come. Something's happened. There are things going on in the world today.'

'Serghiana, tell him,' said the handsome man. 'Or shall I? Your country's been invaded.'

'I just heard,' I said: 'I understood; I was listening—by the Russians.'

'Well, strictly speaking, by the allies of the Warsaw Pact.'

'Don't confuse things,' said Serghiana: 'Don't be pedantic. Just explain, in simple terms, simple enough for him, what's going on. Say what's actually happened.'

'Absolutely,' said the handsome man: 'A reasonable request.'

He began speaking to me in a gentle, agreeable voice. 'You're familiar with the board game Monopoly, yes—you know the rules?'

'Of course.'

'And everyone who plays must abide by them. So: picture this. The Russians have built a hotel on the Champs Élysées, or the Boulevard des Capucines, and, by the roll of the dice, the Czechoslovaks happen to land there, and they refuse to pay. What happens?'

He looked at me. I said nothing. He smiled in triumph: 'Everything breaks down, that's clear enough. The game's over: winner takes all.'

'That wasn't very helpful,' said Serghiana.

She looked up at me again, a bleak expression on her face. 'My child—Russia's always been a dark and potent force.'

'I thought the Russians were our friends now, in a way,' I said.

'Who have you been listening to? A dark force: believe me, because I know—dark and unremitting. They hold what they have, at all costs. We've woken up to find a new order. The West will sound concerned, of course, and pretend to act, and do nothing. That's the picture. It's always the same.'

'And that was helpful, Serghiana?'

'This is Daru,' she said. 'Stephane: this young man, as you can tell, is my nephew, about whom you've heard so much.'

'Nephew?' he echoed, in a quizzical, slightly mocking voice.

'In a diagonal manner, yes. My child—Daru's a very distinguished man. He's an ambassador—and he's an intellect.'

'He's intelligent?'

'Yes—and many people say he's in intelligence as well.'

'Please, Serghiana!' said the young woman at Daru's side: 'Someone might overhear you, and take you seriously. Just think of the consequences—they could be incalculable!'

Serghiana leaned back in her chair. 'Don't dramatise, Josette,' she said: 'Incalculable! What nonsense.'

She got up, and paced about the table, then wheeled round. 'Surely you understand,' she said, her voice low: 'None of us matter now. Our positions don't matter; whatever prestige we might once have had is nothing. We're bystanders. This is the day that changes the map for generations to come. Can't you hear the echo? It's the same lesson as 1956—or even 1939.'

'A fait accompli,' said Daru.

'Precisely. What we think—our opinions, our theories, our predictions—they're all irrelevant. The tank columns are on the move, they're in the streets of another European capital—and we find ourselves here, high up in the Alps, listening to shortwave radio reports, powerless, and wondering what our fate will be.'

'The fate of Western Europe,' said Daru, 'will be to avert its eyes, just as you say.'

'I find myself in strange agreement with you, Serghiana Ismailovna,' said Egon, rather nervously, laughing.

She turned away; her attention had been caught by someone else. In the hotel's entrance lobby stood a rotund man. His face was soft and unemphatic: he wore round-framed glasses, which gave him an owlish look. He waved, and she gestured back.

'What a comical-looking little figure,' said Daru: 'He looks like a travelling shoe salesman!'

'You've always had a discriminating eye, haven't you?' said Serghiana: 'I thought you knew that world. He's the professor of theoretical physics at the Charles University in Prague—and he's got a minder in tow.'

The rotund man now approached, followed by a pale, thin, grey-suited attendant. He bowed to Serghiana, took her hand and raised it to his lips in histrionic fashion.

'*Küss die Hand, schöne Frau!* I've been trying to find out further details.'

'What, Leo—practising your bourgeois airs in preparation for exile?'

'Madame Serghiana, don't joke,' he answered, looking around uneasily.

There were introductions: the group gathered at the table began to disperse. I stood next to Serghiana, waiting. She reached into her handbag for a cigarette: Egon sprang towards her, his pack open.

'Please,' he said.

'A peace offering, Egon? So soon? Show me: yes—Muratti—with the charcoal multifilter! How Mediterranean! My child, a man's choice of cigarette is very significant—particularly when he's a refugee.'

'And what does my choice tell you?' asked Egon: 'Or should I perhaps have had a Black Russian Sobranie in my hand to mark the day?'

She ignored this, and turned to me. 'My child,' she said, in a whisper: 'You already know Uncle Leo, don't you, from home?'

I nodded.

'And you know he's been courting your mother, don't you?'

He was with us now, before I could answer.

'We've met before, my boy,' he said to me, affably: 'Do you remember when?'

'You came to take me out at Easter,' I said: 'Last year.'

'That's right, in St. Gallen—with your mother. We had a good afternoon together, didn't we, that day? I was telling you all about our childhood times, when she and I were in the same language class together at Prague Grammar School. In fact, I often used to do her homework for her.'

'Wouldn't that have been cheating?'

'She was very beautiful. How is she? Is she here?'

'Leo,' said Serghiana, commandingly, changing the subject: 'An update—you promised.'

'This was inevitable,' he said, assuming a confidential air: 'I've known it was coming for weeks. Everyone did—except the leaders. They refused to hear! I spent the last week at an international conference—in Trieste. It was already common knowledge.'

The man standing beside him drew closer, at this, and gave a slight shake of his head.

'Trieste,' said Serghiana, nostalgically: 'Such a mournful place. Sometimes I think we'll all end our days there, waiting at the waterfront, scanning the sea for boats that won't ever come. My child—maybe you should go and ask Josette to take you upstairs to have a look at the Nietzsche vitrine. She's got the face of a little angel; she won't do you any harm. A dose of Nietzsche: that might provide you with more amusement than this unending politics.'

She beckoned to the woman with Daru.

'Were you talking about politics all this time?' I asked Serghiana.

'Everything's politics! Go on.'

'But we've already looked at the vitrines and display cases upstairs together—several times.'

'No: I only showed you the Einstein one, with the picture of him and his wife and Irene Curie, and the one for Empress Zita with the slipper and the glove she left behind. Nietzsche's on another floor. I was saving him for emergencies—as a special treat.'

'And is this an emergency?'

'Certainly—it's a very good time to make his acquaintance.'

The young woman had drifted over to us.

'Would you, Josette?' said Serghiana, rather meltingly: 'I'd be eternally grateful.'

'Better your gratitude than your hostility,' said the woman.

She smoothed her hair back, took me by the hand, and turned, but at that moment one of the hotel waiters who was edging his way through the gathering reached us.

'Madame Semyonova,' he said to Serghiana, almost cringing: 'Forgive me—you have a telephone call—international. Shall I bring across the phone?'

'No,' she said, 'I'll take it in the cabin.'

'Well, I wonder,' said Daru, with amusement in his voice: 'What can that be about? Instructions from the Cominform?'

'I think those days are behind us,' said Egon.

Daru gave him a cool glance.

'Behind us? They're never gone.'

'You believe our hostess, with whom you've been dining happily and speaking very freely, still has affiliations—and of that kind?'

'Some affiliations are permanent,' said Daru: 'You know that very well. There are affinities, and persuasions; there are crevasses and susceptibilities in every heart. You should keep in mind her origins.'

'I've heard she grew up in some wild Caucasian oblast,' said Egon, almost stuttering as he replied.

'The kind of place where dreams of revolution can seem quite natural. Serghiana Ismailovna, with her famous patronymic. She has her loyalties. The regime's in her blood.'

This was said with a little, curling, triumphant smile. Egon glared back.

'Insinuation. How diplomatic! You are aware, aren't you, that the Kremlin killed her husband? Her life's pattern's very clear.'

'I've heard many stories,' said Daru: 'About her; about you, about all of us, and they serve very well to pass the time. Some of them even provide us with a pretext for our lives—a cover, and in due course we may actually come to believe them, and bind them into our selves.'

'Cover!' said Egon, in a heated voice.

Josette tapped me on the shoulder. 'Let's go,' she said.

She steered me away, and guided me up the first flight of stairs, moving slowly and gracefully.

'Did you understand any of that?' she asked me, as we reached the second landing.

'I think so,' I said: 'Did you?'

'I'm afraid I did,' she said.

She stopped in the hallway leading to the guest rooms. In front of us was a little white pedestal, topped by a glass display case.

'Can you see?' she asked.

'I can see a pair of glasses, and a photo, and a paper—and some bones. Is that him?'

'No! I'll tell you what it says. He was a famous philosopher, and he came here, many years ago—in 1873, long before any of us were born. He was looking for peace and quiet so he could write—and he did. In fact, he wrote one of his best known essays here, and stayed here for a whole month, but it sounds as though the hotel got on his nerves. He was constantly complaining: there were too many flies in the salon, the piano was out of tune, he didn't like the food they served in the restaurant. He must have had a very bad temper: one day he decided the piece of chicken on his plate was inedible, so he threw it at the hotel manager's head.'

'Did he hit him?'

'It doesn't go into that much detail—but these are the bones of the chicken, in this glass case: they kept them as a memento of his stay.'

I took all this in.

'You're very quiet,' she said: 'Are you shy around strangers? Don't be. Not with me.'

She bent down until our eyes were level, and stroked my cheek with one finger. 'What is it? Are you upset—about what they were all discussing downstairs? Or are you embarrassed? Is it me? Are you just tongue-tied around me? Do you think I'm attractive?'

'Of course,' I said, uncertainly.

'You don't sound very sure! And how about Daru? Do you like him?'

'Your husband?'

'Oh, he's not my husband. I'm just his secretary.'

'Would you like to be married to him?'

She gave a little smile, and shrugged. 'Perhaps. And perhaps not.'

'Why do you work for him, if you don't like him?'

'I don't mind him—I like him—he found me when I was a translator in the Moscow Embassy—we got on—and here I am. Let's go back down.'

'Wait,' I said: 'The bones.'

'What about them?'

'How can we be sure they're the same ones—that they're really from the piece of chicken that he threw at the manager of the hotel?'

'That's a very philosophical question. How can we be sure of anything? We live in a murky world. You have to take what you hear and what you read on trust—otherwise everything falls apart.'

'And is that what he thought: Nietzsche?'

'I'm not really an expert. I don't know.'

'But Daru would?'

'I dare say.'

'And what happened to him?'

'To Nietzsche? I know the answer to that, at least. There's a special museum devoted to him, at Sils Maria. It's not far away from here. We were there just last week, Daru and I, staying at the hotel. Nietzsche adored the mountains: he used to come to the Alps every summer, for his holidays, to work, of course—and most of all he loved to go on long walks by the lake shore at Sils Maria and at Silvaplana, and up the pathways of the Fex valley, and higher still, towards the bare peaks, always on his own. When autumn came, though, he preferred to travel on to warmer places: Nice, Genoa, the Mediterranean coast. One winter season he rented a set of rooms he'd taken before, with a family he knew in Turin, but by that stage he wasn't very well. Just outside his lodgings, early one morning, he saw a coachman in the Piazza Carlo Alberto whipping his horse. He burst into tears: he flung himself around the horse's neck as if to save it: then he had a complete breakdown. His senses had left him: he never recovered them—he slipped into a coma that lasted for the rest of his life.'

'What was wrong with him?'

Josette pursed her lips. 'I think,' she said, after a moment's equivocation, 'that's probably something for another day.'

Downstairs, the tension had grown. Voices were speaking, loudly, in different languages, men and women were pushing into the hotel lobby and milling round the reception desk. Daru spotted us at once.

'Malzahn's here,' he said to Josette: 'Can you imagine? I had no idea, I just found out. He's staying at the Waldhaus. We have to go across at once.'

'Who's Malzahn?' I asked.

'He's a minister,' said Josette: 'Stephane's deputy minister. A powerful man. He has cruel eyes—I don't care for him.'

Daru looked at her in amazement. 'My dear,' he said, 'your personal predilections are hardly the criterion that should be guiding us now. It's worrying in the extreme that no one told us.'

'Surely he's just taking a holiday: he looks as if he needs one: all those student riots would grind anyone down.'

'For God's sake, Josette!'

'No, for God's sake, you!' she said: 'Can't you see—it's chaos here. No one's in charge, no one here knows anything at all.'

'Here's someone who's in the picture,' said Daru: 'The physics professor.'

He reached over through the press of new arrivals and gave Leo a fraternal pat on the shoulder, and beckoned to him with an air of ingratiating urgency.

'Tell us, do,' he said: 'You must know. Are times of instability upon us? Is this a quick stab—or a change for the long term? Should we be anxious?'

'Anxious?' Leo stared at him: 'You want me to write your whole telegram for you! Frozen times are what lie ahead now—and frozen times are what lie behind us as well. Weren't you posted to my country?

Didn't you have your eyes open when you were there? Or do I have to say more about a truth everyone understands? Wasn't Madame Serghiana with you a moment ago—I can't see her anywhere.'

He glanced round, and looked at me as though I had hidden her. 'What's the meaning of her presence here anyway, I wonder?'

This seemed to be half a question directed to me, and half a meditation.

'Why ask him?' said Daru, and then he saw what I saw: Serghiana, bearing down. She came up behind Leo.

'So here you are—the insider,' she said, in triumph: 'The only man who admits to having had advance warning! And you're keeping an eye on my nephew. In loco parentis. It's touching. I'm pleased to see it.'

Leo took a little step back from me.

'How was it?' asked Serghiana: 'At the Nietzsche shrine, I mean. High up in the realms of the unfettered intellect—beyond good and evil, cold and pure?'

I looked back at her in confusion.

'Josette, didn't you explain it all to him?'

'I tried,' said Josette.

'I'm sure you did. And did you talk about what's going on?'

Daru now broke in. 'Serghiana—I just found out Malzahn's here. Malzahn, of all people! Won't you come across the road to his hotel with us for a talk? It could be enlightening.'

'A talk with the emissary of a hostile power,' said Serghiana, sternly: 'With a junior minister of a bourgeois republic!'

Josette laughed.

Daru glared in her direction. 'In a crisis of this kind,' he said, 'the first hours are the crucial ones. It's good fortune I'm here to restrain him. What if he plans to release some communique?'

'Why should that be any concern of mine?' said Serghiana.

'Some of us here are in the wings,' replied Daru, looking solemn: 'But some are in the flow of history. We all know who you represent.'

'I represent no one. Only myself.'

'And of course you have no connections at all, no protectors?'

'Stephane,' said Serghiana, very coolly: 'Your composure and your capacity for charming dissimulation seem to be deserting you. Perhaps our masks should stay on, at least for the duration of this carnival. Don't you agree, Josette? My child, why don't you come with me into the garden. I want to talk to you—and escape from all this.'

'Madame Semyonova—a message!'

A man in the uniform of another hotel had rushed up, and stood before her, bearing an envelope. She took it, and with a single fluid movement looked at the note, folded it into her pocket, waved him off and strode on; the messenger was immediately engulfed by a group of other guests. I followed her through the crowd until we reached the far balcony's balustrade.

'Are we still going up the mountain today?' I asked.

'Of course. It was a promise. I've already booked the car—it's coming to collect us. Do you really think I'd let a little quarrel in a faraway country between people of whom we know nothing get in the way?'

I stared at her. 'It's not that far away.'

'No, it's not, it's not at all far. And I know a great deal about the people on both sides. Forgive me—I couldn't resist. It was just a glance back in time: a quote—a famous one. Something that started off a war. Of course we're going to go up. Look—follow where I'm pointing. You can just see the top station, where the snow line begins—and you can see the funicular cable glinting in the sun. That's where we're going. Doesn't it look majestic to you, as if it's floating there, in that clear sky? It always seems beautiful from this vantage point, from down below: then you reach the summit, and the beauty's gone, and there's something different, something wordless, in its place.'

I gazed up. I raised my hand to shield my eyes. At last I saw it: the dot close to the peak; the thin, gleaming line, like fire; the blue of the morning, pale, almost transparent, and within it faint, shifting shapes and images that seemed like the negatives of clouds. They shimmered, their outlines took form for a moment, then disappeared, and slowly recomposed themselves—sea monsters, dragons, animals, ghostly figures with tendrils trailing in their wake.

'It resonates with me, this view, today of all days,' said Serghiana.

'Why?'

'Everything seems drenched in sadness. And not just for the obvious reasons. Not because the golden future's ground to dust: that happened ages ago; and not because of what's led up to this, and what's going to come from it, all the things we can't see yet, but can sense; not even because I don't know what I used to hope for, and what I'm going to fear in times to come—but because there's never any escape.'

'Escape from what?'

'Even here, behind this fence of mountains, the wildness breaks in: I can't hold it back. Even when I'm spending my days with you, whom I should be shielding from such things, it forces its way in. You can see how all these people here around us in the hotel are excited by disaster. They feed on it, they depend on it, it's a good trouble for them; a happy sadness for them.'

'Who are they?' I asked. 'Do you know them all?'

'They're the international class, of course,' she said: 'They're diplomats, and businessmen, and backroom politicians—they like to talk to each other. You heard Daru: for them, a crisis is a pretext for a conference, and that's all it is.'

'Great-Aunt Serghiana,' I said: 'Shouldn't we go home?'

She turned to look at me, and gave me a smile—it was a smile that wanted at the same time to laugh and to dissolve into tears: 'Home? And where is that? Where? The place you were born? Where you were growing up? The country on your passport? My child, we're hotel people—nomads, always moving, always with our suitcases packed and ready, always waiting for the knock at the door in the dead of night. And wherever we are, we're in the same place.'

She paused, and shook her head: 'That famous grand hotel—the hotel perched above the abyss,' she said then, and repeated the words, in several languages, each time more softly: 'It's an old joke—and the most absurd thing is that it's true, down to the last detail: there's every comfort, every luxury: and what a vista we have! On the very edge. Do you understand what I'm telling you?'

She glanced down at me: 'Why would you? Sometimes only half-understanding things is a blessing,' she said. 'I remember when I was your age—and the wars were coming: I had no idea at all what my life was going to be.'

'And what was it like, being a child then?'

'It was roads, and trucks, and train carriages. It was always staying with strangers—new people, unkind faces; movement—that's what I have in my memory most of all: school to school, city to city, constant noise, no stillness, no silence or peace.'

'And you never had a home?'

'There were many different homes: one after another.'

'Didn't you like any of the places where you lived?'

'On the contrary: I was left alone. No one cared what I did or where I went. I used to go exploring. When we were moved to Crimean Kerch there were still wrecked houses and piles of rubble everywhere; I found hideaways in the ruins; I went climbing on the ramparts of the old fortress. When we stayed in Uzhgorod, we were in the barracks, right by the cathedral, and I spent all day by myself on the riverbank: there were cherry trees in flower all through the parklands—it was like a paradise. The same in Sukhum, beside the quay: you could watch the changing patterns on the water as the sun went down and there'd be no one else in sight. It was like a stage-set. None of it felt real, or solid, or tied to life. That was what those years were like. People came and went without reason, they would vanish, and then reappear a few days later—everyone was anxious, and hungry, and nothing was ever spelled out. The most substantial places were the hotels—you could feel the power and the safety in their corridors.'

'And that's why you like living in hotels today?'

'Do you think that? Do you really believe I have a fondness for this kind of life? What I think is that hotels like this are theatres, where we're in character, where we're most ourselves. We're on display, we're all actors. Life's richer, it's brighter.'

'And it's safer to live without a home?'

Serghiana was silent in reply: Egon came up behind us, looking flustered. 'Forgive the interruption, Serghiana Ismailovna—I have a request to pass on to you.'

'Egon Keleti,' she said, in a rhythmic, ironic Hungarian accent, drawing each syllable out: 'E.K. The man from the East! I always thought it was a good name you chose for yourself. Cartoonists need a catchy tag, don't they—a label, a signature to scrawl? My child—this gentleman's an artist, he's a gifted individual, he's drawn for all the best European newspapers.'

'I know your godson—wasn't that what you called him?' said Egon, and he smiled down at me, and gave me a quick, uncertain pat: 'We've known each other for years—from previous summers in the mountains, you see.'

'Godson! How formal! How tactful of you, Egon! I must have missed the christening!'

She reached over, and drew me closer to her: 'We're kindred spirits,' she said: 'That's all. That's enough—and it's fallen to me to look after him in these days and weeks. You know the story: perhaps you should give some thought to doing so as well.'

'But what on earth could I do?'

'Draw, of course, show him how to: teach him—or do you have hidden talents I don't know about? Should I consult your file?'

'Please—Serghiana Ismailovna, don't say such things even in jest. I'll help, of course. Whenever you want. We should support each other—no one else will.'

I looked at them both. 'Are you two friends now?' I asked.

'Absolutely,' said Egon.

'Shared background means much more than friendship,' said Serghiana, coldly.

'But I'm confused,' Egon said then: 'I must admit it. A few minutes ago, you were damning me in public, consigning me to the deepest circles of hell—and now we're close, we're allies. What's changed?'

'My mood, for one thing,' said Serghiana: 'Besides, we're going to ride up to the peak—that always lifts my heart. Why not come with us?'

'Oh, no,' Egon recoiled: 'I couldn't. The vertigo! The second I step onto the chairlift I tremble, panic takes hold of me; my head spins, the light in my eyes fails.'

'You're in the wrong place, really aren't you? You came out of the teeming streets of Budapest: these mountains aren't for you!'

'It's true,' said Egon: 'Sometimes I wonder what it is that keeps drawing me back here.'

'You come here because you have to. You come because this is what you are. You linger, you mingle, you make yourself familiar, you spend time on the fringes of groups you think significant, you imagine you're in touch, you're in the swim of things—then back you go, to Berlin, or Vienna, or Zürich, wherever it is you're selling your work now, and you tell your golden summer tales.'

Egon looked at me with a helpless expression. 'Your godmother has a sharp tongue!' he said.

'What would be the point of gentleness?' asked Serghiana: 'And what did you actually want?'

'The message: it's a film idea. A proposal. There's an American here. He asked me: he wants to meet you. He wants you to produce for him.'

'The Vietnam screenplay,' said Serghiana: 'I know: I heard. I already have his message: several of them, in fact. Some people have no sense of timing.'

'Why does he want you to make a film?' I asked.

'That's what your godmother does,' said Egon, a note of venom suddenly entering his voice: 'The truth is she's just the same as me: she needs these people just as much as I do—she makes pictures, she sells stories, she's a broker of amusements.'

'I prefer to call it culture,' said Serghiana.

'And are the films you make famous?' I asked: 'Like westerns?'

'Hasn't she told you?' Egon asked me: 'What reticence! Maybe she thinks you're too young. Of course she's successful: how could she not be? She's an intermediary between worlds. There's no one else like her, no one who can do what she does. We mere mortals look on in amazement, and wonder how she makes it work.'

'You pay me the kindest compliments, Egon,' said Serghiana: 'But I'm afraid this little talk of ours has to come to an end. The car's here. Soon we'll be high up among the peaks—in that pure, thin air where cartoonists fear to tread.'

We rode up in the chairlift, side by side. It was swift, and silent; it carried us high above the paths and rooftops. Streams and meadows passed beneath our feet, the landscape stretched away—then the lines of distant ranges, one after the next, like waves on an icy ocean, came into view: and though years and decades have gone by, nothing has dimmed my memory of that ascent, when the mountains and their geometry of ravines and spurs and rockfaces were shifting their alignments with each second, and a new world of air and void and precipice was unfolding before me: the glaciers shone, the grey screes slanted down into deep shadow, the light picked out each lake and forest clearing. I can still feel the warmth of the sun's rays at the instant they first fell on us; I can hear the sound of the wind, and the abrupt noise the lift made clattering across each pylon in turn.

From the midway station Serghiana and I looked down together on the buildings below. They were arranged in just the way the relief maps in the hotel showed them: spread along the valley floor as though in the palm of a sheltering hand. She made me point out each landmark, and laughed when I made mistakes, and corrected me. She was telling stories, describing the books she would next read with me, and the countries we should explore together: how close they were, just across the alpine passes—what wonders we would see!

Then came the journey's last stage—a closed funicular. The two of us climbed in alone, the cabin door clanged shut. Serghiana's mood began to shift: I could tell the warning signs. She frowned, she stared at me, a hard look coming into her eyes, as if my presence was a burden to her. She swung away, she reached for the safety rail with both hands: she gripped it tight and gazed off into the void: suddenly it felt as though a demon was there with me inside that glass-windowed cage. This continued until we reached the summit. We stepped out. A bare plateau lay ahead of us, and beyond it a line of sharp, snow-covered peaks. The air was cold; we walked. She went ahead, not looking back. I followed, becoming more fearful with each step, feeling more out of place. I had the sense of time in its passage slowing, pressing down, imprinting its every second on me. All I saw around me was set at a strange angle. I had questions: I wanted to ask them; I hesitated. I turned to Serghiana. She wheeled round.

'No words,' she said fiercely; her eyes were blazing, her face was contorted: she looked like a hunting animal: 'Don't speak,' she hissed: 'Don't talk to me! I don't need your childish nonsense now. Just look, that's all you need to do—look about you, keep your distance, stop plaguing me—say nothing—leave me in peace!'

*

After this Serghiana dropped from sight. Days passed. She left the hotel. When she came back there were strangers with her; I heard reports: how she was busy with her schemes and projects, how there were plans underway, political initiatives, and she was at the heart of things. Men and women with serious expressions were gathered at the tables in the hotel lobby; behind closed doors in the conference rooms meetings were held. Then, late one afternoon, I caught sight of Serghiana in the gardens. She was with Professor Leo. She called me over to them.

'You've been very quiet,' she said, her voice almost reproachful: 'I've hardly seen you at all since our trip up the mountain. Has Josette been looking after you properly? And Egon? I hope he's been helping to keep you occupied?'

She made a little gesture to the professor, as though to indicate how impossible it was that the cartoonist could be competent at anything.

'I thought you were angry,' I said to her. 'You were so strange up there, that day: so unfriendly. Don't you remember? You told me to keep quiet; you scarcely said anything to me at all.'

'That's right, my child,' she said, quite calmly: 'For me, it's something like a religious experience, going to those peaks. I thought that would have been plain to you.'

'I used to love the mountains, too, when I was your age,' said Leo, affably, and he motioned to me to sit down by his side.

'Really?' I asked, in a sceptical voice: 'Really, truly?'

'It's absolutely true,' he said, then went on: 'We used to always go to the Tatra Mountains for the summer holidays—to the Grand, in Tatranská Lomnica. My parents, my sisters and I. My father owned factories, but really what he wanted was to be an inventor. He told us he needed to take long mountain walks so he could think. He set out every morning, after breakfast—and I would try to go with him, but he always sent me back. Children and ideas don't mix, he used to say. But I argued with him—I told him that ideas were like children, and children had ideas too.'

'And were you a child, or an idea, to him?' asked Serghiana.

'Both, I imagine,' he said, and laughed: 'I knew even then that I was going to be a scientist. I wanted to prove myself to him: I was determined to show him what I could do. I used to go on expeditions along the walking tracks, alone, and collect the rocks with unusual shapes or coloured veins of mineral: I had a miniature prospector's pick, and a little leather pouch with my initials on it where I could keep my finds.'

'Yes,' said Serghiana, in a nostalgic voice: 'A family scene in the old homeland. An enchanted landscape, like a dream.'

Then she looked at me: 'Have you ever been to the high Tatras? I don't suppose you will, now—the door to that world's just slammed shut.'

'What do you mean?' I asked.

'Are you having trouble understanding what's been going on?' she said, sharply: 'Or do you just not want to know? Life is loss—isn't it,

Leo? Am I not right? We lose everything: places, people, loves, hope. Best to lose them early. Don't look at me like that! If you want someone to comfort you, my child, go and find Josette. But if you want me to tell you a story about these mountains—a story that means something—stay here with us.'

'I'd prefer to stay here with you, Great-Aunt Serghiana,' I said: 'You know that.'

'That's better—brave, and strong, and solitary—that's what I want you to be. Now listen.'

'Don't I always?'

'Don't test me! And let's not weary our friend the professor!'

She gave Leo a glance to signal her exasperation.

'But I understand,' said Leo: 'I was young myself once. And I also spent my days with adults when we were in the mountains: and by choice: but there was a desolation in that, as well as a kind of privilege.'

'Leo—such unexpected depths of sentiment!'

She turned to me again: 'When we were up on the summit together, at Cassons Grat, what impressions came to you: what did you feel?'

'That you were upset—or unhappy.'

'I don't mean about me—I mean about being there—being up above the world. What's the feeling that comes naturally?'

'You say,' I said.

'Didn't you feel how empty it was? How strong that sense is—the nothing behind the silence! I did: that's the feeling that always takes hold of me when I go up into the high Alps. Emptiness. Pure absence: no sign of man; no sign of a presence beyond man. Nature's inert there: it makes no difference how picturesque the view can be: how lovely, how symphonic, light and haze melting into each other, the mountains and the cloud banks like reflections of each other: the experience still leaves one bereft. But it wasn't like that always: these peaks used to be full of life. It's the same for me as for Leo: I can remember the Tatras as well. I spent a summer there—just one summer. It was like a dream of happiness for me. It was the last time I spent with my father...'

'The revolutionary?' I interrupted.

'Yes, the revolutionary,' she said: 'Do you want to hear, or interrogate me? We would go for mountain trips together, and when we climbed at Bystrá, or walked the path to the Kriváň summit, the skies weren't bare like these skies. There was life in the air; there was movement. I'm talking about the lammergeier: the vulture of the peaks—the ossifrage.'

She pronounced those words with great emphasis. I looked back at her.

'Don't tell me you've been neglecting your study of the Old Testament! The dietary prescriptions: Leviticus 11:13. "And these are they which ye shall have in abomination...the eagle, and the ossifrage." Do you remember seeing them then, Leo? Were they in the mountains, when you were a boy?'

'Of course: I loved to watch them—they would soar forever, I used to imagine that they were flying to the sun.'

'And those were your special favourites?' I asked Serghiana: 'Vultures?'

She looked at me. 'By name they were birds of prey, it's true,' she said: 'In a formal sense, if you have to classify—but not in any other. The moment I caught sight of them I was won over: how high they flew; how effortlessly! When they were aloft and tracing out their great circles they seemed to complete the sky. And they used to reign over these valleys as well. That's the whole point of what I'm telling you: once they were everywhere. They were the symbol of the mountains— the guardians of the Alps.'

'What happened to them?' I asked.

'It's the old story. Can't you guess? They were poised, and majestic: they were beautiful. Everything beautiful attracts hate—and the most fearsome raptors aren't in the natural kingdom, they're in the world of man. Whenever a child was lost in the mountains, or animals from a flock in the high pastures went missing, the vultures took the blame. They were wild, and free, and savage-seeming. They were turned into the enemy, the scapegoats, birds of ill omen—the fatal foe. Of course as soon as high-powered rifles came into use their numbers fell away. It didn't take too long. There was an extermination campaign: teams of marksmen fanned out through the ranges and shot them down.'

'They killed them all?'

'And for no reason! Poor creatures! They don't ever take live prey: they don't even feed on carcasses. No! Not for them the vulgarity of flesh consumption. They survive entirely on a diet of bones. All the violence and the bloodshed is over long before the lammergeier flies. They have a different purpose: they absorb death, and the remains of the body, and make new life. They aren't predators: not at all. They're cleansing animals. They bring a new, pure order into the world.'

'I think,' said Leo, uneasily, 'that I detect a political metaphor lurking here.'

Serghiana gave him a cryptic smile: 'Well,' she said: 'It's certainly no coincidence it was western countries that found them threatening, and purged them from the sky.'

Leo had been glancing round as this exchange progressed.

'No need to fret,' said Serghiana: 'No minders anywhere in your vicinity: the situation's become much too confused for them!'

'You could make a film about the vultures,' I said.

'Now there's an idea,' said Leo.

'On the whole, it's best to choose subjects you can actually show on screen,' said Serghiana, rather caustically. 'Rare birds that are only found at high altitude and that have gone extinct across most of their range wouldn't be ideal. But maybe we shouldn't rule it out. There might be potential: Czech directors won't be making their own films for a while, we can be sure of that—and the Carpathian studios in Bucharest might agree to co-production. Leo—you could even be a technical consultant: you've developed a liking for film-sets, haven't you?'

Leo turned to me, in a confidential manner. 'Madame Serghiana was kind enough,' he said, 'to invite me, when I was lecturing in Zürich, last year. I was able to take my departmental colleagues: we drove down to the location on the lakefront where the filming was underway. For me, it was like a brief visit to another world: so many people, working to a single goal; so much excitement, such glamour in the air.'

Serghiana raised her eyebrows. 'Glamour! In a film about Carl Gustav Jung and his archetypes: don't be absurd!'

'It was wonderful,' said Leo: 'When will it be coming out?'

'There were problems,' said Serghiana, now in a deadpan voice: 'In fact, it turned into a nightmare as we went on. The state film companies fought with each other constantly. Midway through the shoot the lead actor became convinced that Jung had been reincarnated in him: he wanted to write his own dialogue. Then he had some kind of breakdown: we had to pull him out. We began looking for a substitute—we decided to cast several actors to play different aspects of Jung instead. In the end I had a great falling-out with the director. He was Yugoslav: you can imagine the risk I'd run in choosing him! It was a bad decision from the start. He wanted to make Jung's dream about the Basel Münster the opening scene—and how, exactly, was he going to film that? I insisted that he bring in a narrator: he refused. We ran over our budget: the Culture Ministry stepped in. It was only through pure good fortune that I had another project—one with western backing—already underway.'

'Really?' said Leo: 'What project? What investors, at a time like this?'

Serghiana looked at him. 'My dear friend,' she said, 'your modest interest in my professional world seems to have deepened. I begin to wonder on whose behalf you ask me such specific questions.'

'But, Madame Serghiana...' he began.

'Enough!' she said. She turned to me and made a quick signal, a summons. In a flowing movement she rose from the table, took my hand and guided me away.

'Vipers,' she said to me under her breath as we walked off: 'Vipers everywhere—and the most venomous are the ones closest to us. And to think I was actually on the point of trusting him. What a collaborator—a time-server, on the lookout for himself at every second!'

'But you called him Uncle Leo when he arrived here,' I said.

'Titles mean the opposite of what they seem to mean—haven't you learned that yet?'

'I'm not sure I understand,' I said.

'I'll explain it all to you, later. In years ahead you'll look back on these times and everything that's happening around us will be clear to you: painfully clear. What makes people do what they do, and what makes them say the things they say.'

'Is it politics?'

'Yes—politics again.'

She let go of my hand, and looked down at me. She drew me nearer, and, absent-mindedly, affectionately, she stroked my head and ran her fingers through my hair. I pulled away from her.

'You don't care for that? You should relish the days when those around you want to smooth your hair, not fire a bullet into the base of your skull.'

I stepped back. 'That's a cruel thing to say,' I said.

'My child,' she said then, in a serious voice: 'Listen to me now! Don't you understand: you're my hope. I want you to fly free—to escape all this: not be trapped, not be caught by who you are and where you come from. I want you to know everything. I want you to be as wide as the horizon and as deep as the sky. I'm not trying to hurt you with my harshness: I'm trying to make you whole.'

We made our way back in silence through the hotel, and upstairs, to her floor.

'Come in with me,' she said: 'What's wrong? Have you used up all your conversation?'

'I've never been into your room before,' I said.

'Don't be ridiculous—it's just a hotel room, like any other.'

She gave me an encouraging prod and escorted me into a vast, elaborately furnished space: it was a corner suite, with doorways leading off into further corridors—a cavern, more than a room. At the far end stood a dining table and a grand piano, both bearing vases full of flowers. There were banks of armchairs and sofas, with coats and jackets draped over them. In one corner was a large work desk, its surface covered by documents and sheaves of typescript; old, ill-folded newspapers and magazines were heaped to overflowing on a low table. The French doors looked out on a wide verandah. Through them I could see two men sitting at a table, talking and gesturing, stealing brief glances in our direction.

'Don't pay any attention to them,' said Serghiana: 'They're the cultural attachés from the embassy: we've got some business to go through. Here—sit with me for a while.'

She cleared away a pile of folders from an armchair to make room. 'Push all that away,' she said. 'All those papers—they don't matter.'

'What are they?'

'Nothing—just radio reports and film scripts.'

'Great-Aunt Serghiana,' I asked: 'How did you actually become a film-maker?'

'I'm not a film-maker,' she replied: 'Making films is the easy part. That's what directors do. I produce them. I organise them, and find the money to pay for them. It's completely different!'

'How did you become a producer, then?'

'That's an easy question to answer: I married a director.'

'Is he going to come here too?'

'God, no! I didn't stay married to him. I don't stay married to anyone for very long.'

'Was he a good film-maker?'

'Very—that was one of his problems. And he was a perfectionist: that didn't help either. Moscow wasn't the right place for him. He went off to the United States. He works there now.'

'Why don't you go there too?'

'I don't think that would be a good idea. I have my own projects. I make a bridge between two worlds—between two systems. It's exactly the way Egon was describing it to you. The art's in the East, the money's in the West—I bring them together—and I can only do that when I'm midway between the two.'

'Somewhere like here.'

'It's ideal here, yes—but these are strange times. No one can really tell what's going to happen in the long term: that's why the people you see around us are so on edge. Everything could be destroyed for me at any moment.'

'And then you could go back to books,' I said, encouragingly.

She raised her eyebrows.

'I thought they were what you loved most.'

'They are. Of course they are. Books are everything to me—and films, the cinema, almost nothing: except in one respect. Books are simple in their texture; films are hybrid. Even the most complex, ambitious book you could ever read goes down a single channel. Everything's passed through the written word: from word to mind, from the writer's pen to the reader's heart. Everything's made from the simplest building bricks, from letters, from words and sentences. But cinema has several distinct channels—images, sound, text, music too. You can run them together, or set them against each other. You can make the viewer feel different things at once—and that brings it close to our experience of life. Division, contradiction, emotions that provoke their opposites! You know the way being aware of your sadness can make you feel a kind of joy—a sombre joy—and being happy and knowing that your happiness is fleeting can lead you to the edge of despair.'

'Can it?'

'That's something to live through, really,' she said: 'To find out for yourself, not to learn about from someone else. And you will. When you're a child, you don't always know what you feel—feelings flow through you, but they don't have labels yet. In a way it doesn't matter what they are, it just matters that they're strong, that they sweep you away. Then, in time, you learn the words for them, and words come like a fence or a fortress wall to protect you from feeling too much.

They file feelings away; you start to think before you feel. You describe your emotions to yourself. You enter the long twilight of adulthood.'

There was a knocking, insistent, at the door. In came Daru, elegantly dressed, with Josette just behind him and an older man, grey-haired, sharp-featured, in their train.

'Here she is—the impresario of our troubled times,' said Daru, and stretched out his hands to Serghiana in exaggerated greeting.

He glanced round the room, and fixed his eyes on me. 'You—here—and not in the nursery! While your protectress, not content with culture, is breaking into politics!'

'Stephane,' said Serghiana: 'How fine you look, in your linen suit: as sleek as a racehorse. But I'm afraid the child won't have the faintest idea what you're talking about.'

'Let me spell it out, then,' said Daru.

He moved to the centre of the room, and made a sweeping gesture towards his companions. 'We know,' he said, in accusing fashion: 'We know you attended a meeting that involves me directly—and told me nothing.'

'A meeting?'

'In Vienna—two days ago. And now I find myself called in to my minister, and I've been kept in the dark: it's left to my colleagues to inform me.'

At this, the older man, who was standing at Daru's shoulder, broke into a sphinx-like smile.

'That may be,' said Serghiana.

'May be?' Daru's voice rose: 'You said nothing, and you know I was trying to lead negotiations. I could almost believe you're trying to damage me, or act against us.'

'I haven't seen you to tell you.'

'We're staying in the same hotel.'

'And do you have some inborn right to know my every move, as if I were your captive here? Are you my guardian? Are you my keeper?'

'I thought I was your friend.'

At this, Serghiana laughed. The smile on the face of the man beside Daru widened. The two men from the verandah opened the French doors and came in.

'I think you know these gentlemen,' said Serghiana.

'I do,' said Daru, 'and I see your betrayal of me is complete.'

They all shook hands, slowly, ceremoniously, without a word.

'You look like dancers in a ballet,' said Josette, nervously.

'Impromptu diplomacy!' said Daru: 'I learn more about you by the minute, Serghiana.'

'Stephane,' she said: 'You lack intuition. You don't know me at all. You like to paint me as some kind of conspirator. You're wrong. If I find myself summoned to a talk with artists from an invaded country, it's precisely because I have no cause to fight for. Because I'm non-aligned. Do I even need to tell you something so obvious?'

'But you will surely report everything back.'

Serghiana made a sign to indicate the two men who had just come in. 'As you can see. Is that a surprise? Is it improper? Have you never felt the need for intermediaries? If someone asks for my help, I give it. If a diplomat like you asks for my opinion, I share it. Otherwise, I keep my thoughts and expectations to myself.'

'And what should we be concluding about all this? That some channel for negotiations has been opened?'

'Not at all. That a private talk of no consequence has taken place. You ought to pay more attention to the surface of events. Don't you know that an agreement's going to be signed in a few hours' time? The first act of the play's over now: there's no more state of crisis. Just the long sequence of aftershocks ahead. It's as I told you it would be on the first morning. The West deliberated, and force of arms prevailed.'

Daru looked at the man at his side, and shrugged, and turned back to Serghiana. 'It's true,' he said: 'It's really true, Serghiana, what they say about you. We're witnessing a masterclass. The truth is that you give nothing, and you disclose nothing. How useful you must be to those who have your loyalty.'

'Josette,' said Serghiana: 'Let me call on you again—time for you to step in and take the child away.'

Josette led me down the corridors. 'I'm glad we don't have to listen to any more of that discussion,' she said.

'They don't seem to like each other very much,' I ventured.

'They like each other very well,' she said, a note of resignation in her voice: 'They understand each other perfectly. That's the world they inhabit: every word they say to each other is said to gain advantage, and when they express a view you can be sure they think the opposite.'

'But if you don't like it, why do you spend your time in that world with them?' I asked.

'Don't pass judgement on me that way,' she said, frowning: 'You're becoming too much like Serghiana. We're here: your room—so—until tomorrow—or the next little dramatic episode. Just be careful that you don't end up living this kind of life.'

*

The following day, in the late afternoon, I was sitting alongside Egon Keleti at a table in the gardens, both of us bent over a block of pale blue sketching paper. In front of him was a wooden box full of pencils in bright colours, and at his side a leather satchel. The low sun lit the branches of the trees above us; the first leaves were beginning to turn.

'I thought you could draw anything,' I said. 'Why not the mountains?'

'I can,' he said: 'Of course I can—but landscapes leave me unmoved. I much prefer humanity.'

A waiter was hovering close by.

'Another coffee,' said Egon: 'Black and strong. We have ground to cover, my nephew and I! You don't mind if I call you that? I hope not. One can never have too much family.'

He gave me a quick look, failed to meet my eye, and picked up his outline pen. With a few quick motions he drew a set of curves and hatch marks on the paper, and pushed it away.

'I'm talking incessantly,' he said: 'I know it—but I'm nervous every time I sit down to draw.'

'Nervous? But you're the best in the world. Great-Aunt Serghiana said so.'

'She also says I'm highly strung. And it's the truth. Fear comes over me, my hands shake, my heart pounds, I feel as if I'm going to pass out. It happens to me every time.'

'Even now?'

'Even now—and I've already finished two cartoons today: I outlined them this morning, and sent them off—do you want to see the drafts?'

He produced a pair of lightly traced out pencil sketches from the folder at his side—scenes of men standing together, gesticulating, arguing, pointing at maps.

'What do they show?' I asked him.

'They're political,' he said: 'Like everything I do. Like everything around us. You've been spending a lot of time with the Red Princess, haven't you?'

His coffee arrived. He drank it in a single gulp.

'Why do you call her that?'

'I think you know—you know very well. You've got the trick of pretending not to know what you know, don't you? I used to be like that. I still am. She's not really a communist, I'm sure you understand—but then no one is, these days.'

'She's looking after me—while my mother's away.'

'It's a mystery to me how those two could ever have come to know each other,' he said. 'I can't imagine how their paths even crossed. Where is she now, your mother?'

'She's on holiday.'

'This is a holiday.'

'She's on holiday from our holiday.'

'I should be honest with you,' said Egon then, his voice uneasy. 'I promise I will be in the future. I know where she's gone.'

'You were tricking me,' I said, and stared at him: 'You've got your tricks, too.'

He looked down, and started to draw lines on the paper once again. His hands were long, and thin, and elegant: they moved in soft and even fashion on the page, and made a gentle, soothing sound.

'Yes,' he said: 'That's right. I've been to see her. I know exactly where she is.'

'But I don't—I only know she had to go to Austria—somewhere near Vienna.'

'Yes—to Klosterneuburg: it's beautiful. It has a famous monastery—and a church with a golden altar, and parapets like crowns around its spires.'

He paused, and toyed with his empty coffee cup, and checked my expression, then hurried on: 'I was very young, you know, when I first met her—I was still in my first year at the School of Arts in Budapest. She spent a month there, on a student exchange. They were hard times, for everyone—it was just after the uprising. Do you know about all that history?'

I shook my head.

'I suppose it doesn't matter, really—it was before you were born, and you don't have to know—the story repeats itself.'

'Were you friends?'

'Not then—she was quiet, and private: she seemed completely unapproachable—and I was very much in awe of her. We all knew she had some official connection: you couldn't travel so freely back then without approval. And we knew the foreign students only stayed with us for a short while. I wouldn't have been able to say much to her, anyway. Slav languages were a closed book to me; I didn't speak Russian—I hated it, I never wanted to learn it. I'd come from a small town in the Hungarian part of Romania. I was very much on my own in those days.'

'So you didn't know her at all?'

'The truth,' said Egon, 'is that she was a kind of ideal for me, a far-off ideal. I didn't want to know her. I never imagined I would in later years. I saw her: that was enough. She had a striking face: a candid face: it conveyed emotions very well. She was a beautiful girl, of course—I'm sure everyone tells you that—but I could see something else in her: an air of tranquillity: a great, accepting calm. It came back to me, long afterwards. I had a strange experience.'

He paused, and turned to look at me. 'Shall I tell you the whole story? I was already in the West, and working. I used to visit art museums constantly, to school myself: to learn. I had a hunger for art when I was young—a wild hunger. I was in Antwerp, and I went to the fine-art collection there: and I saw her. I saw her in a painting—her face—she was in the altarpiece of the Seven Sacraments. She was Mary Magdalen: the figure gazing upwards from the foot of the cross. I was astonished: I saw the resemblance instantly. I spent a long time there, looking, making sure I had it fixed in my mind.'

'Did you tell her about it?' I asked.

'I didn't dare to. You should go and see it in the museum when you're grown up, if you have the chance.'

'Why don't you draw her?' I said.

He shook his head emphatically. 'No—I couldn't,' he said. 'That world's gone. That time in my life's gone. It's nothing but a dream, and one that no one treasures—no one cares about.'

He fell silent. After a few moments, he began crying, very gently, without making a sound. Tears ran slowly down his cheeks. He reached over and touched my hand, as if to console me. 'I'm sorry,' he said: 'I don't even know why I'm crying. I'm not crying for her and what's happened. I'm not sad. I'm actually happy.'

'Aren't they almost the same thing?' I said.

'That's a very profound piece of wisdom from one so young! Did your great-aunt tell you that, too?'

'Yes,' I said.

'Did she, indeed! I wonder why she felt she should say that to you.'

'You don't like her, do you—at least not very much?'

'It's not that I don't like her. I admire her, in the same way one

might admire a glacier, or an alpine waterfall. I don't expect she wants
to be liked. She'd think it better to be feared—and people do fear her.
You can see what's going on around us, here in this hotel, can't you?
Look at that professor from Prague—he rushes to her side because he's
afraid of what she could do to him. And that ridiculous French diplomat strutting about the hotel with his mistress...'

'She's his secretary,' I said.

'His secretary, then—he keeps his eye on Serghiana Ismailovna
in case what she knows could be useful to him. They all run after her
and court her favour: they've convinced themselves she's at the heart of
things.'

'And she's not?'

'Who knows? She was once: she may be still. But they imagine
when they talk to her it's like sending a message directly to the Polit-
buro. They have a black-and-white view of a grey world—and nothing's
greyer or more impenetrable than Soviet politics.'

'But you're not afraid of her like them?'

'On the contrary—I fear her all the more, because of the way she's
been able to present her new face to the West. Everyone believes in
her: she's invented herself, she's made herself up, she's sent her image
out into the world, and it circulates: it has for several years now. I'm
sure the process works the other way—that it wins over her masters
in Moscow as well. And maybe that's enough: maybe the appearance
of influence gives her everything she wants. What's frightening isn't
her, but the way people bow down to her: diplomats, directors, actors,
writers, artists—everyone. As if she had some special, secret source
of information. But if you strip away all the stories that surround
her—who she's worked with, who she's supposed to be connected
with—what's left? I'll tell you! A woman with a faded glamour and an
intellectual cast of mind; a woman with access to large sums of money,
and a fondness for living in grand hotels. It's an unusual tale—and I
know exactly where it began—I know how she was living in the years
before liberalisation came.'

He gave me a smile, and clasped his hands together. 'That's enough,' he finished: 'Too much, in fact. I shouldn't say any more.'

'Go on,' I said: 'Don't just stop!'

'Please!' said Egon: 'Do you think I have no idea what children are like? I know you'll tell her everything I've said. Best for me to fall silent. I'm perfectly aware that in some dark corner of her thoughts Serghiana Ismailovna would like nothing better than to see me dead!'

I stared at him.

'Why the wide eyes?' he said: 'You don't believe me? You don't think she's capable of such unpleasantness? You don't think she's strong, and harsh, and cruel? She's kind to you because you're young, and helpless, not for any other reason!'

'That's a terrible thing to say—what you just said about her. And how can you know why she does what she does?'

'I know she's a monster.'

'Why don't you draw her?'

'That's an interesting idea,' he said.

He brought the sketchpad closer, positioned it, selected a bright red pencil from the wooden box in front of us and began to draw. On the page before me Serghiana's likeness took shape—but it was another Serghiana: her eyes were red, her face was transformed into sharp, contending angles, her hair was piled into a mass of coiling curves. He gave her a dragon's body, with its scales filled in as blurry hatch marks; she had claws, there were snakes wrapped around her arms, smoke puffs came from her nostrils; her lips were open and she was breathing fire.

'There!' he said: 'Your great-aunt as a mountain dragon. I think it's a good likeness, don't you?'

He looked at his drawing appraisingly for a few moments, then wrote underneath it, in capitals: SARKANY.

'Sarkany?' I asked.

'It's the Hungarian for dragon,' he said, and continued writing. 'Serghiana-saurus—rare and implacable.'

I looked at him.

'Implacable means you can't resist. The dragon can't be appeased.'

'It's beautiful,' I said: 'I've never seen anyone draw like that. But it's not very kind. I don't think we should show it to her.'

'No! Of course not. That would be a bad idea. We'll make it our secret, if you agree—just between the two of us.'

'We should do this every afternoon,' I said. 'Draw like this. You could turn everyone into dragons.'

'They're all dragons anyway,' said Egon. 'And you can tell me if you see any new ones, next time you go up to the peaks with Serghiana Ismailovna.'

'That's more the place for vultures,' I said.

'Vultures—what are you talking about? There aren't any vultures in the Alps.'

'She said there were, once.'

'I don't know why she took you up there to the top of the mountain: it's cold, and bare, and empty—and there are walks to treasure down here in the valleys and on the lower slopes: walks that fill the heart with happiness. I could take you on the paths through the forests, to the lakes, and to the cliffs above the Rhine. Would you like to go with me— or would you rather spend your last days here riding up in the funicular with your great-aunt to Cassons Grat?'

I said nothing in reply: he gave me a quick glance, then turned to look at me more closely. 'Did something happen when you went up there?' he asked.

'No—of course not,' I said.

'I caught the expression on your face. You want to be kind to her— but perhaps she's not always so kind to you. She was a strange choice to look after a child. Wasn't there anyone else?'

'She was my choice,' I said.

'I understand,' he answered, quietly: 'Don't say anything. You don't need to. You have to like her. And I have a fondness for her too, I even feel sorry for her, at the same time as fearing her: she looms very large in my life. She had her dreams and her ideals—I'm sure she still does. Shall we draw her another way, maybe—not just her harshness but everything that's strong and pure in her as well? Let's try—let's draw her as one of the avenging angels.'

'What are they?' I asked.

'You don't know about them? The angels sent down from heaven to cleanse the world? They're in the Bible, at the very beginning, when God destroys the cities on the plain; and at the end, too, when the rider on the pale horse is given power over the fourth part of the world.'

'And that's how you see her?'

'Let me show you how I see her,' he said.

He closed his eyes tight for a second; he interlaced his fingers and stretched out his hands: then he frowned, and began to draw again: quick, jabbing marks, long, graceful lines. His expression changed: at first it was mournful and solemn, then determined, then he nodded to himself: he tilted his head to one side, leaned back, looked down once more and pushed the block of paper across to me.

'There,' he said. 'That's what I see in her.'

The sketch bore no resemblance to the cartoon he had just drawn. It seemed to come from a completely different hand. This was a portrait: half illuminated, half in shadow. Serghiana's deep-set, angled eyes, the strength in her gaze, its yearning quality, the scornful, hurt edge to her smile, the hard set of her jaw, her look, her bearing, her presence—they were in the image: he had caught them all. It was nothing but a handful of flecks and lines and hatchings—it was her. It had taken him a minute; she seemed to be there before us, looking at us from the page.

'You can see,' he said: 'I know her well.'

I put the two sketches side by side. 'Why don't you make drawings that way all the time?' I asked him.

'Shall I tell you? There's a reason—a simple one—a bitter one. Do you want to hear it?'

'Would you like me to hear it?'

'Of course, yes. I'd like you to know me, or at least a little bit about me: in case something were to happen. It feels safe to be known by a child.'

He gave a half-smile, more to himself than to me, and gestured at each drawing in turn.

'This one's a caricature; but this one is meant as truth. When I was young, and I was still learning, I believed in drawing truth—I thought you could paint your way to heaven: make perfect images of everything around you—the sky, nature, the faces of everyone you saw—and that would be my place in life, my way of holding back the pressure of the world. I wanted only to be an artist, and be able to draw anything: I knew I would be one: I would make myself one. That's what I studied and what I loved. I drew on the blank pages of old books at home—I had books covered with my drawings even before I went to school. I was my own master and instructor then. I taught myself to make portrait sketches.'

'Like this one?'

'Absolutely—I had my special style: I showed what lies around the features of a face, I drew in negative. I wanted to make the eye believe in what I was drawing, I wanted hands to reach out and touch my images and think they were real.'

He paused.

'And what happened?'

'I was torn apart at once when I went to fine-art school—to that great school I'd dreamed of reaching. I thought it would be freedom and discovery; it was like an unofficial prison camp. There were ways you had to live, and things you had to think, and rules to take to heart: it was impossible to go against the tide. They told me my way of working was old, and useless, and idealistic, and there was no place for that kind of art anymore. I look back now, and wonder at myself: I fell into so many traps. I had no worldliness, no way to defend myself. I was sincere, and weak; that society was for the two-faced and the strong. I was still trying to find beauty in everything I painted—but all around me there was chaos: war, and the memory of war, and the threat of more violence close ahead. They threw me out of that school after my first year there. I was facing time in the army. I decided to run—and that's the end of the story—I reached the West.'

'And you started to draw cartoons?'

'To support myself—yes. I knew how to draw: that was all I knew—or almost all. I understood what people wanted. I could tell what made them smile, and laugh: I'd learned from my teachers how to draw crudely, how to exaggerate. Those were the only lessons they'd taught me. I was in Vienna first. Then Berlin: poor, without friends. No one cared for what I did; all my portraits, all my fine, well-drawn lines and shadings. No one would commission me. So I made cartoons—and they were picked up. That's when I began to see the way things were: the sharper the cartoon, the starker the message, the more popular they became. The more I betrayed myself, the better things went.'

He gave a brisk laugh; it sounded like a yelp.

'At first, when I'd just begun my exile, I hated what I was doing: but not enough. I persisted. My work became known. I had support-ers—and I was useful to them, because I came from the East, I was the victim from the other side. They pushed me, they even told me what to draw—and soon it became easy for me. It's easy now. You saw: I can draw my cartoons like this.'

He clicked his fingers: 'See—a good sound, isn't it? I do them like a magician's trick. The less thought I give my work, and the less care, the better it is.'

I looked back at him.

'I'm telling you a dreadful story,' he went on: 'Do you understand that?'

'I think so,' I said.

'Of course I'm only telling you because I know you can't possi-bly. I might as well whisper a secret to the wind. I'm telling you that debased times like ours need debased art; and when all the dreams and principles have rotted away, caricature's the only truth. Beauty can't mean anything anymore: it has no place. Listen—try to remember what I'm saying. Remember it, even if it can't mean a thing to you now.'

'You think I can't understand anything: you're making fun of me.'

'What I'm doing is trying to warn you—not to do what I've done... There's Serghiana Ismailovna now.'

He pointed her out. She was on the far side of the hotel's garden terrace, surrounded by a group of men.

'She's casting around,' he said: 'She'll see us, you can be sure of it.'

With a quick, stealthy movement he gathered up the two drawings on the table and slipped them into the folder by his side.

'She helped me, you know,' he went on: 'In those days I was describing to you, when I was just beginning to work in the West. She made things plain to me. She gave me to the editors who made me what I am. And now she likes to make jokes about how far I've fallen—as if she believed in ideals and high art still. She likes to think she's a child of the revolution: she's the ultimate in capitalism.'

'That doesn't sound like a good thing to be,' I said.

Serghiana made her way between the tables towards us. She tapped Egon on the shoulder.

'Discussing me again behind my back? It's a bad habit.'

'No, Serghiana Ismailovna—of course not!'

'Was he?' she asked me: 'Don't answer; it doesn't matter.'

'No,' said Egon to her: 'I'll tell you what we were saying. I was telling your child what I know—that we live in broken times; that the past's the only thing that lights us up—and if we gather here in the summer months, it's because places like this reek of pastness. We suffer from a love of what used to be. We're sick with nostalgia!'

'The title, as it happens,' said Serghiana, 'of a film I want to make.'

'I'll tell you what nostalgia is,' said Egon, and his voice rose: 'It's not what people think it is—no! It's the pain of longing, the pain of wanting to return and always knowing there's no home; knowing you can't get back what you've lost. That's what afflicts us all.'

'And that's why you draw as you draw—that's why you're a cartoonist and a caricaturist, and you can't make the great art you were born to make: and nothing good or true is possible. I've heard it all already. It's also why you're rich and successful and well known. Do I really have to remind you? I don't see you struggling to go back into oblivion.'

'And it's why you do what you do, Serghiana Ismailovna: my old friend, my benefactor—it's why you produce films set in a golden past, and peaceful days, in a time gone by that never was.'

'Such delirium!' said Serghiana, in a magisterial voice: 'Child—night's falling. Go and find Josette. It's best you leave us now.'

*

One morning a few days later I went downstairs to the breakfast room at the usual time to find Serghiana. There was no sign of her. The tables were empty; the hotel lobby was quiet. I went out to the terrace, where Egon always drank his black coffee: no one. I waited a few minutes, then went over to the concierge's desk. Mr Balzer was there, talking in a low voice on the telephone—speaking in a soft, strange language I had never heard before. He glanced down at me, nodded to me and kept talking: I leaned against the reception counter and let the sound of his voice wash over me: it was like the call of songbirds, or the flow of a river, or the humming of bees. I closed my eyes, and listened, and felt the cool brass edge of the counter pressing against my cheek. His call ended. He put his hand on my shoulder. 'Young man—is everything to your pleasure?'

'Mr Balzer,' I said: 'I was looking for my great-aunt Serghiana. I can't find her—I'm not sure where she is.'

'And this is a surprise?' he said. 'Really? You must know very well that she comes and goes from time to time. Don't worry—we'll look after you. She wrote you a note yesterday evening before she left.'

He reached into the message boxes behind him, produced an envelope and gave it to me. I opened it: the notepaper was Serghiana's.

Across the top of the page were art-deco motifs, entwined leaves and ornamental flowers, and her name in stylised capitals—'S. I. Semyonova: Producteur – Régisseur.'

I tried to make out the message: she had written in her cursive hand, at speed—one could almost see the words racing across the page: every few words the script jumped from Roman to Cyrillic lettering, then back again.

'My Dear Child,' it read: 'Forgive me—I care for you, I truly do.' The word 'truly' had been underlined with a sharp flourish—the pen had gone through the surface of the paper. 'I must go away for two days to Zürich with Uncle Stephane. The usual stand-ins will look after you while I'm gone. For all your needs turn to the concierge, Balzer, to whom I am entrusting this note, written with great affection in my heart. Trust Balzer—he has hidden depths. From the friendly hand of your great-aunt.'

I finished the note, and looked up at Mr Balzer. 'What does she mean by hidden depths?' I asked him.

He looked puzzled. 'I don't understand,' he said: 'What is it actually that you're asking me?'

'What language were you speaking,' I asked instead: 'When I came up to you and you were talking on the phone? It was beautiful.'

Mr Balzer smiled, and looked pleased. 'That was Romansh—Surselva Romansh, our language from here, the language we speak in this valley, among ourselves—but my mother's family came from the Lower Engadine, and we have another language there, even more beautiful: We call it Vallader.'

'It sounded like music,' I said.

'Yes—people fall asleep listening to it—fall asleep and dream. We don't speak it when the hotels are busy. It's a private language, for our world alone. Old men used to say it was the language of God: my father told me it was the language of poetry and song.'

'Will you teach it to me?' I asked him.

He laughed. 'It's a hard language to learn—and the members of your family already speak too many. Your aunt in particular. She changes and switches all the time: we can't keep up with her.'

'Won't you say something for me—to me—in your language—even if it's too hard for me to speak?'

'Of course I will,' he said.

He looked about the reception, then came out from behind his desk, and went down on one knee alongside me: he pronounced a few sentences in rhythmic fashion, almost in a whisper: a rustling, scurrying rush of words.

'What did that mean?' I asked him.

'The Lord bless you and keep you—the Lord make his face shine upon you and be gracious to you—the Lord lift up his countenance upon you, and give you peace.'

'Thank you,' I said: 'But—Mr Balzer—why are you praying for me?'

'To intercede for you in your misfortune.'

'I see,' I said.

'Do you?' said Mr Balzer. 'It's natural for us to want to help you and protect you. There's more to our work than meeting the needs of our guests—much more. It's best if we can see through the expressions they wear, and look into their hearts; if we can find a true affinity with them; if we know what they want before they know it themselves. Those are the things that make places like this what they are—not luxury and spa treatments and elegance.'

'Can you really remember all the different people who come here for their holidays?' I asked him: 'Do you recognise them from year to year?'

'Of course,' he said: 'We know their stories, and we know their habits. We know the face each one of them presents to the world. A guest like Madame Semyonova, for example: we greet her on her arrival as if we were greeting a respected friend. We know the pattern of her life, we know her hopes and fears, we sense the obligations that weigh her down. We know where she travels when she leaves us at short notice, and we know why: we see everything, and judge nothing.

We try to be of assistance to her in all her tasks. Sometimes it seems to me as if we're an audience, watching a great spectacle, and the guests are actors on a stage. When the play's well scripted and performed, we can feel everything they feel: happiness and sadness, fulfilment and discontent.'

'And what do you feel about this summer's performance?'

'The season isn't over yet. It's too early to say. Last year, though, I felt a great worry—worry, in fact, for you.'

'But it was a good holiday.'

'Do you remember it? For a boy your age, a year's a long time ago. You spent most of it reading with Madame Semyonova. She became your family. You hardly saw your mother at all.'

'I know.'

'She was occupied with other people.'

'What do you mean?' I asked him.

'Will you be paying her a visit?' he went on, in a soft voice. 'If you do, please give her a message on our behalf: tell her that we miss her, and wish her well.'

'You liked her—when she was here before?'

'We care for all our guests—even the most difficult ones: even the ones who fail to notice us and what we do. Especially for them, in a certain sense. Enough of all that now: I want to show you something: a surprise!'

'You're changing the subject,' I said.

'Of course I am: that's also part of what we do.'

'Why?'

'You'll have ample time for difficult, unpleasant things in your adult life. Look behind you—at that photograph on the wall: the panoramic view. I'm sure you have before.'

'Hundreds of times.'

'But look closely. It's an old picture, of course. You can tell that from the landscape: it was taken in the early days of the resort. There are no holiday villas; the pine-tree forests reached much further then than

they do now. And here we are—where I'm pointing: this hotel building already looked the way it looks today. How many floors do you see?'

'There's the reception floor, and one below, and four above.'

'Exactly so. Now—come with me.'

He led the way to the lifts, and pressed the call button. We got in:
the doors closed behind us.

'How many floors?' he asked again, and pointed at the control
panel.

'R for reception, G for garden, and three more.'

'Exactly so! There's one missing. Shall we go up, and see if we can
find it? Let's take a look.'

'Don't you have to stay downstairs?'

'I think I can risk a few moments away from my duties,' he said,
and pressed the button for the top floor.

'But this is the floor where I'm staying,' I said as we got out.

'And have you never wondered about that closed double doorway,
with no bell to ring, and no room number beside it, at the far end of
the corridor? Didn't you ever think there might be something strange
behind it—something you wouldn't expect?'

He produced a key, opened the doors and ushered me in. Before us
was a wide staircase, drenched in light. We climbed it, and it was as if
we had stepped into another world. There was a roof of curved glass far
above our heads; there were chandeliers, there was fan vaulting: iron
columns rose around us; two long, glass-walled galleries stretched away.
On every side, the eye was dazzled: sunshine, the gleaming peaks, the
white clouds, the blue of the sky—everything was shimmering and
alive with light.

'Now, tell me,' said Mr Balzer, stretching out his hands: 'Isn't this
one of the most splendid sights you've ever seen?'

I looked out—then up, into the vaulting, and the sky: the sun
blazed, its light poured down, the clouds raced past—I felt myself
adrift, my head spun.

'Where are we?' I asked him.

'This is the Glass Chamber,' he said, in a dramatic voice: 'It was a ballroom, once—a grand ballroom with a view onto the stars. See how fine the flooring is—Versailles parquet, perfect for the dance. Guests from all over Europe used to come to the parties and the celebrations here. There were recitals in the afternoon all season long; a string quartet from Italy gave chamber music concerts every night. It was a gathering point, it was famous, everyone in Berlin and Vienna knew its name, they all longed to see it with their own eyes—it was one of the marvels of the Alps.'

'And what happened?'

'Tastes change. Nothing stays the same. People come here today to walk in the mountains, not to dance. The hotel's owners decided long ago to close up these rooms. Look carefully: you won't have the chance again. The whole floor's going to be remodelled over the next few months. Nothing will be left of all this. The sun won't stream in through the glass cupola anymore; the snow and ice won't mantle it in winter. Look, and fix it in your memory.'

And doubtless, with the naive good faith of childhood, I wished to do as he instructed, and I promised him I would—but as the years flowed past and the images that came crowding in upon me multiplied, my memory of that morning when the last glow of summer was in the air around us faded. The world of mountains and hotels retreated from me, that whole childhood time—it was gone, with all its surprises and its upheavals. They vanished, I hid them away inside myself, I had no use for them—they came to seem far distant, they were gauzy and disjointed in their texture, and more like a story I had once been told than recollections of the past. My life had turned into a series of staccato chapters: I went from city to city, and from school to school; I looked ahead, not back—my interests and my fears were all in the present and the future tense.

So it was a jolt for me when, one afternoon at the beginning of my student years, I came face to face with a set of images that brought that day with Mr Balzer back into my thoughts. I was with my friend

Beni Anselme: we were both strangers in Paris, we had just arrived, we both felt out of place. We were walking together, on the Rue Champollion: we passed a rerun cinema, the Reflets Médicis. There were black-and-white photos pinned up inside a display window by the ticket office—production stills: I caught sight of a single, striking shot: it showed a boy staring upwards, and a wash of bright light streaming down upon his face. Suddenly I could see myself standing beside the hotel concierge all those years ago, gazing up at the crystal chamber's vaulting, and through it, to the sun's disc and the clouds as they raced by.

'Stop,' I said, and pulled at Beni's arm: 'Stop—we have to go in, Benoit—we have to see that movie—now.'

'Don't tell me you haven't seen it before,' he said, screwing up his face in a pantomime of scorn.

'What film is it?' I asked him.

'You don't know, and you want to go and see it? That's crazy! It's *The Silence*—Bergman's *Silence*—it's a very well-regarded work: in fact some critics believe it's a masterpiece—though not me! Still, I don't think anyone could consider themselves cinematically literate without knowing *The Silence* inside out.'

'I haven't had the benefit of your grand-bourgeois upbringing,' I said.

'You know how to hurt! What about all your filmic connections?'

'Knowing film people doesn't mean you necessarily know much about films.'

'Well, why now, anyway? We've got lectures.'

I explained.

'You're telling me that in all seriousness you want to spend the whole afternoon in cinematic darkness because a single publicity still reminds you in some vague way of something you saw years ago?'

'Can you think of a better reason to see a film?'

'Not really.'

'Let's go in, then.'

We did: the film enveloped us. Its plot is straightforward. Two women and a young boy travel by train through a strange country whose language is unknown to them. There are tanks patrolling in the streets; the atmosphere is redolent of the Cold War years in the Eastern Bloc. The older of the two women is gravely ill: they have to break their journey; they find accommodation in a dilapidated grand hotel: the boy explores his new surrounds; the rooms, the long, empty corridors. A lone waiter befriends him; a troupe of dwarf performers amuse him, and amuse themselves by making mock of him. The older woman—a translator—makes lists of words in the mystery language; her sickness worsens; the younger woman pursues a brief, wordless liaison. The two are sisters, but not close; they bear each other grudges: they argue, they speak harshly: it is the climactic scene. A brief coda follows: the translator lies still, eyes wide, awaiting death; the younger woman and the boy travel on; their train pulls away, rain falls, the film ends. We left the cinema: I was silent, and greatly moved.

'So,' said Beni: 'See any parallels?'

I looked back at him, and tried to smile.

'That's a wan little smile,' he said.

'Analogies, maybe,' I answered: 'Not exact parallels.'

'You must have had quite a childhood!'

'The mood was familiar, certainly, that's all I mean. I've been in places like that. I'd like to see the film again.'

'Don't pay too much attention to films that seem to retell your own story,' said Beni: 'The whole point of cinema-going's to experience something new.'

'You don't think one can learn from seeing familiar themes explored by different eyes? You don't think art illuminates?'

'I'm sure you think your life's richer than a quickly thrown-together piece of arthouse angst.'

I said nothing, and we walked on, and I turned over what we had seen: the details of the story, the pacing, the words exchanged, the things unsaid. Even as the film was screening I could see the half-rhymes it made with my own experience of childhood: it stayed with me—but only long afterwards did I come to realise that encounters with *The Silence* were playing an unusual role in my life.

I was in Budapest, and it was night, a summer night in 1989. I was travelling with a photographer and a team of documentarists: we had been together since the start of August, and we were nearing the month's end. It was the midpoint of that year of revolutions: the world I had known all through my youth was being remade before my eyes. The next morning, the border with the West would be opened: a first breach; a fatal breach: we could sense it—for the regimes of Eastern Europe the end was drawing near. We had an apartment in a new building by the Chain Bridge and the Danube. I looked out onto the flowing river and the moon's gleam reflected in its current, and the dark mass of the castle high on the opposite bank. I watched the river barges steaming past at speed; I watched the tail-lights of the cars on the far embankment driving by. In the plate glass of the window I could see the flicker of the television on the wall behind me. Something made me pay attention. I turned, and looked: the scene was familiar—the boy from *The Silence*, running down the hotel's empty corridor. I had found some western cable channel and left it on. I sat close before the screen, and watched, and let the story take hold of me again.

In the south of France, six months later to the day, I had the same experience. It was in Toulouse. That afternoon I walked past a book-shop close by the Place du Capitole. There was a copy of Céline's *Bagatelles pour un massacre* in the window: it was in mint condition, its pages uncut—a collector's item. For years I had searched for this bitter manifesto, and dreaded finding it. I bought it, at vast cost, exchanged complicit glances with the bookseller and went back to my hotel room. I began to read the book, which is unsurpassed in the violence of its language and the force of hatred it conveys. I read through it, as much as I could bear, and fell asleep. In the small hours I woke. The television was still on: *The Silence*, with Spanish subtitling, was being shown:

I could see the actress Ingrid Thulin, as the translator, writing her notes and staring into the void.

The same, too, in Moscow, on the day of the failed coup that brought about the Soviet Union's end: a signal again, a private sign. I was there collecting eyewitness accounts, quite unsure what the past few hours on the barricades had meant and what the day ahead would hold. Night fell. I looked in vain for enlightenment from the official television news broadcasts, and switched over: I saw the first scenes of *The Silence* unfolding on a foreign channel, and knew at once more risk and danger lay ahead. And I could multiply this sequence of coincidental broadcasts of the film at fateful moments, at points of change in my life's course— but even as I set these words down I realise no one will ever have such experiences again: it is no longer possible. The days when films were rare, and exquisite, and one went to any lengths to see them, and paid heed to the times when one saw them, whether in the cinema or on the television screen, are gone: and a vital part of their magic has gone as well. They can no longer serve as harbingers, as tokens of life's mystery—they are ubiquitous, and so the lustre of chance recedes from our world.

*

More days went by: I spent them with Mr Balzer and Josette. Serghiana came back at last one night, very late. The next morning I found her seated at her usual table on the garden terrace, talking to Professor Leo and Egon Keleti in a low voice.

'Stalemate,' she was saying as I came up behind her: 'Pure intransigence. Nothing will happen now: they had bargaining power, or at least the ghost of it—the power of the unjustly condemned—they let it slip away.'

I touched her on the elbow: she gave a start.

'My child,' she said: 'You appeared so silently!'

'How soft it is—your pullover,' I said to her.

'It's cashmere, from Afghanistan: a special kind of wool. It's not from sheep. It comes from goats, mountain goats that live high in the

Hindu Kush. They have thick fleeces, and a down that keeps them warm—it's gathered from them every spring.'

'That doesn't sound very pleasant for the goats,' said Egon.

'Nonsense!' said Serghiana: 'The hair's combed out when the moulting season comes. The goats don't mind at all: they like it.'

'In fact, they're happy to live in servitude and give of themselves to fulfil their part in global capital's great production plan!'

Serghiana raised her eyebrows, and turned away from him. 'My child,' she said, 'we were just talking about you. The season's almost over. It's been a perfect summer.'

'A profound summer, certainly,' said Egon.

'A perfect summer,' repeated Serghiana: 'Look: the splendour of the sky, the leaves just turning in the trees around us, the cold stealing into the air, the first hint of storm formations headed to us from the south. Such wonders! Don't you feel swept up by emotions, Leo, when the alpine autumn comes? Happiness of course, because it's the most poignant of the seasons; sadness, because pure joy in life's no longer possible, it has to be a painful joy, you realise the great lesson once again—all things of beauty have to fade and die. And there's the special sadness of these days we're living through as well. I think we can agree to call these tragic times, Leo—wouldn't you say?'

He gave her a wry smile.

'No view, Leo? Nothing? A man of your stature and your knowledge, with nothing to say?'

'What should I say, Madame Serghiana? My field is science, not politics.'

'I thought the two were intertwined in your academy! You don't share my sense of disillusion—of dismay? You don't feel you can confide in us? There aren't any minders with us now; the child's not going to tell stories to anyone, and Egon's too deep in his own maze of contradictions to care. I'm asking you—in all seriousness.'

There was silence between them. Leo kept his expression fixed. She gave a little laugh, and spoke again:

'No,' she said: 'Really? You've got no answer to give me—just your smile: your wise, well-calibrated smile? But isn't it plain to you? Don't you know me well enough by now? I only wanted to see where you stand—and when you say nothing to me the answer's clear. Don't stay silent, Leo—don't make me see you as the scientist of the state!'

She stretched out her hands for a moment towards him.

'How magnificent you look, Madame Serghiana, when you plead with me like this,' he said: 'That's what I'll remember of you when I travel back to Prague.'

'And you wonder why I despair of you and your kind! Here you are, dragging out the last days of your sabbatical while your country's being pulverised and turned to dust. How full of caution and irony you are. You won't take a side, you won't allow yourself to have principles: all you have left is your accommodations and your ambiguities.'

'Madame Serghiana,' said Leo, 'you think you can embarrass me by speaking to me this way: but you know very well it's not possible for someone in my position to have principles. To be candid, you know it better than I do.'

She smiled at him, in a measuring way, and tapped the armrest of the wooden bench she was sitting on. 'Sit here,' she said to me: 'Don't just watch. Sit with us. What will you remember of today, when you look back, and see us all again in your mind's eye? Will you remember the blueness of the sky above the peaks: that blue that goes into white, and wavers when you stare at it, and blinds you? Will you still see that?'

'I'm sure I will,' I said.

'Picture us all now, and the backdrop of the mountains. Carefully. Keep the image. Try to hold it in your thoughts. Childhood's the blessed time! Truth's very close to us early on. Everything's clear—you can sense what you are: then all that's overlaid, by experience, by what comes to meet us—and we spend the rest of our lives trying to recapture that essence of ourselves we once knew well. What good fortune it is that we've been here, in the mountains, during these days when your world was turned upside down.'

'Why?'

'So that you remember, of course—so these days make an impression. So they sink in. Really, you should never come back here, to this valley—that's the best way to preserve the memory—preserve it without taint or overprint.'

'For God's sake, Serghiana Ismailovna,' said Egon: 'Don't be so extreme!'

Serghiana paid no attention to him. She placed her hand gently on my back, high up, between the shoulder blades, and left it there.

'We have to decide what to do with you,' she said.

'What do you mean?'

'School. We can't send you back.'

'Can't I stay with you?'

She looked at me pityingly.

'And what would you do? Read bad film scripts with me in my hotel room?'

'Why not?'

'So charming. Be careful. Charm wears off!'

'Why do the mountains matter anyway?' said Egon to her.

'Because the mountains are a stage: they intensify thought. The eye looks into the distance; the mind follows. They're a screen for the imagination: they aren't real.'

'Please—they're as real as stone!'

'My poor friend—you've never really understood. You think you've found your way into this world of ours, this little society of the lost, this Bohemia—but it's not so. The mountains are only for true artists: for those who want to see beyond, and bring back what they've seen. They speak to the child, though. I could see it in him, up on Cassons Grat, when we left you behind and took the funicular that day.'

'Is that right?' said Egon, in a sardonic voice, and looked at me.

'Yes—of course it is. Do you think I could be wrong about such a thing?'

She turned to me. 'You should make sure you go to Luzern, when you're old enough. To the museum at the Gletschergarten: they have old panoramas of the mountains, perfectly preserved. All the history's laid out there before you. Artists and writers have been coming to the Alps for centuries: Byron, Wordsworth; even the Russians, even Dostoyevsky and Turgenev. I went there with my husband when I was travelling for the first time in the West. I'll never forget it: I was very young—it was a golden time.'

'Which husband?' asked Egon.

'The geologist-engineer, of course—the one who made me what I am—the one whose name I take.'

'You know, Great-Aunt Serghiana,' I said, 'I'll have so many places to go and see I won't have any time to do anything else.'

'He has a point,' said Egon, laughing.

'Pay no attention to him!' said Serghiana: 'Do you remember what we were reading, last year, when we spent our afternoons together in the gardens of the park hotel? The French novel—the *Princesse*?'

I nodded my head.

'And you realise I didn't choose it for you just because it was a fine romance—a pretty costume drama. No. It was something much more than that. It was fiction beyond fiction—the most serious kind of book. And now I can see the deeper reason why we were reading it. It's a story about the arrival of misfortune. There's a lesson in its pages. It tells you not to trust others, not to give way to sentiment: to close yourself off, and live hard and cold.'

'And that's the lesson you want to hand down to your charge?' said Leo, speaking softly: 'That's what you're going to leave him with, as you cast him aside, and go on your way?'

'Uncle Leo seems to have concerns,' said Serghiana in a velvet voice, and she fixed her eyes on me. 'But he doesn't understand: he doesn't see how close we are.'

'I'm sure that's a great consolation to the boy!' said Leo.

'Nothing can come between us,' said Serghiana: 'Can it?'

'It's an impressive display you're putting on, Madame Serghiana,' said Leo, and he shook his head.

'Can it?' she asked me again, and took my hand in hers.

'No,' I said: 'Of course not.'

'And that book will be with you always. It'll come back to you, and play its part in your life. Great books become true for their readers. They shape the lives of those who give themselves to them: that's their hidden strength.'

'Please, Serghiana Ismailovna,' said Egon: 'Stop confusing him!'

'Are you confused?' she asked me.

Egon leaned across towards her, and took her arm, as if to restrain her.

'For my part,' he said to me, 'I hope you remember these days kindly, and all of us as well—and I hope you come back here often in years to come, and make it a place with depth and meaning in your heart—just as your mother did. There's nowhere more beautiful. I'm thankful that I found this tranquil paradise.'

Serghiana stood up. She reached across to me, and took me by the shoulders, and held them. 'You'll see, both of you,' she said, in a triumphant voice. 'And he knows already. The look's there in his eyes. He knows words have force. A strong thought's spoken out loud, and it's as good as true. He won't come back. The forests and the peaks will haunt him, and always be inside him, they'll remind him of the time we've spent in each other's company, and the memory will stay. Happiness and sadness joined together—that's what he inherits from us. We'll be gone, and years will pass, and everything in the world will change— and that will stay. He may long to be back here, he may even set out on the journey, he may tell himself it's a necessary pilgrimage, but he'll always turn aside. This will be a place of imagination for him, and nothing beyond that—a place to keep in the past and keep unspoiled. I know it. I know it for a fact.'

She looked into my eyes, then across at Leo and Egon. But at that moment one of the hotel's concierge staff came bustling up, and made a little obeisance to Leo, and the tension between the three of them dissolved.

'A phone call for you at the desk, professor.'

'Who can that be?' said Leo, an anxious look crossing his face: 'Nobody from the university knows that I'm still here.' He hurried off.

Serghiana watched him go. 'He has the look of a hunted man about him, doesn't he?' she said.

'He may well be one soon, Serghiana Ismailovna,' said Egon: 'If anything you suspect him of is true.'

'Stars above!' she said: 'Who'd have thought that out of my two faithful companions here this summer it would be you, dear Egon, who would prove to be the more amusing, the more blessed with insight and the more profound!'

Leo returned. He was beaming. 'Good news,' he said: 'Ady's coming! I can't wait to see her. She arrives tomorrow.'

'That showgirl!' exclaimed Serghiana: 'Already! It's not what we agreed! She's coming to claim him. To exult. And so our little idyll comes to its close. How convenient that I'm booked to leave today.'

'You're leaving the hotel?' I said.

'I'm leaving the country, my child. It has to be. I have work. Don't worry—we've made arrangements.'

'But you didn't say.'

'Aren't you and Ady friends?' Leo asked her: 'You must move in the same circles. Don't you have a great deal in common with each other?'

Serghiana glared at him. 'In common! With her—a Carpathian peasant—a dancer from the Viennese stage—a failed actress—a fraud in the world of culture. What could I have in common with someone like her? What? I'd like to know, Leo!'

'Madame Serghiana,' he said: 'One of the most engaging things about you is the intensity of your dislikes. But even so I'd have thought at least you would have an admiration for her new husband—or husband-to-be. After all, he's a brilliant man.'

'A brilliant man embarking on his tenth marriage!' snapped Serghiana. 'Doubtless destined to a long duration, like all the previous ones. Who knows how she ensnared him? Although I can guess, of course—he's always been a satyr. All conductors are!'

'What's a satyr?' I asked.

'Even in the nineteen-sixties,' she said, 'it's something bad.'

'Are you talking about Ady Palafay?' said Egon from his corner of the table.

'You know her?' said Serghiana, indignantly.

'I do—and you must know her too,' he said to me. 'She's a friend of your mother's: your mother always calls her Adela, and of course soon she won't be Palafay anymore—she'll have another name.'

'Do you know her?' said Serghiana, giving me a furious stare.

'You shouldn't be so hard in your judgement of her,' said Egon: 'She comes from a different world to us.'

'And what world is that?'

'The world of pleasure and amusement.'

'Yes, and of course you're such a devotee of wit and hedonism, aren't you—the committed joker, the secret humourist in the swamp of gloom.'

She wheeled around to look at me. 'And you,' she said: 'You carefully kept quiet! Is Egon right? You know her?'

'Aunt Adela? I've known her since I was little.'

'And you like her?'

'I love her—it's wonderful spending time with her.'

Serghiana gave me a radiant smile. 'Aunt Adela—and you love her! You love her! It's too perfect. Everything falls into place. She can look after you now—and pay for you, and drag you around Europe with her like a lapdog, along with all her dresses and her monogrammed luggage and her chauffeur. I'll leave you to her devices—and to these gentlemen!'

And she tossed her hair back, gathered up her coat, turned, strode off without a backward glance and disappeared into the lobby of the hotel.

III

Corviglia

A YEAR HAD passed, and more. I was at a school I disliked in the Engadine. In the afternoons I used to sit alone for hours in the gardens that overlooked the valley: I could see the narrow river far away, the roofs of the village, the tall, thin church spire, the silent streets and shuttered houses. There was the school courtyard, immediately beneath me, and the senior classroom building with its tower and the clock that never told the right time, there were the neat pastures full of grazing cattle, there was the narrow road that led towards the national park and the Austrian border in the west. I could just make out a small vehicle coming from the direction of Samedan, at speed. Its windscreen gleamed as it caught the sun. It was a sports car, steel grey. I watched as it drew nearer, then turned, and began the climb up to the village. It swung round a farmer's cart and straight up the no-entry street, and vanished from view. I could still hear it, screeching round the corners, accelerating up the alleys—then suddenly I saw it again, close by, turning into the school's main driveway: it braked sharply and came shuddering to a stop. A handful of older students standing in the main quadrangle stared in curiosity: by the standards of the Lyceum Alpinum, this arrival was already an event. I looked on as the driver's door opened. A man of slight stature in a dark suit jumped out, smoothed his long, greying hair and rushed round to the passenger's side. He made a little bow, and offered his hand in formal fashion, but the woman who emerged from the car waved him off, then paused for a moment and rearranged the scarf at her neck. There was something familiar about this figure. I looked more closely: not young, not old, foreign in manner, extreme in elegance. She glanced round, screwed her face up in an expression of distaste, reached down into the car, extracted a pair of sunglasses and put them on.

'What a place,' she said loudly, in an accented voice: 'These archways, these colonnades and blank windows. It's like a cross between a monastery and an asylum. Let's not waste time here. Quick—go and find him, go.'

She turned while speaking, and I realised I was staring down at my aunt Adela—my honorary aunt Adela Palafay, whom I had been very fond of years before, when she first spent time in our company. She had seemed quite fascinating then to my eyes, with her golden hair, her voice redolent of far-distant, mythic regions, and the bright clothes she wore that gave her the look of a bird of paradise at rest. I smiled at the sight of her. I was on the point of calling out, but one of the teachers from the senior school had spotted her, and came up.

'Young man,' she said, and extended a hand in his direction as if she expected him to kneel before her: 'Fetch me the headmaster—right away.'

The teacher scuttled off. I made a slight movement. She wheeled round and saw me gazing down. At once she broke into a radiant smile and waved to me. 'My treasure,' she called out: 'My soul! I knew you'd be waiting for me; I knew you wouldn't have forgotten me. Don't just stand there staring—come down, I've longed for you, I've missed you, I've so much to tell you.'

She turned to the grey-haired driver, who had remained with her. 'Hurry, Muscatine, go and meet your new friend. Try to be civil to him.'

The man in the dark suit came clipping up the stairs towards me. At that moment across the courtyard the main door to the tower building opened and the headmaster, pursued by his deputy and several members of the teaching staff, strode out, beaming, both arms stretched before him in greeting. Ady put her hand to her chin, and tilted her head in her most feline fashion. She stretched out her hand once more: the headmaster bent, and kissed it reverentially.

'An honour,' he said: 'And a surprise!'

'Bring me my boy,' she said, her voice stern.

But the dark-suited man was upon me, panting as he came up to the garden balcony. He spoke my name, pronouncing it between his teeth as if he was tasting it.

'That's you, isn't it? Why are you hiding up here?'

'I'm not hiding,' I said: 'Who are you?'

'I'm Muscatine,' he answered, frowning as he spoke the syllables.

'And what do you do?' I asked him: 'Are you a chauffeur?'

'No, of course not,' he said, and gave me a look of undisguised hostility: 'I'm the Maestro's accompanist.'

'The Maestro?'

'Novogrodsky, Madame Ady's husband.'

'Novo-grodsky?'

'Yes—don't you know who he is? Don't you know anything about musical culture?'

'Lots,' I said: 'They teach us Beethoven, and Mozart, and Haydn, and we have singing lessons, too.'

'Beethoven—Mozart,' said Muscatine, and raised his eyebrows: 'Is that all? You might as well be studying mediaeval plainsong!'

He had long hands with manicured fingers—he flicked them dismissively, with the air of a man used to passing judgement on great swathes of European civilisation and finding them deficient.

'Novo's a more modern figure,' he went on: 'Much more modern. He has a contemporary philosophy, he reaches out to concert audiences. He's a conductor for these times.'

'And you travel with him? You accompany him?'

'I'm a musical accompanist,' he said: 'Not some kind of travelling companion. When the Maestro rehearses his scores, it's with me, always: it can only be with me. We spend our days together; I even collaborate with him when he composes. That's the way it is.'

Ady called to us from below. 'Come down,' she cried: 'The headmaster's been telling me interesting things!'

'Of course, madame,' Muscatine called back, cringing, and glanced at me again.

'That shriek,' he said in a low voice: 'That woman!'

'You don't like her?'

'Don't presume—and don't make trouble. Be quiet, be tactful!'

'Why?'

'Because all the people round Novo these days are like piranhas. She especially. You're related to her, aren't you?'

'In a kind of way. Does that mean you don't like me either?'

'Not yet. You have to earn being liked. Let's reserve judgement on each other. Come on!'

With that, he gave me a prod. We went down the steps together.

'Madame,' he murmured in deferential fashion, and made another little bow.

'Headmaster Grafhorn's been entertaining me,' she said: 'What a charming man he is! Such courtesy!'

'You're too kind, Madame Palafay,' said the headmaster: 'But it's Ganzhorn, actually.'

'What's Ganzhorn?'

'My name.'

'Your name's a detail, mister headmaster,' said Muscatine in a sharp voice: 'But madame's is something quite different: it's Novogrodsky now. Don't you think you should take care to know the correct titles of your benefactors?'

'As in?' asked the headmaster, clearly overwhelmed by what he had just heard.

'As in,' said Muscatine, grimly.

'How wonderful! All my regrets—I cover myself in apologies.'

'It doesn't matter,' said Ady, with a magnanimous wave: 'I don't mind keeping the names of my different husbands. I like it—it keeps one's memories of them vivid. Like a sediment of men. If you place them in the right order their surnames make a good anapaestic cascade—it goes with my accent, very well. You should pronounce it my way: Ady de Znajm Novogrodsky Palafay. See how it flows off the tongue!'

'Admirable,' said the headmaster.

At which point she made a sign to me—I was hanging back on the fringes of this exchange—reached out, drew me to her, bent down and kissed me on the cheek, once, twice, three times in the most dramatic fashion.

'My delight,' she said: 'At last I see you. How long? A year? Too long! But what are you doing in boarding school anyway?'

'It was you who sent him here, in fact, madame—you and Egon Keleti,' said Muscatine.

'Yes, yes,' she said: 'There's some vague truth to that, but really it was all more complicated.'

She turned back to me. 'And do you like it here, my prince?'

'He's a dreamer,' said Ganzhorn. 'He's always off somewhere else in his thoughts; he's scarcely with us here at all.'

'I hate it here,' I said.

Ganzhorn laughed, and glared at me.

'An unbroken spirit, Madame Novogrodsky,' he said: 'As you can see! Give us time. We'll make a proper Western European of him. It takes a while for a child to change cultures. New languages, new friends, a new way of life. It's something difficult we're asking of him.'

She took a step away from me, and towards him. 'Difficult? You don't mean it! There's nothing easier in the world than changing cultures. I do it myself six times every day. Do you at least educate him properly?'

'Madame,' he said, 'we pride ourselves on offering a moral framework. That's our goal, just as much as an education.'

'A moral framework: interesting! Not that the details of one's schooling really make much difference in the long run, do they, Mr Ganzhorn, if we're being honest with each other. I paid no attention in the classroom: I know whatever I need to know. I can make conversation on any subject, I speak every European language that matters, and some that don't as well.'

'And they all sound the same,' said Muscatine in a low voice.

'Rein in your hostility, accompanist,' she said: 'You think you're indispensable. You don't know yet who I am! What I'm saying's true. It's background that's important; it's the milieu a child's exposed to. Not learning, not information. Wouldn't you agree with me, head-master?'

Ganzhorn gave a prudent smile, and interlaced his fingers. 'Indeed. You touch on our great advantage in what you say.'

'And what's that?'

'Tradition, a grounding in the framework of tradition. We have the children of many titled heads among our students here.'

'Titled heads! I like this school less by the minute. Privilege—I spit on it. Heredity—I spit on it. I want my little prince to belong to the natural elite of the modern world, not some network of old museum pieces. You told me your establishment was democratic, meritocratic: I don't even remember what adjectives you used. You made it sound like paradise on earth. That's why I enrolled him with you in the first place when we met and spoke in Vienna. You knew I had to choose at once. I took you at face value. That's the reason I sent him here. Was I wrong?'

'Perhaps, Madame Novogrodsky,' said the headmaster, making a pleading motion with his hands: 'Perhaps you might care to inspect the music block?'

'The music block. Why? Do you think you have another maestro in training to show me there?'

'Please—it would be an inspiration for our students!'

'Anything for the sake of art,' she said, sighing theatrically: 'My treasure, go and get your things.'

Things for what, I wondered, and she swept off.

'Amazing,' said Muscatine, standing beside me: 'They bow down to her like servants, don't they? Like slaves? And she's got no real idea about music, no understanding in any depth, I can promise you that!'

'You seem to bow down to her as well,' I said.

'At least I offer a little resistance.'

'And why do they do that, do you think?'

'They can smell the money and the fame, of course. The reek of it! It comes off her like a sweat, like some hormonal secretion. Like scent from a gland. People are drawn to her and the Maestro the way flies are drawn to a corpse.'

We spoke on. Soon the others returned.

'How was the grand tour, madame? Enlightening?' asked Muscatine in a waspish voice.

'Don't be so arch and so contrary,' she said: 'It was just what you'd expect, like almost everything in life.'

'And we discussed certain topics,' said the headmaster in a satisfied voice, and looked at me: 'Such as the problem of your absconding.'

'Absconding?'

'Running away. Madame Novogrodsky agrees with me that we should take steps to discipline you.'

'Discipline him?' she said at once, indignantly: 'Do you want to crush him, Mr Ganzhorn, is that what you want? Anyone with spirit runs away from school. It's a good sign, not a bad one. Can't you let him fly free? Life will discipline him soon enough. There are Ganzhorns everywhere, lying in wait like guerrillas in ambush in the dead of night.'

'But, madame,' said the headmaster: 'You said you agreed with me. You said you'd back me up.'

She laughed. 'And you believed me? You really thought I'd take your side against the child?'

'We have to control our students, madame. He misses whole days of lessons, he runs off, we even found him once on a walking trail in the gorge at Celerina. Last term he got as far as Zürich railway station on his own. And it goes beyond him, madame, far beyond. He's always trying to slip away, and getting other students to lie and cover for him.'

He paused, and gave her a look of entreaty.

'You look to me like a man of some experience, Mr Ganzhorn,' she said: 'Such a noble, handsome face! You're German, aren't you?'

'North German, Madame Novogrodsky.'

'I hardly thought you came from Bavaria. Now let me tell you something: something you should already know. Children lie constantly—but they don't lie as much as adults.'

She turned from him, and made a sign to me: 'My blessing: you come with us. We're here to take you for a drive, aren't we, Muscatine? It's an important day. I've got things to talk over with you. Private things. I'm sure you don't mind my taking him away from you, Mr Ganzhorn, now we've cleared the air. I won't damage his moral framework—at least not too much.'

'Usually, madame, we like to have some advance notice—for administrative reasons.'

She stared at him. She held the stare. He flinched.

'But of course, in this case,' he continued, 'that's perfectly in order. We don't object, as long as you bring him back by nightfall, when the study period starts. We're happy for you to have him. And dare I ask something in return?'

She cut him off. 'I know what you want. Muscatine, what's Novogrodsky's schedule?'

'Full, for two years ahead. Completely booked, scarcely a free day for anything.'

'But I feel sure my poor overworked husband would see the merit in paying a brief inspection visit to Mr Ganzhorn's music students. So he can meet the concert pianists of the future being educated here, maybe even rehearse with them, play through a piece or two with them. Don't you think we could possibly persuade him, find a little flicker of generosity in his chilly heart?'

'I'm sure you could, madame.'

'That's right. We're in agreement, headmaster?'

The two of them shook hands, ceremoniously, like generals at a treaty signing. Ganzhorn retreated, with his retinue in tow.

'My life,' she said to me, and beckoned to me: 'You look so pale and ill. Living in this barracks, I'm not surprised. And how do you find me?'

'Just the same,' I answered.

'The same? The same! You're supposed to say—Darling Ady, how wonderful you look, as lovely as a meadow in the spring, as dramatic as an alpine storm, as ever-changing as the waves of the sea. You're supposed to charm and enrapture when you're speaking to a woman like me. What do you actually remember of me, from last year, and the years before? What do you think of when you think of me?'

I looked back at her.

'My God, don't say nothing. That's the worst thing to do. Just say the first thing that comes into your head: how you picture me.'

'I remember...' I began, then hesitated.

'What? Go on, don't be like that, don't keep it to yourself—say.'

'I remember that you never wore the same dress twice all through the summer holiday; and they were always dresses in bright colours; and you smiled, and played cards with yourself; and your voice always made everything sound important, and from the way you spoke it seemed as if you knew a special secret, as if there were things you kept just beneath the surface and wouldn't ever tell.'

'Absolutely. Hapsburg irony. Happiness and sadness and appraisal and withholding all in the same breath.'

'And you were always kind, and talked to me, even though we never went on walks together.'

'And I bought you coffee Ischlers at the Konditorei every afternoon, don't forget. You see, Muscatine. He's a natural. I think we have the makings of a little Casanova here.'

'What's a Casanova?' I asked.

'That's something that'll be clearer later on. But you gave a good reply. I knew you would!'

'Thank you,' I said, 'Aunt Adela.'

'No!' she took me by the shoulders, and grasped them: 'You mustn't call me that. Not aunt—that's much too familiar. I love you more than I would if my own blood were running in your veins. Never call me that. Never think of me that way. Call me by the name that those I care for use with me: Ady. Call me Ady. Say it.'

'Ady,' I said.

'No. Like this. Ady—from the back of your throat. Ady—like the name of the poet.'

'What poet?' asked Muscatine.

She rounded on him. 'I thought you were a man of culture: Ady Endre—the lush romantic, Ady with the handsome face and long flowing hair, Ady who died in freezing January, in a dark room in a dark house in a dark street of a dark capital. That's what we used to say of him. I think of him every time I hear my own name on someone's lips, and it makes me happy to share that sound with an artist as pure as him. Now: time for us to make our getaway. Into the jump seat, Muscatine. I'll take the wheel.'

'But, madame,' he protested.

'Don't worry,' she said to him: 'I'm a good driver, when I put my mind to it, especially with coupés like this. They suit me; I know the way to treat them—just as if they were living things.'

'I'm not talking about your driving,' said Muscatine, in a voice of outrage: 'I'm talking about the jump seat. It's too small. I can't fit. He's a child, and I'm a grown-up. Let him sit there.'

'You're being objectionable. Try. You'll fit easily. Just fold up your legs. My happiness, get in, here, beside me. Let's drive.'

And she reversed, and swung the car around. We sped away.

'Muscatine, my cigarettes!'

'In the glovebox, madame, as always,' came his voice from close behind me.

'My life, find them for me, and light one up! Light me a Lucky! Isn't this village charming? Unspoilt surrounds! Don't you like being here, at least?'

'Too many animals,' I said.

'No. *Too many animals, Ady.*'

'Too many animals, Ady.'

'I can't see any. In fact, for a Swiss village, it's astonishingly animal-free: as if they'd all caught some strange plague and dropped dead.'

'Yes, there are,' I said, and pointed to the gables on the house facades in the square. 'Look. Up on the buildings, and even painted on the walls, and on the church front—storks, eagles, chamois.'

'If carvings and images and statues count, of course it's a menagerie. And that's a good sign. Love for animals is a proof of humanity. Never trust a man who doesn't care for them. Never stay in a home without them.'

'No chance of that in any of your houses, madame,' said Muscatine.

'My husband adores dogs—Salukis and Afghan wolfhounds. He prefers them to human beings. He spends his time with them so he doesn't have to talk to visitors. Isn't that true, Muscatine? But Muscatine doesn't care for them. They're almost the same size as him, and they pester and intimidate him all the time.'

'Madame, that's not fair. I don't like them because they're always shedding their coats and their hair gets onto everything. Clothes, carpets, furniture. It's as if we were working in a kennel, not a home. They sleep on the piano stool, they howl all through rehearsals, they jump up and paw the sheet music: they're impossible.'

We were on the main road through the valley now. Ady sped up. The wind blew past us, the sun was strong. I reached into the glovebox and found only a slim pack of cigarettes with a stylised white flower on the front.

'They're not Lucky Strike,' I said.

'It's just an expression,' said Ady: 'From the movies. Those are Edelweiss. Very alpine! Light one for me. You know how?'

'We're not really allowed to smoke.'

'Today's a day for firsts, and breaking rules. Give me one—it's like this!'

She demonstrated.

'Try. You see. It's easy: you didn't even cough. And do you know where we're going? No idea? You can't guess? We'll be there soon. Somewhere that might mean something to you. See the peaks above us, leading back towards the Tyrol, and all in snow, so bright you can't look at them for more than a split second? That's the way to our true home. Yours and mine. They can be like a sign for us, reminding us of where we're from—and what we've lost.'

'We're from the same place?'

'All the East's the same. It's all Mitteleuropa, it's the opposite of everything that's here around us. But there's something else that's special about it. You understand that, don't you? You have to! It's no longer really there. We come from somewhere that's disappeared. They still mark those countries on the maps, but we can't travel to them. They only exist for us now in our minds. They're gone, all gone, they're in the shadows of our memory. Isn't that so, Muscatine?'

She turned round to him even as she swung out to overtake the car ahead.

'Madame, please, the road.'

'There's no danger,' she said: 'Not with him here. My talisman. Look down the valley now, to where I'm pointing. What can you see? Shield your eyes. Look now, before the turn comes, look beyond the peaks. It's not just distance that you see there, and the light greying and fading, is it? No, it's as if you can see right through to another time. Sometimes I think that horizon's speaking to us, telling us what lies ahead, whispering its secret to us, telling us we'll never reach our home again. Broken life for you, it's saying. Broken life, memories and dreams that escape from you and have no end.'

'How bleak you are with him, madame,' said Muscatine into my ear. 'Such dark thoughts for a mountain drive.'

'Bleak! Is there only sadness in what I'm saying? Or is there a secret happiness as well? The happiness of having nothing. Nothing that ties you, nothing that binds you, nothing that stops you from remaking yourself. Wait. Slowly now, it's coming up. Here's our destination, just ahead.'

She turned abruptly off the valley road onto a side track, braked hard and came to a stop. There was a straight, stepped pathway ahead of us. It led up to an old church and belltower.

'Let's walk,' she said: 'Come with me. Muscatine, you stay here.'

'What, madame? A sudden religious inspiration?'

'It's a bad idea to make fun of me too often, Muscatine!'

She stretched out her hand to me. 'Take it. Follow.'

We climbed the steps in silence. Inside, the light was dim. There were painted patterns on the roof beams above us; there were frescoes on the far wall behind the altar, almost too worn and faint to see.

'Sit with me now,' said Ady.

Her manner had changed. Her voice was serious. She was speaking softly.

'I brought you here because I want to tell you something. A story about my younger self, a simple story. Would you like to hear it?'

'Of course,' I said: 'But why here?'

'Because it happened here. In this church; in San Gian, a long time ago.'

'How long?'

'More than a decade ago. Before you were born. Let me set the scene for you, even if when I think of that time now I feel as though I'm watching some old, flickering film in black and white. It was an episode, it led me to the life I lead today, but when I picture it, I see a stranger, someone I hardly know. I was working as a translator then. Have I ever told you about that time? No? I was a diplomatic translator. At the mission in Geneva, at the UN. It was after the great uprising in Budapest. Everything was already over; the reprisals were underway. Our days were tense, and there was a drama in that tension, it felt like being on stage, or in one of those dreams where the menace is never clear and never goes away. Each morning I waited to be summoned by the staff attaché and hear I'd been dismissed and called back home. I was full of fear, and also full of hope, and those two feelings fed each other—because I'd fallen in love.'

She paused, and looked across at me, and smiled.

'With one of your husbands?' I asked.

'Of course not. Women only get married to the kinds of men I choose after all their ideas of being truly loved in this world have gone.

No. I was caught up in a wild romance, it was under the star of impossibility, that was the entire point of it, I knew it would end in disaster before it even began, I just didn't know what form that disaster was going to take. Does that sound peculiar to you? Grown-ups give in to temptations like that all the time. You don't believe me? Don't be shocked by what I'm saying! He was Russian, posted to Geneva, and full of charm. Handsome, a wondrous depth of culture, a perfect proletarian background. I look back now and I realise: he was working for the state security.'

'He was spying on you?'

'He wasn't what he seemed to be, and I'm sure I knew that then, in some part of me, but it made no difference. My head was full of books and stories. My life until then had been just an emptiness. Wartime, all the horror. And post-war, a drab parade of interludes that never seemed to end. I wanted life. I thought I'd been denied it. I'd survived, and been given nothing more. I'd forgotten survival's the greatest gift—and has its own responsibilities. I was only beginning to know him, and have a sense of him. We used to meet by the lakeside, at the Rousseau statue, every afternoon. I thought that was exciting and clandestine, like affairs in the movies. We'd walk together hand in hand along the embankments, past the Beau Rivage and the Angleterre, I'd look up to the villas at Cologny, and beyond, to the Mont Blanc massif in the clouds, and I wanted nothing in that picture to change.'

'And what happened?'

'The picture didn't last for long! He vanished. I went to the Rousseau Island late one afternoon, and waited by the statue. He didn't come, that afternoon or any other. I never heard from him or of him again. I don't know if he disappeared into some camp in Siberia or Kazakhstan, or if he took a new identity, or even who he really was. At first I was afraid he might have been punished because of me: because I was from a fraternal country turned unreliable. I was frantic, I don't know what thoughts took hold of me. I waited—a week, two weeks, then I summoned up my courage. I went to the Soviet permanent mission. I asked for him. "And this was an individual you felt you knew closely?" they said to me. "We no longer have that name here; we no longer know it." I walked back to the lakeside, along the embankments, past the jetties and the monuments, across the footbridge to the island. It was as if I was seeing it for the first time. A standard nineteenth-century statue, a little park with trees, and pigeons, and passers-by, rain in the air, traffic blaring on the streets. That was the end of my diplomatic life: the very next day they called me in.'

She gave another little smile, and shook her head.

'It's a sad story,' I said.

'That's not the story, my treasure. It's just what happened first, before the story starts, and I was listening to my voice as I was telling you all this. How trite it sounded. A little Cold War drama, nothing else. At least there's more adventure in what happened after that. I knew very well there'd be no hope for me if I went back to Budapest. They thought I was a meek young woman, and I'd just follow whatever orders I was given. They booked me on a train back home through Switzerland and Austria. Can you imagine! A minder went with me. I knew him a little. He was old, and kind. He liked me. I'm sure he knew I wasn't going to finish the journey with him. We had to change trains at Zürich main station. I lost him there. I left my suitcase. I ran.'

'And that's what made you take my side,' I said: 'About running away to Zürich.'

'I was on your side all the time. I was just pretending to the headmaster. Surely you can see by now you have to pretend a great deal in the world of adults? People are always pretending. Those who don't are usually the worst.'

'I see,' I said.

'Do you? Let me tell you what came next. I had no aim in view. I was amazed at what I'd done. My life had just been transformed. How instantly! How easily! By getting off a train. I walked and walked. I went all the way down the Bahnhofstrasse. At last I reached the PostAuto terminal, and I saw the different buses lined up, and their destination boards. My father had owned a villa in the Graubünden once, on the lake at Arosa, before the war. I'd never been there: I knew nothing about the place. I don't think I even knew where Arosa was. There was a Graubünden PostAuto just leaving, for Chur and Zernez. I jumped on board. It headed off. You know that journey, don't you, how it has a rhythm? Zürich, the view across the water, the peaks advancing towards you and retreating, the mountains, their walls of rock, the little towns along the lake, the clouds, the peaks in snow. I stared out at them. I had no idea where we were going. Soon it was mid-afternoon. We were high up. Whenever there was a stop, I found myself listening for the three notes—the PostAuto horn.'

'I do that, too,' I said.

'It was a happy sound for me that day. It still is. We crossed the Julier Pass. I could see the valley of the Engadine spread out below: Silvaplana, St. Moritz. I thought it would be a bad idea to get off somewhere so well known. The next village was Celerina: here—where we are. Dusk was already falling. I could see this church tower, standing on its own, surrounded by green pastures, lit up by the last sun. I walked up this pathway, up the same steps we climbed. I pushed open the church door, and came in.'

'And this is what you saw?'

'It was less well-kept then. The murals were fainter, everything was in half-darkness. I remember it—a strange, suggestive shade. I went up to one of the front pews, before the altar. I was going to sit. It seemed best to kneel. All through that day I'd been insulated from my feelings. Suddenly I was overwhelmed. I was happy at what I'd done—I regretted it. I imagined the new life ahead of me—I missed everything I was leaving behind. I was excited—I was afraid. I leaned forward; I rested my head on the wood of the bench in front of me. I could feel myself crying, but almost silently, I was sobbing, my whole body was trembling. Then a hand touched my shoulder, and I heard a voice, a woman's voice. "Don't cry," it said. "Don't cry. Let your feelings leave you. Let them go." And it was such a soft, sweet voice that I did stop crying.

I straightened up, and looked round. There in the murk I could just make out the profile of a young woman, standing in a shaft of light. She sat down, moving very gently, like a bird alighting on a perch, and she took my hand in hers and held it. "There," she said to me: "Be still." And I was, for the first time in many days. I was still and calm inside. It was as if she was some kind of modern angel, coming to me in my time of grief and need. We began to talk. I told her what had happened to me.'

'And who was she?' I said.

'Can't you guess? We sat side by side, the two of us, close to where we're sitting now. "I'm no one," she said to me: "Or no one at all unusual. I was here when you came in. I was at the back of the church, I was in the shadows, and I heard you, and watched. I thought you might not want to be alone. I thought you might need to feel someone's presence close to you." I could see she had a particular air about her, I noticed that at once. A distant air, as if some part of her mind and being was always somewhere else.'

'And she became a friend of yours?' I asked.

'Yes, that's right,' said Ady, softly. She was whispering now. 'A special friend. I know her still. I've known her ever since, through everything—but—but it's been some time since I've seen her now. Some time—and I don't know if I'll see her again.'

She stopped speaking, and put her head in her hands.

'Was it who I think?' I asked.

'Of course it was,' she said after a few moments: 'That's why I brought you here. The scene's very vivid for me. Clear, as if I were living through it again—or maybe you make it stronger. What was she doing there, at nightfall, in a village chapel, I wondered. I wanted to know. "I'm asking for a blessing," she said: "A blessing for my unborn child." How well I remember that. It moved me very much.'

'How do you remember things so well?' I asked.

She let my hand go, and stood up. 'Time for us to move on, I think,' she said, abruptly, in a stronger voice: 'Let's join the Romanian. We can talk about memory and its pitfalls some other day.'

'Join who?'

'Muscatine. He's Romanian, or at least he comes from Romania; he's actually Gagauz, I think, or Tartar, he comes from some little town at the far end of the Danube. Brăila, Tulcea—somewhere like that, some place at the ends of the earth. And he was a prodigy in his day, a real keyboard star. He was selected for the Warsaw competition. That's how he met Novogrodsky and fell in with him.'

I followed behind her, half-running down the steps to keep up. Muscatine was waiting by the car, a long-suffering look on his face.

'Madame,' he said: 'Where would you like me to sit this time?'

She gave him the keys. 'Here, Ludo,' she said: 'You drive us.'

'Madame Novogrodsky! You've never called me by my name before!'

'Is it an honour, or an insult? Run us up to the palace of fantasy! Take us to Badrutt's!'

The trip was brief. We pulled up in front of a high-arched hotel entrance. A figure in uniform helped us all out, took the keys from Muscatine, jumped into the front seat and drove off.

'Don't worry,' said Ady to me. 'He's not going to steal the car! Come, follow. We'll go straight to the back drawing room.'

She led the way, but she had only taken a few steps into the hotel's crowded lobby before she was accosted by a solidly built man in a grey suit.

'Eppler,' she said: 'You don't have to greet me personally every time I walk in.'

'But I do, madame, I do,' he said: 'It's the little tribute Badrutt's pays to genius.'

He bent down, and shook my hand in exaggerated fashion.

'And who's this?'

'My nephew,' said Ady.

'But you said...'

She raised her hand to cut me off.

'Any relation of the Maestro's is a friend of the hotel,' said the suited man in a grave voice, as though pronouncing a sacrament. 'Shall I find one of our housekeepers to sit with him?'

'He's at school here in the Engadine, Eppler. It's part of his cultural education to see Badrutt's, don't you think?'

'Undeniably so!'

'And you know what I'd most like him to see?'

'I do. And I'll give the historical account personally, of course.'

'I'd expect nothing else.'

'And will we eventually be able to welcome Maestro Novogrodsky here with you? Any word?'

'He's still in Hamburg, conducting the Philharmonic State Orchestra, and doubtless harassing the first violins as well.'

'I don't think I heard properly, madame—it's high season, such a crush of guests. Too noisy here in the great hall. Let me take you through.'

At that moment I caught sight of a face I recognised. It was Josette, standing in the middle of a group of men. She saw me, waved, and came towards us.

'What a surprise,' she said: 'I thought I'd never see you again. You vanished so suddenly back to school. There's Stephane, just over there. He'll be pleased to see you, too.'

She pointed out Daru, and beckoned to him. He paid no attention.

'He's ignoring me! As usual! He thinks he's with important people. I'll go and drag him over here.'

'Who's that?' said Ady, acidly: 'She looks like a French waitress in that short skirt, and she sounds like one, too.'

'It's Josette. I know her from last year. She looked after me, for weeks; she was the only one who did.'

Daru came up, with Josette firmly grasping his hand.

'You remember our friend, don't you, Stephane?' she said.

'I do,' he said: 'How could I forget our happy days together?'

He was about to turn when he noticed Ady. His manner changed. He brushed past me towards her, extended his hand, and smiled a radiant smile.

'Madame Novogrodsky,' he said: 'Please! What good fortune. Let me introduce myself: Stephane Daru—and my wife, Josette.'

I looked at Josette questioningly. She gave a nod back, and a quick, almost imperceptible shrug.

'And what brings such a glamorous couple here to Badrutt's?' said Ady, in her most sardonic voice: 'You look just like a pair of movie stars—but I suppose that's what one finds in the great resorts of Europe now, isn't it? No more consumptives and Russian exiles, only jet-setters and escapees from Hollywood. And how do you know my nephew?'

'Nephew?' echoed Josette: 'Really? I'll never work your family out!'

'Nothing's more ambiguous than Central European relationships,' said Ady, sternly.

'I believe we met through Serghiana Semyonova,' said Daru.

Ady turned on him: 'That Bolshevik! How appalling. Is she a friend of yours? Are you two communists? You certainly don't look the part!'

'Madame,' said Daru, 'I have the honour to be the ambassador of the French Republic.'

'Almost the same thing! Ambassador to where?'

'To Switzerland: to Berne.'

'And where before that?'

'Prague.'

'So you specialise in postings to small, insignificant countries?'

'I have other tasks. One in particular that may be of interest. That I'd be keen to describe to you.'

But Ady turned her attention away from him, and towards Josette. 'I was married to an ambassador once,' she said: 'He was always sleeping with his secretaries.'

'Fancy that,' said Josette, uneasily.

'Yes, blondes, with hair just your lovely colour, for the most part. It was as if the ministry had a limitless supply. One gets used it. But there's always a way to master a man!'

'Indeed?'

'It's simple. Would you like me to tell you? You have to find the special attribute in them that's present to excess. That's the weakness in their psychological armour. There's always something. Aggression, or shame, or cowardice, or self-love: it's obvious what it is from one individual to the next. You identify it, then you highlight it constantly, until they suppress it in themselves. That's the trick to psychoanalysis. You make the patient do the work. No point being married to a man who isn't properly bridled. They need to be broken in.'

She gave a quick tug on an imaginary rein to illustrate the point. 'Like this. You have to keep them off balance. Otherwise they're no good, to you or to themselves. Otherwise they surrender to their love of power. They give no quarter, they don't compromise, they believe they can run their worlds alone.'

'But this gives me a perfect opening,' said Daru, enthusiastically: 'Compromise in politics! Let me escort you into the salon. I'll tell you all about the first session of our European conciliation council. It's only a month away.'

And he offered his arm to Ady, who took it, and went ahead with him, glancing for a second at Josette.

'I'm so susceptible!' Ady said: 'You understand. The charm of a diplomat!'

We followed in their wake through a series of reception rooms.

'Who is that woman?' Josette asked me, almost under her breath. 'She doesn't sound as if she's related to you. She's obviously Hungarian. And why doesn't she like Serghiana?'

'She's not. Not really,' I said: 'She's a family friend.'

Ady stopped. 'I heard that—my treasure! My burden! Don't deny me that way! Family friend! Wherever did you pick up that awful expression? If I'm not your family, who is? If I didn't care for you, and pay the tuition fees for you, who would? And you—you want to hear why I don't have any liking for Serghiana Semyonova? Obviously you don't know what she's capable of doing, and how few principles she has.'

'She's always been kind to me,' said Josette.

'Kind! Anyone can be kind when it suits their purposes. True kindness, selfless kindness, that's something very rare, and it's not present in her. I've had my dealings with Semyonova, and I can tell you: she was brought into the world to spread chaos and darkness, not harmony and light.'

She gave me another glare even as she shifted her attention back to Daru. 'Now—this conference you were telling me about.'

'Council. A gathering at governmental level...'

'And you want Novogrodsky.'

'Madame,' said Daru: 'Let me explain!'

'Do you think this doesn't happen to me every day? Drop the preliminaries! When and where?'

We were standing at the entrance to a large, lavishly decorated drawing room with a view of distant mountaintops. The manager appeared at Ady's side.

'Eppler! Rescue me!'

'A minute, madame,' said Daru: 'One minute—that's all I need to convince you.'

'One minute, then,' said Ady, an amused expression on her face.

Daru breathed in, like a diver about to plunge into the sea. He began: 'I could tell you all about our hopes and dreams; about our longing for a peaceful, reunited continent; I could tell you how we believe culture must light the way for politics, how pivotal our first meeting will be—but I want to speak more simply. It was my idea to approach your husband, mine alone. I was still a student when I first saw him perform. He gave a concert in Paris—symphonic, very beautiful—well-judged, well-paced, professional. Then he played an encore, a set of keyboard pieces. Just him: a dark stage, a spotlight, a harpsichord. He played Rameau. Up until that moment I believed I knew that composer's works very well. I listened, from my seat high up. I felt I was being given the keys to understanding the music, that I was hearing the notes for the first time, that they were being passed directly from his hands into my heart. It was a visit to the realm of the sublime. I still see that evening and the scene before me: Novogrodsky did what no other performer has ever done for me—he lifted me up above the passing flow of time. That's why I ask you. Not because of his prestige, not because of the celebrity that attaches to his name.'

'Bravo,' said Ady, and made a quick clapping motion with her hands. 'Superb, in fact. I'll give him to you. Muscatine! Muscatine?'

She looked around. 'Where is that man? Impossible! We'll make time for your council, I promise you. Novogrodsky was going to record a film next month, about the mountain origins of *Parsifal*, of all things. One of those mad ideas the publicity departments of record companies dream into being. They wanted to have my poor husband tramping up and down on the edge of the Suvretta glacier, and telling everyone how Wagner drew his leitmotifs from nature, how the music reflects the skyline of the Eastern Alps. Only a philosopher could come up with something as deranged as that. It has the smell of Nietzsche about it, doesn't it?'

'Remember him?' I said to Josette.

'I remember that day very well,' she whispered back: 'The chicken bone!'

'What are you two murmuring about?' said Ady.

'I was just saying it must be inspiring to be married to such a man,' Josette said.

'Inspiring! It's like being tied to a panther in the jungle! He has no self-awareness. Everything in him is instinct. An impulse comes to him—he follows it. A need arises in him—he pursues it. Consideration for others is one tune that's not in his repertoire. Do you know why he laid siege to me? Why he chased me round the world for years?'

'Because he was in love with you? Because he thought you were beautiful? You would have been a great prize—even for a man like him.'

'No: it was something else. Novogrodsky went on his hunt for me because he knew we were both made-up people, and he liked that— but above all he thought I made a visual rhyme with him. Really he married me because he knew I photographed well at his side.'

'But why did you agree to marry him?'

'Why did you say yes to your husband? Novogrodsky never gave me any peace. The easiest way to be rid of him was to accept him. I knew exactly what he was: an absence, not a presence, a man hollowed out by all his art. I accepted him as an exercise in self-denial. That must be plain enough!'

She glanced back and spotted Muscatine scurrying towards us. 'At last,' she said: 'I'll never know why my husband feels the need to employ staff from these obscure eastern ethnicities! He had a Vlach chauffeur when I first met him: the things that man believed! What have you discovered on your travels, Muscatine? We've been looking for you high and low!'

'Madame,' he said, panting: 'A call for you at the lobby. It's the Maestro! His performance—it's about to start. And flowers have arrived for you as well—from Hamburg: I've had them arranged in your bedroom upstairs.'

'What a sweetheart,' said Ady, almost purring: 'How well he knows me! I'll be back. These little phone talks only take a minute: he likes to hear my voice.'

She hurried off, Muscatine behind her giving chase.

'Such a magnificent creature,' said Daru, watching her as she went. 'So fitful. So flamboyant!'

'It's not hard to win you over, is it?' said Josette.

'How fortunate,' he went on, 'that we stumbled on our young friend!'

'Stephane,' she said, 'try not to make too much of a fool of yourself.'

'But this is like a dream come true. It lifts our project up into the skies. And I believe the president of the republic himself has a strong admiration for Novogrodsky. Truly a lucky day!'

The hotel manager was upon us. He tried to take me by the hand. 'Don't worry,' he said: 'I'm not going to arrest you! I'm here to show you our great treasure, just as Madame Ady asked. See it, there, at the far end of the drawing room, in the place of honour, in the golden frame?'

'The painting?'

'More than a painting. The Madonna, painted by the hand of Raphael. Raffaello Sanzio. You know his name?'

'I don't think art scholarship has been a feature of his upbringing,' said Daru.

'Stephane!' said Josette: 'What a thing to say!'

'So: have you spent much time in the company of Raphael?' said Daru to me.

'Maybe not,' I answered.

'See! How could he have?' said Daru: 'He's been living in the East. To know Raphael in any serious way, you need to know the Louvre— or the Vatican.'

'With one great exception, of course,' said the manager: 'The twin of this painting—the Sistine Madonna, lost from our world, alas, marooned in the gallery in Dresden: but if you look with clear eyes, the version here at Badrutt's is even more perfect. Even more sublime.'

'Are there degrees of sublimity?' Daru murmured to Josette.

Ady had reappeared. She stood beside us. 'Tell him the full story, Eppler! Leave nothing out. Tell him about the artist, but don't forget the mystery and the intrigue. It's such a story! What do you think, my treasure? Isn't it a lovely vision—so poised, so full of grace? We came here specially to see it—and there's a lesson to be learned from it. Listen carefully, and afterwards I'll give you a little test!'

She gave me an encouraging tap on the shoulder. I gazed up at the canvas: the pair of bored-looking angels leaning on the parapet at the base of the composition, almost level with my eyes; the virgin and child in the centre, flanked by a pair of adoring saints; the speckled background, greyish, full of gauzy, angelic figures, hovering and indistinct.

'She's floating on clouds, in the air,' I said: 'The artist should have painted a bench or a platform for her to stand on.'

There was general laughter.

'How ridiculous,' exclaimed Daru to Josette.

'How delightful,' said Josette.

'Don't make an exhibition of yourself,' said Ady: 'Be an adult among adults—and be on guard. Remember others are always assessing you.'

'She floats,' said the manager: 'Yes, she does, because the aether is her realm. She belongs above our world, she looks down upon us, contemplating the sins and sufferings of mankind, and the fate of the child she holds in her hands...'

'Eppler, we can leave the theology to one side,' said Ady, interrupting. 'Introduce your hero!'

'At once! In years gone by, our founder, Caspar Badrutt, was raised in this valley. He knew the beauties of the Engadine. He had a dream of what it could be. He built this palace, and it was his masterpiece: the emblem of its age, the model for a hundred other grand hotels across the Alps. But Caspar Badrutt was more than a businessman, more than a visionary in his special field. He had received an international education...'

'Just like the one I've arranged for you, my treasure,' said Ady in a stage whisper, and gave my hand a reassuring pat.

The manager paused, and looked across at her for approval. She nodded: he went on.

'Yes! He had a deep culture—a great love of art. It so happened that his father, Johannes, had acquired the painting you see before you, and many others, in the course of Italian travels, and this Madonna was a well-known work, a version of a famous masterpiece, one of the most famous paintings of the Renaissance. It was hung in its place of honour here soon after the completion of the new hotel—and all who came here praised its beauty, and saw it as an adornment to the palace Badrutt had christened with his family name. A version—a studio copy. But is it? Is that all it is? You can look for yourself. You can judge. Does it seem to you a workshop imitation, by a lesser hand, with the stiffness and lifelessness that all copies have, or is it rich and poignant and full of the breath of life? Caspar Badrutt was an intellect, but he also had something of the detective about him. He began to investigate the painting. He found out the details of its history, he chased down every lead. He came to his conclusion: that the work his father had acquired was the original, and the celebrated altarpiece in Dresden the copy. He set out his thesis in a monograph—a challenge to the art historians. It was a lavish publication—it was widely noticed.'

'Of course it would have been,' broke in Daru: 'And it was also invaluable publicity for the hotel.'

'A hotel like this one is not in need of advertising,' said Eppler, firmly: 'Not then—not now. Caspar Badrutt merely wanted a public comparison of the two works to be made. That was enough for him. He was sure the painting itself would persuade the most celebrated experts—that it would win the day. And he had good reason to think that.'

'What can you possibly mean?' said Daru.

Eppler turned to him with an air of triumph. 'The canvases themselves tell the tale. You surely know Raphael took great care in the preparation of the portraits and the altarpieces he completed in his workshop. He preferred to paint on wood. When he made a work on canvas, he would select a single piece of material—and yet the Dresden Madonna is a poor, coarse patchwork of canvas pieces, sewn together along two crooked seams, while ours is on a single piece of linen damask, the finest of the day. Now: you answer me. Which is more likely to be the original, the genuine Madonna, from Raphael's immortal hand: the misty painting in the Dresden Gallery, or this one, austere, and clear and soulful—as you can see with your own eyes?'

He paused, and glanced round at his audience, and held up his hands in expressive, pleading fashion. 'Caspar Badrutt was willing to put his ideas to the test. He travelled to Dresden to make his case. He took our painting with him. The comparison between the two canvases did take place, but in private: no outsiders. And the Dresden gallery director behaved as you would expect. He dismissed Badrutt's painting out of hand. He dismissed Badrutt as well. The canvas was brought back to us—and how happy we are to have it here. Those of us who see it every day can feel its magic. It shows us something new each time we see it. Our guests admire it, our new visitors are struck with astonishment the first time they come face to face with it, and the Madonna still casts her calm light over us, and over the entire valley below.'

'Admirable,' exclaimed Ady: 'Eppler gives such a good account of everything. Listening to you, we almost feel we were present as these events were unfolding. Quite remarkable.'

'Too kind,' said Eppler.

'No, it's the truth. But there's something else about the painting. Something I wanted the boy to see.'

She beckoned to me. 'Come: sit, sit here with me, and look. What mood does the artist conjure up inside you? What feeling does he leave you with? Tell us!'

'Is it a sad painting?'

'In a sense,' said Ady: 'But it speaks to me of something else—it speaks of longing.'

'Longing for what?' asked Josette.

'Longing itself. Pure longing. I saw the painting in the Dresden gallery when I was a child. In those days it was a rite of passage: you were without culture until you'd been taken on that pilgrimage. It was like a stamp in your passport, proclaiming that you had a tradition, and eyes with which to see the splendours of the past. You were following in the path of Goethe and Dostoyevsky—or you were downstream from them in a great flowing river. I remember that trip very well. There were people from all over Europe, East and West together, standing before the painting, as if they were inside a church at prayer.'

'That time's gone,' said Daru: 'Perhaps forever.'

'But I long for it. I long for it so much the past still seems present for me.'

'A natural reaction to these days we're living through, when the whole world round us seems to be dissolving.'

'You make it sound as if it's just sentiment, and weakness,' said Ady: 'But that longing lies at the heart of everything. Sometimes I think all we are is longing. If we didn't feel the loss of what we care for, we'd scarcely be alive. If we weren't always longing for what's vanished from us, what's been taken from us, if we weren't gazing back towards the past we've left in our wake, what would we be? The Madonna longs for the grace of heaven to be spread among us; the artist longs to recreate the original of his image; we long to know what he once knew. The circle of desire and longing goes on its great chase through the world.'

'But you don't find,' said Daru, 'that the work's just a little—how can I put it tactfully—old-fashioned?'

'You're forgetting that I'm Viennese, and it's been several decades since anyone in Viennese society had an appetite for art that calls itself new.'

'I thought you were Hungarian,' I said.

'My treasure, no one truly Viennese was actually born or brought up there.'

'I see,' I said.

'And what would count for you as modern, anyway?' she said, then to Daru: 'Today's new will look older by tomorrow than what seems antique to your eyes now.'

'But, madame, surely you'd agree the Renaissance has nothing new to say to us? Don't we know its great truths already? Aren't they commonplace, aren't they familiar in every way?'

'Stephane,' said Josette: 'Don't be so contentious!' She turned to Ady. 'Forgive him. He always has to have the last word.'

'No need to jump in to protect me,' said Ady: 'In cultural arguments, I can fend for myself. It may please your husband to see me as some kind of exotic from the backlands of Eastern Europe...'

'But women like you are rarely what they seem?'

'Exactly so!'

'That's not how I see you at all!' said Daru: 'But could there be anyone more strongly in the camp of modernism than you? Married to a champion of new paths in music: a Darmstadt modernist, no less.'

'And this rules out any admiration for art made in centuries gone by? What is it you object to? Tell us truly. Is it the angels, the cherubs, the saints?'

'It's not the most socially engaged and committed work of art I've ever seen.'

'You'd prefer a painting that addressed the horrors of the moment? Vietnam, perhaps, or Laos, and Cambodia?'

'Naturally. It's our duty to highlight what's being done there.'

'Your duty as a great power diplomat, or as a man of sophisticated European morality?'

'Both, of course.'

Ady leaned across, and took Daru's hand for a second, then let it drop. 'When you realise that everything you're speaking of is addressed in this painting, and in fact it addresses nothing else, then think of me,' she said: 'And the same thing goes for you, my badly behaved treasure!'

She tapped me lightly on the knee. 'I brought you here to open your eyes: to show you this. It's an important occasion. You reward me by joking about it, by not paying attention, by speaking ill of me to others, by looking bored. Don't make light of the image here in front of you, and think you can fool me. Don't be embarrassed. I can tell what you really feel.'

'How?'

'Such defiance! Such inwardness. Your eyes, of course—they show what's inside you—they give you away.'

'It's a special moment!' said Daru: 'The beginning of an education in the arts—and life.'

'Maybe he'll become a connoisseur,' said Josette.

'Maybe not,' said Daru.

'It might be so,' said Ady: 'I have an instinct for these things. The image will stay with him. It'll haunt him, and he'll haunt it, no matter what he thinks now.'

'You mean I'll come back here?'

'Somehow, I don't think the Palace Hotel and St. Moritz will be your natural environment in years to come, young man,' said Daru.

'Why not?'

'There's a secret visa that you need to spend your days in places like this,' he said, and laughed a little.

'I was really thinking more of Dresden,' said Ady, in a wistful voice, and gazed at me: 'Dresden, in some future when all the walls and barriers come down. I was thinking of the Raphael that's hanging there. I imagine you on the day you first go to see it. What agitation you'll feel inside you! You'll be happy and sad at once, for a hundred reasons. You'll stare at it obediently, and admire it, because you've been taught to do so. You'll think it holds great mysteries, but it'll take a long time before you make out its depths: a long time—and then, perhaps, one grey morning, alone in the gallery, ages afterwards, half a lifetime afterwards, you'll see: see the mother in the painting looking back at you.'

*

And though years have passed since that afternoon at Badrutt's, it stays with me. Ady's words stay with me. I can picture her still as she was then, her face set in a calm and serious mask, her eyes like bright lamps shining into mine, and I hear her voice, speaking gently, with its insistent rhythm: 'Look back on this. Look back, and think of what I'm telling you.'

My life took its course. I passed through schools; I travelled. I saw sights and met strangers. I plunged into traditions, I rejected them and returned to them. I wrote, I began stories and despaired of them. And all through this time I believed I was charting my own path through the world, and failed to see how much of my trajectory was already clear to those who set me on my way.

I was at the end of my student years when I made my first trip to Dresden, as though in fulfilment of a promise. It was still an East German city, it had the atmospherics of a mausoleum, it was sombre, its streets were cloaked in brown coaldust and noxious fumes. Inside the famous gallery all was quiet. Visitors strolled here and there, and spoke in whispers. I found the Raphael hanging in its special alcove. I stood before it. I let my thoughts roam. People drifted in, and lingered, looking up: a school party, a group of Red Army soldiers, all Kazakhs, in uniform, clutching their wide-brimmed caps upon their chests. After some minutes a young man in an overcoat came in, and stood beside me. He had a light meter in his hand. He held it up and took readings from several angles, went closer, pressed the meter against the picture's gilded frame, repeated the performance, frowned, nodded to himself and then glanced back at me.

'You look disappointed,' he said: 'Don't you like the painting? What were you expecting? To meet the mother of God in person? Where are you from?'

I told him.

'The decadent West! Exciting! I never met a westerner until I moved to Moscow. They still seem strange to me: always in a hurry, always unhappy, always on edge.'

He came nearer, held out his hand, took mine, shook it very formally and gave a little bow.

'Are you a photographer?' I asked him.

'A film-maker. Can't you tell?'

'Aren't you quite young to be making films?'

'Not at all. It's a time for the new generation now. New thoughts, new approaches, in all fields of life. I'm making my graduation film: the true story of the Sistine Madonna. It's a project that would only be possible in times like these—in Glasnost times. I have it on good authority that the General Secretary himself has been briefed about my proposal. I mean to tell the truth about the painting and its special role in Soviet life.'

'Starting with Dostoyevsky, of course.'

'So you know about the painting, and its place in Russia!'

'A little.'

'You must surely be a scholar—a worker with ideas?'

'I wish I was,' I said: 'I just go here and there, and look for things to write about.'

'And seek out the patterns and the clues in life; find ways to know yourself by studying the world. I understand! We're on the same path, we two. And the nineteenth-century story of the painting and Dostoyevsky's special feeling for it draws me in as well. In fact, I made a great discovery about Fyodor Mikhailovich the other day. Would you like me to tell you about it?'

'By all means,' I said.

'You know the famous scene in *Karamazov* with the devil? When Ivan sees the devil in a nightmare—or someone he imagines is the devil—a man of modest property, middle-aged, shabbily dressed, wearing a brown jacket with a foulard at his neck. Do you remember it?'

'Not really—but go on.'

'Not really? Nothing in all Russian literature's more vivid! For us, growing up in the provinces, the classics were everything, they were our breath and life, they gave us hope, they opened up the world. Even when I was a boy I knew the story of the Karamazovs by heart: I used to dream I was Alyosha. But there was one detail in that scene that troubled me: the ring—the devil's ring. He wears a ring with an opal set in it. But how did he come by such a ring? The story's from the 1870s, and the great new-world opal fields were only found years later. Where could the stone have come from, and why would he wear an opal? I asked, and found no answer. I read the great works of literary criticism: nothing. I asked professors at the academy: they had no idea. At last I went to the geological institute—and that's where I learned about the old opal mines of Slovakia. I set out at once on a journey there.'

'You don't do things by halves, do you?'

'With obsessions, you have to go right to the end! I went deep into those mountains; I saw the mine workings; I saw the antique opal rings and stones in their museum. I even made a short film there. An experiment—a montage. I'd told myself I knew exactly what to expect. Legends, pagan superstitions: there were very few of them. In some south Slav folktales, opal stones can shield you against the evil eye, or make you invisible—but the devil's ring in *Karamazov* comes from elsewhere. From a book, in fact. Can you guess? No? I was surprised myself. Dostoyevsky loved the works of Sir Walter Scott. He read through them all one summer, when he was twelve years old: they made a strong impression on him. One of the Waverley novels tells the story of a Swiss baroness who wears an opal in her hair. Holy water spills on the stone. Its colour fades at once. The woman who wears it sickens and dies. The book was a great bestseller across Europe: the idea of the opal as the devil's jewel and bringer of bad luck took hold, and it lingers still. Extraordinary! Think of a book having such power today! Once you know, you can see Scott in Dostoyevsky, everywhere. In the unending tension, in the back and forth of voices, crowding round the reader, competing for attention, in that sense he gives of every single story taking place on a small, constricted stage. He even weaves Scott into his own stories—in *The Double*, in the "White Nights". It's a literary descent line. A secret one.'

'So you're going to be filming a biography. Of a writer as well as a painting.'

'In a sense, but I'm not lost in looking back. Not at all. My script takes things forward—to our time. And you know the present's much more troubling as a subject than the past.'

'Go on!'

'Come with me,' he said then, in a conspiratorial way: 'Of course Fyodor Mikhailovich stands at the heart of everything. Of course he's the one who made this painting famous all through the Russian lands. But there's a sequel. It's important. Come. The time's not right yet to talk about this where people can overhear.'

We walked out to the Zwinger Gardens; we made our way around the lake. He became expansive. He told me the details of his plot: the fate of the Raphael in modern times: in war, when it was hidden away for safekeeping in a salt mine deep underground; in peace, when it was transported to the Soviet Union and kept in hidden storage for a decade.

'And then came the great exhibition of the painting in Moscow—a profound event. Every theme in our history was brought together. War, sacrifice, the memory of our triumph, our yearning for and rivalry with the West. All the masterpieces from Dresden were there: it was the first time they'd gone on view. The crowds were overwhelming. They waited patiently to see those paintings, they queued all day long outside in the pale spring light.'

'How do you know so much about it?'

'It's a well-known story. I've heard it told often by men and women who were there: that's the only way the real truth of the past gets handed down. And it was something for them to remember, in those grey times. But it was an event for our great writers, too—for Shalamov, for Grossman. You know them? Our secret masters?'

'Their names, of course,' I said, but he hurried on.

'What they experienced made its way into their words—clandestine words. The little story Vasily Semyonovich wrote about that morning was passed from hand to hand in Moscow for years afterwards. People whispered to each other about it, they wept and wiped the tears from their eyes as they read through it. It was their own story, it was gold, it was a special treasure of the underground. When I found out it was to be published at long last—officially published—that's when I knew the time had come to make my film. It's all clear to me already, the structure—I can see it all so well. I begin with the writer's own opening. Listen. I'll recite: "And so, on the cold morning of the thirtieth of May, nineteen-fifty-five, I walked along the Volkhonka, past the lines of policemen controlling the crowds who wanted to see the works of the Old Masters. I entered the Pushkin Museum, climbed the stairs to the first floor and went up to the Sistine Madonna." That's the way he sets the scene: how direct he is, how stupendous, how unadorned. You can see at once, can't you? It's cinema—pure cinema—it's a tracking shot! He describes his feelings then in simple fashion. No other work besides the Sistine Madonna has so conquered his heart and his mind. No other work's immortal in the same way. No other work will continue to live for as long as people continue to live—and if mankind were to die out, then the creatures that inherit man's place on earth, whether wolves, or rats, or bears or swallows, will also come to look upon the Madonna's face. He leaves the exhibition. He walks back through the streets, through the cold sunshine, confused by his feelings, overcome.'

'Another tracking shot?'

'Precisely—and he travels further in his thoughts. He summons up the image of the holy mother, and her son: he sets them against the backdrop of modern times. He realises that he's seen them, mother and child together—he's seen them everywhere. On the frontline at Stalingrad, in war, in famine, in chaos. In his mind's eye he even sees them in the darkest of all places: there they stand, alone, in death's antechamber—his thoughts dissolve into an image-stream.'

'And you mean to film all this?'

'No point in trying to capture anything on film that isn't almost impossible to show. You must know it's the magic art—it goes much further than mere words. I'm taking the sentences Grossman set down on the page. I'll raise them from their burial in print: I'll be the one to give them new life. Don't you see it? I can portray what he only describes: the mother walking barefoot across the dark earth, cradling her son in her arms. She belongs to our world, she lives among us, she's trudged through the snow, she's walked the autumn roads, she shares the dark gruel the soldiers drink from their tin cups every day. How long the path is that stretches ahead of her—from Oboyan near Kursk, or from the black earth of Voronezh—all the way to the taiga, to marshy forests beyond the Urals, to exile in the sands of Kazakhstan. He remembers when he saw her during the years of famine, in Konotop in Ukraine, at the station there—her face was dark and drawn from hunger, she came up to the window of the express train, and begged for bread, wordlessly, only moving her lips; he sees her as she was in Lenin-grad and Moscow, in the time of purges and night arrests, holding her son in her arms for the last time, saying goodbye, then heading down the ill-lit stairs. A black car waits for her in the street below, a wax seal is already placed upon the door of her room—and how silent the tall buildings seem, how strange and solemn the silence of the dawn. All this he imagines, and her journey to her new home, to sentries, watch-towers, barbed wire. All this, and he feels himself filled with wonder at the majesty of life. That's my project—my dream! To shape these frag-ments, to make them into a necklace of shining jewels—bring them into life up on the screen.'

He paused, and turned his anxious eyes on me. 'So,' he said: 'What's the verdict? What do you think?'

'Just you?' I asked: 'You're going to film it all yourself?'

'Just me. I'll go with my camera—wherever the road takes me. I'll make myself a modern Dziga Vertov—I'll go to Karaganda and see the Kazakh steppe, I'll go to Voronezh, I'll take my tripod back to Moscow and set up outside the Lubyanka, right underneath Dzerzhinsky's eyes, and see who stops me.'

'I'm not sure that's such a good idea,' I said.

'You're trying to hold me back! I thought you'd be in favour. Isn't that what the West dreams of? A Russia reborn, and in the arms of faith? You'll see—I'll make a film so rich and strange you won't be able to drag your eyes away.'

'I look forward to it,' I said.

'You don't believe me. Do you think I'm just a fantasist? You say almost nothing.'

'Do I have to take a position?'

'You hold yourself back. Is that what a free man does? It seems I'm freer than you, and I've lived all my life in chains.'

'Everyone's in chains,' I said.

'Or perhaps you think I'm some kind of provocateur. Is that it? You think I'm trying to entrap you. Do I look like that kind of person? Is that how I strike you? Really?'

'The thought had occurred to me,' I said.

'I expected more from you when we began talking, you know,' he went on, in a low voice: 'Much more. I thought to myself: here, a conversation partner, what good fortune. Someone to trust who'll trust me. Someone with western eyes, who's lived in truth, who's made the pilgrimage to the Sistine Madonna—who feels compassion for the world, and sees beyond the boundaries of himself.'

With that he produced his light meter, held it up to my face and, in silence, before leaving me, gave me a long, appraising look—and this little scene and its conclusion might be less vivid in my thoughts, were it not for a chance encounter a few months later in a very different setting that brought it back to me. It was near the end of summer: I was in southern Italy, in the town of Trani, whiling away my days, waiting to meet a schoolfriend of mine who was following a course of lectures at a college nearby. I had a room at an old hotel beside the cathedral and the little harbour and its fishing boats. From my window there I could hear the seagulls calling, and see the sunlight glinting on the waves. All was quiet. Life's burdens seemed far away. I went downstairs one morning, and began to read in the reception. Slumped on a low chair across from me was a young man in jeans and a thick green work jacket. He seemed about my age; he had tousled hair and pale blue eyes. For some minutes he stared in my direction, then he came over.

'You have my room,' he said: 'I need it. We have to change rooms—right away. You take mine; I'll have yours.'

'Why?' I asked.

'I'm a novelist.'

'That's not really enough as an explanation.'

'I'm doing my field research.'

'More like an anthropologist, actually?'

'And you've got the room I need for that.'

'Tell me more.'

He sat down beside me, and gave me a defiant look. 'Why are you here, anyway?' he said: 'Do you need that particular room?'

'What's so special about it?' I asked him.

'It's the room the film-maker Tarkovsky stayed in, when he came here, just a few years before he died. He was hunting for locations for his Italian film. You've probably seen it: *Nostalghia*. It's a great masterpiece. It won a few prizes. They say it would have won the Palme d'Or in Cannes but the Soviet authorities stepped in behind the scenes. You're not familiar with it? I know it perfectly. I know every shot in it and every idea that went into its composition. I know every piece of dialogue. I know the whole film as well as if I'd made it myself.'

'And that's what you're writing about? A book about a film?'

'Of course,' he said: 'All my life's given over to the task.'

'Art about art?'

'Exactly! Is there any other kind? I'm using the story to retrace the last stages of Tarkovsky's life: his thoughts, his feelings, the ideas that came to him in the places he visited—the way that exile sharpens everything.'

'But why him? You're not Russian, are you? You don't sound as if you are.'

'I'm not, but art's not an affair of nationalities.'

'It's universal?'

'No. The opposite! It's specific. Everyone has their own nature. We're confined in what we are. How rare it is that an image of a film or book reaches into us. Don't you find that? If you come across a snatch of music or a dramatic scene that speaks to you, that's a treasure, that's something to hold on to. It's the reason why you have to seek out the artist who speaks to you—seek out the art that's on your wavelength: pursue it, keep it in your vision. It's the way to see yourself clearly, amplify yourself—know yourself more—grasp your purpose in the world.'

'And this is yours?'

'Naturally.' This was said in a voice of complete assurance, with a proud glare.

'And what's it going to be called, your book?'

'I'm going to call it "Nostalgia for Nostalghia". The obvious title, don't you think? Though I had thought of calling it "From the Madonna to Portonuovo", but that didn't seem to flow so well.'

I had the strong sense I knew where this talk was going to lead.

'Go on,' I said.

'He was a believer, of course, Tarkovsky, that's clear enough. Every film he made was a quest for the divine in life.'

'Truly?'

'Of course. In *Stalker*, God is radiation; in *Solaris*, God's there when the planet gazes at the cosmonaut; in *Mirror*, God's in the mother's eyes; and in *Nostalghia*, he's in the sputtering candle flame. In my story Tarkovsky ends his quest in the little seaside town of Portonuovo, up the coast from here. He finds a Russian icon hanging in an empty church. He realises that his life's course is run. The gates of heaven are there before him. Suffering is at an end.'

'And where does it begin?'

'In Moscow, of course. It begins with the Sistine Madonna. He saw it when he was a young film student there. It was shown at a famous exhibition, in the Pushkin Museum. That had an impact on him. What you hear and see when you're young shapes what you turn into. We think we're free: we're not! We go down tracks prepared for us—prepared a long time before. Why do you smile that way? Is this all amusing to you?'

'No. It just reminds me of a talk I had, not so long ago: and it makes me think how life seems to go like that—repetitions, echoes, half-rhymes, as if the world was trying to tell you something, get a point through to you, and it keeps on telling you, and you can't help seeing the pattern and wondering what it means.'

'But isn't that what I've just been describing to you? Isn't that the task of art—to trace those hidden links and joins? The task of life, even—to see the resemblances? What we have awareness for?'

Maybe it is, I thought then as I listened to him—maybe that's just what it is. He spoke on, I said nothing, and pictured Ady in my mind—Ady as she was that day at Badrutt's Palace, long years in the past, fixing her stare on me.

*

'What a look,' said Josette to her: 'As if you were condemning him!'

'And perhaps I am: condemning him to complex times.'

Muscatine drew towards them at that moment, with Eppler and a stranger, a new arrival, tall, middle-aged, elegantly dressed. The stranger stopped, gave a little bow of the head, clicked his heels together and extended his hand towards Ady. 'Amborn,' he said.

'Do we know each other?'

'In an adjacent way. I'm just a humble music lover, madame. I have the Amborn Foundation. We support the Tribschen recitals your husband's going to give this year. I was with the Maestro last week, in fact, in Hamburg. It was a blessed time for me, a dream. How forthcoming he was—full of warmth.'

'Madame,' said Muscatine: 'The foundation's bringing out a book, and holding an exhibition, too. On Wagner and the Maestro.'

'*Valhalla Redefined*,' said the new arrival, savouring the syllables as they rolled off his tongue: '*A Study in Affinities*. That's our title. We made the plan last autumn, together, just the three of us—your husband and I, and our friend Muscatine.'

'How intimate,' said Ady.

'And we realised as we were talking what an opportunity we had before us. The time for the revolution of ideas has come round—for a breakthrough in our understanding of music's last hundred years.'

'I see,' said Ady: 'So many revolutions in the air.'

'Yes. Novo's Wagner is the new Wagner, that's evident: a tumultuous Wagner, unstable, melting, boundless in possibilities. I like to say that in the Maestro's hands the whole Ring Cycle is open to our eyes once more—open, and full of mystery. His *Parsifal*'s the pursuit of a godless grail. How perfectly he understands the composer—he sees into his heart.'

'And what's in there?' asked Ady, in a smooth voice.

'A galaxy—a whole whirling, exploding galaxy of contradictions: love, desire, hatred of desire, the life instinct, the death instinct—under his baton the music pulls apart our certainties.'

'Clearly for you it's not just notes on a printed score. I'm sure you're going to tell me that the music's the shattered mirror of our times, or something grandiose like that.'

'Absolutely, madame,' said Amborn. 'You phrase it well.'

'Shall I tell you the real truth about Novogrodsky's Wagner,' said Ady then: 'What the poor man actually thinks? What his aim is? Why he can't ever stop himself from performing these works—time after time, the same repertoire, reworked, refashioned, year after year? Would you like me to do that? Do you dare to know?'

'Please—I always have the feeling when we're talking that the Maestro holds himself back—he veils his words.'

'You know my husband was born in eastern Poland. You know he lost his family. You know what he witnessed, in his years of boyhood there: you know what befell that world: you know of his escape. You can imagine, then, that for him the case of Wagner is a special one.'

'Of course, and for us too—the shadows are always present in our hearts...'

'The music is the enemy,' said Ady, sweeping on. 'The enemy for him—the threat, the ever-present danger—the danger to be subjugated: to be neutralised, torn apart and remade—and that can only be done on the podium. When he stares out over the orchestra and its gleaming instruments he's looking out across the camp of death itself. For him, the music's something to be destroyed in public, the notes are there to be mastered and reclaimed—he's colonising the composer from within.'

There was a silence.

'How wonderful,' breathed Amborn: 'Of course: it must be so. And our task must be to help—in any way we can.'

'A noble thought,' said Muscatine.

'Yes—to plunge into the storm: go headfirst,' said Amborn: 'That's the path ahead: it's clear. And you, madame? Does our project speak to you? Our exhibition? Does Wagner loom as large in your thoughts as in ours—or your husband's?'

'Do I seem like a Wagner lover? Listening to him puts me in fear of dissolving—as if I was soaking in a bath too long. You need a fondness for complication over simplicity to be a true Wagnerian. The music closest to my heart is the music composed here in these valleys: the Four Last Songs.'

'Richard Strauss: a pure taste,' said Amborn.

'Music like light,' said Ady to him: 'Like air.'

'No. Music like you!'

'Ah, gallantry,' said Ady, and she turned to me: 'Take note, my treasure. Charm's only charm when glancingly deployed.'

'And now a suggestion for you, madame,' Amborn went on: 'A request, even.'

'Of course!'

'How honoured my wife and I would be if you and your husband cared to join us. We have an evening planned, next month—at home, nearby.'

'Home?'

'An estate on the Bodensee,' said Muscatine into Ady's ear.

'A modest affair,' said Amborn: 'By the waterside. And I hear there's some hope the Maestro will accept.'

'You hear that, do you? And who from?'

'Ludovic's been very helpful.'

'Has he, indeed—the faithful accompanist.'

She turned to face him. Muscatine quailed. 'And what else have you been scheming about behind my back?'

'It'll be a select gathering, I promise you,' said Amborn: 'Only like-minded souls, only the finest flowers of the cultural world. And I believe we have a special friend in common—she'll be there.'

'Oh—and who might that be, in these revolutionary times? I'm not sure I know myself who I could still count as a special friend.'

'I mean Serghiana Semyonova, of course. We know how close you are.'

'Close! To that fellow traveller? How much longer will she dog my steps! Muscatine, if this is your idea of a refined insult, if you're behind it, your days in my husband's service are at an end.'

'Madame, I'm innocent. I've said nothing, I know nothing.'

'Those may be the only true words that have passed your lips all day.'

'Forgive me, Madame Novogrodsky,' said Amborn, with a little pleading gesture. 'It was Serghiana Ismailovna herself who told us. She came to us with a proposal: for bridge-building between East and West.'

'The bridges at the heart of Europe seem to be working quite well already,' said Ady: 'You may not have noticed the Soviet tanks making use of them a year ago to stamp out the Prague Spring.'

'Exactly so. The need to soothe the tensions is as great now as at any point in our lifetime.'

'And she means to do this how?'

'By making a film: Mozart's journey on the road to Prague. The famous tale, freely adapted, with a cast drawn from both sides of the continent—East and West—and she believes the Maestro should conduct the music. All Mozart compositions, of course.'

'The great unmade film! I've heard the fantasy. If she's even read the book she hasn't understood it. Nothing could be less well fitted for the purpose. Surely you know it's something like a sacred work for us, in the Hapsburg lands, that novella, with all its sweetness and its charm. And now kolkhoz hands reach out to grasp it! What treasure of ours is there they won't try to take?'

She looked around the silent room. Everyone was watching. Guests, waiters, the manager, Amborn above all.

'Madame,' he said again: 'Forgive me. Such an error! I would kneel at your feet if I thought it would make a difference.'

'I'd like to see that, my dear industrialist!'

'I'm not an industrialist. Our enterprise makes precision instruments.'

'A minor detail. I meant what I said!'

'What, madame?'

'I'd like to see you kneeling. Right here, right now. In the ladies' salon of Badrutt's. Make the gesture! Back up your words. Or are you embarrassed, in front of all these staring eyes? Perhaps you don't want to spoil the press of your Knize suit?'

'If you wish it,' said Amborn, half under his breath.

'I do. I do wish it. With all my heart!'

For a few moments no one spoke. Gradually, uneasily, almost in slow motion, Amborn fell to his knees, placed his hands before him on the carpet and bent his head. Ady looked down at him, a cold expression on her face. She gave a soft, mechanical laugh—a laugh directed inward, for herself, not for the watching room to hear.

Beside me, Daru was whispering to Josette. 'It's not every day that one sees one of the continent's grandees kneeling before a Viennese cocotte.'

'I couldn't hear you exactly, my dear diplomat,' Ady called out to him: 'But I can guess the sentiment!'

Amborn looked up at her with beseeching eyes.

'Just like Saint Sixtus in the painting on the wall,' she said: 'What a pose. What piety. Up, now—enough playacting.'

She made a sign to Amborn, stepped away from him, paced towards the window and back, and turned. 'I'll tell you the true story of the Caucasian and her Mozart fantasy. Why not? It's almost funny, in an irritating kind of way. She came to Vienna for a visit. Somehow I doubt she filled you in on all the details. Picture the scene. The Ring, beside the Stadtpark. A dull, grey morning, rain in the skies, a cold wind. The doorbell rings at my town palazzo—my modest affair. A housemaid opens. There she is—standing on the steps: the queen of the red screen herself, the all-powerful Serghiana Ismailovna, with an Italian in a leather trench coat at her side. No appointment, no advance notice.

They were shown in. I came down. I'd only just returned from a long trip with Novogrodsky. We were both exhausted. Imagine the astonishment I felt. She made her pitch, in a stumbling, nervous way—the same one she made to you: bridges, Europe, a shared space and common culture, all the nonsense from the propaganda mills. She gave me the usual promises: state funding, governmental backing from the East. "And," she said, "you surely know Luchino, who's agreed to direct!" She'd brought Visconti with her. Can you believe it? Of all the drawcards she could have chosen, she'd selected him—a count from a line that goes back to the thirteenth century. At least he'd been a communist, and had a fondness for opera. He sat obediently by her side, chain-smoking, smiling unhappily and listening to her, and not following a word of any of the languages we were speaking. "I came to you because we're almost sisters." That's what she said, I promise you. Almost sisters. "We're strangers," I replied. "On opposite sides of the barricade." "But we used to be so close, we belonged to the same milieu. Won't you consider the idea? For the sake of the past!" What was I to do with that absurd pair of grotesques in my reception rooms, sneaking glances here and there to see if they could catch a glimpse of Novogrodsky ghosting about? I had an army of Salukis and wolfhounds to walk. I handed the two of them over to Muscatine. I felt I could rely on him to bore them half to death.'

'I did as you would have wanted, madame,' said Muscatine.

'So you're a mind reader now, to go with all your other hidden talents. For subterfuge, for double-dealing, for ill-treatment of animals?'

'What?'

'I see you kicking the dogs off the piano stool at home, I see them flinch whenever you come into the room.'

'That's not fair.'

'If you're looking for fairness from a woman in my position in the world, you're looking in the wrong place! We're not here for you to air your grievances.'

She turned to me suddenly, placed a hand on my shoulder and drew me to her, and looked down, an amused expression on her face.

'Why are we here, in fact,' she said, 'my treasure?'

'To have tea, and cakes?'

'Not exactly, although it's always a good time for tea and cakes. We'll arrange ourselves at the round table, over there, beside the window and the chaise longue. Eppler. Dear Eppler. Would you mind terribly? See if you can arrange a selection to be brought to us. Everything that's sweet and crumbles on the tongue. Say, a plateful of Ischlers and Florentines, a Religieuse or two for our Parisians. Mohnzelten from the Waldviertel to make my nephew feel at home. And Mozart cakes as well, the finishing touch—why not?'

Eppler retreated.

'And chamomile tea, of course,' she called out after him: 'For everyone. Yes, everyone.'

She made a sign to Amborn. 'Stay with us. You too might be interested by what I have to say.'

'I'm sure of it.'

'And our French friends, also.'

'Of course,' said Daru—but Josette took a step forward.

'I have to tell you this,' she said to Ady, and gave a quick, defiant toss of her hair.

'Indeed?'

'You're being unfair to Serghiana. You shouldn't speak that way about her in front of the boy. She looked after him all through last summer. She cared for him as if he was her own flesh and blood. She took him to the peaks and forests; she sat with him and read through books with him, every day, for hours on end; she showered him with affection, she gave her all to him. I saw it. You may have your differences with her. That's no reason for you to tear her down in front of him.'

'A pretty speech. You think I don't know what was going on last summer? Keleti told me everything the day that I arrived. Hungarians have no secrets from each other. I know all about the reading sessions in the gardens, and the little classes in French literature, and the long conversations at the dinner table: words, words, words, day and night. I know what she was doing. Shaping him, training him, making him her own—reading him those sickly mediaeval stories that tell her own life's tale. I know her ways—much better than you do. My disagreement's not just with her but with what she preaches: the religion of art she's being pouring into my treasure's ears. Art above all things, art as the purpose of mankind, art as the royal road to self-fulfilment, to paradise on earth. It's a sickness women like her fall prey to. She idealises art because there's no life in her, she's parched and dried up. Women like me are quite different: I understand what life is. Fear, mystery, beauty, laughter, tears. Art reflects life. That's all it is. A mirror, a mechanical thing. I put it in second place.'

'Despite being married to a great artist?' said Daru, but Ady paid no attention.

'The truth is that my doctrine's darker still. Isn't it, Muscatine? At home in Vienna we're surrounded by art. The best of everything. We hear music constantly, the walls are hung with tapestries, there are prints in the reception rooms that should be in the Albertina, not a private home. Every conversation's about art, it feeds us, it chokes us. And yet in my inmost being I know the truth. That it's next to nothing, it's an illusion, or not even that, it's a dreamed-up realm, it springs from our needs, it's a symptom in our psychology. We need art in a godless world, we make it the special, holy element, life's vanishing point, we build it up. We tell ourselves the notes in music are lovelier than birdsong, and more meaningful, that we stand far above mere nature, that art's more than craft, and skill, and subtlety in design or story-telling—yes, much more, it reaches to the skies, it gives us our one earthly chance at transcendence, it makes us companions of the gods...'

'But it's really a cult,' Daru broke in: 'A form of false worship. An idolatry: it's a bowing down before the golden calf.'

'How well you listen—and that's exactly why we came here today, why I dragged my poor nephew all the way from his place of incarceration to this menagerie.'

'Oh, no,' I said: 'The school! The study period! Remember what the headmaster told us? About being back there?'

'He's right,' said Muscatine: 'The sun's going down. We're going to be late.'

'Quiet, both of you. We're at the heart of everything. We're in the special sanctum where the gilded come to pay each other their respects and incline their heads before the art that reminds them all how privileged they are. But there's no standard to gauge what's good and true—none. It's completely arbitrary! Here's a canvas, hanging on the wall before us. A thing of beauty. If Badrutt was right, it's this one that should be worth millions of Swiss francs, this one that should be revered instead of its twin in Dresden. Pure chance decides which version prevails, which one we decide to crown as perfect. And there are hundreds of other paintings to admire across the length and breadth of Europe, thousands. There's no good reason why one stands above another, or one artist's elevated above all others. It's we who feel the need to make our chosen favourites into something more. To find value, to make value. It hardly matters what we choose to look up to. We need the peaks, we need the distant heights our eyes strain to see: we need to believe. That's why I brought you here to see this painting, my treasure. So I could show you the deserts of illusion that surround us in life. That's my lesson for you. Do you understand?'

'I think so,' I said.

'In time,' said Ady, 'perhaps you will. And in time you'll find you have a choice to make. For now, all this may seem like an amusement—but the day will come when it's clear to you that there are two ways to live. You can live for ideas, like Semyonova, or live like me—live for what's around us—all the wonder and the strangeness of the world. Ideas are easy, and dangerous, and sterile. Life and truth bring happiness—and pain.'

'You're so harsh,' said Josette: 'He's still too young for words like that.'

'It's the judgement of Paris, the choice you put before him,' said Daru: 'Only we're lacking one goddess!'

'That's not right,' I said: 'We're not in France!'

Daru gave a quick, sharp laugh.

'He means a different Paris,' said Josette. She came up close to me, and leaned on the arm of the chaise longue. 'The Paris who was a Greek hero, in *The Iliad*.'

'A villain, actually,' corrected Daru.

'You really think no one can be complete without all your majestic knowledge of the past, don't you?' said Josette. 'Your classics, your old, musty cultures. Always thinking in Alexandrines! The perfect Énarque!'

'Do you want me to repudiate everything I stand for?'

'Stephane, I despair of you,' said Josette, but Ady interrupted her.

'We're not in a history seminar,' she said: 'It's an afternoon tea at a Swiss mountain hotel.'

'*The* Swiss mountain hotel, madame,' said Eppler, reappearing.

A train of waiters came behind him. They took up their positions, approached in unison and dispensed an array of silver platters, each one piled high with cakes and biscuits, creams and jams. Tea was poured; tempers calmed.

'What sport,' said Ady, then she looked across again at Josette and Daru, and gave them both a measuring stare: 'I realise you two are in Semyonova's orbit. It's normal. You have to be. She holds sway in your world. She has connections. She's really the informal Soviet consul, isn't she?'

'When she speaks,' said Daru, 'we can almost see the nuclear missiles gleaming in the European sun.'

'Indeed. While I, alas, have nothing to offer you beyond season tickets to the Festspielhaus.'

'I'm prepared to rethink my allegiances, Madame Novogrodsky,' said Daru: 'On a personal level, of course.'

'Of course. And why are you still here with us, as a point of curiosity?

The pleasure of my company? Or is there something else? An invitation from the plutocrat, perhaps?'

'Thoughtful of you to remember us.'

'You make a strong impression.'

'It's extraordinary,' Josette whispered in my ear: 'She hates Serghiana, but she's just like her!'

'Serghiana's more frightening, and Ady's got more money,' I whispered back.

'You two again: you find our talk so dull.' She turned back to Amborn. 'My dear industrialist, don't go, don't leave us. Surely your party by the lake wouldn't be complete without the French envoy and his dreamlike wife? Let me present them to you.'

Daru jumped forward to introduce himself.

'Amborn!' said Amborn. Another click of the heels, another little bow.

'How pleased we'd be if you could join us,' he said to Daru: 'Your deputy minister's already promised he'll be there.'

'He spares no gathering of significance his company.'

'I like your husband, I must tell you,' said Ady to Josette.

'Truthfully?'

'Truthfully. He has no shame.'

'It's one of his strongest qualities.'

They laughed, and so the afternoon flowed on. The last sunlight faded. Ady's mood began to shift. She and Amborn fell into a lengthy discussion of art and politics. Muscatine watched them like a nervous animal. I looked round, and left the table and went over to the fireplace on the far side of the salon, where Josette and Daru were talking in low voices, making expressive movements with their hands.

'Malzahn,' Daru was saying: 'Why would he bother with such nonsense? Amborn must surely deal in armaments.'

'Hello,' I said, and gave Daru's sleeve a gentle pull.

He spun round, and gave me a black look. 'We're speaking privately. What do you mean by eavesdropping like that!'

'You're talking about the man with cruel eyes, aren't you?' I said to Josette.

'Did I ever say that in front of you?'

'Last year. Last summer. You said you didn't care for him.'

'My God, did I really? You've got a good memory.'

'Let's hope he's not storing up everything we say in the back of his mind,' said Daru: 'Think of the consequences if he were to say something to Semyonova.'

'I wouldn't do that,' I said.

'Is that supposed to reassure me! Children are like sponges. They soak everything up, but they don't know when to keep quiet.'

'You could show him some gratitude,' said Josette in a sharp voice: 'If not for him we wouldn't be here having tea at Badrutt's with one of Europe's best-connected women. We'd be taking another dreary walk round the lake, or looking at the shop windows, and you'd be making vague conversation about diplomacy and ministerial politics, and wishing you were with your Asian mistress and not with me.'

'Any other secrets you'd like to broadcast at this juncture?' said Daru.

'Is it a secret—or just something I'm not really supposed to know too much about?'

'Go on,' said Daru to me: 'Go back over to your aunt and the captain of industry. Be tactful. Surely you can tell this isn't for you to hear.'

I did as he instructed. Ady and Amborn were sitting side by side. Muscatine was hovering in front of them now, dutifully pouring out fresh cups of tea.

'I promise you,' said Ady, laughing, as I came up to them: 'That morning, standing there in her mink coat, she looked just like a character in a Keleti cartoon.'

'Who are you talking about?' I asked.

'Don't interrupt like that, my treasure. Your special friend—the protectress who abandoned you—the one who likes to call herself your great-aunt.'

'How is Egon?' said Josette, who had followed me across the salon: 'I haven't seen his drawings in the newspapers for months now. There's nothing else remotely like them—one feels their absence very much.'

'Don't you know?' said Ady: 'He's in Klosterneuburg. He's in the sanatorium.'

'I had no idea,' said Josette: 'I'm sad to hear it.'

'What's wrong with him?' I asked.

'My treasure, it's hard to explain it to you. There are illnesses of the body, and illnesses of the mind—but there are also illnesses of spirit, illnesses that have more to do with grief and melancholy than with health itself.'

'Will he be there long?'

'Poor thing—it may be so. Did you like him very much?'

'We used to draw together.'

'You must think everyone from Central Europe ends up there. It's not that way: it's only like that for people who are too sensitive, who feel the sting of exile or displacement very strongly, who find it too much to bear. I made a visit to him not that long ago, from Vienna. He wasn't in great shape. I told him I was going to take a trip to the mountains specially to see you. He made a little drawing for me to give you. He did it while I was there.'

'What was it of?'

'It was strange. It was a sketch: an imaginary creature. A dragon, yellow, quite like Polomoche in the Babar stories, actually. I didn't think that was a good sign. I told him not to be ridiculous. I said you were much too grown-up to want something like that.'

'Did you bring it with you?'

'I don't believe I kept it, my treasure.'

'But I like his drawings of dragons. We used to make them together, every afternoon. They were wonderful. I collected them. I loved them.'

'Don't whine. Don't be childish. That's not the kind of drawing you should want from a great political cartoonist like Keleti, even now he's fallen in the shadows.'

'Maybe we should go back to the school,' I said.

'Sulking! Worse and worse! Let's turn to the education question, then. Let's accommodate your wish. Muscatine, go and fetch the telephone.'

'The cabins are near the reception, at the entrance to the great hall.'

'I know that perfectly well. I want a telephone brought here, to this table. Find Eppler again: he'll arrange it. I need to have this discussion in front of the boy!'

A telephone was produced, and installed. Muscatine called the school, and tracked the headmaster down, and spoke to him: there was a brief altercation.

'Yes, I realise we're a little late, it's quite true, I accept that, Mr Ganzhorn,' he said in an emollient way.

'Hand it to me,' Ady commanded: 'Glanzhorn! Where are we? We're at Badrutt's, of course: where else would we be? Yes, that's why I'm calling you. The child's not coming back. I'm withdrawing him. Why? Can't you guess? These should be the happiest years of a boy's life. I arrive to collect him for an afternoon outing, and I find a sullen, subdued, dejected creature. He looks as if he's been on a starvation diet. And he shows no sign of having learned anything. It's intolerable. No, I will not reconsider. Don't worry, you can keep the endowment!'

She put the receiver down, and pushed the telephone away, and made a face, as though it was a contaminated object.

'Well, that's done. What a dreadful man. He started talking to me about detentions and punishments. You can't go back there!'

'What happens to him now?' said Josette, and looked at me.

'There are always options. After all, this country's famous for its education. Einstein went to university here, remember!'

'I don't think he's quite at that stage yet,' said Daru: 'But there are international academies in Geneva, important ones, with a good name, and all round the lake shore, as well.'

'We don't really want him to fall into the French sphere of influence, at least not too much,' said Ady: 'Think of it—a young Cartesian. However would I be able to talk to him?'

'Madame, if I may,' said Amborn: 'The Rosenberg in St. Gallen is very well regarded.'

'I've already been there,' I said.

'Is there anywhere you haven't been?' Ady asked me: 'What about Austria?'

'That would be wonderful. I could come and stay with you then, in Vienna, couldn't I?'

'There's probably only room for one child in our household, my treasure. Any other suggestions?'

'I was sent to school in Salzburg for a brief period,' said Amborn: 'With the monks.'

'A good education? Broadly based?'

'Certainly, but it wasn't for the faint of heart.'

'Are you just going to decide like this?' said Josette, in a voice of outrage: 'Right now, on the spur of the moment, as an afterthought, an entertainment to follow on from the tea and cakes?'

'I take no pleasure from these circumstances, I can assure you,' said Ady: 'I feel almost like the Madonna before us in the painting, thrusting her child into the harsh world!'

'What a comparison!' said Josette.

'Quite original,' said Daru.

'We have a plan, as it happens,' Ady continued, in a calm voice: 'Don't we, Muscatine? It's a good plan. I simply wanted to know whether any of you had ideas for us. I'd hoped to wait another year, but I just don't see any way of avoiding it. We have a school in mind already. I'm sure it'll be a good surprise.' She gave me a look: a look that blended sympathy and aloofness.

'Where?' I said.

She turned to Muscatine. 'You've already enrolled him, haven't you, as a precaution?'

'I have, madame. Though I feel sorry for him. It's such a momentous change.'

'You mean it's all already decided?' I said: 'You knew all the time you were going to do this when you came to collect me today: everything you were saying to the headmaster, about your husband visiting, and rehearsing with the music students, it was all made up—it was just a game, a game you both were playing with him?'

'Don't work yourself up into such a state,' said Ady, almost laughing: 'Muscatine and I do that all the time. Games and acts are part of life. You'll be master of your own destiny soon enough, I promise you: for all the rest of your life, and there are times when that bitter freedom seems to last forever. Thank me for making decisions for you. For thinking of your interests. It'll be a dream come true. You'll adore it—won't he, Muscatine?'

'Of course.'

'But where are you sending me?' I insisted.

'To America—where else? The promised land.'

IV

Chastè

THE STEWARDESS LED the way downstairs into the arrivals hall, her hand clutching my wrist. She glanced about. I did the same. She watched me.

'Do you actually know the person meeting you here?'

'By initials, perhaps,' I said.

'What? But look—over there—that must be him, wearing blue jeans, in that strange khaki jacket. Yes—see—he's got a placard with your name on it.'

She pointed out a youngish man with long, floppy hair and a bored expression on his face, standing at the end of the walkway and holding up a piece of cardboard.

'Spelled wrong,' I began to say, but the stewardess had forged ahead.

'You're from the film company? This boy's for you.'

The man looked down at me, and touched the plastic badge around my neck. 'Unaccompanied Minor,' he read out: 'Sure—I'll take him.'

He turned to me. 'Let's make tracks. Your flight came in very late. No way we'll get to where we're going before dark.'

'Who are you?' I said.

'Don't sound so suspicious. I'm Lipsett. But we can be informal: Corey, to you, I think. Your aunt sent me. I'm her production assistant. And now I'm your driver, too.'

'She's my great-aunt, not my aunt.'

'Don't be stupid—Madame Semyonova's not old enough to be any-one's great-aunt. Besides, she's already told me the story—how she's looking after you, and making a path in life for you—out of the kind-ness of her heart—not that it's so very obvious to me she has one!'

'Why are there all these police with machine guns everywhere?'

'They're not machine guns, they're submachine guns. Much more effective against terror. The weapon of choice. Don't you read the news? Zürich airport gets hit all the time.'

'For real?'

'Frightened? No need—we're not going to be hanging around. Is that all your luggage—just one little case? Come on, then—let's pile into the cruiser. Where did I pull up, now? I've been waiting for you so long I've almost forgotten.'

I followed him. We roamed through the airport car park, up and down the rows of vehicles. At last he stopped in front of a low-slung red sports car.

'Is this yours?'

'Sure—you think I'm just going to drive off in one at random? Doesn't it meet with your approval? It's an Alpha—a special model GTA.'

'It's very small.'

'And very fast, and super-cool. You were expecting a limo? A big, shiny black Russian ZiL, perhaps?'

'Where are we going?'

'To Sils Maria—don't you know anything? You don't look very happy to be here. Not many schoolboys I know would complain about a free trip to the mountains in the middle of term-time.'

'I'm missing things at school.'

'Don't kid a kidder! I spoke to them myself. I fixed the whole thing. They were cool with it. They said it was family week. And you're here to see your extended family. What could be more natural?'

'It's family weekend, actually. And the idea is that the family comes to the school.'

'Family weekend—how harmonious that sounds. They didn't have that in my day.'

'You went to school there too?'

'To the same kind of place—a while ago. Things have moved on: but I know the vibe, that's for sure. You should be grateful to us for getting you out of there. When I was your age I'd have killed for a week or two off school—and to be in on the first stages of a movie project as well. What a blast! Hardly anyone gets to have that kind of experience.'

'And that's what I'm doing here?'

'Madame Semyonova told me she sent you all the details in a telegram.'

'It didn't say very much. I've got it with me—it's folded up in my passport—see.'

He reached out. 'Hey—I've never seen one of these before: "Československa Socialistická Republiká—Cestovní Pas"—from the other side of the Iron Curtain: that's wild!'

'You're pronouncing it all the wrong way!'

He opened it, and glanced through its pages. 'Here you are. What a photo! As if you'd just emerged from some communist detention camp. And look at the personal data! They seem very interested in the colour of your eyes, but nothing else.'

He held it up, and looked into my face: 'And they even got the colour wrong—they're blue, not grey. Typical Eastern Bloc efficiency! A passport like this wouldn't take you very far in this part of Europe. It's about to expire as well. What will you do then?'

'I'm not sure.'

'Don't look so worried—I'm just joking. And this is the telegram? Let me see a second.'

He read it out loud. '*Ticket waiting—all arranged with school—CL—* that's me, of course—*to meet you at Kloten—scoping new film: rendezvous at Waldhaus—bizous, Serghiana.* See—what could be clearer? And she must really like you. *Bizous!* She's never normally affectionate that way with anyone. Okay, then: ready? Let's move.'

He set off with a screech of the tyres and took the main road leading into Zürich. He drove fast. Soon we were in the downtown, near the river, in a maze of crossing streets.

'I think I'm lost,' he said.

'That direction, go there—along the lake shore—then you just follow the signs—Chur—Sargans—Julier Pass: lots of twists and turns.'

'You know your way around!'

'Of course I know the road—I was at the school in the valley near St. Moritz all through last year.'

'So you know the hotel too.'

'The one with the tower, and the battlements?'

'That's it.'

'You could just see it, sometimes,' I said: 'On walks, or from the funiculars and chairlifts, once you were high up and the landscape was spread out below you—all the lakes, and the lines of the peaks—it was in the distance, above the roofs of the other buildings, on its own—it looked like a castle in another world.'

'That's exactly what it is—especially these days.'

'And that's where you're going to be making your film—in a hotel?'

'No—it's just the base camp. The hotel wasn't even there in the plot time. You know the story, don't you: the Nietzsche saga?'

'I know lots about him,' I said.

'Like what? He's a mystery to me, and I've been researching him all year. Go on—tell me!'

'Well: I know he was Swiss, and a writer, and—and he spent time in the mountains—and his life didn't end that well.'

'And?'

'And—that's it.'

'Nothing else?'

'And now I know Great-Aunt Serghiana's making a film about him.'

'Thinking about making it. She's always got several projects under-way. S-Film's branching out—that's why she brought me in—to write the Nietzsche script.'

'S-Film?'

'Her new company. She's got an unusual take on the story. Don't you want to know? Or is it all too complicated for you?'

'Of course I do—I'm not a child.'

'You're not—what are you, then?'

'We're taught at school to say we're young but empowered, we're the new generation—we're people of potential.'

'Is that what they're teaching these days? Well—Nietzsche's definitely for you. And Semyonova sees him as a young hero. She's starting with the romance, of course—you have to if you want a modern take on him.'

'The romance?'

'The great affair—the impossible love. Nietzsche and Lou, the drama of his life. No—that rings no bells? Listen—I'll fill you in—I'll even pitch the story to you. It's good practice for me.'

'Pitch it?'

'Yes, while we drive. So: you pretend you're running a film studio—and I'm the screenwriter, coming in to your office in Hollywood to run through my script. You're the executive in charge of productions, a movie mogul—I'm trying to win you over: okay? I'll break it down for you: the basics—the pattern. Let's call it "Nietzsche in Love"—that's just a working title. We meet our hero: he's a prodigy, he's troubled, he's on edge. He's thrown over his professorship, he's on the move, he's looking for a place to work, for peace and quiet, he's tried everywhere—mountains, the Mediterranean, the south. Pure chance brings him to the Engadine. It becomes his special haven: the secret home from home where he can write. It's the 1880s: and that's the great decade for him: his ideas are pouring out. We hear them on the soundtrack when we first see him—a mesh of different voices, all conflicting, all fading in and out. But it's not just a film about him. No film worth anything's ever about what it seems to be about: there's always a higher theme.'

'Really?'

'Of course—that's the way with every work of art. Subtexts, opposites that complete the initial picture, and also undercut it, and give it dimension and relief. It's a film all about light—the light that blinds; light, insight, alpine light—and enlightenment as well, the world of reason that the hero loves, and hates, and overthrows. In light he sees destruction—and that's not a metaphor, believe me—he can barely see, his eyes are so weak the gleam from the blue sky almost destroys them: light fills the screen all through the movie, but at the end there's darkness, there's a fall, disaster comes, and with it a new mood, new visuals—suddenly everything's refracted, filtered; the focus blurs, there's nothing but sepia tones. How does that sound?'

'It sounds complicated.'

'I didn't mean how it sounds to you—that was a prompt—for the studio guy I'm pitching to.'

'The imaginary one?'

'Yes—anyway: we've met the hero. We meet his foil, too—his best friend: a handsome, engaging, rich young man—Paul Rée: and Rée's like a brother to Nietzsche, kind and understanding—but Rée's also a tormentor, just because of all that kindness and understanding. He's everything Nietzsche can't be—he's calm, he finds ideas intriguing rather than oppressive; the world he sees is something straightforward he can master, it holds no deep secrets, it wears a pleasant face. And then there's the love interest who divides the two of them—she's a creature made for film: Lou Salomé. If she wasn't in Nietzsche's life you'd write her into it; she's brilliant, and beautiful and unpredictable. And the plotline's in a perfect shape already: three acts, meeting, romance, dark climax—and curtain: a potent end. We'll close it all out with music—Wagner, of course.'

He made a dramatic hand gesture for emphasis: the car swerved. 'Don't worry! All under control.'

'And that's it? The whole movie?'

'No—that's just the outline. Then there's the casting to talk through. Almost more important. The story's got big characters— we need big stars. The female lead's the key—I must say I had Julie Christie in my thoughts. I think that's the point when the studio guy laughs, and inwardly he starts to pay attention. And I say to him then, sure—it's an ideas film, that's true, but it can be a star vehicle as well: it's made for grand performances. It's not some trite costume drama: it's nothing like that. It'll be modern, it'll be a film worthy of its hero.

The critics will sit up and take notice of it. We'll use intercutting, we'll break down the walls of place and time. Flashbacks, of course, and flashbacks within flashbacks: the whole script's structured as a memory: Nietzsche's already left the world behind. We see him as he was in Rome, when he and Lou first meet. We see the three stars together in Luzern: a brief, golden interlude, they set off from there exploring, they take little excursions, they're happy, friends. We see the primal scene, of course—at Orta, on the holy mountain, where Lou and Nietzsche have their romantic moment. What a backdrop—it's perfect cinema. First his memory of that day's shown; then hers—they don't match. That's the dream; the lovely dream that breaks—then, right on its heels, the nightmare—his collapse: he's in Turin, in the piazza. And after that the fadeout. Dementia takes him—he lives on for a decade in a bedroom in his sister's house, the sickness slowly eating his brain and spinal column away.'

'What?' I said: 'That's horrible!'

He looked over at me. 'You told me you knew all about him. You don't—do you? How can I explain it tactfully?'

'There was a dark force in him?'

He gave a short laugh. 'I guess that'll do: for now, anyway. So: try this out: how I see it opening. First shots: we ride with him, the camera's with him, in tight close-up. Then it pulls back—we see his face, half-lit and half-shadowed: remember, he's the hero and the anti-hero at the same time. We're high up in the peaks—but he's no alpinist, his eyes are so shot he has to wear dark glasses whenever he's outside, and he wears a hat and a kind of veil as well.'

'That would look funny, wouldn't it—in a movie?'

'Yes—it's a problem—but not the only one. The key scene in the script's a vision, or a visitation, after all.'

'What kind of vision?'

'You could see it as a meeting with an angel—or a devil. Semyonova's got some way of showing it—but she won't tell me what it is. She's still looking for her director. Sometimes it sounds as if she wants to set the whole film in modern times, and turn it into a kind of Cold War parable. I know exactly what I'd do: shoot the vision scene in black and white, bleached out, overexposed—the way Bergman does sometimes, for nightmares, and for waking dreams.'

We were making good time—the roads were clear. Lake Zürich was already far behind us: the late sun was shining on the peaks. I gazed out.

'How strange it is,' I said, 'coming this way and seeing all this.'

'Like coming home?'

'In a way. Like coming back to somewhere I thought I'd never see again.'

'I used to feel that way about Williamstown, Massachusetts! Can you believe that, dude? And now here I am!'

'But how did you get to be here? And get to work for Great-Aunt Serghiana?'

'Oh—contacts,' he said, vaguely: 'Recommendations, networking, that's the way this world runs. The human element. I don't exactly work for her: I'm more like a student of hers, or an intern, in a way. But she's coming to rely on me, more and more. We've got plans. It's just she's got too many old projects and old hangers-on. She has to change: that's what I keep telling her—to move to international productions, to America. And that's where I come in. She must have thought I could help her because I had a background in American film.'

'You do?'

'God, no! I majored in Russian literature and twentieth-century politics. I wanted to take the State Department exam. The last thing I expected then was to wind up working for a communist like her! But you have to start somewhere, don't you? Not be too doctrinaire. I would have stayed on and done a master's, that would have been the safe thing—but the time just wasn't right: it was the end of the sixties, those were days of madness. I wanted drama; I wanted poetry and adventure. So I took a Pan Am flight to Paris instead—I had to see the revolution on the streets. When I tell Semyonova that she just laughs at me: but I did. I was there, I saw it all, I soaked it up. I fell in with the

Cahiers crowd there: movie journalists: in-touch people. They'd heard about this project early on: they steered me this way, and here I am—almost by accident—right at the vanguard of international film-making.'

'Super-cool,' I said.

'You're good to talk to—you know that? You're cool, in fact.'

'So we'll be friends?'

'There's a significant age difference, but what the hell: why not! And where are you with music, anyhow? What do you listen to, in that grey castle in New England, when evening comes around? Hendrix—Santana—The Doors?'

As he was speaking he pulled out a strangely shaped plastic assemblage from the glovebox and levered it in to a cavity between us on the dashboard.

'Music's not really allowed until the senior years,' I said. 'What's that thing?'

'It's an eight-track cartridge. Never seen one? You really do lead a sheltered life up there, don't you? Here we go: Creedence Clearwater.' With a flourish, he pressed a button on the console. 'Take a listen—Vietnam music—I'm really into this right now.'

The speakers gave a quick, loud hiss, followed by a whirring, grinding sound.

'Oh, no—it's jammed—jammed again! Too bad. You'll just have to listen to me talking film theory all the way.'

We spoke on. Night fell. The road wound upwards. A PostAuto, its headlamps gleaming, its horn rising and falling, came towards us and went rushing past. The hairpin bends began: they had a regularity to them: straights, acceleration, gears changing, then a braking, a sudden slowing, long, languid turns, the engine dropping low. It was a lulling rhythm: I leant my head back, and closed my eyes, and almost drifted into sleep. Some time went by, with Lipsett's voice in the background. Eventually he shook me, and gave me a reproachful glare. We were stationary: he had pulled off the road; we were looking out over the still surface of an alpine lake.

'How can you fall asleep to West Coast music!' he said: 'Come on—come with me—quick detour. I'm going to show you something. Something special—it's just a short walk. It won't take any time—and we can see everything beautifully. Doesn't it look like a landscape in a dream?'

Outside, the whole valley was bathed in moonlight; the peaks and forests rose steeply all around us: there were town lights in the distance strewn along the valley floor.

'I know where we are,' I said: 'It's Lake Silvaplana. We're almost there.'

'You're right—and that's the waterfall—see, the ribbon of its spray, high up there, tumbling down. Listen—you can even hear it, can't you—you can just catch the sound. So bright, isn't it—a real day for night.'

A few steps more, and we had crossed a footbridge over a rushing stream: onwards, and the path came out by the lakeside. Lipsett stopped, and looked at me, an expectant expression on his face. 'So—see where we are now? What do you make of it?'

'Make of what?'

'The Nietzsche stone: here it is—right in front of you! The symbol—the stone of revelation.'

'This one here, next to you, like a little climbing pyramid?'

'Like a mountain. It's where he came up with his great idea: the eternal return. I can even recite what he wrote about it for you. Would you like that? I know the whole passage off by heart.'

'In German?'

'In translation—but I'm sure it's just the same—in fact it's probably better this way.'

He assumed a dramatic pose, one hand stretched out, palm up, fingers curved and trembling, as if the better to extract the essence of the words. 'How,' he began, then paused a moment for effect, and fixed me with a stare: 'How if some day or night a demon were to sneak after you into your loneliest loneliness and say to you, this life

166

as you now live it and have lived it, you will have to live once more and innumerable times more; and there will be nothing new in it, but every pain and every joy and every thought and sigh and everything immeasurably small or great in your life must return to you—all in the same succession and sequence—even this spider and this moonlight between the trees, and even this moment and I myself. The eternal hourglass of existence is turned over and over, and you with it, a dust grain of dust!'

He lowered his outstretched hand and bowed his head reverentially. 'Magnificent, isn't it? The hero tears down the walls of his prison cell, and finds another set of self-created bars surrounding him.'

'I liked the loneliest loneliness,' I said.

'That's all? What about the idea itself? That we're all trapped, every one of us—we're in a cycle, going round and round the same life all the time?'

'Wouldn't we remember?'

'Yes—well, that's a good point to make.'

Lipsett stepped back, and leaned against the stone, and looked up at the sky. 'No stars: the moon's so bright. It must be just the way he saw it when he went walking out from his lodgings, in the cool summer nights. You know—I've come round to him. When I started working for Semyonova, and reading him for her, I wasn't tuned in to him at all. I couldn't tell what's deep in him from what's shallow, what's real from what's nonsense. I thought he was unbearable—violent in his thinking, self-centred too. Now I see a life—a life full of suffering—and suffering goes down very well on film! The more I've listened to him, and followed in his footsteps here, the more it all hangs together: the idea that you just go round and round in repetition, that we do things again and again until we find a way to get past them. Don't you ever feel like that—like you're caught in circles you just can't get away from? No?'

'Sometimes,' I said, 'I imagine I can see into the future—I imagine seeing myself a long way ahead in time, and I look at what I'm doing, and hear the words I'm saying, and wonder—where I am, and who

I'm talking to—or I imagine being older and looking back, and seeing myself now, seeing that perfectly. Being in two times at once.'

'See, kiddo—a philosophical idea if I ever heard one.'

'Does that ever happen to you?' I asked him. 'Do you imagine like that?'

'I get caught up in obsessions, things that keep coming back to me: ideas that become a part of me, and stay. Returning experiences, remembered dreams.'

'And remembered places?'

'Memories of places too. That's part of what Nietzsche was thinking: and the thought came to him right here. He used to lean back into the rock—I can see him doing it: he says so in his letters: he'd lean back, and rest his body in the folds of the stone, like this. Try it. Lean back. Rest your head back: listen.'

I did as he said, and looked up at the moon blazing in the darkness, and the peaks shining by its light. I felt the cold, rough surface of the rock against me.

'And maybe,' said Lipsett then, 'just maybe, you'll hear something—a voice, a whisper, the echo of a heartbeat—as if you've been here before, many times before—as if the mountains and the valley were welcoming you back home.'

*

Morning came. My hotel room was flooded with light. I made my way down the grand staircase to the reception, listening for voices and counting the steps as I went. The lobby was empty; the salon beside it too. I tried the garden terrace. There, seated at the centre of a long table, surrounded by a group of men and women in outdoor clothing, was a familiar sight: Serghiana, holding court. Her face was serious and severe. She was giving instructions. Everyone hung on her words. I came closer: she saw me and her expression changed.

'Come—my child. Come and sit here next to me.'

I went up to her, a little tentatively.

'My child! Don't look so unsure what kind of greeting to give me. I'm the person who cares the most for you in all the world.'

She stretched out her hands. 'You can give me a kiss on each cheek if you're feeling Central European—or a handshake, if you want to be transatlantic in your manners, I suppose. I can't tell you how much it pains me that I haven't sent for you before. Everyone—this is my...'

She stopped, and frowned. 'Yes—what, in fact, are you? And what should I be now to you?'

'Great-aunt,' I said: 'Don't you remember?'

'Perhaps adopted son,' said one of the young men at the table, smiling.

'Skating on thin ice there,' said Serghiana sternly: 'Advance team—it's a good time to break: you can head off.'

They all rose to their feet obediently, pushed their seats back to the table and trooped away.

'They're the set-up crew,' she said: 'They're checking the locations in Fex valley this morning—then back to Zürich later this afternoon. Now—let me look at you. Taller, thinner, distracted-seeming. You're growing up—you're losing your simplicity. Well—it has to be!'

Lipsett had appeared, and was hovering beside her.

'You've met Corey—you've been exposed to his dazzling personality and charm. Did he try out his Russian on you? For a westerner, he speaks it well. And he took you on an excursion, I gather—a moonlight drive.'

She turned to him. 'You seek out Nietzschean places all the time, don't you? You're insatiable: I should just give the running of this project over to you!'

'Thank you, Madame Semyonova,' he said, inclining his head deferentially.

'I'm not sure it's entirely a compliment. Now—my child—but it's really true, isn't it: you're not one anymore. My young adult—my adolescent—those won't do. What on earth am I to call you?'

'The airline gave him a badge saying Unaccompanied Minor,' put in Lipsett.

'No. We'll stick to child! It's decided: now—and forever. It's a tradition with us—we'll keep it going. Nostalgia's best. Corey, go and check for overnight messages with the concierge—you know what I'm expecting.'

'I sure do!' He retreated.

'And look now, there behind you—see who's coming over to us,' said Serghiana to me: 'Step by fretful step.'

I turned. A round-faced, worried-looking man in glasses was weaving his way between the tables in our direction. I struggled to place him.

'My boy—we meet again,' he said in a friendly way.

'Surely you remember Professor Leo, who was so very interested in your poor mother? Leo Loewy, the lion of East European scientific theory, the genius of Prague. But no longer a hero of actually existing socialism. Don't ask him about the old country—he's made the break!'

'Please, Madame Serghiana,' he said unhappily: 'Not so loud—it's not necessary to advertise!'

'Leo, Lyova, Lyovushka—nothing's louder than defection. The look in your eyes—there's nothing like it: exaltation, excitement, fear. Everyone who needs to know already knows. Everyone can tell. Sit—we'll have a good talk. It's been so long since the three of us were together. My child, Leo's found a good position, don't worry for him; he's a professor now, in Zürich—we saw each other there when my last project was underway.'

'Your great success with the comrades,' said Leo, in a reproachful voice: 'No need for you to feel any sense of worry.'

'Calm down,' said Serghiana: 'Calm yourself, dear friend. No one's going to trouble us here, it's like being in heaven.' She patted his hand, and gave him a reassuring smile.

'Did you see it? Or hear about it?' she asked me: 'My film—the new production?'

'It was very widely discussed,' said Professor Leo: 'Here and all through Western Europe, when it came out a few months ago. I took care to follow the reviews and the feuilletons.'

'What was it called?' I asked him, and he began to answer, but Serghiana broke in:

'Don't you know? Whatever are they teaching you in the place that ridiculous woman sent you to? I should never have gone along with what she wanted!'

'What do you mean? You chose the school—along with Ady?'

'Do you really imagine I'd let her make decisions about you by herself? Don't think that just because you don't hear from me I'm not watching over you. Do they at least teach you some kind of modern history there?'

'I didn't know you two spoke to each other,' I said: 'I didn't want to go to America.'

'What a voice! Don't be that way. Don't be resentful: you have to go to school somewhere, after all: why not the new world rather than the old? I was talking about our Lenin film. You didn't hear anything about it? I suppose you don't read the culture pages of the newspapers over there; there's not much to read about anyway.'

Professor Leo leaned forward: 'It was very well done,' he said to me, in a soft voice, as if imparting a confidence: 'It was wonderful, in fact—such an original idea.'

'Modesty prevents me from telling him—Lyova, fill him in.'

'Madame Serghiana had the idea of casting Vladimir Ilyich's life in a new way—by giving the story of his time in exile—before the revolution came. He spent a whole year living with his wife in Zürich, in the downtown, on the Spiegelgasse. Maybe you remember all this—from your school lessons from before?'

I shook my head.

'No? I didn't really pay attention to all that party history myself when I was studying, I can confess it now! But some points I still remember—they made us learn it all by heart. Ilyich was busy: he was writing all the tracts that became famous in later years. The lodgings he found were very humble. There was a sausage factory round the corner from them: they couldn't open their windows in the daytime because of the smell. But it was an interesting neighbourhood. Just down the road, only a few doors away from them, was the Cabaret Voltaire.'

He paused for impact, and glanced at me.

'I've heard of that, I think,' I said.

'Good, good. The name's famous now: it's become a sacred place of modern art—where the Dada movement began. That's why the film has a double title: "Dada Lenin". It's the story of the two revolutions—in art and in politics—it sets them side by side. I believe it found strong support in party circles.'

'There was the usual disagreement between the usual factions,' said Serghiana.

'They must have been happy to see you coming back to approved subject matter.'

'I heard whispers. They thought the Dada scenes were suitably decadent. They were relaxed about Ilyich's long walks by the lake shore, which he found so very beautiful, and wrote about in letters home. The only episode they cut was one that showed him and Krupskaya on the crest of the Zürichberg, lying in the grass and eating Swiss chocolate: of course he couldn't be allowed to show any fondness for capitalistic products.'

'No, no,' said Professor Leo. 'Naturally not! And you've heard no echo of all this at your new school, my boy? Of course, European stories must all seem remote and inconsequential over there. How are you finding it? Tell us. I imagine the change was difficult.'

'There's a lot of mathematics,' I said, 'and science.'

'Good, good,' said Professor Leo.

'And it's not a very friendly place.'

'You think you're among strangers—you're always on edge?'

'Exactly.'

'Yes—I'm familiar with that sensation myself, these days.'

'Lyova,' said Serghiana: 'Don't encourage him. Pull yourself together, stop wallowing—it's a new chapter for you now, a new decade. Thank heaven the sixties have come to an end—what a dark, disconsolate stretch of years that was!'

'I liked them,' said Lipsett, who had just returned to the table: 'Wild times!'

'Did I ask for your opinion, Corey?' Serghiana shot back: 'Have you lived through any other decade as an adult to compare them with? No—you haven't. What news?'

'There's a long message. Everything's arranged: the delegation from Moscow's already left: they'll be here in two days' time.'

'What delegation?' asked Professor Leo in a voice of alarm.

'Naumov's coming?' asked Serghiana: 'That's confirmed?'

Lipsett gave a solemn nod. 'Absolutely,' he said: 'With a support cast. It's all in the telegram.'

'Who?' asked Professor Leo again.

'The deputy culture secretary from the Central Committee,' said Serghiana.

'A powerful man?'

'In some ways. Well connected: that's what matters.'

'A friend of yours?'

'I doubt he thinks so, though he might say he was.'

'And you—how do you see him?'

'Naumov—I've dealt with him for years; I know him well. A facade of liberal-mindedness, a surface of civility; educated, able, fluent in the western languages he speaks, fluent above all in the system and its ways; complex enough to seem a moderate—an artist in the exercise of power behind the scenes.'

'A true believer, then?'

'Who could say? In name and deed a communist—a believer in the policies and causes it's prudent to believe in. Efficient, once he's been shown the necessary tasks to fulfil.'

'A minor devil, in that case, in the scheme of things?'

'Correct.'

'But why are you dealing with such a man?'

'Funds. But not only funds. It was his backing that first gave me a position; a part to play in this world. No point in deluding oneself. It's very clear: I wouldn't still be afloat in this business if I hadn't kept that tie with him over the past two years, and been careful to maintain the ambiguities.'

'Serving the interests of both sides?'

'Serving as an unofficial contact point, yes—but also nourishing the dreams of both.'

'Dreams!' said Professor Leo: 'Do people like that really dream?'

'Desires,' said Serghiana then: 'Priorities. For westerners, there's always the longing for new commercial arrangements, for distribution in the East; for Naumov and his kind, the mirror image: more co-productions: more dramas from the war years and the revolution's glory days: anything to change the climate of opinion they face in western capitals.'

'Cultural politics—that's become your specialty now?'

'Diplomacy by another means.'

'And that's the real reason why you still choose to live the way you do, on the border between the two worlds? It was always a mystery to me.'

'Of course that's why—but it's exhausting, it's a constant balancing act. You can go from film to film and place to place: everyone you deal with is suspicious of you—suspicious even as they use you for their own ends. At least Naumov and the comrades understand the situation. Since Prague, I've been convenient for them, I've been an intermediary they can call in at will. But that landscape's changing. They don't need me as much as they used to once; and I certainly don't need them anymore—there are French producers I've found who want to work with us, Italians as well.'

'Fortunate!' said Professor Leo: 'Because I don't think Nietzsche's a figure who'd appeal to your Kremlin friends. If I'm not mistaken, when I was a young student he was marked down as a proto-fascist. I can't believe there's been a rehabilitation since.'

'You might be surprised,' said Serghiana: 'I've had indications. You're forgetting something—or someone. It's a Russian story—through and through. Lou Salomé was Russian, born in Petersburg—and she was a woman of radical ideas as well.'

'That's very clever!'

'It's nothing but the truth—remember what she represented for Nietzsche—what he called her—*die interessante Russin*.'

'Your precursor!'

'What a thought!'

Serghiana shook her head, then gave me a quick, cryptic look. 'As a matter of fact, I've invited another interesting woman to come and join us at the breakfast table: an old friend of yours, my child: Josette—and her new husband. They're staying here. You'll get a surprise when you meet him. They'll be down soon, I'm sure.'

'But I've already met her husband,' I said: 'Don't you remember—he was with us on the last long holiday we spent together—and I saw him a year ago as well, after they got married.'

'I know all about your escapades last year,' said Serghiana: 'I'm not talking about Daru. I mean her new husband.'

She turned to Professor Leo and dropped her voice to a discreet whisper: 'She's extraordinary, that woman. If things go on the way they are she'll end up sleeping her way into the Élysée!'

She was about to say more, but at that moment a tall, grey-haired stranger drew towards our table.

'Madame Serghiana!'

She glanced up, and frowned.

The stranger grasped her hand, held it in his and sat down beside her, staring fervently into her eyes. 'I came to greet you. I had to. To share my grief! I'm Fridolin—remember? The publisher—from Graz.'

Serghiana looked at him, and hesitated.

'My grief about poor Teddie, of course.'

'Of course,' she said then: 'Such a loss!'

'A tragedy,' he went on. 'It seems like yesterday we were all sitting together. There—at the end of the terrace, where the garden looks out over nature—that was his table, with the view across the valley and the lakes and the deep, dark blue of the sky. Do you remember—how he used to stare up at the peaks, as if he could annex them; how he would paint word pictures of each one in turn!'

'You must miss him very much,' said Serghiana.

'I used to meet him here—early in the summer season, every year without fail. He was an inspiration to me. Although it's not as if he's lost altogether—such a treasure house of words remains behind him—but that can never substitute for the living presence. Words in print are dry, they're skeletons of the moving, breathing thought: we delude ourselves if we believe we preserve the spirits of our friends in what they leave behind for us on the page.'

'A sad reflection,' said Serghiana.

'But you know how he was! It's nothing but the truth. I think all the time of how we used to take our walks together, and the talk that swept us up would last for hours; sometimes until the sun was down behind the mountains, and evening was falling, and we'd have to hurry to find our way back to the hotel. How wonderful they were, those days. He told me all about his childhood, and his memories of Amorbach. And I told him he gave me too much of his precious time, he was too kind to me: I joked with him: I said he must be one of the thirty kind angels sent down to the world.'

'Thirty-six,' said Serghiana sternly.

'What?'

'There were thirty-six of them, not thirty: it's a legend in the Talmud. And they weren't angels. They're the hidden figures of humility, sent to save mankind from hell. I don't think Teddie was quite that kind of person. He was clever, though: brilliant, even, in his particular and labyrinthine way.'

'The only true genius I've ever known,' said the publisher then, in a fervent voice: 'The only one. And what those students did to him! I'm sure it brought about his end.'

'Yes,' said Serghiana: 'A dramatic exit. I wonder what Mann would have thought. Although "Der Tod in Visp" doesn't have quite the same ring, does it?'

'No—and how quickly we all pass into history.'

'Or oblivion,' said Serghiana.

'He was very fond of you. I can tell you that now.'

'I know.'

'How could you know that?'

Serghiana glanced round at us, a look of slight vexation coming into her face.

'How could I not? *Il me faisait la cour—constamment!*'

'It was a passion,' the stranger said. 'He spoke of it to me for hours. I think he liked the idea of a red romance!'

'Doubtless thinking of Benjamin and Asja Lācis!' said Serghiana, in an acid voice: 'But you can't borrow someone else's life. It's a mistake often made by people who read too much.'

She tapped me on the knee. 'Child, don't drift off. Pay attention—we're talking about a great philosopher.'

'Can you read too much?' I asked.

'History's made by people who don't read—and studied by those who read all day.'

'You're speaking of Adorno, aren't you?' exclaimed Professor Leo at that point: 'How wonderful! He spent his summers here in the Engadine? He was like contraband for us—when I was—you know—over there.'

He gestured with one hand in the direction of the border and the ranges to the east, past Samedan. There was a pause in the flow of conversation. In perfunctory fashion Serghiana introduced the two men.

'Just think,' she said to Professor Leo: 'Had you left two years earlier you could have spent hours talking with Adorno in person—exploring your shared interest in the pangs of unrequited love! Although his conversation tended towards the monologue.'

'In truth music was his greatest and most enduring passion,' said the stranger.

'Indeed so,' said Serghiana: 'Every evening he would serenade me on the grand piano in the winter salon at the back of the hotel. His own compositions—all in minor key. One was a sound portrait of the landscape—very funereal. He told me the bare high slopes of the mountains reminded him of industrial slagheaps and mines, and showed nature's true face: bleak and empty—sad. And it is a sad valley. Look at the people who find themselves drawn here. Sad fates for them all: Anne Frank, Annemarie Schwarzenbach—Nietzsche, and now poor Teddie too. But he'll become an institution in the end. The graven, frozen, captured image of originality. What he most feared—and always longed for, despite himself.'

'You judge him harshly,' said the stranger.

'He was a harsh judge as well. And in the end, utterly a bourgeois, no matter how fervent his denunciations of the bourgeoisie.'

'What is a bourgeois, exactly, Great-Aunt Serghiana?' I asked her.

She laughed, and looked at me, and touched my hand. 'Something we all fear turning into—like Kafka's insect. The class who will inherit the earth—indeed they already have. Look, here are two, coming down from the bridal suite to join us!'

I shifted in my chair, and followed the direction of her eyes, and saw Josette gliding through the hotel foyer, a man with hawklike features at her side. She scanned the terrace, saw our table, and waved and beckoned. I turned to Serghiana.

'Go on,' she commanded. 'Don't be unfriendly! Go across and say hello to them. Josette's been looking forward to seeing you.'

I did so. Josette shook my hand in solemn, formal style. 'Our paths cross again,' she said: 'Under changed circumstances. I want you to meet my husband: Henri Malzahn—a name you've heard before.'

Then she bent down, as if to give me a kiss on the forehead: 'Be tactful,' she whispered. 'Say nothing.'

The pair of them walked the full length of the terrace, Malzahn making little signs of acknowledgement as they passed by various tables, then, still in perfect tandem, they both swung round and retraced their steps to where Serghiana was waiting and watching.

'Come, Henri,' she said: 'Come and sit by me.'

Malzahn raised her hand to his lips obediently. 'Madame Serghiana,' he replied, 'I can think of nothing I would like more.'

The three of them then began speaking at once, swiftly, in animated fashion, jumping between subjects, finishing each other's sentences, paying no attention to the others at the table.

Lipsett leaned across to me. 'Do you know these two?' he asked: 'She's magnificent! They've been spending a great deal of time with Semyonova in the last few days.'

'He's a kind of minister,' I said: 'I think—a deputy one.'

'Don't whisper, my child,' said Serghiana: 'Is all this too boring for you: politics, culture, the future of Europe East and West? This is the way we manage things: it might seem as if we're talking about nothing, but really there's serious business going on. Isn't that so, Henri? And I should let you know how our groundwork's progressing: we've found the lead—an actor from Limoges, of all places, can you imagine? He's the philosopher incarnate—commanding, frail, neurotic.'

At this, Malzahn inclined his head, and made an appreciative noise.

'We'll have to dub him, but in every other way he's perfect—and we have our strong heroine, a Russian, from Mosfilm: German-speaking, born in Saratov.'

'You didn't tell me any of that,' said Lipsett.

'If you'd learn to read between the lines of the paperwork you handle, or listen to the words being spoken all around you, Corey,' she said, 'you'd already know—but you do at least know the investment picture. All resolved: European interests. Your support at the outset was everything to us, Henri.'

'It was nothing, Madame Serghiana.'

'On the contrary. French prestige counts for a great deal.'

'It's a cultural fund,' said Malzahn: 'It's supposed to fund culture. And I was pleased to hear of their decision.'

'We appreciate their trust,' said Serghiana.

'And we trust in your art!' he said, and interlaced the fingers of his hands, and smiled majestically.

Waiters came and poured fresh coffee; the talk continued, it broke into currents round the table, there was that sense of different tides of words and repeated phrases flowing in and out. I pushed back my chair to leave.

'Child,' said Serghiana: 'Hurrying off already?'

'Serghiana,' said Josette, 'let him go: let him have a break from all this grown-up talk. Life will put its chains on him soon enough.'

'But don't you know what I'm trying to do with him, my dear—make him a master of the chains, so he doesn't have to wear them.'

'For me, Serghiana—let him go—he's only just arrived. I'll take him outdoors, and give him a quick tour of the gardens and the grounds.'

She got up, took me by the hand and led me away through the lobby and out.

'I can walk without a guiding hand,' I said.

'So cold,' she said then: 'What makes you like that? What makes you look so disapproving? I'd like to talk to you—properly.'

'Why? Do I matter? Am I someone?'

'Of course you are—I need to talk to you. Aren't you my little companion—my special friend?'

'You mean talk here—now?'

'No—I have to go back to M.'

'M for minister?'

'M for Monsieur—M for Malzahn—M for man. Come and find me later—this afternoon. I'll be down in the pool—down there below.'

'Is there a swimming pool here?' I said, looking round at the sloping lawn and fir trees that surrounded us.

'It's indoors—on the lower level. Newly built. It's an engineering wonder—that's what everyone says, anyway. Maybe a change of scene will lift your spirits.'

And she turned on her heel and strode back in.

Afternoon came; its hours dragged. Serghiana and her location hunters held a meeting in one of the salons; Lipsett sat in on it. I left him there, and scouted round, then made my way down to the lower level. It was sleek and new: soft lighting, marble, glass partitions, mysterious corridors. I found the sauna, and a spa and a little reception desk, unattended—and beyond it a long, low chamber, slightly humid, dimly lit—the pool. Josette was there, alone, lying on a daybed beside the windows at its far end. She lifted herself up on one elbow and looked across.

'Come over,' she said. 'You managed to escape Serghiana's clutches!'

'She's having talks,' I said.

Josette laughed. 'And you're wandering around a hotel alone, as usual.'

I looked around. 'It's very quiet here,' I said.

'A strange quiet! It's like a stage-set: you have the feeling something's about to happen, any moment, but nothing ever does: the light reflects in the water, the power supply hums, and the men and women upstairs pretend to enjoy themselves.'

There was a pair of large black-winged silhouettes on the plate glass of the windows looking out across the valley. I pointed to them. 'What are those?'

'They're hawks, of course—hawk images—to stop the birds outside from flying into the glass and killing themselves. A symbol of death to prevent death: like mutually assured destruction.'

I looked back at her.

'You know what that is. I'm not going to explain. It's all around us—I think you know that concept very well.'

She stared at me in a diagnostic way for a second or two. 'You've changed,' she said: 'It's natural. How much one changes in a year at your age! But there's something else.'

'What?'

'I don't know—a slight defiance, maybe. I'm not exactly sure yet.

I'll tell you when I've worked it out. Aren't you at least happy to be summoned back here—to your favourite part of the world? Don't you like the mountains anymore? Didn't you once tell me they were your promised land? You said it was a secret you'd only ever tell me.'

'That's right,' I said.

'And I kept your secret, faithfully. Nobody else knows. Nobody else realises that the forests and the peaks are your temple, your private paradise. Who would you share it with? Who would you allow in? Serghiana? Ady Novogrodsky? Me?'

'It's not a real question,' I said.

'But if it was?'

'It's wrecked anyway,' I said: 'You can see that.'

'You mean it's not the way it used to be. Isn't that the whole point of paradises? Otherwise there wouldn't be any reason to dream of them. It's a famous commonplace: a paradise wouldn't be a paradise if it wasn't already impossible. But it's too early for you to have ideas like that. Everything's still to come for you; you shouldn't be thinking as if your life's already been lived and you're looking back at a remembered world that's gone.'

'It's just that everything's changed from before—it all feels unfamiliar—wrong.'

'And do I seem unfamiliar—aren't I the same?'

'You seem changed too,' I said.

'Well! You can tell there have been some developments in my life—but I'm still the same person—the same Josette.'

She reached towards me, and made a sign to me to take her hand. I stayed still.

'Honestly—you're impossible. Many people would love to be in your place right now, sitting in an alpine resort, alone with a young woman who cares for you, and wants the best for you—but here you are, quiet and sullen, as if you've just been handed a death sentence by some dark and dreadful court.'

'What happened to Daru?' I said.

'Is that it? Are you actually worried about him? I can't believe it! He never liked you. Surely you knew that? All through those weeks when I was looking after you, you were just an irritant to him.'

'It wasn't hard to tell.'

'Don't fret on his behalf. He's got what he always wanted. I was good for him. He's been sent to South-East Asia, to the embassy in South Vietnam. He was brought up there, you know, he speaks the language perfectly—in a sense that's where he belongs.'

'But you told me you didn't like...' I stopped.

'Like who?'

'Your new husband. I heard you say it—in front of Daru. I remember.'

'Yes, yes, I know you remember things. What would you expect me to say, when I was together with someone else? You'll understand, in time. One moves through stages in life; feelings grow cooler; the logic of the world comes in. Are you disappointed by what I'm telling you—about myself?'

'I thought you were different,' I said: 'Different from the others, all around us. I believed you.'

'You believed in me, that's what you mean. It's not the same thing at all. Don't get hung up on my arrangements: they don't have anything to do with you, or how I think of you. I can still see you, you know, just the way you were the day I met you, when I was travelling with Daru on our first holiday: that day the Prague Spring died—and Serghiana made me take you upstairs to get you away from all the adults talking politics, and she thought I'd be glad to escape as well.'

'She was ordering you about then,' I said: 'And here she is, treating you like a queen.'

'It's a noticeable shift!'

Her expression and her manner changed. A waiter had come up. He placed a tall glass and a bottle of Évian on the bench beside her.

'Here,' she said: 'Put it just here. Leave it. I'll pour it. You can go.'

She sighed, took the glass, tipped out the ice cubes and flung them imperiously into the pool.

'I wanted no ice. They never learn. Come here.'

She touched my chin momentarily with her cold fingertips.

'What a shame it is. You're so perfect now—so unspoiled. On the brink of knowing, on the threshold, but not there yet. You just drift through the world and time. I wonder if you can see what's lying in wait for you—what's all around us—the wild chase of life.'

'Like upstairs?'

'Everyone working everyone else. Everyone wanting something, every word disguising what they really want. That great châtelaine Serghiana being the prime example. I can't bear it—it wears me out to even think about it.'

She lay back on the daybed, and yawned, and stretched out languorously, and smiled. 'You're quiet again. Why are you looking at me like that?'

'It's you who sound like Great-Aunt Serghiana,' I said: 'Cold and hard, the way she used to be.'

'That's enough,' said Josette, and she sat up. 'Leave me alone now.'

'Just like her!'

'Enough—go back up to her if you want to—if you think your salvation lies with her—your cherished blood relation! Go!'

*

It was almost daybreak, and a hand was on my shoulder, shaking me. I looked through the half-light. There was Serghiana, her face close to me, her eyes staring into mine.

'Wake up,' she whispered.

'What time is it? Is something wrong?'

'It's early—and nothing's wrong.'

'Have you been here a long time?'

'It's the only way truly to know someone—to watch them while they sleep. Are you well rested, my child? Any dreams?'

I shook my head.

'No? A good sign. Intelligent people don't remember their dreams.

The trapped and brainwashed dream to order—the order of Freud. Who could take such a man seriously? Let's walk, just the two of us, the way we used to. It can be our field trip—our private exploration.'

'Where to?'

'You'll see. It'll be a surprise. Get ready. The hotel's prepared a picnic lunch for us.'

'What's in it?'

'Oh, I don't know. Their usual—bread, chocolate, strawberries, two splits of champagne.'

'Champagne?'

'Generally they think in terms of older guests.'

'Are we celebrating?'

'Always. Survival. Life itself. Hurry—I'll be at the reception, waiting for you.'

And there she was, a few minutes later when I went down.

'Come,' she said: 'While the light's still so pale—so beautifully ambiguous.'

She was wearing a thick coat and headscarf; she looked me over and frowned. 'You'll be too cold,' she said, and with slow, stately movements she undid her scarf, tied it round my neck and folded it carefully into place.

'But what about you?' I asked.

'I'm used to these temperatures,' she said: 'Remember where I'm from. The wilds beyond the edge of Europe. This gentle cold is nothing to me, nothing at all.'

We set off. The valley was still plunged in shadow; there was a scatter of frost on the grass.

'This path we're on—it's the way down to the lake, isn't it?' I said after a little while: 'Is that where we're going? Are we going to walk all the way round?'

'No, child—there, ahead of us, where the fir trees are—that's where we're going: the peninsula—it's called Chastè.'

'That's a lovely name,' I said.

'It is—it's Romansh. All the names here are magical. If the world spoke Romansh there wouldn't be any sadness or wars.'

'That would be wonderful,' I said: 'Wouldn't it?'

She looked sceptical, and made no reply. We went on: soon we had reached the lakeside: the track led up toward the banks and outcrops where the promontory began.

'Of course, there's no escaping from him,' she said: 'This is where Nietzsche used to walk, this way, every morning, when he spent his summers here. There's even a memorial to him at the tip of the point: the kinds of people who come to Sils Maria for their holidays in this century have a fondness for memorials. But it can be our idyll, even so, can't it? Never mind him.'

'Idyll?'

'Like a dream.'

'But you said intelligent people don't dream.'

'Consistency's an over-praised virtue.'

'I see,' I said.

'Do you remember how we used to walk together, years ago—in the mountains, and down in the valley, through the forests: how happy you were when the songbirds were singing from the treetops; how frightened you were when you saw the poisonous red mushrooms growing in the shade.'

'Of course I do,' I said: 'I can still see it all. I see it in my mind all the time when I'm at that school.'

'And do you remember the trip we made up to the peak at Cassons Grat, on the funicular—how perfect that time was, up in that clear air, in the bright morning, high above the world; and it was a precious thing for me to go up with you, that day of all days—it helped me see into the future: I thought of you living on after me.'

I looked across at her as we walked, but she went on speaking, with barely a flicker of a pause in her words.

'And that's why I wanted you to come here. Not so you can hear about Nietzsche: there'll be time for that later on—ample time, when you're condemned to studying him somewhere. I wanted you to be here with me; I wanted you to see the lake and Chastè together with me. I wanted to see it together with you.'

She took my hand. 'Do you understand how important that is to me?'

'Because it's an important place?'

'It's important, yes, in a way it is. Writers tend to come here, if they can: it makes them feel exalted. Musicians, though, above all, it's like a rite of passage for them. You should see the hotel's guestbook: it reads like the performing schedule for Salzburg or the Vienna Philharmonic. But it's not because of that. I came here for the first time years ago, years into the past, when I was a very young woman, and those were days that meant a great deal to me—that's the real reason I brought you here.'

She smiled at me, and stopped speaking, and stood still. There was a strange expression on her face: it combined happiness and distress.

'Are you sad, Great-Aunt Serghiana?' I said.

She let go of my hand and, for a moment, covered her eyes. 'Always, inside,' she answered: 'Ask me something else.'

'Was it very different here, then?'

'It looked like heaven, because everywhere else was in ruins.'

'You can remember everything?'

'Perfectly. You know how to aim your memory, don't you? No? I think you do know; you know by instinct, and very well. You make your mind into a cinema: you place the characters inside it, as if they were standing on a stage-set; you place them in their positions, their exact positions, one by one; you build the scene that way before your eyes. You picture everything, every detail—but you leave yourself out of the picture.'

'Why?'

'Because if you're in it, vanity and pride come with you, and distort everything. Remove yourself: then what you've seen and heard comes back to you. All the words, all the looks and gestures. It's all still there in the record chambers of the mind. I wish it wasn't that way. I wish things could be erased. Ask me something more.'

I asked a question; and another. Suddenly it seemed essential to fill the air with words, with questions and with her responses, to be speaking constantly, to protect her and envelop her, to prevent her from having to stand in silence even for the briefest instant. There was a sense of crisis in those moments, it mounted, it was strong, then abruptly that strength subsided, it became weaker and weaker: the scene lost its menace, it became amusing; it passed. The distraught look had left her face. We walked further.

'We'll talk about those days another time, my child,' she said eventually.

'Because they haven't gone?'

'They can't disappear. It's all still real, everything that's happened to us. Those experiences haven't gone anywhere, or faded away somehow into time. Time's not real. It's nothing—it's a measure. We invented it.'

'And you're still caught in those days you can't talk about?'

Serghiana ignored this, and went ahead of me. The path narrowed. There was a steep headland: we rounded it together. Ahead we could see the curves of the peninsula and the early sunshine gleaming on the lake.

'How blissful,' she said softly: 'Nature's what gives us peace, not man. But look—above the pass—those clouds. There'll be a storm: this morning, soon—it's coming fast.'

She stopped, sank down on a low, weathered wooden bench beside the path, and made a sign to me to sit beside her.

'Great-Aunt Serghiana,' I began, then hesitated.

'What, child? Such calm: I don't know whether to fall into the quiet forever or run from it. Another question?'

'These seats and benches with names carved into them—the ones along the path: what are they? Who put them here?'

She laughed. 'Remember yesterday, when you asked me what a bourgeois was? Now I can show you. Show you to perfection! These are bourgeois seats. They're the memory seats; that's what they're called. People who come here in the summer each year claim them, they buy them up, and stamp them with their names, and have them put in places with a view. It's become a fashion. Children dedicate them to their parents, and parents to their children—and married couples as well, you see benches commemorating them and their long-lasting unions, too.'

'Because they love each other?'

'Because they love themselves, and they want their names to live on! That's what the bourgeois want. To be remembered after death. To be missed. Soon the whole Chastè peninsula's going to be covered by these benches, there'll be one every few metres, they'll form a perfect record of a class and its longing for permanence.'

'But won't the benches all rot away and collapse—the way old trees do?'

'Yes—they'll be ruins in the end, or earth art, and decay to nothing.'

'Would you like me to put one there for you?'

'The wrong thought! I'd rather be remembered in your mind than on a block of wood along a footpath. Anyway, I don't think I fall into the category—I may be many things, but I'm not a bourgeoise!'

'No,' I said then, triumphantly: 'You're the Red Princess!'

'Wherever did you hear that expression? Who have you been listening to?'

'It was Egon the cartoonist who called you that.'

'Is that so—the poor deluded man!'

'I don't think he meant it in a bad way. But princesses can't be bourgeois—can they?'

'Nor can communists.'

'What about Ady? Is she one?'

'Now there's a question that opens up the depths! Everything about her's made up—even her name. I suppose that's forgivable.'

'It is?'

'Everyone in this part of the world has an origin story, and they're all false.'

'Even yours?'

'Of course not! Do you want to know the true story of Palafay and where she came from? I'm sure you've heard the cover version.'

'I know she likes to keep the names of all her husbands.'

'That's one way of putting it. Her father was from the Bukovina, from some marshy shtetl. There were pogroms: he fled them; he made his way to the city: he failed in business in Vienna; he tried again in Budapest, and opened up a shop there with borrowed money, selling toys, and trinkets, and ladies' clothes. That went well, he expanded, he did the right people favours—he became a big capitalist; and his daughter was a little student by then, at a private school high on Gellert Hill: she was pretty, very pretty, in the usual lighthearted Hungarian way: she survived the war somehow—who knows how, and who knows where. I remember her in party circles, afterwards, in those years when the war was over and everything was being remade; I know I saw her once, at a meeting in Romania of the Cominform—then suddenly she was in the West: she had a singing voice; it gave her a screen career she doesn't like to be reminded of—and that's when her real days of performance began: she went out and found her husbands, each richer than the one before: there was a count, and after him a diplomat, and now a maestro of the music world. The class terms don't exist to describe someone who's lived their life like that: she's what bourgeois women dream of being, rather than being one herself. I've seen her mansion on the Vienna Parkring: the interiors make the Hofburg look modest. Quite a tale, isn't it? From the proletariat to the plutocracy in two generations. Does that fit with anything she's told you?'

'Not really,' I said.

'Well—why should it? Her life's just the raw material for her self-reinvention. No one would begrudge her that. What matters more is how she treats you. Do you actually like her? Has she been kind to you? Does she ever come to see you? I know she hands you on to those Upper East Side intellectuals for your holidays.'

'You know everything!'

'You didn't answer me. You told me once you enjoyed her company; you said you loved her. I think you know—that cut me like a knife. But now I wonder: now you're under her wing, is it still the same: a year, no, two years later? Do you like the treatment you get from her? Do you still care for the life that's been sketched out for you by Palafay?'

She turned, and gave me an inquisitorial look. I stayed silent for a moment.

'See!' she said then: 'See what you've become. I ask you a simple question: and you stop, you think. Your face doesn't move, it's like a mask, but inside you're considering what to say. You're no longer a child at all: in fact you're quite grown up in your behaviour. You've become calculating. What things you've learned from Palafay!'

'But I hardly ever see her,' I said.

'I know it's not your doing,' she said then, in a gentler voice: 'But you understand, don't you? You had a place in my life. And she has you now. Does she mother you, does she fly in to see you, and spoil you with her gifts?'

'In a way.'

'So she's claimed you—with a glance, and a smile, and some Hungarian patisseries?'

'You're not being fair.'

'Fairness isn't in my repertoire. Truth, principle, loyalty and faithfulness until death—those are qualities I recognise. The world doesn't know fairness or justice; it knows their absence. It knows danger and destruction. Look up. See there—the storm's almost on top of us. That's the way the world is—random bursts of violence—look, there—you can see the lightning flashes deep inside the clouds. Don't flinch! Have you become afraid of storms now? Should we go back—or are you still actually the same inside—brave and fearless, the way you were when I was shaping you?'

'I love storms,' I said: 'Of course. Let's stay, and watch it coming in.'

'Well—why not? We'll stand right at the water's edge. Let's see its fury. See the true face of the nature we try so hard to love. There's the rain, there—pelting down, on the far side of the lake—like a column pouring from the clouds. It looks just like Dürer's dream.'

'Whose?'

'An artist—from long ago. He had a famous dream—I know—another dream. But this one counts. He made a watercolour sketch of it, so we know what he saw—or what he imagined he saw. And he wrote about it too.'

'What did he say?'

'There's a long description: it's in the collection in Vienna. I've seen it, I've held that page from his workbook in my hands. It's a striking image—the storm looks like an atomic bomb cloud, just after the detonation—but he made it hundreds of years before anyone ever thought of atoms and nuclear tests. He often used to see imaginary paintings and artworks in his sleep, and as soon as he woke up they'd vanish from him and leave no trace—but this was a different kind of image: clear, precise enough to draw: a wide column of water falling from the sky, and spreading out before it hits the ground, with smaller jets of water falling all around it, close by and far away, just like the rain veils in the tropics. Beneath the image there are several lines in his handwriting, very neat and elegant, and his signature as well. He says in his dream there was a furious noise, and a wild wind, and the force of the flooding drowned the whole landscape in front of him—he woke trembling, he had no idea where he was, he had to struggle to get control of himself.'

The rain had drawn closer as she was speaking, the clouds were rearing upwards, they formed white towers, rising and shifting, with voids between them through which shafts of blurry sunlight came pouring down; there were plumes of vapour hanging low like ragged curtains stretched across the lake. Blots of cloud raced in; their shadows pressed down on us. The wind had strengthened—it whipped up wave crests, the surface of the water turned to foam. Serghiana dropped down to one knee beside me, she clasped her arm around me and held me by the shoulder, tight. Her face was touching mine; her breath as she spoke blew on my cheek.

'It's near,' she said: 'How wonderful! Almost like the storms of years ago.'

'Were they different from the ones today?'

'Very. They were dramas, they were violent, they had a progression to them—like a piece of music. First a thunderclap—the statement of the theme—then variations, and a quiet interlude, then, suddenly, out of nothing, the finale, fierce, profound: you'd see lightning bolts come down on both sides of the valley, the thunder would roll across the sky and jump between the mountaintops, and there would always be a double rainbow at the end.'

'Here in the Alps?'

'In the country I came from. Wilder than here—higher peaks, like needles and like blades. And here, too, once, when I was here, a long time ago. All that's gone. Everything's a pale imitation now—for me.'

'You always say that!'

'It's true. Now—hold my hand—take it, and stay still beside me. This downpour's come for both of us together. Fix this image in your mind—if you ever think of me, think of me like this, here, with you on the water's edge.'

She looked up. The rain was on us now: it gathered force, it came beating down.

'Look up with me,' she commanded. 'Look at the storm—open yourself to it—look into its heart.'

I did so, and saw her face beside me, tilted skywards, into the rain and the swirling fury of the clouds.

*

It was morning once again, light was streaming through the windows, the sun was high in the sky. Someone was prodding me. It was Lipsett.

'Hey, kiddo,' he said: 'Wake yourself up. It's all going down.'

I covered my eyes with my hands, and looked through my fingers at him. 'How could I wake myself up if I was asleep? Anyway, you already have.'

'You sleep too much.'

'You need your sleep when you're growing,' I said.

'And what—you think people who aren't growing don't? Hurry! The show's already started.'

'What show?'

'The Reds. I was there, by the entrance, when they drove up. Want me to tell you?'

'Sure—you could make it like a pitch again, to the mogul in Hollywood.'

'It was quite cinematic. First one black Mercedes, then another—not a ZiL in sight. Bodyguards in both the Mercs jump out.'

'Any submachine guns?'

'What?'

'The weapon of choice—you said; don't you remember?'

'None that I could see. That's not the point. Get ready—let's go down. Semyonova sent me to find you. I was sitting with her, in the foyer, killing time. They were late; she was nervous. She took me into her confidence—I think. It's the first time we've ever spoken that way. She told me things: about the main man, Naumov: where he came from, how he began in the party; how he rose so high. How to read him, too: the little signs that mean everything. She said he'd come up to her, shake hands for a brief moment, then kiss her on the cheeks, very ceremoniously, three times—and if that doesn't happen on occasions like this, something's seriously wrong, But isn't that too friendly, I asked her—she said not. It's the fraternal socialist kiss of greeting, like a password—you could say it's a sign of shared beliefs. For men like Naumov, Semyonova's the head of a progressive organisation, she's actually a comrade in arms.'

'I know how it works,' I said: 'Next scene!'

'The little cavalcade pulls up. Out jumps the driver, he runs round, opens the passenger door and jumps to attention. Naumov gets out first: he's a cool cat—distinctly cool: tall, middle-aged, handsome enough, in a reptilian way, clean-cut, the usual Soviet type. Two others fall in behind him, like wingmen: they come through to where Semyonova's waiting, dressed in black, standing still and proud. He smiles at her as if he's seeing an old friend. Her hand's stretched out to greet him, but she keeps her face expressionless: "My dear friend," he says softly to her, there's the swift handshake and the three kisses on the cheeks, and they're real kisses, tender ones: he's still clasping her hand, she pulls away. "Everything's arranged for us, Pavel Pavlovich," she says then, and glances at the other men behind him: "We're in a private salon, it's quiet there, the winter salon—in the back of the hotel." He gives a sombre laugh at that. She makes her first thrust. "I've got one of my young directors with me—and there's a western friend of ours staying here: a backer, in an indirect way. He'll join us. You know him: you held talks with him in my company, two years ago." "Serghiana Ismailovna," Naumov says, in a calm voice: "Nothing you do surprises me anymore. I was almost expecting his presence here. It would be lonely without him." She turns to me: "Go, Corey—find Malzahn: he'll be expecting you. Tell him the delegation's here." I track him down out on the terrace. Malzahn's with the babe...'

'The babe?'

'His wife—I give them the message, but I also let him know about my time in Paris; I tell him what I'm working on with Semyonova as well. He makes a show of being interested. "We'll follow you," he says: "Lead on." "But, Henri," says the babe: "Surely you can't." He looks at her. She tries again. "Perhaps," she says, "you shouldn't be sitting down with them—at least not so publicly." "I'm always grateful to you, my dear," he says then to her, very smoothly: "For your thoughts on what I can and can't do and should and shouldn't do—but in this case, it so happens that I have a reason. A little bird told me something interesting: it'll be announced today. News of interest to the Soviets. It might be quite worthwhile to listen in—and you should too." "We're on holiday,' she says: "Our first together." "You know very well a holiday's just a chance for unofficial contacts," he replies: "For real contacts—the only kind that count." I feel it's a cue for me. I jump in. "If you like,

Madame Malzahn," I say then to her, very politely, "I'd be happy to take you for a drive around the lake: I could show you St. Moritz, and the sights." No response. I think she was wavering. You know her: any prospects, down that avenue?'

'What?'

'Never mind. She's quiet for a second—she even manages a little blush. I press the advantage: "I know the valley well," I say. She attacks: a good sign. "And you presume I don't know it? In any case, I'm a married woman—I can't accept invitations from strange men—not in my husband's hearing, anyway." They both laugh, as if it's an in-joke. Game and first set to her. We troop off together to the salon. Everyone's there already, sitting at a long table, the two groups facing each other, Semyonova opposite the main man, just like in the diplomatic meetings you see on television; there's her new Italian director beside her, and that professor you were with yesterday as well. They're already talking in several languages—and jumping between them; there's laughter too—the mood seems warm; there's a great fussing over Malzahn when he comes in. He and the babe sit at the empty places on Semyonova's side of the table. More pleasantries, the waiters appear. They have the mineral water: they pour it. But it's Vichy, for God's sake—like in *Casablanca*. What a choice! Naumov glances at the label and gives a sardonic little smile. Semyonova's furious. "Bring us new glasses," she commands. "And more water—Badoit, Vittel, Volvic—anything—but not this." At that moment she sounds at a loss: she looks almost frightened by the men facing her. "Another meeting with unusual atmospherics, Serghiana Ismailovna," says Naumov then: "At the end of a long journey for us. And another of your westernising proposals." "You've gone through it," she asks him: "The dossier I sent through to you?" "Of course," he says. That's when she begins to push back at him: "I don't flatter myself, Pavel Pavlovich," she says. "It's not my way. I don't think for a moment you've travelled such a distance to go through project ideas with me. You were coming anyway—to Locarno, to the festival. And you have a demand to make of them: you're going to insist they not screen certain Soviet films." Naumov's obviously annoyed. "As always, very well informed," he says in a soft voice, and there's a sudden feeling of unease in the air.'

'Go on,' I said.

'That's as far as things have gone. That's when the bodyguards came in. They called Naumov and the two underlings beside him from the room. And Semyonova made a sign to me then, and told me to run upstairs and fetch you. Time to head back to the salon: come with me. Just don't move around and fidget and be a nuisance.'

'Am I that way usually?'

'No—you're quiet and subdued—like a typical young private-college boy—safe and tamed: the way I was.'

'And still are?'

He gave no answer, but led the way. We went down together, slipped into the room by the terrace doorway, and found a quiet corner table.

'That's Naumov,' said Lipsett, leaning over to me: 'See, right there, he's the one standing beside Semyonova. Did you hear—they're waiting for some message to come through, I'm sure that's what he just said.'

There was confusion round the long table. Naumov and the men with him spoke in whispers briefly, then seemed to come to some agreement: they took their seats.

'Of course,' he said to Serghiana, looking straight across at her: 'You know you had a success last time—a great success, it pleased the right people, you know that very well. It was a clever idea. And so you have the high cards in your hand. Freedom of a kind—this time—but only this time.'

'I'd be astonished if it was otherwise, Pavel Pavlovich.'

'Yes—your star's high—but I've seen it low before—and maybe it will sink again one day.'

'I've never seen yours low, Pavel Pavlovich,' she said.

'No—and that's not a coincidence. I'm guided by principles that are clear.'

'And those principles will allow you to grant us your actress?'

'For this project? That's not so straightforward.'

He tapped a folder in front of him, and sighed, and held up a type-script page with notes written in its margins.

'So many problems,' he went on: 'So many potential pitfalls. A Russian heroine from the nobility—who passed her adult life outside the motherland. A woman who chose to practise Freudian psychotherapy! And you want our actress for this part? No other suggestions? No other scripts, more suitable ones? You know how rich the archives are in untold stories.'

'I know the past, Pavel Pavlovich.'

'We all do, in our different ways—but this story of a life of the mind—this particular hero-philosopher—a German hero—for us?'

'There are a hundred other projects we could set before you, Pavel Pavlovich. All you need do is say the word. We could show you a screenplay of the life of Dostoyevsky, or a portrait of Chekhov, seen through the mosaic of his stories, and set in Yalta as his life ebbs away. And there are others, but I don't see the point of mentioning them to you—stories from more recent chapters of our history—stories set in the furthest reaches of the Soviet state.'

'Don't mention them,' said Naumov: 'Don't.'

He shook his head in a regretful way—at which point one of the bodyguards came back in and whispered to a young man at the end of the table, who jumped up and murmured something into Naumov's ear, then left the room.

'A necessary interruption, Serghiana Ismailovna,' he said then. 'The cable from the embassy—it's being brought in now. And so: we understand each other, don't we? We're clear what's been decided. Proceed—another film set in these mountains, in this blessed country. You must like it here. Perhaps it's becoming your true home?'

'You know my purpose in being here, Pavel Pavlovich,' she said.

'They're fencing with each other,' said Lipsett into my ear. 'That's the way it's been right from the start. It's becoming like a duel between the two of them.'

'And it agrees with the gentleman at your shoulder, too!' Naumov said: 'The time's come for you to present him to us. I believe the face is familiar to me. Am I wrong?'

Professor Leo was sitting beside Serghiana. He looked uncertain. He turned to her.

'Pavel Pavlovich,' she said, 'on matters of detail, I've found you're rarely wrong. But there's no reason you should know Dr Loewy, our friend from Zürich: he assists us with the screenplay background.'

'Indeed—Dr Loewy—Leo Loewy—in fact from Prague. I remember. It's such a distinctively—well, what should I say—such a Czechoslovak name! And should I congratulate you on your change of country, professor?'

'I'm surprised you would even know of me, Comrade Naumov,' said Professor Leo in a mournful voice: 'Very surprised.'

'It's my task in life to know such things—and know the company my fellow communists are keeping, day by day—and every single movement across borders helps us to see the correlation of forces between East and West. How critical that work is, in these times of tension, when matters stand so delicately poised—and when the safety of socialism in your country, professor—your old country—is under such determined threat.'

'It's best by far if I step away from the table,' said Professor Leo: 'My presence can only be a hindrance to you—I don't have an important part to play.'

'No, no,' said Naumov to this, and he made an expansive gesture, and glanced round at the figures on his side of the table. 'It's not necessary, Professor. It makes no difference. Just so you know we know.'

'That goes without saying, Pavel Pavlovich,' said Serghiana.

'Stay, then. It's settled. You can remind yourself of the rigour of our ways—ways, Comrade Professor, that you once were careful to observe. And perhaps there's something fitting in your presence here.'

He held up the sheaf of paper resting on the table in front of him again. 'I glance through these notes—the tale of a learned man, a genius of a kind, isolated from the people, unwanted in his own country, led astray by a Russian, doomed to madness and a long, lingering death in life—and the thought comes to me that the tale may hold some faint resonance for you.'

'Still the same, Pavel Pavlovich!' said Serghiana, and she fixed him with her stare: 'How much I admire your consistency. True to the line, impervious to events. Fluent in your professions of faith—as flexible as the creed itself.'

'I understand your meaning,' said Naumov: 'And you doubtless understand where words like those will lead you in the end.'

'Wild, isn't it?' said Lipsett to me: 'She's something else!'

The tone of the exchanges was becoming sharper. Serghiana was speaking in her most languid, irony-laden voice. Naumov had a look of irritation on his face.

'Yes,' Serghiana said to him: 'Your consistency. Your orthodoxy. Don't you see I'm paying you the highest of compliments—old friend. There are times when you remind me of the old southern commissars, of the wartime years, when it was my father who gave them their commands. Or I can cast my imagination even further back: how furious you are in your pursuit of enemies—like the borzoi from czarist times that would chase down their prey and hold it by the throat, immobile, until their master with his serrated knife rode up.'

There was a sudden commotion as she said this. The young man came back into the room, almost at a run, and thrust an envelope into Naumov's hand. Naumov opened it, unfurled a sheet of folded paper and read it. Silence. He frowned, glanced at it again, then handed it to the man at his side, and leaned over and spoke a few words, and the man inclined his head.

'Do you know about Serghiana's father?' I asked Lipsett.

'Only that he won battles in the war,' he whispered back: 'Great battles—and lost his life.'

Then Serghiana began to speak. At once Naumov clapped his hands together.

'Quiet!' His voice was hard. 'No more. This is an outrage. A provocation. I have here before me proof—if it was ever needed—of the forces drawn up against us, and the lengths to which they go. A scandal—and among the worst.'

He shook his head in dramatic fashion, and looked around him, as if measuring the complicity of all those present in the room.

'October the eighth, nineteen-seventy,' he said: 'The date will live in memory—a day of infamy—a day that will be marked forever by our people.'

'But Pavel Pavlovich,' said Serghiana: 'Whatever are you talking about?'

He stared back at her.

'Fury in those eyes,' murmured Lipsett.

'I shall read you the note that was just handed to me. A communiqué. It comes from Stockholm.' He spat out the words.

Malzahn made a little movement and looked across to Josette.

'Issued this morning by the Nobel Foundation—our well-known foe, the same club of academics who wished to honour Pasternak. And now they find another anti-Soviet activist to crown. I quote for you: "The Nobel Prize in Literature nineteen-seventy was awarded to—to Aleksandr Isayevich Solzhenitsyn for the ethical force with which he has pursued the indispensable traditions of Russian literature." Ethics! Literature! No! They give their prize to swill, to incoherence, to reactionary propaganda—to slander against the Soviet state. I can almost hear the laughter in Washington and New York. And as I speak, I reflect that there are other western countries where the leadership may not wish us well.'

He looked down the table to Malzahn and glared.

'Yes,' Naumov continued, his voice falling very low: 'Tact prevents me from expressing my thoughts—but I ask myself, Serghiana Ismailovna, if your friends came to listen and advise you, or came with foreknowledge, to gloat.'

Malzahn held up his palms. 'I hear this now for the first time,' he said: 'I give you my word.'

'And I accept it,' said Naumov to him: 'Naturally—I have to. No more for today. Serghiana Ismailovna—you understand I must cut short.'

'Wait,' she said, her voice full of urgency: 'Wait, Pavel Pavlovich. Listen to me—before you go.'

'What can you have to say to me now?'

She gave a short, surprising laugh. 'Don't you understand the opportunity you have? Step back. Consider. Think like a strategist.' She was smiling. There was excitement on her face.

'Serghiana Ismailovna,' said Naumov, 'I don't know what you mean. I don't think I want to know.'

He picked up the slip of paper before him, and looked at the men at his side, who all flexed their muscles: like birds about to fly from their perch.

'Listen,' said Serghiana, 'Pavel Pavlovich: listen to me—we know our respective roles—we know them well; we know what's expected of us.'

'And?'

'It's my task to see your situation clearly, and advise you. Yours is to use culture as a weapon: a means to advance the cause. This is more than just an international prize for literature. It's a challenge.'

'It's an assault, Serghiana Ismailovna. An ideological attack.'

'And what do you do when an enemy comes rushing at you? You turn the blow—you use his strength to your advantage.'

'I can promise you the matter will be handled just as was the case of Pasternak twelve years ago. Our leadership will stop the so-called writer Solzhenitsyn from collecting his award. Or we will send him out, then not let him back.'

'Why not welcome it, the way you did with Sholokhov, five years ago?'

'There's no similarity. Sholokhov was a hero of socialist literature—this person aims to undermine the state.'

'So it seems wise to you to send him into exile, and make him even more famous than he will be after today's news—turn him into a megaphone, prove the truth of every criticism that he makes!'

'What do you propose instead, Serghiana Ismailovna?'

'Seize the chance. Take control. Announce today in Moscow that the award's welcome, it shows the depth of Soviet culture—rehabilitate the writer—receive him in the Kremlin, even.'

'Reward him for his slanders?'

'Exploit him—rather than let the West make use of him.'

'How?'

'Can't you see it, Pavel Pavlovich? You have the chance to lead opinion, to shape it. Co-opt ideas, not stifle them. Be the master—pile laurel wreaths on the author and his works, praise them for their position in the mainstream, no, the vanguard of socialist endeavour—commission a dramatic, splendid piece of cinema made from his words.'

Naumov laughed at this—a hollow, unpleasant laugh. He glanced at the men alongside him, who gave their own short, gruff laughs as well.

'This is a dream, Serghiana Ismailovna. I suppose you think the film should be of *One Day in the Life of Ivan Denisovich*—and the responsibility for making it should be given to you?'

'It doesn't matter what book or story of his you choose to turn into a film, or who makes it. Commission it today. Neutralise your enemies—proclaim it to the world.'

'Such foolishness. You really think the idea escaped us? You think we didn't consider *Denisovich* and weigh up its argument, its message? We could have filmed it at any time. After all, we published it: have you forgotten that? But the decision was made. And events have justified it.'

'Events, Pavel Pavlovich?'

He gave a smile of triumph. 'Perhaps, Serghiana Ismailovna, you're not as well informed about western cinema as you like to think you are. As a matter of fact a film of *Denisovich* has just been completed, in Norway: they have their own cold, icy landscapes there. We know something of its content.'

'I'm sure you do.'

'Yes—we have sources. It's just what you'd expect. Pure anti-Sovietism.'

'Pavel Pavlovich—you know a film made by our side would be different—and have a different impact.'

Naumov interlaced his hands; he leaned slightly forward. 'You've been away too long, Serghiana Ismailovna. The truth is you don't know our country anymore. And this so-called author, this prize-winner—propped up by tiny cliques of activists and backed by western money—you don't know him: you don't know what drives him on. But we do. We know what he's been writing, in secret, hiding his typescripts away, using copyists across Moscow to shoulder all the risks for him. He thinks he operates without our seeing, but we know. We know what he thinks and what he plans before he even sets it down on paper. We have the new pages he's written every day before the sun goes down. And do you know what his great plan is: the vast betrayal he's embarked on now? He means to send a history of the Gulag to the West. And why? To harm the reputation of the state. He exaggerates the troubles of times now long gone, he takes no pride in our achievements.'

'Please, Pavel Pavlovich,' said Serghiana: 'I know the speech already; I know every word by heart.'

'Do you see what she's doing?' said Lipsett into my ear.

'Not really, no,' I whispered back.

'I think she's actually trying to provoke him. As if she wants him to lash out at her. I almost think she wants a great dramatic scene, a show-down—maybe so she can make a film of it.'

'Pavel Pavlovich,' she was saying: 'Credit me with some ability to think. I've put forward a proposal to you—the best course of action for you now: in fact, the only one that makes any sense. Everything this writer writes is well known. Do you imagine there's a single family in the entire Soviet Union that has no knowledge of the past; that hasn't lost a parent or a grandparent to Kolyma, or the Karaganda steppe, or frozen Magadan? Can that be what you think—that all this is a state secret? Everyone knows—at home, and in western countries as well. It's common knowledge, wherever people want to know. Our young generations may keep silent, but they've been told: about the purges, and the trials and deportations. All of it: what happened to the priests and believers and landholders—the intelligentsia as well. So many secrets, stored up in every heart. Don't you see how much the Soviet people would appreciate such a film, how proud they'd be to see it, how it would be a gesture of honour to their missing and their dead? The truth—what a sign of hope such a film would bring.'

'Serghiana Ismailovna—please! You want to make a monument to a traitor—a man who hates his country and its cause. That's who you want to honour and promote; maybe you want him to be received in the Hall of Facets. Should he be given a banquet by the leaders of the party? Or should we all sing songs in his praise? I can hardly believe it's you who's saying these things. I look across at you, and a strange question rises to my thoughts—I have to ask myself: have you become an enemy of your own people—of your country?'

'Pavel Pavlovich,' said Serghiana then: 'Must you really sink so low? You understand exactly what I'm proposing to you, and why.'

Naumov was silent for a moment. He stared at her, and glanced round the table—at the men beside him, at the figures sitting opposite. He interlaced his fingers, and pursed his lips. When he spoke his voice was almost a whisper: dry and cold.

'Serghiana Ismailovna,' he said, 'you stand on a knife edge. You don't see yourself: you don't see what you're doing. You don't see what you've become.'

'How fortunate I am, then, to have you here to make that diagnosis for me, Pavel Pavlovich!'

'Shall I tell you what I see when I look at you,' said Naumov: 'You—the daughter of a famous revolutionary. You, the Red Princess, who received everything from the Soviet state. Everything—your education, your privileges and your connections, your place in life. All you are, you are because of our system—'

'I know what made me what I am, Pavel Pavlovich,' she broke in: 'And I know you too. You forget how well: your career, its beginnings, your sudden elevation, the heights you still aspire to. I know the patronage you received, and the alliances you depend on. Who you've spoken against, who you've raised up; what you've done, and what you've tried and failed to do—'

Naumov interrupted in his turn. 'My actions speak for me—my record.'

'Your war, and your gilded version of it—I know that also,' said Serghiana: 'In fact, I know you well enough to see the fear in your eyes today. You're afraid this isn't just a little problem for the cultural authorities—another minor nuisance like the Pasternak affair. You see the threat, just as I do, but you see it as a threat to your position. I still remember what you told me two years ago: you said that after Prague, every ideal was smashed. The only thing left was power—Soviet power, the power in Soviet hands, hands like yours—and that, you said, was quite enough.'

'And there was something else you might remember that was said in that talk, Serghiana Ismailovna: I made you a promise. I said we'd send you all the funds you need for your productions—on condition that you stayed abroad. You've received that backing, you accept it happily enough—and you play your role well as our facade. But that's all you are today. Our front. Our instrument.' He looked at her: it was a testing look; it had amusement in it. 'Do you deny what I'm saying?'

'Why should I, Pavel Pavlovich? It's the truth. Although it was in confidence—our discreet arrangement.'

'A deal, in fact—a business deal, made in another time of troubles, when East and West were poised, and on alert. I told you then that we should stay on guard; that we'd see new attacks and provocations, new attempts to probe our resolve and strength. And this is one. It detonates in front of us—you hear the news, and your first thought is to help our adversaries. You want to film a piece of anti-Soviet propaganda: you want to do their work for them.'

'I didn't know any of that,' said Lipsett into my ear: 'That there was a deal like that.'

At which point a troop of hotel waiters appeared in the doorway. Serghiana beckoned to them; they approached. Naumov had been about to say more. He stopped; everyone around the table, as if by tacit agreement, froze.

'The Badoit you asked for, Madame Semyonova,' announced one of the waiters in a nervous voice: 'Will it be acceptable?'

Serghiana laughed. 'A well-timed interruption,' she said. 'For this gentleman opposite me, first of all. He has a thirst—for many things— and he feels himself pre-eminent. Pavel Pavlovich, will you join me in a drink—of blameless mineral water? You can drink with me and undermine me at the same time, can't you?'

The waiters set down new glasses in tandem, opened the bottles with a co-ordinated flourish, poured and hurried out. Even as Serghiana finished speaking, Josette leaned across and murmured something to Malzahn. She slid from her seat and made for the terrace door; she noticed us and paused.

'Hello, my little someone,' she said, and perched on the armchair I was sitting in: 'Still cross with me?'

'All this talk must be boring you, Madame Malzahn,' said Lipsett: 'Want to take me up on that offer and make a getaway?'

'Do you know this low-life?' Josette asked me: 'Is he a friend of yours?'

'He's the production assistant for Great-Aunt Serghiana,' I said.

'Thanks for the glowing reference, kiddo,' said Lipsett.

'Production assistant,' echoed Josette: 'What kind of creature is that? Driver, maybe.'

'That too,' I said.

'Thanks again!' said Lipsett.

'He's just trying to help,' said Josette: 'He likes to have things clear: to know exactly where people stand—don't you?'

'Are these two friends, or enemies,' Lipsett asked her: 'Or both?'

'Can't you see what they are?' said Josette to him: 'They're poker players—and it's a high-stakes hand. Just listen: how tense it is across that table!'

'You'd finished, Pavel Pavlovich,' Serghiana was saying: 'But I've scarcely begun. Of course we should be on our guard: not your way, though—it's a trial of tactics just as much as strength. Your real adversary's not the dissident setting down his Gulag memoirs in some tiny upstairs room on the corner of the Arbat.'

Naumov gave a little start.

'Yes—I already know the story of his secret manuscript and your spying on him: it's the talk of Moscow. I hear about it—even at this distance. But it's not his challenge to you that matters—he's nothing without the West. This is their signal—don't you see? They're warning you: they're saying to you—we stand behind your dissident, we'll raise him up and make him our symbol. It's the end of the era of peaceful co-existence. A new landscape. That's what this prize means. It's not an insult. It's a message. And I've shown you the way to answer it—the only answer that's confident and strong—an answer that would serve to raise your name up as well.'

'If I put my name to this idea and sent it forward it would destroy me, Serghiana Ismailovna,' said Naumov: 'I think you know that very well. We've reached the limit of what we have to say. This is the end of our pleasant talk.'

He turned and gave a sign to the men beside him. He gave his bitter laugh again.

'Stop,' said Serghiana: she leaned across the table and stretched out her hand towards Naumov: 'Use my name.'

He took up his papers and handed them to the man beside him.

'You think your name still counts for something, Serghiana Ismailovna? Really? It has an old flavour, like the smell of a field after harvest in the days of childhood.'

'The most poetic thing I've ever heard you say, Pavel Pavlovich.'

'And you're taken aback—because you don't believe anyone except you and your circle could have fine thoughts or beliefs or ideas. It's true we're not the same, but the difference between us is simple. In your heart you believe the system your father helped to build is weak, and set on unsure foundations, and always under threat. And I believe it's as strong as shining steel, and just as permanent. You think a pinprick from the West can tear down our defences. When I hear you list the dreadful dangers that surround us, the realisation dawns on me: you long for the disasters you describe.'

'You're going too far,' said Serghiana.

'No—I'll say it. Let's speak plainly to each other—for once. I'll tell you the truth. I used to admire you, I looked up to you: when I first came to Moscow you were at the heart of everything: and when your darkness fell, you had your dignity, you were even more a heroine in my eyes—one who'd suffer silently for the greater cause. Only now do I begin to see how damaged you are.'

Serghiana smiled: a smile for herself. She made a quick cutting movement with her hand.

'It's as you say, Pavel Pavlovich. The time for talking's done. You've always been limited in your thinking. You're caught out by the news you've heard. You're lost. You don't know what to do. I hand you the solution. You refuse it. You turn your face away. You don't even have the courage to present it to the Kremlin gods.'

'Present it yourself, if you dare to! You're the one with a great protector—but when he goes, what will you be? No one will save you then, no one will care what you say or think. I should have known it was a mistake to make this visit to you—to come to your court: your exile palace. I should have sensed what you've become: a woman of the West.'

'That's your view of me, is it, Pavel Pavlovich?' said Serghiana in her most contemptuous tone of voice: 'Your view as a communist?'

'It is. I see your true colours, I see through your disguise of loyalty: I see you as you really are. And I also know why you're the way you are. You've never put aside your own misfortune or recovered from it. You never learned from the criminal acts of your husband Semyonov all those years ago.'

There was a silence then. Everyone around the table seemed to sense the weight of those words. Serghiana leaned back in her seat. She was calm. Her eyes bored into Naumov in silence. He looked away.

'Criminal acts,' she said softly, and repeated the words: 'Criminal acts. You have to lie, don't you, Pavel Pavlovich, and repeat all the old party lies you've learned—and you have to believe those lies as well. You insult the memory of a great man—a man with a faith far purer than yours. You might as well spit in my face. Go ahead—here it is before you. Lean across the table. Go ahead. It would be the same for me as the words you just said. And it's easy to speak that way, isn't it? Easy to defame the dead. It's almost second nature for you—you do it before you can stop yourself.'

Naumov ran a hand through his hair; he shook his head: 'I'm sorry, Serghiana Ismailovna. Forgive me. I shouldn't have spoken that way about him. It was wrong of me.'

'Forgive you! Forgive!' She was laughing at him as she spoke: 'No, Pavel Pavlovich, no. You can't undo words like that. You can't. You showed me your true face. The worst thing is that I've listened to men like you, apparat men like you, saying the same words before—often, very often, in the dark years, in the time before his rehabilitation came, and I stayed meek and silent. I betrayed him too, my unmoving lips betrayed him—I was quiet to save myself. No longer. It's I who can see clearly now, Pavel Pavlovich: I who can see you for what you are. In my eyes you're an animal—no, worse than an animal, much worse; animals are loyal, and proud, and true. You're that special kind of beast they call human—a socialist human—the wildest of the wild. You pollute the air with your breath—you insult the mountains by your presence here. I renounce you—you and your kind.'

There was a pause. She held herself straight and defiant. Her face was flushed.

'Do I understand you?' Naumov said.

'You do,' said Serghiana, and she breathed in deeply: 'I renounce you. Take the message back—carry it back like the servant that you are.'

'I can't bear it any longer,' Josette said to me then in a low voice. 'Come with me, let's go—we shouldn't listen to this.'

'What's happening?' I asked her.

'She's destroying herself.'

'They're destroying each other,' said Lipsett: 'It's like we've stumbled into the last pages of some unknown Russian novel!'

Naumov leaned back in his seat again. His features had relaxed. He glanced around the table. He began to speak—his voice was almost nonchalant. 'So—it ends this way.'

'It does,' said Serghiana.

'What an adversary you've become. Such ferocity! You want to escape, to flee from what you are. Be sure of what you want. You can be sure of the consequences.'

'Pavel Pavlovich,' she said: 'There's nothing you and your kind could ever do to me that would be worse than what you've already done. I've lived with lies for years, in a kingdom of lies. And today the break comes: a crack in the ramparts. You say your defences are made of steel: but I know their secret—those tall watchtowers that protect you are really like pinnacles of glass—glass crystal. Not without elegance of structure, but weak, with hidden flaws. Like this glass, in fact.'

She picked up the glass in front of her, tilted it in her fingers, and gave it an appraising look.

'Bohemian crystal,' she said: 'The finest. You probably don't know much about the properties of glass crystal, Pavel Pavlovich—after your childhood in the workers' camp at Chelyabinsk. It has a tendency to shatter completely when struck; it makes a satisfying noise, a clanging noise—like this.'

She brought her hand down as she spoke and smashed the glass on the surface of the table. It exploded into fragments, they caught the light and gleamed, they hung in the air a moment, then fell in a shining circle all around her. At once the figure at Naumov's side jumped up and began brushing the shards from his jacket. Naumov lifted up his hand.

'You've made your point,' he said: 'Very clearly.'

'If I go on making it and remembering the past and my silences and your words until Judgement Day, it wouldn't be long enough.'

'Antique superstition—how far you've fallen, Serghiana Ismailovna.'

'A Caucasian trait. It must be ancestral. It's fitting, in a way, Pavel Pavlovich, that it should be you who came here with the news that's brought us to this. You, the grey comrade, the specialist in propaganda, the system man, always serving, always stealthily advancing; you who never understood a thing about Soviet culture, what it was in all its glory—what it could become—and yet you hold its future in the palm of your hand—and it's plain from everything you say: you mean to choke it and strangle it until nothing's left. You talk, you repeat your slogans, and I hear the voice of the party, and hear what it's become.'

Malzahn rose from the table as she was speaking, and came towards us.

'Let's go,' he said to Josette: 'This is in danger of becoming an incident.'

'Becoming! It already is,' she said to him: 'It's wonderful!'

'It's dangerous. This is the kind of absolutism that starts wars. Come—it's best to leave. We should have gone long ago.'

She turned to me. 'Come too,' she said: 'Or do you want to stay in this pandemonium with her? We could find a place for you, couldn't we, Henri?' she said, and looked round, but Malzahn was already on the terrace, beckoning to her furiously. She paused a second, then hurried out to him.

'It's just us now, kiddo,' said Lipsett: 'Just us.'

'We'll leave you, Serghiana Ismailovna,' said Naumov, in a calm voice: 'I doubt our paths will cross again. I'll make the report you want. I'll convey it in person. In detail. But it's the wrong choice you're making. You're comfortable here—in another country. Too much at ease: I can see it; everyone says it: even your defenders. But your judgement's in error. You'll miss the world you came from. You'll regret your decision. You're going into a great wilderness.'

'I know where I'm going, Pavel Pavlovich,' she said, also in a low voice, almost in a whisper: 'I was in the wilderness already—I've been there for years. In my mind I'm always in the frozen north. So I'm grateful to you—for speaking as you did, for being what you are, and showing it so plainly to me. I'm grateful to you—for being my foe.' She gave him a tranquil, beatific smile.

Naumov shook his head, and glanced round again. 'Enough of your paradoxes. You'll survive, of course, Serghiana Ismailovna: we both know that: you'll prosper, you'll see rewards, this will be the making of you in the West. I've suspected for a long time that things would end for you this way—since I first met you, when you were in your glory, when you were the young bride of a great man of science, and I was nothing.'

'Nostalgia, Pavel Pavlovich! And self-pity! Truly? Your parting shot?'

'I watched you,' he went on: 'How could I fail to? It was splendid, you were the party's favourite child—but I knew—I could see there was a fatal pride in you: it lifted you too high. You thought you were safe forever, the machine would never touch you, the state security was for other people, the knock on the door in the dead of night would come for them but not for you. And then, one day...'

'I know the story, Pavel Pavlovich, I know it very well. Do you say all this to ease your feeling of complicity or to cause me fresh pain? No more! Be off—go on your errands. You can remember the day when you drank from crystal glass in a grand hotel and saw the Red Princess of your dreams go over to the West. Remember it, and laugh at me—but it's time for you to disappear—you don't belong in a place of light like this. You don't: I renounce you—I'll never deal with you or any of your kind again. I promise myself that—and I promise you, in front of everyone, and I'm happy as I tell you—I'm joyful in my tears.'

V

Passirio

ZÜRICH AIRPORT ONCE again, the arrivals hall: late afternoon, a year on. I looked round for familiar faces: a driver I knew, perhaps, or even Muscatine. No one. I went up and down expectantly, dragging my case behind me, until I noticed a young woman, tall, with long, dark hair and angled eyes, studying me. She beckoned.

'Come,' she said, in an accented voice.

'Who are you?' I asked.

'Elista,' she said, and reached for my suitcase: 'Madame Ady's assistant. Give!'

'I've never met anyone called that before.'

She stared back at me. 'Don't you like the name? Don't you recognise it from somewhere? Geography not your strongest subject at school? Quick—there's far to go.'

'I thought we were going into town—to the same hotel as usual. The one by the river.'

'Change of plan.'

'Where's Muscatine?'

'With the Maestro, of course, where do you think? We left them in Salzburg. We drove all the way here to collect you. We're going south.'

'Who's we—and where to?'

'Questions all the time! Let's hurry. What's wrong—don't you believe me? Do you think I'm trying to steal you away? Are you always so suspicious? So on edge?'

'I've never heard Ady mention your name before. I'd have remembered. Where do you fit in? Have you only just started working for her?'

'You're not very well informed, are you? You could say I play the role you used to play in Madame Ady's life—that I'm replacing you, in fact.'

'I didn't realise I had a role—or that I was being replaced.'

'Ask her yourself.'

'Where is she? I can't see her.'

I looked towards the concourse; I peered over the young woman's shoulder—at which point a pair of gloved hands slid over my eyes.

'I'm here, right here, behind you,' said Ady's voice.

I swung round. There she was; she held me by the shoulders and gave me an appraising stare.

'How tired you look, my treasure: those flights! Each one a trip through purgatory. Has Elista made you welcome? Are you being pleasant to him, my dear? She's been dying to meet you; she's heard so much about you.'

'I gathered that,' I said.

'And you're forgetting something—something critical!'

'I am?'

'Your upbringing: take my hand, touch it to your lips, my poor treasure who's growing up so fast. Quickly, now: we're heading off on an adventure together.'

'We are?'

'Yes, we're going to the landscape of my childhood—to the Dolomites: to Meran. Come—follow me: you won't be sorry.'

She strode off towards the exit from the terminal. I followed in her wake.

'Where—where are we going?'

'The name says nothing to you? Nothing at all? It's called Merano now, and it's a backwater—but it used to be the centre of the world—at least in summer, and in Austro-Hungarian times. I'll show you the valley, I'll show you the old town—I'll show you everything: it was the magic kingdom of my childhood; it was a paradise. I spent my happiest days there—and my saddest, too. I haven't ever been back, since that time.'

'Why not?'

'I never felt I could—but with you here: we can excavate the past together, can't we, explore it hand in hand? And there's someone staying there you might remember: someone you might like to see.'

'What about the hotel in Zürich?'

'Don't worry so much—it's just a side trip we're making, two days, three days—no more. We'll be in Zürich again soon enough: you can go back to walking round the lake shore and feeding the swans.'

'That's not the only thing I do all day when we're in Zürich.'

'Don't argue—it's good to see new sights and travel to new places: the mind stays fresh.'

She stopped in front of a large Mercedes. 'Jump in.'

'Into this? You've changed cars since last time.'

'You think perhaps Novogrodsky and I have only one? We change them often—but never the make, or the colour. Always grey metallic— always the dark grey of Bukovina skies. Slide across to the middle of the front seat, sit between us—we can talk along the way.'

The young woman opened the car door and inclined her head towards me in a slightly mocking fashion.

'I should be the one opening the door for you,' I said to her: 'Not the other way around.'

'Heavens,' said Ady: 'You've remembered your gallantry. Don't try to charm the staff—I won't allow it. She is lovely, though, isn't she? Aren't you, Elista?'

'If you're kind enough to think so, madame,' she replied, 'that makes me happy!'

'Her name,' said Ady to me: 'It's a romantic story: shall I tell it to you now? You don't mind, do you, Elista? Her father was an academician, from Leningrad: he specialised in eastern religions; he studied in Kalmykia: he fell in love there—can you imagine, in those Buddhist wastes—he brought his daughter back with him to the city; she grew up in a grand apartment on the Fontanka: golden privilege—until things changed, the way they do in that part of the world.'

'And that's where you met?'

'No: that's not exactly a milieu for someone with my kind of past— you know that. It was elsewhere: you won't ever guess; we found her during last year's concert tour. She was a language student; she was interpreting for the Slovak opera. We extracted her. I felt we had to. She reminded me of myself when I was young: proud, and lost, and helpless. Of you, too, actually—you the way you were before I took you in hand.'

I glanced across at Elista during this little speech: she said nothing; her expression stayed unchanged.

'Believe me,' Ady went on: 'She's gifted: very. You can practise your languages on her—or have you already forgotten everything in that foreign school? You could even go exploring together. You've never been to Merano, have you, Elista?'

'No, madame—you know that. I've never been anywhere except with you.'

'Another thing to thank me for! Drive, then, fast. I want to be well across the border before night comes.'

'The border?' I said.

'Yes—of course—we have to go over the mountains: into Italy.' Ady's face softened—her voice became nostalgic. 'I loved crossing the frontier, on journeys like this, when I was a child. We'd drive from Vienna, my father and I, just the two of us: we'd set off early in the morning, so we could make the whole trip in a single day: through Innsbruck without stopping, and up, across the Brenner—on the old road no one takes anymore. I can still picture it the way it was: the barrier that had to be rolled away for each car going through, and then rolled back again—the guardhouses painted in national colours; the soldiers on both sides in their uniforms, saluting: all the signs and all the flags. Even then, I understood it was more than a frontier between countries.'

'It was, madame?' said Elista.

'Much more—it was the dividing line between north and south. Every time we made that trip, I longed to see what lay ahead: I'd wait for the moment when we first caught sight of the high peaks and the cliffs, and the waterfalls and landscapes far below. I told myself I'd always be happy if I could stay in Merano. It was everything I dreamed of as a girl: bliss and harmony, warmth and light. And the border—how majestic it was to my eyes—it was like a heaven there. We'd stop at the pass, every time, and sit still, side by side, saying nothing, looking out, as if there was only us two, only my father and me in all the world.'

She fell quiet; I listened to the engine's hum; night was falling. I leaned back against the seat.

'Don't sleep,' commanded Ady: 'Stay awake with us. We'll be driving through the Engadine; your old home away from home—and then the road runs straight as a line. You'll feel the change as soon as we reach Merano: it's like the Mediterranean—there's a softness in the air: there are vineyards and orange groves in the hills all round the town, palms and frangipani along the riverbanks. I knew their botanical names—I memorised them all because I thought they were so beautiful. Everyone went there in the season: everyone who mattered: the cities emptied out. Schnitzler had a great romance there; Zweig went each summer; and Strauss, and Schoenberg: Rilke, naturally, but Rilke was everywhere. Doesn't it sound appealing to you? I used to think every piece of music or writing worth anything came from the Dolomites. And it's where self-knowledge and the science of the mind began.'

'It is?'

'In a certain way. You know all about Freud by now, don't you?'

'We've just begun studying him,' I said: 'And Serghiana used to talk about him—all the time.'

'I'm sure of that,' said Ady, rather acidly: 'Not that he'd be much help to her, the way things stand for her now. But it's really true: the whole story started for him in Merano: his first great case: the one that showed him everything. Do you want to hear?'

I leaned back, and half-closed my eyes.

'He calls her Dora,' she began: 'But that wasn't her real name, of course. She was Ida—Ida Bauer. She was a lovely, gifted child. When she grew into a young woman, men who shouldn't have been were drawn to her, with the usual consequences. And it all happened in my paradise—in Merano. Here: rest your head on my shoulder.'

'Maybe we should let him sleep, madame,' said Elista.

'My dear, it's character-building to stay awake for long periods at a stretch—to master the body with the mind. And it's a story you should hear as well. Besides, car journeys are ideal for case histories like this: you're disconnected from your surrounds, it's dark outside, your thoughts are free to range, the shadows of the landscape go rushing by. It's almost like being in analysis—you plunge into yourself, you can never be sure what's going to come to light.'

Ady spoke on, her voice low. The car braked; we began climbing the hairpins of a mountain road.

'I'll begin in Bohemia,' I heard her saying: 'Bohemia, where all good stories start.'

I listened, and let the tale drift into me. Freud's childhood; his first discoveries; the account he gives of Dora's early life: the setting, the characters, the tensions between them; the primal scene in Merano's central square, its sequel on the Garda shore—all this in word pictures, pictures so evocative I saw the drama unfolding as if excerpts from an old movie were flickering before my eyes.

'Madame,' I heard Elista's voice saying: 'I think he's almost sleeping now.'

'That's ideal,' said Ady: 'He can hear it in his dreams—it's very suitable—perfect for the subject matter. Things sink in deeper, much deeper. When I look back I realise everything I've learned has come from dreams.'

'Truly, madame?'

'Can you doubt it? Don't you always see through what your mind's telling you? Your conscious thoughts? All that's nothing—what we think. That's why Freud works so well—at least for Central Europeans: one look's enough to tell you what kind of creatures we all are: made up of obsessions, and complexes, and buried desires.'

'Him too? Is he like that?'

'Naturally. It's part of him. It's a cultural system; it's general—there aren't any exclusions.'

'And is that why you sent him to a school so far away?'

Ady gave a sigh: 'Perhaps it was,' she said then: 'Perhaps I hoped he could escape the pattern.'

'And now you've changed your mind—and here he is.'

Ady shrugged, and my head moved with the movement of her shoulder; I shifted, and fell back into a fitful sleep.

*

Bright daylight; the hotel room. I woke with a start. Through the open French windows came a seething, high-pitched noise. I went to the balcony and looked out. Beneath me, across a narrow promenade, was a river, straight and fast-flowing, with rapids in its channel and rocks and boulders protruding from its bed. Beyond was the vista Ady had described the night before: peaks, green slopes with vineyards, the facades and roofs of buildings, a slender spire. I made my way down several flights of stairs, through the lobby, out, and across to the balustrade above the stream. Its sound was deafening; the braids and flecks of water went racing past; they threw up flares of spray that hovered, gleaming, in the sun. For a few moments I watched, until something made me turn, and look around. High above rose the hotel's facade, blue-grey, with an imposing emblem on the pediment: 'Meraner Hof'—and there, leaning against one of its entrance pillars, arms folded, watching me, was Elista. Her face was sombre; her hair was pulled back.

'Hello, replacement,' I said as I went up to her.

'Don't talk to me,' she snapped: 'I'm in disgrace. I thought Madame Ady was going to send me away this morning.'

'Why?'

'It's your fault. You fell asleep on my shoulder while I was driving.'

'So? I was tired. You know that. You said so yourself.'

'Wrong shoulder. You should have chosen Madame Ady's.'

'I didn't choose anyone's.'

'Surely you know she's possessive about you—you've worked that much out, haven't you? Aren't you something like a child to her—the child she never had?'

'I hardly ever see her,' I said: 'I scarcely know her anymore.'

'Is that so?' she said, sarcastically. 'She doesn't seem to think that way. She talks about you all the time.'

'I thought she was getting ready to say goodbye on this trip.'

'It may be so. That would only add to the pull—affection rises up when it's about to come to an end.'

'Actually, I thought she was treating you like a favourite. Don't you and she get on? You seem to—just fine.'

She stared back at me. 'You believe it's a relationship of equals? Be serious. What choice do I have? I'm just another in the long parade of underlings from Eastern Europe she and Novo collect and make use of and then discard.'

'And am I that, too?'

'You want me to do your thinking for you? That's for you to work out.'

'I see,' I said, and went back over the balustrade.

Elista came up. 'Did it work, anyhow?' she asked in an abrupt way.

'Did what work?'

'Her stories—while you slept. Did you have Freudian dreams?'

'What should I have been dreaming about?'

'Don't you remember any of what she was telling you? You ought to know all that anyway. It's famous. Dora's dreams: the dream of the house on fire, the dream of the strange forest. No? Nothing? You should go inside now, and find Madame Ady. She was asking for you. She told me to go and wake you. She's on the terrace, over there, with the director from Bregenz. I'll show you—I've got a message for her. I have to interrupt them.'

'Then we can explore, afterwards?'

'She'll take you. She's in a good mood. Their little negotiation's been going well. She wants Bregenz to program Novo's Eastern Orchestra for next year: his youth orchestra.'

She looked at me expectantly. 'The new project,' she said: 'You must know all about it.'

'Are you part of it?' I asked.

'Are you?'

'I'm not that musical,' I said.

'Everyone is,' said Elista, rather scornfully: 'We are music: haven't you heard all that before?'

'What?'

'The Maestro's doctrine: what he teaches in every masterclass. We're each one of us like phrases of music—we have to find them inside ourselves and express them: sing ourselves into being. No?'

'You seem to know everything about your protectors,' I said.

'And I have the feeling you've still got some things to learn about them.'

She said this in an offhand fashion, almost laughing, speaking over her shoulder as she led the way back into the hotel. There, at a table in the sunshine, was Ady, leaning back in relaxed fashion, shading her eyes against the glare. A grey-haired, earnest-looking man was seated opposite her, speaking to her in an animated fashion, his hands interlaced.

'That's the festival director,' said Elista in a low voice into my ear: 'And I think you've already come across the man sitting at madame's side.'

Next to Ady, whispering something to her, was another figure, younger, wearing a linen jacket, his back to us. There was something familiar about this individual—I looked again. I told myself he looked almost like Stephane Daru. At that instant the man turned his head, noticed me, nodded and even waved: it was Daru—his face tanned, his hair longer than when I had seen him last years earlier, a fret line stamped on his forehead—but it was him. Ady had also spotted us; she made a sign for us to wait.

'You understand, madame,' the stranger said: 'If only your husband would agree to conduct.'

'No,' she interrupted in a forceful way: 'If only you'd understand! It's an orchestra for the young. My husband's seventy-five years old.

And it's an international project—the conductor's magnificent—we're lucky to have him—he's from the conservatory in Kiev. It's not a cause that speaks to you?'

'It's a dream, madame—an unfulfillable one. Brotherhood across borders—concerts in the public squares of eastern capitals. It's as if you and your husband believe the twentieth century isn't real.'

'Not at all—we simply want to bring it to an end. What seems permanent can be made provisional; what seems hopeless can be the start of hope. When you've lived lives like ours, you tend to believe in lost causes—the wildest dreams—they're all that's left.'

'But that makes things very political for us, madame.'

Ady reached over, and tapped the grey-haired man's hand, and looked into his eyes. 'That's exactly the point,' she said: 'Don't you want to do something worthwhile with your position? Don't you live and breathe for that? Wasn't that what you dreamed of when you were appointed? I seem to remember you came to visit Novogrodsky less than a year ago and told him so yourself—told him exactly that.'

She paused then, and laughed in her most engaging way. 'Best not to answer. You know what I want—what we expect. I'll leave you two together to come to some kind of understanding.' She got to her feet.

Elista leaned over to me. 'That's what she always does,' she said in a low voice: 'Creates a vacuum around herself: a mystery out of nothing. It's her favourite trick.'

'Is it a trick?'

'That's what all power is.'

Ady was upon us. 'You two—how pleased I am to see it: just like brother and sister, whispering to each other: getting on so well.'

'Madame,' said Elista: 'Frolich from the record company rang and left a message for you. He's in Zürich already, waiting for us. For the meeting you arranged. I called him back. He's worried something's wrong. He's afraid you're going to cancel. He says he absolutely has to see you. He has an idea he wants to outline: to propose to you.'

'An idea,' echoed Ady, in a voice of amusement: 'That's when record-company people become dangerous.'

'And he needs to fly back in two days' time.'

'How did he sound?' said Ady.

'Insistent.'

'So let him come here. Call him again. Tell him to drive over to us. It's not that far. It'll do him good to see the Alps in autumn. We can fit him in, can't we? Tomorrow morning, just as arranged. We can all enjoy his company and his eloquence.'

'That's the message you want me to pass on to him, madame—you're sure?'

'Don't I sound sure? He's American: it won't make any difference to him what grand hotel we meet in—or what country.'

Elista retreated. Ady took my hand. 'Treasure,' she said: 'Come with me—I've arranged a splendid breakfast for you at the table. All my favourites from my childhood here: I had the concierge go specially to buy them: fresh patisseries, from König's on the Corso—walnut cakes, strudel, tiramisu.'

'I don't know if I can manage all that.'

'Of course you can—you need nourishment for all your studies. And they're light, and delicate. I loved them when I was your age—if you're still hungry later we can go there and try their Meranertorte this afternoon. I've nearly finished with our friend from Bregenz: then we'll set off. We'll follow the river, walk the summer promenade as far as we can go.'

Daru had made his way over to us. 'It's done, madame,' he said: 'And as you wished.'

'You know my handsome peacock already, don't you?' said Ady to me: 'I'll leave you with him a moment.' She let go of my hand, as if signalling the end of a dance.

'You look as if you've seen a ghost,' said Daru to me. 'Are you so surprised?'

'I thought you were far away,' I said: 'I thought you were still a diplomat—an ambassador, in fact—in South Vietnam.'

He recoiled as if he'd just been dealt a blow. 'You shouldn't mock me that way. It was the dream of my heart. I'd be in the skies of happiness if that were true. Whoever could have told you such a thing?'

I hesitated.

'Don't say—I can guess. Believe me, I asked for that posting, I pleaded for it—but as you can see, my career in diplomacy hasn't advanced. Your aunt was kind enough to take an interest in me. I was able to put my ideas to her: it was at the time when her husband was just setting up his orchestra. So I work in his interest now.'

'And is that better than what you were doing before?'

'It's wonderful—to have a cause to believe in.'

'And that's a change?'

'It's as if I'm returning to what I once was: music was my special refuge—my only refuge—when I was a boy growing up in an empty house in Saigon. I loved the piano: I played from very young—I even used to compose my own pieces—in the style of Ravel, and Debussy: I wanted to found a school of hybrid music there: West and East together; two traditions into one.'

'And do you still want to do that?'

He looked into my eyes for a moment. A pained expression came over him.

'Do you have hopes of that kind?' he asked. 'You should hold on to them. The dreams of childhood are the best things we have in life.'

'You seem very different,' I said.

'People change sometimes, when their circumstances change—or they come back to their true selves. I wonder if you still see Semyonova?'

'Not recently,' I said.

'You mean you're in Madame Ady's orbit now?'

'I suppose I am.'

'We both are! I don't lament Semyonova's fate, I have to say—although I admired her, and feared her, and made use of her as well—whenever I could.'

'What fate?'

'She's nothing, now—or at least not what she was. No connections. When she gave up Moscow, she gave up all her power. It's as if she's vanished from the landscape here. She still produces, films on art, I think, and period dramas, all in California—but here in Europe you rarely come across her name. You're better off with Madame Ady anyway. She's a gentler kind of autocrat.'

'If you say so,' I said.

'Believe me—I can make the comparison. I know.'

He gave me a slightly distracted smile, and went back to the table.

'You don't seem very comfortable with Stephane,' said Elista, coming up to me.

'Do you know him well?'

'He's only just started working for the Novogrodskys.'

'He was always very cold towards to me—until now,' I said.

'Really? I've never met someone whose personality I find more warm-hearted and open. There's a lightness about him: I can't imagine him being anything but kind. Perhaps it's more you: your nature. You seem to be on guard always—with everyone.'

'If it's me, and something in my nature, how would I be able to tell?' I started saying, but Ady swept towards us again.

'Come,' she said to me: 'We'll go off to inspect my birthright. Elista—I leave you with the peacock. Call the record man. And don't forget your appointment: Fragsburg at midday—then down again to meet us.'

She turned back to me, and took me by the arm. We walked in silence for a short while.

'I saw you talking to Elista before,' she said then: 'Outside, by the river. As if you were arguing: sparring with each other.'

'That's not true,' I said.

'Perhaps I was imagining things—but that's the way it looked to me. She's still finding her place among us. Be kind to her: be friendly. Try. I can tell you don't care for her. It's natural. She's my new companion—you're jealous.'

'I'm not. I was never your companion.'

'Yes, you were—of course you were—but now you're growing up, becoming what you should be—what you really are: a watcher of life's parade, a composed and well-defended creature: safe in yourself. That's what I wanted you to be. That's what I promised I would do for you. And our paths are separating; they won't cross so much in the years to come. You know that yourself already; you've hardened yourself against me. I can see it in you.'

'Please,' I said: 'Don't think that.'

'My treasure—you look so sad, suddenly. Don't be: life's sad enough as it is. Just open yourself up to me one last time—will you: will you do that for me?'

I nodded my head.

'And don't be confused. No need. This is the way we agreed things would be.'

'We?'

'Your first guardian and I felt it would be for the best—if you had every choice, if you were bound to nothing; as free as you could possibly be.'

'You mean Serghiana Ismailovna?'

'How Slavic of you! I do mean Semyonova.'

'I used to think that you and she never agreed on anything. That you were enemies. You always made it sound as if you were.'

'It's not quite that way. It never was. Enemies are the people whom you fight. It's simply that we're unlike each other. You understand that, don't you? We couldn't ever be friends—our backgrounds are too different; the things we care about are different, the way we live our lives is different; in fact the only point we have in common that I can call to mind is you.'

We had reached one of the river bridges: Ady stopped. 'How I love that sound,' she said: 'I always have: the song of the river—its name's much better in Italian: Torrente Passirio: with its glacier water—deathly pure and icy cold. Take my hand again, but do it properly, this time, gracefully, casually, as if we were strolling together on the Ringstrasse, and without a care in the world. Stay in step: we'll do the rounds—see all the sights—sights in the town of ghosts.'

'Why do you call it that?'

'There's a ghost at every corner for me; behind every facade. I've thought of this place so much—it's in my dreams each night. I've come back here so often in my mind. Can you tell what I'm thinking: right now, when I look across the river, and see the Kurhaus and its statues, or Theaterplatz, with its gabled houses and its colonnades? Can you?'

'You're smiling,' I said. 'You look happy: but thoughtful, as well.'

'The mountains don't change,' she said: 'That's what I was thinking. And the faces of the people are still the same—only the buildings change. So much new; so much gone. Down that street, that was the way to the Waldpark, to Bermann's sanatorium—my father knew him well, and Balog, too, and Lustig: he knew every one of the specialists: the pioneers who offered radiation cures.'

I looked at her.

'You don't believe me? It's true. The hills are radioactive. That's why the soil's so fertile, and the vines and fruit trees grow so well. That's why Merano became famous in the first place, and so many of the doctors who were already famous in the capital moved their clinics here. They used to prescribe a special diet of grape juice—juice and thermal baths: they wanted to irradiate their patients back to health. And there were doctors for the mind and heart as well: people crossed the mountains to come here as though they were travelling to a promised realm of happiness.'

'But what about you? Why did you leave Vienna? Why did your father bring you here?'

'I'm telling you the story. Just listen. It was for a different reason. The obvious reason. He saw ahead. And of course he loved the mountains—but in another way. He liked to say they were our barrier, our secret fortress, they were a wall of granite, protecting us from harm; but he always said it jokingly: I was still too young when we

231

first arrived here to understand what he meant. I was constantly asking him to take me walking on the mountain paths; he said the time might come, and I should read the guidebooks; and I did: I studied them.'

'At school?'

'No—I had tutors—I would have gone to some school for young ladies in due course, I imagine, in France, or Switzerland, maybe—but I wasn't much older than you are now when I saw Merano for the last time. Come—keep up with me.'

She looked round, and smiled, and stretched out her hands: 'How strange the feeling is. Like walking through a world of crystal. Everything I knew and cared for here has vanished, it's gone, but I can see it still. That's where the Villa Steiner was, and there, over the bridge—the Post Bridge, with all that latticework of gilt and silver—the first building on that side was Wassermann's, the photographic studio: I had my picture taken there on my birthday, every year; next door was the jeweller, and then it was just a few houses to Feldschareck's, the piano school: that's where I went for my lessons: Tuesdays and Thursdays, at three in the afternoon.'

'You remember everything!'

'No—it would be more truthful to say I've built a life on hiding memories from myself: on looking past them, never coming back to them.'

She walked on for a while, then stopped abruptly in front of an imposing townhouse with a covered entrance and heavy, dark-painted double doors. There was a new expression on her face: tender, uncertain, dismayed.

'Where are we now?' I asked her: 'This must have been something grand.'

'It was a great landmark. Can't you picture it? Can't you guess? This was the headquarters of my father's empire across the mountains: his trading bank—the Bank of Vienna and Tyrol. I came here every afternoon to collect him, and the staff gave me little salutes of greeting when I walked in: I'd go up to his office, his secretary would announce me, and then, whatever he was doing, whoever was there with him, he'd break off; we'd go out together to the balcony and watch the sky changing colour, and we'd talk as the sun went down. That was our ritual: I looked forward to it every day. Let's not linger: it's changed too much. Everything has. It hurts me just to be here—more than I thought it would.'

'You expected it to make you sad, and still you wanted to come?'

'We came so I could show you all this. Don't you think it's a proper part of your education? No one's wholly European or civilised unless they know the stories of old Meran: the charm of its past, the charm that lulls.'

'I see,' I said.

'You don't sound very sure. Look around you. The literature of longing—on all sides. There, on the Corso, or on the Post Bridge, you could have caught sight of Ungaretti; in the town castle's courtyard, Julien Green; along Portici, the architect Orlando; down the Winkelweg, poor Morgenstern, who came looking for health and found only illness and decline. Name me the dreamer who hasn't washed up here. The prince of them all, as well! I had Stephane find the villa on the Maiastraße for us. It's not far from here—the Ottoburg, where Kafka stayed, sitting on his terrace in the sunshine and working on *The Trial*—you know all about him, at least, don't you?'

'And the metamorphosis, yes.'

'Metamorphosis, and many other things. He liked it here: he wrote to Milena in Prague, and told her all about the south—the land beyond the mountains: how exalted it seemed, how free he felt. And I think if he'd been able to live his life as he wished, he'd have been quite happy here, wandering round Merano and the lakes: he'd have been a tranquil, romantic figure, lazing in deckchairs and pacing up and down the promenades of Gardone and Salò. You can see it in the stories, if you look carefully, and know how to read them: you can see the way the Hunter Gracchus really wants to come ashore—and if Kafka could somehow make a trip back here, I think he'd be proud to see the Via Franz Kafka signs on the Riva waterfront. Don't you? You're very quiet. What's the matter?'

She stopped and gave me a questioning look.

'Why do you have Daru working for you?' I asked her.

'Stephane? Why not? You don't approve of him? Another member of the staff you don't care for? Perhaps you'd like to screen everybody we come into contact with and give them your certificate of approval? He's been a great discovery for us; he fits into our lives as though he always belonged: I thank the fate that brought him to us. Novogrodsky adores him, Elista's half in love with him, even Muscatine gets on with him. He's been invaluable. And very informative about some details you never thought to mention—my treasure.'

Her tone had shifted. She leaned against a stone barrier and turned towards me, and gave an operatic sigh.

'What details?'

'You kept very quiet about Serghiana's new supporters in the West. You said nothing to me. Don't look surprised—I know you know: the French culture fund. I needed Stephane to tell me who was paying for her documentary about my husband. You didn't even let slip that you spent last summer with her on location in Sils Maria—when we were just a few kilometres away—a short drive down the valley at Badrutt's: you never called; you never let us know you were so near us—you didn't breathe a word.'

'Was I supposed to tell you about the French? Am I a spy for you now?'

'No: you've become a keeper of confidences. Concealing things from me, editing things out. I know you feel more in tune with Semyonova than you do with me.'

'That's not true!'

'Of course it is. I know it, and I know why. You feel loyal to her, you think she's a tragic figure, noble and suffering, and intellectual and profound—whereas here with us you're in a world of idle luxury and

234

froth and sweet patisseries and pointless chatter, and the theme tune's a Vienna waltz.'

'None of that's fair,' I tried to say: 'It's not fair at all'—but she spoke over me, her voice sharp and cold.

'It's not hard to work out. Remember, I've known you all your life—I know the kind of child you were, I know what's gone into you, I know the flavour of your personality—very well. You turn things back to front. That's your way. False is true for you and down is up. But things in your world aren't the way you want them to be. In fact they're quite clear and straightforward. Semyonova's harsh and remote with you, she neglected you, she abandoned you, just the way she neglects and abandons everyone: I care for you and support you, I smother you with affection and with gifts—yet you imagine Semyonova's the one watching over you, you think she holds you in her heart. Stephane tells me you actually call her "great-aunt". What delusion! She's a wild Cossack from the Terek River, there's nothing she has in common with you, she's not fond of you the way I am: but you treat me as if I was the stranger from the backlands: you make quite sure there's no warmth between us—no tie as close as blood. Nothing like it. It's embarrassing; it's hurtful. What did I hear you call me once—I'll never forget it—you said I was just a family friend.'

'But you told me never to call you Aunt Ady! Don't you remember that? It was on the day you came to collect me from the Lyceum, from Zuoz. Muscatine was there. You said never. It was an instruction; a command.'

'And you took me literally! How little you know about the world.'

I hesitated, and looked across to her. 'I didn't mean to upset you,' I said, and listened to my voice as I was saying the words: 'It's strange, sometimes, it's hard—being so far away, half a world away—then suddenly back here—back into your life. I don't mean to seem cold towards you. I don't feel that way—at all.'

She stared back in silence.

'Aunt Ady,' I said then, and she smiled, and stretched out her hand towards me, her manner completely changed.

'That's all you needed to say. I understand how things are for you. Of course I understand: I see it in your eyes. That's why you're here with me now, that's why it's only us here, the two of us, walking together. All those others at the hotel are just the figures in the charade. You're the one I'm close to. You're the one I chose—long ago.'

'Chose for what?'

'Chose for what, *Aunt Ady*.'

'Chose for what, Aunt Ady.'

'To be my memory child.'

She looked at me carefully after saying this, and made a sign to me to come closer. 'Do you understand the term?'

'Maybe.'

Very gently, she put her arm around my shoulder, and rested her hand on mine. 'Maybe's not really good enough in this instance. It's something important: an obligation—a task. I want you to know what I remember from the days when I grew up here—everything. I want you to remember it in your turn. And remember me when I'm gone from our world.'

'Please, Aunt Ady,' I said: 'I hope that day doesn't come.'

'Don't be sentimental: not about this! It's much too serious. There are two deaths—for everyone. The first when we leave the world, and the second the real extinction—when the last person who remembers us and cares about us dies as well—and then the final trace of us is gone; then we're just names, names to be forgotten; whatever we once were has vanished, it can't ever be brought back; no one will ever know again the way we looked, the way we smiled, the scent of our skin, the way we moved and held ourselves, all our gestures, all the clues to our nature, the little things that give us away. They go—into oblivion—but for as long as you live on in someone's mind, the mind of someone who loves you, and holds you close, then what you were and what you cared about hasn't entirely disappeared or died.'

'I see,' I said.

'Don't sound so uncertain! That's how we survive—the only way— in the memory of others. We're given a second, paler kind of life:

an afterlife that's like a purer version of our own: filtered—stripped of what's inessential, made more perfect, crystallised. Preserving that new life, that second, echoed life—that's the task that we perform for those who go before us, and others in turn perform for us: that's what I'm asking you to do for me. Will you?'

'Of course I will,' I said.

'It's a binding promise. Don't give it unless you mean to keep it. Remember where you gave it—in the sunken garden in Merano, across from the Kurhaus, next to the cypress tree.'

She put her hand on my heart, and held it there a moment. 'That's my assurance; that beat's your pledge. We're kindred now—kindred by choice.'

She gave me another long, assessing look. 'Thank you—my treasure,' she said then: 'And with my gratitude comes a burden for you.'

'A burden?'

'The burden of remembering. There's so much to tell. I should have begun with the villa—of course we should have gone there—but we wouldn't have had the time—not now, at any rate, not this morning.'

'What villa?'

'My father's retreat. The Villa Sorgenfrei—ill-named! You can see the site from here, quite clearly. Look—follow where I'm pointing. Train your eyes towards that peak, then along the cliff face, halfway to the old castle and its tower: there—in the folds of the landscape, with the last vines in rows beneath it.'

'It looks almost like a blur,' I said: 'Is that it?'

'A blur—a stain—a darkness. Yes—that's where it was—but it's a ruin now.'

'What happened?'

'It was blown to pieces—bombed into rubble in the last days of the war. No surprise. It was a grand creation: it was much too beautiful to last. My father designed it himself, with his favourite architect—that modernist—the Slovene who'd worked for him in Vienna and Prague. They built a monument. The stone of the facade was all Istrian marble—it gleamed like a Roman temple in the sun. Inside, everything was sleek and sparse; you'd have thought you were in a building devoted to scientific study, not a private home—until you reached the pavilion at its centre; you went through glass doors and came out in a world of growth and flourishing—a conservatory, a glass-roofed hothouse, full of palms and bamboos and scented flowers from the tropics; you were dazzled by the light pouring down above you, you had to shield your eyes.'

'I think I've seen another glass chamber very much like that,' I said.

'Really? Surely not one sited like that, so high up, almost in the clouds. When you reached it, it seemed like a paradise. There was an English garden sloping down, and a reflecting pool in front of the entrance, and a balcony and belvedere: you could look out towards the Bernina—you could see south too, down the valley where the railway runs—it was always bathed in sunshine—you would have thought it was the track to happiness.' Her voice trailed away; she gave me a little smile.

'And did you spend much time there? So far away, so far above the town?'

'No—on the contrary. Once it was finished, my father never went there again. He'd laboured over its detail for so long, he'd expended all his enthusiasm and care on it, he'd made it perfect in the abstract—but when he saw the completed building it displeased him. It was exactly what he'd wanted, every detail was correctly executed, but he felt it was a monstrosity: he said everything about it seemed wrong.'

'And after that—what happened to it?'

'It was left empty for a year: then it was the summer guesthouse for his friends and his business visitors, and whenever anyone stayed up there, he made a point of apologising for its shortcomings: in the end he gave it to one of his factory managers from Brixen. When the war broke out it was requisitioned; they turned it into a barracks and an observation post. It was destroyed in the first Allied raids: the fire burned on for days and nights.'

'And then?'

'Nothing—no thought of trying to save it. No one missed its presence up there. People in Merano used to call it the Slovene folly: they thought it was repellent, and foreign: they would have been happier if we'd built another imitation castle in the hills. My father had wanted it to be a landmark, a glory for the ages, like Novacella or the Marienberg: in less than a decade it was gone.'

All through this account she had kept her eyes trained on the mountainside; she looked at me, and smiled a little. 'We'll wind our way back towards the river,' she said: 'We have an appointment to keep.'

'Who with?'

'It's a surprise.'

'A good one?'

'Very.'

'Do we have far to go?'

'Not at all—just through this park, across the bridge with the decorated railings. And look, see—there—that statue? The woman with a book in her hands.'

'This is who we're meeting?'

Ady smiled. 'Well—that would be something! This is Sissi. She used to be the most famous woman in Central Europe.'

I looked at the statue with more attention.

'The Kaiserin,' said Ady, in a prompting way: 'She came to Merano often.'

'Of course,' I said.

'You're familiar with her story?'

'The name perhaps,' I said, 'in a vague way—yes.'

'They don't teach the history of Hapsburg Europe at your school? Sissi's story: Empress Elisabeth—the beloved of her people, the long-haired anorexic, the pale emblem of a pale and dying kingdom?'

'Not directly, no.'

'My stars,' said Ady then: 'I wonder now what I've done in sending you off there. I thought I'd be preserving you and saving you from all the troubles that were tearing at our world...'

'What troubles?'

'Invasion, foreign occupation, the constant sense of conflict close ahead—that's what I wanted to keep you from, but more and more I see there's a change in you: you're not exactly European anymore, are you? You're becoming a young American—in your voice, in your accent, even.'

'Wasn't that the idea?'

She gave a quick, sad-edged laugh. 'I don't know that there was any well thought-out idea at all, my treasure: there rarely is. Let me introduce you to her—Kaiserin Elisabeth: Empress of Austria, Queen of Hungary and Bohemia, and—oh, many other places. When I was your age I used to come to this park in the afternoons and sit and read the story of her life and cry bitter tears—or at least I thought I should be crying, and I thought my tears should be bitter, like my heroine's tears for her dead son as she walked the paths of Gödöllő or Trautmannsdorf—but now I look back and I think they were tears for my world of childhood. We could see it fading even then, we could tell that it was dying, it was fragmenting in front of us—every day, with every headline, it drifted further into oblivion. And she was the incarnation of that world: lovely, weak, enslaved by her worship of her own image: the bereaved princess, surrounded by misfortune, remote, refined, unhappy, but always in a lovely way. You know what happened to her, don't you?'

'Something bad?'

'Obviously.'

'But a long time ago?'

'In 1898—a year of terror all across the continent; quite like the present, actually. She was travelling in Switzerland, incognito, without a bodyguard, only a lady in waiting for company. She'd reached Geneva; she was staying at the Beau Rivage; somehow a journalist found out, and wrote about her visit. An Italian anarchist named Luccheni read the story, and chose Sissi as his target. He followed her and ambushed her: he stabbed her with his stiletto—straight through the heart.'

'But that fits perfectly,' I said.

'It does?'

'It's another link to you. Don't you see—she died in the same city that you went to as a diplomat; you told me all about that time.'

'You remember! I wish it were true, but it's not quite. Luccheni stabbed her as she was about to board a paddle steamer and make the journey across the lake to Montreux; she survived long enough to walk to the landing stage, she even went onboard, and the steamer sailed. It wasn't clear how badly she'd been hurt; the weapon was so thin the wound was almost painless; there was scarcely any blood. Then she fainted away: there was a great panic, the captain turned the boat around, but there was nothing to be done: she died before they reached the shore. And ever since I first read her story, I see the image of her in the saloon of the paddle steamer, sinking into her chair of velvet, sighing, fanning herself, passing gently, imperceptibly away—and when I make a trip to Geneva, or to Vevey or Montreux, and I look out to the landing stages on the shoreline, and catch sight of the white steamers on the water, sleek as they are, and streamlined and low-slung, I imagine something very different—I see them as vessels of ill omen, bringers of grief and death.'

She shook her head, as though to dispel the image.

'I hope you never see the world that way: full of symbols; full of unseen meanings. Come with me—let's not be late. It's only a short way now. Back over the bridge we crossed before—then we're almost at the Wandelhalle. She'll already be there, waiting.'

Ady set off. After a second I chased after her.

'Who—who's waiting for us?'

'Elista, of course—I told her to take an outside table.'

'Elista again!'

'Your new friend. You don't find her elegant, and interesting—attractive, even?'

I gave no answer.

'So quiet! Don't be embarrassed. It's only natural. She's a very high-grade kind of ornament. You find figures like her on the periphery of artistic talent—often. Proficient, engaging young women, with a mission to complicate the lives that swirl around them.'

'And is that what she does around you?'

'That's what she's here for, my treasure: to create tension, to tangle things up. She had an affair with Novogrodsky, naturally, when she first met us: she's gravitating towards Daru now.'

'You don't mind?'

'You could say I encourage it. I much prefer dealing with women who've already betrayed me, rather than with ones I expect to.'

'And we're here to spend time with her?'

'Of course not. I brought you here to see the man who's sitting with her. Look—can't you see—there, directly across from her, at the restaurant table in the sunshine, beneath that climbing vine in flower—the man in the pale summer suit and dark glasses, staring down at his hands as he talks. You don't recognise him? He's changed, it's true—but not that much.'

I shrugged.

'You can't see who it is? It's Keleti! Your old friend. You used to like him, anyway.'

'Egon the cartoonist? But you said he'd gone to—to that place.'

'To Klosterneuburg. I did. He did go there: there was an episode—an injury—he knew he had to be looked after: to be admitted. He went of his own accord. And now he's made steps towards a recovery, and he's been discharged.'

'I see,' I said.

'You look sad. It makes you think of another patient there?'

I turned my face away from her.

'But, my treasure,' she said then, 'I think you know in your heart the one you hope to see from Klosterneuburg will never come. Look— Elista's spotted us; she's waving. That was a wave of relief! We'll go over and rescue her. But let's be careful with Keleti when we're talking to him.'

'In what way?'

'Careful not to excite him—not to talk about difficult things.'

'What are they?'

'Things that might upset him—best just to listen to what he has to tell you. You're good at listening. And be gentle with him—people like him are full of self-loathing: they blame themselves.'

'What for?'

'For surviving. The last time I went to see him at the sanatorium we spent a long time together. He showed me the drawings he'd been making for himself. I can't begin to describe them to you. They were wild: without structure. They looked to me like pictures of the world's creation—or its end. At that stage the doctors were still afraid he was a danger to himself.'

I glanced at her.

'Don't ask—you know very well what I mean,' she said, her voice rising: 'And what a ridiculous expression that is—as if life was a thing to steal; how can you take something that's already yours? They medicate him now, quite heavily. It seems to work: that problem's gone. He was always very fond of you: he used to speak about you and ask after you whenever I went to see him. You remember: I told you all about him, and what had happened—that day we came to fetch you from Zuoz. That's why I thought seeing you again might bring him a little happiness. And it might be good for you to see him too. So you can be face to face with him.'

'Of course,' I said: 'I liked him. We used to go on long walks together, explorations, just the two of us; especially that last summer we spent with him.'

'Not for that reason,' said Ady, sternly: 'More so you see with your own eyes what's become of him. What can happen. How vulnerable we all are. How fleeting the life and the wellbeing that's given to us can be. Say no more now.'

She led the way between the tables, gave Elista a quick glance of acknowledgement, placed her hand on Egon's shoulder in greeting, and bent down and kissed him ceremoniously on both cheeks. He gave her a thin smile.

'Palafay,' he said, in a soft voice.

'Stay sitting,' said Ady: 'Don't strain yourself. And look who I've brought to say hello to you!'

Egon peered up at me through his dark-tinted spectacles, and frowned: his hands were clasped tight against his chest, and they were encased in green suede gloves. He unclasped them and stretched one out in my direction, then withdrew it.

'I won't shake hands,' he said: 'I still recognise you, child: you haven't changed that much, in all this time: same look, same searchlight eyes. Do you still remember me the way I was? Do you even recognise me? I've been in the wars—dreadful wars—internal wars.'

'You look wonderful, dear friend,' said Ady: 'Unchanged. Treasure—tell him so.'

'I'm not unchanged,' said Egon: 'Everything's changed in me. I don't know myself anymore. I wonder what my surviving characteristics are—my qualities? I'm a stranger to myself. Perhaps I always was.'

He gave a little laugh; he turned to look at me. 'Sit,' he said: 'Next to me. Look at me. The good thing about being ill's that you're allowed to think this way. What do you see now—in my face; in my eyes?'

'Keleti,' said Ady: 'Please—be calm.'

'I am,' he said: 'I'm happy. Happy that you've come. You didn't answer.'

He lifted up his glasses, and stared at me, and widened his eyes. 'Do I have the look of a composed, creative being? Do I?'

'Yes,' I said to him: 'Of course you do. You always have.'

'I know what I look like,' he answered: 'I draw myself. Lined face, skin like parchment, eyes reflecting nothing. You shouldn't lie—it's a bad habit to get into. Not to order, anyway, not just because you've been told to by Palafay.'

'He's not lying,' said Ady: 'He's being perfectly truthful. Of course you're still open and creative—no one can take that from you—not even you yourself. Stop trying to: you're always working; you're creative every day.'

'Too much so, if anything,' he said: 'The images are constantly flowing in. I try to hold onto them; but everything's provisional with me—nothing stays, nothing's still inside me. It's the same feeling I had before.'

'Don't speak of that now, Keleti,' said Ady: 'Don't. You have to guard yourself. Don't look back—those times are all gone now. Look around instead: and don't put those blind man's dark glasses back over your eyes; see—it's the magic time of year—late summer, when the season's at its most beautiful, and it's saying farewell.'

'You're right,' said Egon, in a resigned way: 'The peaks almost free of snow, the sky deep blue like the sky of an altarpiece—a day so lovely it makes me think all God's angels brought it to us. How thankful I am to you for bringing me here!'

He turned to me. 'I'm staying in a kind of earthly paradise. Your aunt insisted: she thinks I've been confined in hell: but hell was really where I was before, when I was an artist with a reputation in the world.'

'He's in Fragsburg,' said Ady: 'It's high up: the view's magnificent.'

'It's the castle on the hillside,' said Egon: 'In past times it was a hunting lodge—the trophy heads of dead animals are everywhere—they're looking back at you, whichever way you turn.'

'It's calm there,' said Ady, breaking in: 'That's why we chose it for you. So you could be quiet, undisturbed. There's a famous rose garden: it's been cultivated for hundreds of years.'

'You should come to spend a day with me,' said Egon: 'We could sit, and look out like two invalids, and think up new names for all the mountain peaks: names that suit them, names better than the ones they have now.'

'We're making a short visit here,' said Ady: 'There's not time for that.'

Egon paid this no attention. 'I imagine I seem frail to you, my child. I'd like to speak to you alone. May I?'

'Of course,' I said.

'I think I was asking someone else's permission,' said Egon.

'Elista,' said Ady, 'order for us: what we always have. And for the treasure a chocolat liégeois.'

'But that's not what I really want,' I said.

'Perhaps you'd prefer to drink a Kir Royale like the rest of us?' she said in a strained voice: 'Take what comes.'

'Won't you trust me with the child?' said Egon to her: 'Don't be angry with him for saying yes to me. I care for him more than for life itself. Let me spend a few minutes with him.'

Ady looked at me. 'Would you like that?' she asked in a clipped way.

'It'll remind me of when we used to walk in the mountains,' I said: 'And everyone we used to see.'

'Very well,' said Ady, rising from the table. 'As you wish. We'll leave you two together for a short while. You can talk about your special things. Elista—come—we'll take a stroll up to Castel San Zeno and back.'

'Off they go,' said Egon: 'Such lovely creatures!' He followed them with his eyes for a few seconds, then turned to look at me.

'Are you afraid—to be alone in my company? Don't worry. I'm perfectly well; I'm in control of myself. I think clearly. That's a large part of the trouble. I don't deceive myself about the life we lead. And when I look at you and remember times before, it's true—a sadness steals over me. I haven't seen you for so long. I've wanted to. I wanted to explain to you why it was I dropped from sight. And tell you other things: about where I was sent, and what I saw there: who. But now you're here: and I find I can't.' He smiled at this, and stopped speaking.

'You don't need to say,' I said to him. 'I'm sure I know it all: or I can guess.'

'And some things we know by instinct, without knowing: of course that's so. But I wanted to be truthful with you. I made you that promise, once, long ago. I want to tell you—but I don't have the words.'

'Perhaps there aren't words for everything in the world,' I said.

'We'll be quiet, then, a minute—speak in other ways—and think of other things.'

He reached for the satchel at his side—it was the same one he had with him years before. He produced a sketchbook and a charcoal pencil.

'You find drawing helps?' I asked him.

'I make sketches all the time. How could you think I wouldn't? For a long while, after I went away, I hoped you'd come and visit me: and I used to make drawings for you, I made them every day.'

'Of mountain dragons?'

'Yes—naturally. That was what we were drawing when we were together. They took them away in the end. They thought the dragons were signs of unhealthy tendencies.'

'And you don't draw them anymore?'

'No.'

'Why not?'

'I came to an agreement with my doctors: the dragons don't exist.'

'And what do you draw instead?'

He laid the sketchpad between us on the table. With the gloves still on his hands he began outlining: bands of pattern, a central axis, abrupt, sweeping curves; he made a series of dark smudges, he traced out fine cross-hatchings and thick straight lines. The image took shape. I leaned over and craned my neck to see it better. He frowned and turned the sketch towards me.

'There,' he said: 'For you—the way I used to draw for you.'

It was a butterfly—a butterfly in black and white and shades of grey—but with an iridescence imparted somehow to its wings: they seemed to tremble in the light, they gleamed as though the sun were shining on them.

'What's the verdict?' he asked, and added in a final flourish, and laid the pencil down.

'How wonderful,' I said, 'that you still makes sketches like this.'

'You're not just saying that because you were told by Palafay to humour me: to keep me calm?'

'I'm not just saying it.'

He brushed away the charcoal dust from the paper, and looked up. 'You like it—really?'

I nodded my head.

'I'm pleased, then—pleased for you. All true Europeans should be entranced by butterflies. The gardens at Fragsburg are full of them. I've been studying them: closely—blues, nymphalids, Vanessas, swallowtails. I watch them every afternoon. They have no fear. They fly where they please. They fulfil themselves. I try to draw them in a scientific spirit. I want to know them. I'd love to see as they see. Of course I have my favourites—but I haven't reached the stage of Aby Warburg in the Bellevue. Do you know his story? He used to talk to the moths and butterflies around him in the sanatorium grounds; he heard their voices and their whispered conversations outside his window every night. I hear nothing. Nothing at all. I'm not as fortunate as him— to be given beauty from beyond this world. I draw the beauty that's in front of me—here before my eyes. That's what's been vouchsafed to me. My subjects are all living beings—not visions seen by dark of night.'

A waiter from the Wandelhalle appeared just as he finished speaking, and hovered by our table, balancing a tray of drinks on the palm of his hand.

'May I,' he began, then stopped: 'But it's you—it is you, isn't it, Signore Keleti? The artist—E.K.?'

He placed the glasses before us with great formality, and glanced at the drawing on the sketchpad, and smiled.

'It is,' said Egon: 'Or it used to be.'

'How poised the image is,' said the waiter: 'You expect the insect to quiver its wings and fly away.'

Egon looked up at him, an uncertain expression on his face.

'A pleasure to see you here in our valley, with your son, for these last days of summer,' the waiter said then: 'How much joy your paintings and your sketches bring me! I saw the exhibition last year: I made the trip to Venice specially to be there.'

Egon made a slight grimace, and touched my hand with his gloved fingers, and inclined his head.

'Thank you,' he said.

The waiter gave a little bow, and retreated.

'You see?' I said: 'He loved what you do. He said so. You could tell what he saw in your work.'

Egon glanced at me, and, for a second, covered his face with his hands. 'The things other people see in us can't save us,' he said: 'It's not enough. Not even close to being enough.'

'What more could you hope for?' I said: 'It must be every artist's dream to be admired like that.'

He was quiet for a few moments, then looked across at me. 'What now?' he said, in a low voice: 'What will it be? Talk, or draw?'

'Draw first,' I said. 'Like before. Draw Ady—why not? Draw her the way you used to draw Serghiana, all that time ago—not as a dragon, though—you could make her a butterfly.'

'I don't think she'd approve,' he said: 'I'm sure her picture of herself would be quite different. And she'll be back soon, and I don't want to upset her. I still can't believe she came with you all the way from Zürich—just to see me. You know she used to live here—when she was a girl: when she was your age—just growing up.'

'She said.'

'Her father moved his companies here, and his bank: that was long before the war years came. He made himself the magnate of the Tyrol, he owned everything—and when the Germans moved south and took the valley, he didn't run. I've heard it said he traded his life for hers—on the day the round-ups began. And at a stroke her world was changed—changed completely: from everything to nothing. Has she told you that?'

I shook my head.

'Nor me—but it's true. It's a well-known story here: people still remember. She may have a different name now, but at Fragsburg they know exactly who she is. Maybe we should draw her in dark colours instead: for grief, for mourning; draw her as a moth that returns to the scene of a death. Or draw nothing—nothing more. My preference. That's what I think would be for the best. Would you be disappointed? Do you mind very much?'

He clasped his hands together again and held them tight against his chest.

'Of course not,' I said: 'But why do you keep those gloves on all the time—even when you're sketching? You never did before. Don't they get in the way?'

'You don't like them?' said Egon: 'They're the finest doeskin, from the glove maker on Stephansplatz: the same ones they wear at the Spanish Riding School. I've always loved this colour—forest green, the green of the woods in spring. I'm sorry if they don't appeal to you.'

'It's not that,' I said.

'More that they stand out too much—they're startling—shocking: that's what you think?'

'Something along those lines.'

'And that's one reason I wear them. Don't you ever do things like that, for the strength of the gesture—purely for yourself, to prove you have some freedom—some?'

He held his hands up, turned his palms towards him, then away again, and gave the gloves an appreciative glance.

'But there's another reason as well,' he said: 'The true reason. Do you remember what I told you once, that year when Serghiana was looking after you—about my life when I was young? How I came to be here, in the West?'

'I remember it all,' I said.

'After that summer we spent together, everything changed.'

'Why?'

'You know very well: it changed for you, too. It was the end of the Prague Spring. And you became like me in a strange way then—didn't you? Set loose. Lost. Having to make your way on your own. We tried to anchor you—that's why we sent you to that school—the Academy.

I went to inspect it for Ady: I knew then it wouldn't work, I knew you'd be unhappy: you didn't belong there—it was like a seminary—or a collective farm. But for me that year was a time of triumph: in those months, after August, my star rose very high. Everything I drew was snatched up: everyone wanted new work from me. I began to write—stories from my childhood, sketches in the feuilletons, little parables of politics—and it was all published: the world was spread out before me.'

'Because you were against the Russians?'

'Because I was useful at that time to the people who had power—because my drawings were useful to them. Disaster was good for me. Tanks and demonstrations in Prague were good for me. I was like the crown prince in those days.' He gave a marvelling shake of his head.

'I know,' I said. 'I used to always see your drawings in the newspapers—and in America as well, later on. They even taught them in my classes at school.'

'And did you tell them that you knew me?' Egon asked.

'I don't think they would have believed me if I'd said anything.'

'And then one day you heard some vague story of what happened to me—and you didn't understand?'

I nodded.

'I was riding so high then; I was tense from all the triumphs. There were books of my sketches coming out, there were television programs, films, interviews—newspapers and reporters all the time. I began working with galleries, I had dealers, and promoters, I had international agents: there was even an exhibition of my work in Munich, at the Kunstverein. They thought I was some kind of exotic hero—an artist-hero from the East. That's what I'd longed for; to be known as an artist, not just as an émigré who drew nice cartoons—and it had happened, almost overnight. I'd become one—but I'd become something else as well—or I'd been turned into something: a symbol of resistance, a spokesman for a cause. And that wasn't a role that suited me.'

He stopped, and glanced up at me, and gave a low laugh. 'What cards you've drawn,' he said. 'What bad luck you've had! Look at the people who've taken an interest in you and your fate. Serghiana, who lives in her self-created world of troubles; Ady, who's been caught in Novogrodsky's golden cage; me, nothing but a shadow of myself.'

'You're not a shadow,' I said: 'Not to me.'

'A shadow of a shadow. A shadow's dream. But I can tell you things about how to live when you're surrounded by people you don't trust: things worth remembering.'

'Like what?'

'Survey yourself as if you were a stranger. Fight your feelings. Suspect your motives—see everything around you with cold eyes: cold and clear.'

'Is that the way you were leading your life then?'

'No,' he said. 'I'm afraid not: I couldn't ever step aside from myself. I had no capacity for any of that. And that's why things came to a head for me. It all went very fast. It happened in Munich—in July: on a hot high-summer day: the day of my exhibition's private view. Everyone came: it had been turned into an event on the social calendar. The minister-president and his staff and entourage were there; the bohemians, too; Ady made her usual grand entrance, with her husband in tow, and his accompanist; there were writers and film-makers, photographers, television camera crews: I felt I was being lifted up by a wave that kept rising—I was becoming an image myself—an object—and at first that was a pleasant feeling, it was delightful. The politicians spoke—my gallery director from Vienna spoke—Navratil. Then it was time for me. I went up to the podium, and I saw my drawings and my pastels and gouaches—my own work, all around me: the painted bookplates I'd made as a student, my dream sketches, my portraits of the army conscripts I'd seen in Budapest; my village pictures too, my memories of childhood, even the photos I'd taken of the barbed wire on the borders between East and West. Everything I was, everything I'd ever been: it was hanging on those walls. But I felt crushed by all those images—it seemed to me I had no right to be there with them: they were my bid for perfection, they were all that I could hope to make in life: I was overjoyed to see them—and at the same time I thought they were vulgar, they should be taken down at once—they should have lived on as imaginary things, to have made them into artworks was a proof of vanity—a sign of pride: and they were potent, too, at least to my eyes—they were hostile; they dissolved me—they removed the need for me to exist and have a voice. I said nothing: I couldn't speak a single word. I bowed my head, and it must have looked as if that was my gesture of gratitude; everyone in the room before me burst into applause. There was a jazz group: they started up. That was our chance to slip away. I left with Navratil. "Thank God that's over," I said to him. "I felt so on edge." "It's only just beginning," he said to me: "There's a party for you, of course, a celebration—you have to be there—at the hotel." We strolled back together to the Vier Jahreszeiten: and as we went, with Navratil talking and joking and laughing, I had the sense I was no more than a character in a film— acting, playing myself, performing the role of the art maker—that's how it seemed to me: that I was betraying myself with every step I took and word I spoke.

'We reached the hotel; we could see a crush of people milling round the entrance. Inside, in the great reception, it was even worse: there's a cupola of stained glass that hangs over you in that foyer, and it seems always on the point of crashing down: it's gleaming, and threatening, you raise your eyes up to it—it's an emblem of the four seasons, but it has the fire and fury of an atomic cloud. More talking, more speech-making. This time, I had to find some words. An art critic gave an introduction. Our dear Egon, he'd called me: Our Keleti—one of us—the new conscience of the West. "He might as well have called me their mouthpiece," I said in a whisper to Navratil: "Their puppet—as if I belonged to them—as if I ever belonged to anyone!" The men and women round me smiled and clapped their hands again. I felt a nausea. How had I been so vile as to make my art a slave to politics? Navratil was close beside me. He had his hand between my shoulder blades, and he was trying to tell me something; his voice rose and fell—he patted me as if I was a skittish horse. "Go on now," he said then into my ear: "Listen to me—don't be confused, don't pay any attention to that nonsense; that's what speakers at openings say—whatever their audiences want to hear. But they want you now. They admire you; they adore you. Say something—anything. Give them a few words from your heart to go home with; that's what they're waiting for."

'The crowd was getting thicker; they pushed forward: they were smiling, grinning, standing close around me, they were so close I could feel their breath on my skin. I stammered something: it made no sense. There were words in my head, but they were in the wrong language: my thoughts had flown back to my childhood; I saw the faces of the people I cared about when I was a boy: a parade of faces—eastern faces, from far away, passing before me one by one, as if they were telling me their fates. I was so nervous that I was on the verge of laughing. "I feel shame," I said, then—it was a whisper—less than a whisper. I should never make another sketch, I told myself—I should never make another drawing. I should take the stiletto knife I use to keep my pencils and my crayons sharp, and I should drive that knife's blade right through my drawing hand. It was plain—it was obvious—it was my task. I shook my head. There was a burly, broad-faced man standing near me, right in front of me, close enough to reach out and touch. I was looking at him as these ideas went through my head. I saw him mouthing words at me—I knew what he was saying: it was clear: "Don't forget what you are," he was telling me: "What you always will be. A knife, yes, by all means, why don't you—but both hands, be sure, like a crucifixion, if you want to be one of us so much—both hands." Had that happened? Did he say that? I was dazed, I looked round for Navratil, then back, and the man was lost from me in the press and movement of the crowd. "I need air," I said, and turned, and pushed my way through—out into the lobby with its blood-red marble floor. There was Navratil, almost at once, pursuing me, with a reporter and a photographer in tow. "Our conscience," he called to me, as if it was something amusing. I was outside now, on the pavement—it was bright daylight

254

still—you know how the sun goes down so very late there at that time of year. "A quick likeness," said Navratil to the photographer as they overhauled me. He put his hand on my shoulder: "Stay a moment," he said to me, and then: "It's his day of glory. Go on—immortalise him." "Please," I said: "I have to breathe—I have to be on my own—I have to walk my thoughts away." The camera clicked, once, twice, ten times. "My thanks," said the photographer, in that sympathetic, half-guilty way they have. "Alone can be bad company," said Navratil—and he and the photographer exchanged looks and went back in.

'I turned: I made my way along side streets. I passed the Residenz: I reached the English garden: there were couples strolling on the pathways, smiling, holding hands. How calm it was there: how pure and true the colours were. I drew deep breaths, as if I'd been suffocating all through the afternoon. I walked and walked—for hours—or it seemed that way. I saw the little rise that leads up to the Monopteros temple: what a place to make one's destination! A vacant shrine—a shrine to abstraction—to emptiness. All round me was elegance and beauty—a perfect vista—landscape, sweet, soft light: but there was only dark inside me. I leaned against one of the temple columns, and felt its coolness on my cheek, and I stared up at the decorations inside its dome. How even they were in their spacing; how lovely—how meaningless. I know what I saw then, and realised: I saw that meaning lies in nature and her creations, only nature—not in man.

'After the sunset I came back through the twilight to the hotel: the crowd had disappeared. Navratil had booked me into a suite—the King Ludwig suite—can you believe it? There were portraits of him everywhere, those cold, dead eyes of his were looking out. I sat down at the working desk, with the view of the city and its lights before me. I took my stiletto knife: I gripped it tight. I think I closed my eyes then. I drove the blade straight through the palm of my drawing hand. I twisted it at right angles, and pushed harder: I could hear it grating against the bones. For some while there was no pain at all—only clarity, sublime clarity. My fingers moved, they clenched and unclenched by themselves. I felt remote from what was taking place in front of me; I watched the blood come spilling out in a rich, thick flow. I felt pleased that I'd done something I'd wanted to do so much. The other hand, I thought: it still held the stiletto: but how should I complete the task? It was a logic problem. Then the pain arrived. It swept through me like fire—I lost consciousness. When I came round I was in a hospital, strapped to a bed. Everyone who came to visit me was very kind. Palafay looked after my affairs. She brought me to Klosterneuburg. It took two years before feeling started to return to my hand. There's not too much discomfort now: it comes and goes.'

He gave a slight smile. 'Would you like to see the scar?' he asked me then, in a soft voice.

Without waiting for an answer he raised his hand in front of me; in a single fluid movement he clasped the fingertips of the glove, pulled it off and spread his fingers wide.

'See,' he said: 'It has a certain wayward elegance, don't you think?'

There on his palm was a patch of pale, uneven skin, almost symmetrical in form, with serrated edges and neat cut marks in the form of a cross.

*

Morning once again, and in the room that same seething, constantly shifting river sound: it had pursued me in my sleep all through the night. I went downstairs, walked over to the bank, leaned on the iron railing, and watched the foam and water swirling by. After a while I looked round: there was Elista, standing in the same spot as the day before, beside the hotel entrance, her arms crossed in front of her. She came over with languid steps, brushed her fringe away from her eyes and gave me a challenging look. I stared back.

'Well,' she said: 'What now?'

'Hello, Elista,' I said.

'Do you have to call me that?' she said. 'It's not my real name.'

'It's not?'

'Of course not. Madame Ady invented it. Whoever would be mad enough to name their daughter after a city?'

'What city?'

'The capital of Kalmykia: where I came from—that's Elista—it's on a plain north-west of the Caspian Sea.'

'It must be wonderful there—it sounds wonderful—like a citadel of domes and spires.'

'Names aren't everything. It's very drab, and very flat. I hope I never see it again.'

'It's not the place you think of as your true home?'

'Home! I'm an exile ten times over. I'm an exile much more than you and all your kind. I don't have that Central European nostalgia for lost places and times.'

'You don't have any fondness for it?'

'How could I? We left when I was very young—I only went back once, while I was still a student at the institute in Leningrad. I couldn't get out of there fast enough: I saw dark sights.'

'Like what?'

'I had a glimpse of something.' She paused: 'Is there some reason why I should be talking to you about this?'

'Why not—just for the pleasure of the telling.'

'What pleasure is that? Who are you to know anything of mine? You wouldn't understand a single word of what I'm saying anyway—there's zero chance.'

'No danger in saying it, then: keep going. You had a glimpse—what of?'

'Questions, all the time. Questions to ward off questions. It's not other people who have the answers that you need in life.'

'You're not saying because it's a secret—or it's something you don't think I should hear?'

'There are always reasons for saying—and for not saying as well. If you speak about some things too much you destroy them—or make them real. You still want to know—truly? You won't thank me.'

Another stare of challenge. I nodded my head. She allowed herself a slight smile.

'I'll tell you, then—what I saw on my journey to Elista: my return to the promised land: the first morning I was there. I went to see the Lenin statue. My pilgrim act. It's the great monument—there's nothing else. And even there, in the heart of town, you can see the grasslands in the distance stretching away: but I saw further, for a moment— through all the dust and through the haze. I saw much further—do you understand me?—I could see the world beyond this world.'

Her voice had fallen low; she looked me in the eye, and held the look.

'Everyone believes paradise must be beautiful—it must be some kind of lovely garden, full of streams and flowers. But when I was standing there I saw past the edge of things: to what's waiting for us—a dull, flat plain that stretches to the horizon, and further, beyond that line—forever. That's our heaven, and that's our hell. Nothing profound, and nothing complicated. No dictators; no God. Just silence, and emptiness and a grey half-light, on and on. What do you think of that—Mister Interrogator? Nothing to say? No response?'

'I wish I could see something like that,' I said then: 'Just once— once would be enough. Maybe I should make a pilgrimage to Elista.'

'The capital of exiles. I'm sure they could make room for you.'

'But if it's not really your name,' I asked her, 'why does Ady call you that?'

'She has names in code for everyone. Haven't you noticed? Me, Stephane—you too—treasure. That's the way, with her: devices and diversions, schemes to keep the world at bay.'

'And if it's not Elista, what should I call you instead—what's your real name?'

She leaned towards me again, put a hand on my shoulder and whispered something softly in my ear: a sibilant, then a sudden, whir- ring sound, like a gust or flurry in the wind.

'I didn't hear properly,' I said.

'Don't worry—it's almost unpronounceable. I like to keep it as a secret anyway. Maybe if we ever know each other later, I'll whisper it to you again.'

'I'd like that,' I said, in an uncertain voice.

'Would you? What ideas you have! Do you think I'm some kind of friend in the making for you? I'm not that. And you should get away from this little world and Madame Ady—as fast as you can. There's nothing here that's good for you: it's an airless world; it's drowning in memory; these people live through the wounds of the past; they're all damaged—they go forward looking back.'

'So why don't you—get away?'

She gave an ambiguous smile. 'Perhaps I'm misguided like you. Perhaps I believe there's a role for me here—for now.'

'I see,' I said.

'I don't think so—those in the drama can't ever know the plot—or everything would break down. Did you like your reunion with the poor cartoonist? You looked so sad afterwards, when I took him back.'

'Of course: I was happy to see him—and sad it had to end. We used to spend our days together, years ago.'

'In the golden past again. You do realise he's completely deranged?'

'Perhaps he's seen the darkness at the world's edge too. Maybe you should think kindly of him—maybe you should even try to like him.'

'I never said I didn't. Stop now: we should go in. The record-company man's arrived—with all his reports and documents. They've begun their talk already. You missed the start: the game-playing, the finessing, all the opening stratagems and feints.'

'That doesn't sound like anything that matters.'

'You're completely wrong—that's the key to these meetings. The best part. That's what I try to study most of all.'

'Why?'

'To see and understand what Madame Ady does.'

I turned this over.

'You don't look as if you approve of that,' she said.

'Are you doing it so you can imitate her; be more like her—become her, one day?'

'I'm here to be her mirror—complement her. Isn't it plain? She needs an audience. She needs someone dependent on her—otherwise she doesn't feel alive. Let's go—they're out on the terrace again, smiling at each other—smiling and contending, with daggers drawn.'

'Words as daggers?'

'The sharpest kind.'

'Just, in fact, like yesterday.'

'Just like most days in Madame's Ady's world.'

We went back in. It was as she said: Ady and Daru were at the long table on the garden terrace; a man of middle age in a pale summer suit was facing them. All three were laughing and gesturing, there was a flow to their conversation, the mood seemed easy and relaxed. Elista and I slid down onto the bench at the far end of the table, and listened, as if to a play joined in mid-performance.

'You're wrong, dear Frolich,' Ady was saying, in an amused voice: 'Of course Novogrodsky will continue. He'll conduct until his life comes to its end: it is his life. Performance makes him what he is—you know that.'

'But, madame,' said the man across the table, and spread his hands in front of him.

Ady cut him off. 'Frolich,' she said: 'Don't look so disconsolate. Even if we can't agree on anything, you should be grateful to me for bringing you to this paradise: consider it a part of your education.'

'I thought that was over many years ago,' said the man in a joking tone.

'A very American attitude,' said Elista into my ear.

'You like to generalise, don't you?' I whispered back.

Ady looked in our direction—she made a sign of disapproval. 'You two: bitter enemies one day—best friends the next. Stop murmuring like conspirators. Treasure, here. I ordered for you. Your favourite—café au lait.'

'Learning,' said Daru at that point, sighing melodiously: 'We're all in deficit. It's the times. So much revolution, such upheavals, disasters every day—too much news to give oneself the time to study—too much even to feel free to reflect.'

'Or, it seems, record musical masterpieces,' Frolich said: 'Music to outlast us all.'

Ady gave him a steady look. 'How fast you jump!' she said: 'You really mean to change my husband? Transform him: into a sound on a record, not a presence on the concert stage?'

'I didn't come to dispute with you, Madame Novogrodsky—it's not in my thoughts: it's certainly not what I want.'

'I'm pleased to hear it. The truth is you've come to us with a plea—haven't you?'

'An idea—a proposal—a strong proposal. One that should overcome any concerns the Maestro has about his studio work.'

'A proposal that you need to take back to New York agreed and accepted,' said Daru.

'A proposal that you told me would be welcome, Stephane.'

Ady raised an eyebrow at this.

'Welcome, naturally,' said Daru in a hurried way: 'But only if it meets the Maestro's guidelines.'

Frolich gestured towards Ady. 'And naturally it's true that it would help me, madame, if you could give me some sign of your support.'

'You're forgetting something,' Ady said: 'You promised Stephane a document—you left me endless messages about it while we were in Salzburg—and we still don't know what's in it.'

Frolich touched the folder before him. 'It's here. The idea's original: unprecedented. But can I be sure of one thing? That the details stay between us—that no word of this will travel?'

'You can be sure of us. Can we be sure of you?'

'Of course, madame!'

'I have a confession to make to you at this point, dear Frolich,' said Ady then, in her most honeyed voice: 'I have to tell you. An anxiety afflicts me. I've heard stories from your boardroom—stories I find hard to believe.'

'Indeed,' said Frolich, uneasily: 'And what are those stories?'

'Can't you guess?' said Ady: 'The tales you've told them all: how my husband's firmly in your grasp; how you've won us over through poor, pliant Stephane—how safe your deal is: how Novogrodsky will record for you—and soon.'

Frolich started to speak; he hesitated.

Ady reached her hand across the table, and took his for a moment. 'You're embarrassed. You don't need to be. We understand—isn't that so, Stephane? We know there's a place for subterfuges in your world: little truth improvements to boost collective confidence.'

She turned to Daru and gave him a quick glare.

'Of course, madame,' he said.

'And we don't mind, do we? Not too much, anyway: we've come almost to expect it. But it makes us wonder: what can it possibly be that you want my poor husband to do for you? Fly into outer space and record the music of the spheres?'

'No, madame,' said Frolich: 'Not that—but something as remarkable: a complete Mahler cycle. All the symphonies and all the songs!'

Ady burst out laughing. 'That's what all this was for! All the build-up: the suspense. That's why you flew to see us from New York: for Mahler—that poor afflicted man? That victim overwhelmed by his own avalanche of sound? I couldn't have imagined that. You surely realise that Novogrodsky's never conducted Mahler—not a single work?'

'She knew,' said Elista to me at once in her low, confidential voice: 'She knew already—what his offer was!'

'How can you tell?'

'Everything about her: her manner—her tone. When she seems spontaneous she's at her most rehearsed. And hear how sharp she is now? She has her prey—the scene's coming to its crescendo—and its end!'

'Another argument in favour of our project,' Frolich was saying to her: 'And let me reassure you. Promise you, in fact. For the Maestro: anything. Complete control: free choice—among all our artists—anyone he wants to work with, any studio or auditorium. As much time as necessary—no limit. We believe it should be done. A modern Mahler—clear, and cleanly read—for Mahler's sake, and for the Maestro's too. And it seems fitting to tell you all this here, right here.'

'And why is that, Frolich?' asked Ady: 'Because Mahler spent his final summers here?'

'Exactly so—in this valley, nearby. His last pieces were composed in these mountains, close to where we are today, thinking of him, remembering him.'

'And you want me to present this case for you?' said Ady: 'Seriously? To my husband? Isn't it obvious to you why he's never gone to Mahler?'

'We thought it would be a natural pairing. They have a common background, after all—they're almost fellow countrymen.'

'Countrymen from nowhere, you mean: perfect cosmopolitans—figures with no home.'

'There are other things they share—they've conducted the same ensembles—in the same opera houses and concert halls.'

'Novogrodsky won't conduct other conductors,' said Ady, folding her arms: 'And for him that's what Mahler was—that's all Mahler was: a composer of orchestral noises—a composer with a conductor's tricks. When my husband hears a Mahler symphony he's afraid the whole auditorium's going to dissolve in sentiment.' She turned to me. 'Treasure—you know all about Mahler, don't you? The kind of music that one hears in films; you would have gone to see his birthplace—it's not that far away from Prague.'

She gave me a questioning look.

Daru leaned forward. 'Yes,' he said, 'Mahler symphonies—all sentiment, pure sentiment.'

'But popular,' said Frolich: 'Very—especially in Manhattan.'

'And this is an argument?' Ady's voice rose: 'Novogrodsky's turned down other projects of this kind: complete works, months in the studio, complete this, complete that. Surely you know why?'

'It's a mystery to us,' said Frolich: 'What we hear now—that he prefers live performance to the studio: why? It's madness—he's limiting himself.'

Ady assumed her most regal manner. 'Frolich,' she said: 'I'm surprised to hear you think that way. Perhaps I can shed some light.'

She glanced at me again. 'Treasure—listen carefully. Elista—pay attention too.'

'But I always pay attention, madame,' said Elista, sounding nervous.

'When you're not complaining about my faults and weaknesses.'

'Madame!'

'It's normal,' said Ady to her: 'And without significance. We're human—we're all full of flaws and shortcomings. Just remember—I know what you think before you even have the thought. And here we all sit, with the master of a musical conglomerate—a man who's decided how my husband should live his life. Who believes a studio session can be made perfect. Nowadays, it seems, perfection can be captured on a disc of vinyl: it can endure forever, we can be immortal through it—engineer our own Elysium.'

She turned from us; she fixed her eyes on Frolich. 'But for Novogrodsky, it's different, Frolich—very,' she said to him, her voice turning sharp: 'And I think you know that. For him, to record a work's to kill it. For him, music only comes to life between performer and listener: it's made from nothing—made new every time. The orchestra's nothing, the conductor's nothing, his art's a thing of nothing—built from silence—from the dark. There's no blueprint, no ideal version to be preserved forever. And if a conductor believes there is one, if he ever thinks he knows a piece of music, or holds its secrets in his hands, then he's a dictator at the podium—a tyrant, parading his own glory on stage.'

'So extreme, madame,' said Frolich to her: 'I find it hard to believe you mean the words you say.'

'Is my tone ambiguous? I seem so uncertain?' She looked across at Daru. 'Stephane?' she asked.

'You make your meaning very plain, madame.'

'Novogrodsky's meaning. His! He says when he conducts, he feels a current passing through him: it comes from elsewhere—it's made from harmony, from dissonance. It's not from here.'

'Madame,' said Frolich then, 'you know I worked alongside the Maestro once—I booked his concerts, I arranged his tours, I travelled with him: I never heard him say such things. And if he thought them, that didn't stop him recording in the studio—until now, that is—until now.'

'Perhaps his ideas weren't clear to you—or he didn't confide in you. Perhaps you never really understood him.'

'I find that hard to believe as well, madame.'

'Of course you do. And you know better than him, don't you? You know what my husband should be doing. You've decided what he should devote himself to, and where, and how.'

'Madame, I only wish the best for the Maestro—and for you.'

'On the contrary,' said Ady, quite amiably, 'I'm sure you wish the earth would open and swallow me up.'

Frolich spread his hands before him and shook his head. 'We all have to live in the age of recorded music, madame. Even the purest artist must bow before technology.'

'That's it: how well you say it! You want Novogrodsky on his knees. You want him as a trophy—a name for your collection—your back catalogue. But you knew he'd never agree to your proposal—that's why you came to us, through Stephane—with all your inducements and your promises.'

'Madame—this way the Maestro would live on. It would be his legacy.'

'Frolich, we realise you want to make him profitable after his death —we know that very well.'

'He's profitable for us already—of course. This is for him—for you—as much as for us.'

Ady turned back to Daru. 'Stephane—would you advise me to take this message to my husband? Say to him: *Dear one, you're going to die soon, we all know it—so do as Frolich says and he'll make sure that you survive in memory—survive as long as his kingdom lasts.* Should I carry those words back with me? A message from the board of directors—conveyed by Nathan Frolich—your old and trusted friend? Or shall we place a call to him, Stephane? Call him now: right now—call him at the hotel in Salzburg: why not? And tell him what his friend Frolich thinks—that I've changed him since our marriage, that I've manipulated him, that he's a poor, lost creature, under my spell—trapped in my net. That's what you believe, after all—isn't it, Frolich?'

This was said in a calm voice.

Frolich looked back at her: 'If I thought so,' he said eventually, 'it would be an observation, not a judgement.'

'And now the time's come, hasn't it, Frolich?' Ady said to him: 'The time for you to leave us. This amusement's run its course.'

'Please,' he said: 'Another moment.'

'You don't think our talk's at an end?'

'I have something for you.'

'Oh, Frolich—you shouldn't have!'

'Not a gift: a letter. Our formal offer. Don't you want to cast an eye over it—before you make your decision final?'

He reached into the folder before him, extracted a sealed envelope and handed it across the table. Ady stared at it as if it was contaminated. With the tip of one finger she pushed it across to Daru.

'Stephane,' she commanded: 'Take a look. See what it is our guest wishes us to know.'

Daru opened the letter; he glanced at its contents. 'A few polite sentences, madame. Some specifics, the outline of a contract.' He paused.

'Go on,' said Ady: 'What?'

'A sum of money's mentioned,' said Daru then: 'The sum's significant.'

Ady turned to Daru. 'Give it back to him.' She gestured towards Frolich.

'Take your note,' she said: 'Take it elsewhere. Take it to Abbado, or Bernstein—take it to someone who might want to receive it—take it away from here.'

With that, she stood up, and placed her hands on the table for a second. 'And now, goodbye, Frolich. Our thanks for the kindness of your visit. I doubt we'll be seeing each other again.'

She looked in our direction. 'You two—come with me—there's nothing more to keep us here.'

She swept into the hotel. We chased after her.

Daru came hurrying in her wake. 'Madame,' he said: 'What now? Is it really over?'

Ady sighed. 'Talk to him, of course—like yesterday. Come to an understanding with him. You know what we want from them. What we spoke about.'

'Concerts only?'

'Yes, propose it—but stealthily—go step by step. Talk around it—let him think it's his initiative, seem unpersuaded, hesitate. He has to go back with an agreement: you can hear it in his voice—it's in his face as well. Why am I instructing you? You've done this before: many times. You used to be a diplomat.'

'Diplomacy's not always like that, madame.'

'Stance, appearance, seeing into the heart of your adversary—seeing what he only half-suspects himself: what else is there in diplomatic relations? In life?'

'Those are the skills of a mind-reader, madame. You'd have made a good poker player.'

'I play often, as it happens, Stephane,' she said: 'But only with marked cards.'

'Truly?' said Elista.

'How shocked you sound! Of course not—did you believe me? It's just a line I heard once in the movies—years ago. I've longed to use it ever since.'

'It's not a strange time for joking, madame?' said Elista.

'There's nothing more serious than humour: it only has its place when heartache's drawing near. Come—treasure: such a scene—did it reach you? Was it interesting—worth keeping in your thoughts?'

'Did it go the way you expected it to?' I asked her.

'Of course it did. Elista—you stay with Stephane.'

'Madame—where are you going?'

'It's not a secret, exactly,' said Ady: 'But it's something between the two of us.'

She stretched out her hand to me. 'Come,' she said again, in a soft voice: 'Back into Merano with me. It's time.'

She led the way: across the river, past the Kurhaus, into the mazy old town: the streets were quiet.

'How did all that seem to you?' she said, and then, without waiting, answered her own question: 'It was an exercise in bad faith. Could you tell? The purest duplicity.'

I shook my head.

'That man: he'd been to Vienna—before coming here. He went behind my back. He met with Muscatine: he had a contract in his hands: the same one he just waved before us.'

'Mr Frolich? How do you know?'

'Muscatine's not disloyal. He told me the whole story.'

'But you didn't say anything—at the hotel.'

'I didn't—but by the end Frolich realised: he could see I knew.'

We had made a circle along the arcades and streets; we were at the promenade again, close by where Egon had been sitting the day before.

'There's a story I've been saving up,' said Ady then: 'You already know that, don't you? And you know I've waited until now.'

She smiled at me. Suddenly her face seemed full of sadness. 'It's what I saw here; what happened here—and that's why we made the journey here from Zürich: that's the only reason—but now I find it hard to tell you—I don't even know how to begin.'

'You could tell it as if you were talking to a stranger,' I said:

'Or like a story you heard somewhere—from someone else—not something that involves you—at all.'

'Wait,' she said then, and paused, and looked round.

We were by the entrance to a palm-tree garden above the river-bank; there were steep pathways; the slope plunged down beneath us: the noise from the rapids surged and fell.

'Somewhere you remember?' I asked her.

'The very first day we spent in Merano I found this place,' she said: 'The river was higher then, it flowed faster, it was even louder, it had a hundred different notes in it: I could hear whole symphonies inside its sound. I used to come here with my governess—after lessons, every day—we walked all through the gardens, and on, further upstream, as far up as San Zeno. And every autumn when we went home to the city I drew pictures of this garden, and dreamed of coming back—then, one year, we came for the summer, my father and I, and never left.'

'And he thought you'd be safe here?'

'We were safe—for a long time. Behind our mountains, far away from everything. I lived in books—in stories: that was how I hid away. Our apartment was close to here, on the Sandplatz: it had a roof terrace. I spent hours by myself there, whole afternoons on end—reading—daydreaming.'

'Reading what?'

'Oh—the kinds of books young girls in those days were told to read: romantic books, wistful books: Stifter, Hoffmann, books you'd never hear of now. And we went to concerts at the Kurhaus, too, my father and I. When we were first here it was all still the Viennese—Mozart, Schubert, Haydn—but once the war came that changed—everything was Italian then: the pianists played sonatas by Scarlatti; the quartets were always Boccherini: one night the orchestra played a Respighi tone poem: I thought that was the last word in elegance. But if we stayed at home the nights were quite different: no music. I'd sit with my father in his study and we'd listen to the radio broadcasts: there were days when we could pick up foreign stations very clearly; we heard their reports and bulletins—there was a map of Europe open on the table, and we'd follow where all the different armies were, advancing, retreating: it was like an evening drama that went on forever: we never spoke about it in the day.'

'But everything was quiet here, in the valley—there wasn't any fighting?'

'Not until the end came near. Merano was a hospital town: for a long time we saw the planes flying far above, and the patrols high up, near the frontier passes—that was all.'

'And you never went up into the mountains—you never went exploring there?'

'Once. With one of my tutors: her name was Pavlikova—she came from the Tatras, from Késmárk: I liked her very much. She took me with her on a trip to the guesthouse in the hills above Sankt Martin: there was a steep path—nearly to the snow line. We were looking for chamois—and we saw them, we came close to them: a whole family, standing still: we watched them through binoculars—then there was some sound—a detonation in the distance—from a quarry, or maybe from manoeuvres, far off—I watched them springing away, all together, without a sound, as if they were soaring through the air. "I wish I could run away like that, almost flying," I said. Miss Pavlikova glanced down: "Poor Mademoiselle Adela," she said to me: "Don't you see—how the mountains keep you and your kind in? There's no way out for you here in this valley: you're in a cage." That was the first time anyone had said something like that to me. I remembered it.'

'But your father never thought of escaping; trying to get away?'

'Escape to where? Get away to where? We were in safety—we'd already escaped: that's what he thought. For him, it would have been unthinkable to run from Europe. He felt safe here, he was sure all would be well under the Italians—and for years he was right. But you know how this story ends, don't you? It ends here—by the riverbank: by this cold torrent.'

We had retraced our steps as she was speaking; we had crossed the bridge with gilt and silver railings. Ady sank down on a stone bench; she made a sign to me to sit with her.

'We could go back to our table from yesterday,' I said: 'It's just there, in the sunshine.'

'No—stay with me—beneath the climbing vine in flower—it's always flowering here. It was a day like this when things changed for us: it was also in September. We had no warning: the Germans came. There was a fleet of transport trucks with soldiers in them—aircraft for the officers. That's where they set up their headquarters—right there, in that building, across the river, see—that one, the Palace Hotel. There were guards at the gate, and flags flying—they even draped their banners over the Kurhaus facade. They took back the Tyrol—this whole valley—it happened overnight. Everything beautiful can be destroyed.'

She hesitated for a second.

'Or it wouldn't be beautiful?' I said.

'Indeed not. They marched in—and our paradise became our hell.'

She looked over to me. 'Prompt me,' she said, in a whisper: 'Please—I can't go on.'

I did as she asked: once; twice. She thanked me: her voice grew stronger.

'The next day, there was a proclamation, and a rally in the old town; they gave their orders; we saw their soldiers searching everywhere. My father held a meeting in his office for the directors and the managers—even the ones from Chiusa and Bolzano, from furthest away. They began early; it was evening before they were done. Then they all came back to our apartment. We ate together. They were guarded in front of me—but I understood. I asked my father that night: "What will happen to us?"'

'Aunt Ady—do I have to hear the rest of this story?'

'You do. You wouldn't be the child of my heart if you didn't. After they'd all gone I stayed up with my father—we talked into the small hours. You know how close I was to him; he'd always sheltered me.

That night he told me everything. We were sitting in his study, in the half-light, surrounded by his treasures: his Egyptian figurines, his vases from Crimea, his statuettes of Scythian gold. "And now I have to say goodbye to all these things," he said to me: "I have to leave them behind—this one, and this, and this; I chose them and collected them: I loved them all—but they mean nothing to me beside you: and I have to say goodbye to you too. We'll say our farewells now, here, just the two of us—and when tomorrow comes, show no emotion. Master yourself. Always hide your feelings from the world. Never weaken. Never show your grief or pain to anyone." I sobbed and cried in front of him. I cried my heart out. That was the last time. Never since. He saw far into the future. He told me what to do—how to live in the years ahead. Go out into the world: stake your claim: survive. Never forget; never drop your guard. "How quiet it is tonight," I whispered to him. "It's the way things always are in times like these," he said: "Still everywhere, still and quiet. The servants are all gone; I sent them away. They won't be coming back." I fell asleep beside him, there in the study: I slept until the morning light. When I woke he was leaning back against his work desk, watching me. He was dressed as if for a country outing: a suit of linen, a shirt and cravat. "Did I dream it all?" I asked him. "No," he said: "Our dreams are all cancelled—gone. Memories—those you can still have—it's harder to steal them away." We talked more: about his childhood; about what I remembered from when I was a young girl and we still lived in our house high up on Castle Hill—we went on talking as long as we could.'

'About what?'

'Little things—foolish things. I remember every word; I'm grateful for every word. Then the time came: we walked out together—from the apartment to this bench, beside the riverbank—it's not far. I wanted that walk to last forever. "Does it have to be like this?" I asked him. "Everything's arranged," he said to me: "As much as it can be—of course, though, one can never think of everything. How beautiful the mountains and the slopes and orchards look today. It's the time of year I love most—late summer, with the faintest hint of autumn in the air. Go back to the apartment. You'll find Pavlikova waiting at the entrance. She'll take you; she knows her way in the mountains; she knows what to do." He touched my hand. "Don't be afraid," he said. "I'll watch over you." Two officers in black uniform were standing in the little park beside the Palace, talking to each other casually, laughing. Then one of them looked at his watch, and made a sign. They began walking towards the bridge. "My child," my father said, "these men are here for me. Remember everything I've told you. Now walk away from me—walk away from me as if you don't know who I am—walk fast and don't look back.'"

*

Years went by—a decade, more. I studied, I chose a path in life: I made my way. I had fallen out of touch with Ady; I was becoming what she had wanted me to be: I was an observer in the worlds of others; I recorded their impressions and masked my own. We were in the last days of 1989: the turmoil of that autumn in Eastern Europe was near its end. I was staying at a hotel in Zürich, waiting for a new photographer to join me. He was coming in by plane: his flight was late. I set aside my work and walked down to the lake shore, and watched the last cruise boats gliding in. Sunset; a clouded sky; winter chill. How long it had been since I was last there! An age ago: in childhood. Why not use the empty hours? Why not retrace my steps—walk along the Mythenquai, walk down its winding paths, walk and feel the wind from the lake blowing? There was the lido, where it was always too cold to swim; there was the villa, high up, where Wagner used to live; and here, close by, the old museum with cactus plants and desert flowers: through its windows I could see the palms and the tree ferns, the orchids and the mosses too, and long rows of hanging bromeliads, just as they were the last time I set eyes on them, their spines and gaunt leaves lifted up like sentinels. All remembered—all familiar—as if the past was still present there for me: as if it was claiming me and calling me. It seemed near enough to step into in those moments—and that would be an end: an end to everything. How unmoored I must be, I told myself, how lost on time's ocean—pulled here and there by the faintest recollections—by vestiges—by sights and sounds. Night had fallen: it was hard to keep one's bearings. Time to double back: back to the old town, to its narrow streets and spires and cobblestones. Christmas lights in the shop windows; laughter, voices mingling in the air. I passed a hotel—Ady's old favourite: there was a crowd in the lobby; piano music, a party, a jazz tune playing. And beyond—beyond was silence, calm: the river, the bridge by the town hall, the little balcony where I used to feed the swans—and two swans came gliding by on cue, and tilted their necks enquiringly. I pressed ahead: walking for the sake of movement now, walking to be without thoughts. Onwards—down a flight of steps, along the covered passageway above the riverbank: a colonnade of shopfronts: I was halfway: I stopped. A jolt went through me. But why—why there? I was outside a recessed window. It was nondescript, a square of glass like all the others: it was half in shadow—then I recognised it: it had fallen from my memory, but I knew it: I knew it well. It had been the temple of my childhood summers—a haven for me. It was an artist's studio—a workshop: its window held displays of little figurines—and they were still there—maquettes of dancers: dancers seated, dancers stretching, dancers mid-pirouette. What tales I used to picture in that shadow world! I gazed down. I was shielding my eyes and peering through the light reflected in the glass when I heard footsteps just behind me.

'Hello,' said a lush, accented voice—a voice I knew: 'My treasure.'

I turned. It was Ady—it could only be her. She was smiling her soft smile: there was a familiar expression on her face—her special look that teetered between self-admiration and self-mockery. She was wearing a long fur coat and a cap of black astrakhan. At her neck was a knotted silk scarf. Two elongated dogs with pale beige coats stood by her side, panting, the cold turning their exhalations into brief plumes of misty spray.

'Aunt Ady—how wonderful to see you—how wonderful you look!'

'You charmer—even now you know the way into my heart. You learned the lessons that I taught you—you learned them well.'

She stretched out a gloved hand towards me, as though to touch my cheek—then paused in mid-gesture, and slowly, with a slight smile, pulled her hand away.

'Do you still think of me sometimes, my treasure?' she asked.

'Very often.'

'And do you remember that last summer that we spent in the mountains—when we made our journey to Meran?'

'Vividly.'

'I'm glad. That's what I hoped for. It must have been a hard year for you—a sad summer, with the news we had—from that place whose name you don't like to hear.'

'No—that was later.'

'Truly? So many departures: so hard to keep track. Where do we all go, I wonder—where am I bound for? We're always in flight in life, aren't we—hurtling onwards—on through space and time.'

She looked stricken. I felt I should jump in.

'How strange to find you here,' I said: 'Out walking, on such a cold night. Are you visiting someone in Zürich?'

'My treasure, didn't you hear—don't you know? I gave up the house in Vienna: it felt too empty after Novogrodsky died. It's being turned into a museum, of course—like the whole city, really.'

'But I thought you loved being there! You told me so.'

'My poor treasure—the places you love the most are the ones you leave.'

'And where do you live now?'

'Here, of course. In the Storchen—where we used to stay. I have a suite on the top floor. It looks out over the river: it's a perfect view. Besides, the hotel reminds me of Paracelsus—he stayed there, four centuries ago—and I think the world of him.'

'You do?'

'Yes—he was the first person to recommend the waters at St. Moritz. And the Storchen's convenient, too—for the salukis—my darlings.'

She glanced down at the dogs, and gave their leads a little shake. 'We go for walks around the lake shore, as far as the Rietberg, sometimes further—just after sunset, every day. Do you remember them? Did you ever meet them? Bartók and Haydn?'

At this mention of their names, the dogs lifted up their thin muzzles, looked at Ady and gave, in unison, brief, half-stifled howls.

'How thin they are,' I said: 'Tall and thin—you can almost see through them.'

'Yes, that's true,' said Ady: 'We're all transparent, though, aren't we, one way or another, after a while.' She laughed—a soft laugh, with a slight distortion inside the sound.

'And I see you're covering your bases,' I said: 'Politically, I mean: culturally.'

'What on earth are you talking about?'

'One dog named after an Austrian composer, one after a Hungarian.'

'My treasure—what can you be thinking! There's nothing more Hungarian than Haydn's music. He's not Austrian—not in any real sense. You know very well he composed his best work at Eszterháza! If you listen to him closely you can tell—Magyar themes; Magyar rhythms everywhere. Isn't it plain to you? Hungary's the fount of all music: it always has been. I already knew that when I was a little girl in Czernowitz.'

I looked down at the dogs: they stared back with unblinking eyes. 'They don't seem very friendly,' I said.

'Of course they are—they're being friendly. If they didn't like you, they'd already have jumped up and ripped out your heart.'

'That's reassuring to know,' I said.

'Come and visit me—you must: I've so much to tell you. Come one day—come tomorrow.'

'I can't, Aunt Ady,' I said: 'I'm meeting a colleague of mine: we're leaving in the morning—we're going to drive all the way to the frontier post at Arad, and then to Bucharest. If we can, that is—Timişoara and Bucharest.'

She frowned on hearing this.

'You don't approve?'

'On the contrary—I've always had a soft spot for Romanians— such conspiratorial people.'

The dogs shifted; their leash chains gave a chinking sound.

'They're impatient,' said Ady: 'Time to go. With companions like these two you have to keep moving.'

'I'll walk you back to the Storchen,' I said.

'No, no,' said Ady: 'Our walk's only just beginning—we go deep into the night. Don't worry—they look after me. Au revoir, my treasure—au revoir.'

And she turned and waved goodbye, and was quickly lost from view in the dark of the passageway.

VI

Clemgia

COULD THIS REALLY be my destination? I gazed up at the facade: spires, ornamental arches, balconies and French windows, turrets, colonnades—more like a museum of eccentric architecture than a grand hotel. I found the entrance: wooden doors, palatial, heavy: I pushed my way in. Murk; half-dark. A reception, cavernous: the usual furnishings: armchairs, tables, desks, tall vases full of flowers. Ahead a grand staircase: gilt scrollwork, decorated handrails—but no movement. Nothing. I cast about: down one corridor, then another. At last I made out a sign at the far end of the lobby. 'Bureau,' it announced, in art-nouveau lettering. There, in the shadows, was a counter, and behind it stood a young man in uniform. He was watching me, a sceptical look on his face. I went up to him.

'What a place!' I said: 'Like the landscape of a dream.'

He stared at me for a few moments, his face unmoving. 'A guest,' he said at last: 'A late arrival. Unusual. The name?'

I told him.

'No booking,' he said, rather haughtily.

'I wonder if I'm at the right hotel?'

'That depends,' said the receptionist, and his voice took on a softer tone: 'There are many hotels in this valley—for different purposes: some for cures and some for culture; some for solitude and some for company; some for sadness, some for joy—'

'But this is the Waldhaus, isn't it?' I interrupted.

'It is,' he answered: 'I can confirm that.'

'So I'm where I should be,' I said then: 'I'm meeting someone—a guest who's already here.'

'Unlikely—it's the start of the season—we have hardly any visitors. Only a single group, in fact. And the name of the person who expects you?'

At this riposte I hesitated. 'I'm not entirely sure what name you'd have it under.'

'Try,' said the receptionist, now in a cajoling, coaxing tone of voice: 'Don't give in to doubt. Stand firm. Give me the name you have.'

'Semyonova?'

'No!' he replied, sounding almost triumphant. 'Another name, perhaps?'

'I know she's here,' I said: 'She sent me a telegram. A Russian woman: from the Caucasus: a commanding kind of person—always takes a suite, or several. Tends to travel with a retinue. Sometimes involved in producing films. Serghiana Ismailovna Semyonova.'

'But you mean Madame Serghiana,' he answered, and his manner changed. 'That's all you had to say to me! The rooms were reserved by her studio. We've been waiting for you—you're the missing guest!'

'Wasn't that quite obvious?'

'I thought it might be you. I couldn't know for sure: you don't look like someone from the movie business.'

'At last I've found a hotel that's harder to get into than Kafka's castle!'

'It's been the choice of many well-known writers down the years.'

A porter had appeared; he took my case.

'Please,' said the receptionist: 'Go with my colleague—go—hurry—they've been waiting for you—for hours now, in fact—in the reception suite, in the rotunda: you'll find them there.'

I went up. The door was open: music, laughter, voices speaking in several languages: a throng of faces, smoky air. I stood at the threshold and took in the spectacle: a full salon, a blazing chandelier, high windows open to the night, men and women clustered in tight knots, smiling, gesticulating, darting here and there. In one corner, a buffet table piled with food and drinks: waiters with long-suffering expressions on their faces poised behind it. I plunged into the crowd: I navigated through, and searched for Serghiana. There: I could see her—standing at the open doorway to another reception room where more guests were gathered. I made a sign—she gave me a distanced wave, then turned back to the tall woman at her side and said something that made them both incline their heads. How strange the mood around me seemed: at once elated and serious. Then I caught sight of someone else I recognised: Professor Leo, in the ill-fitting jacket he always wore. Beside him was a figure with a lined, pensive face: familiar too, in the way half-famous actors are—and here was a much younger man with dark brown hair and a full beard, bearing down on me.

'Hey, kiddo,' this man said, and gave me a tentative half-hug: 'All grown up now! Great to see you!'

It was Corey Lipsett, both his look and his manner changed. He seemed taller; there was an air of greater substance about him.

'Corey, is it really you?' I said: 'I didn't realise you still worked for Great-Aunt Serghiana.'

'I don't—otherwise I'm sure I'd have been pistol-whipped until I agreed to fetch you from the airport. No: I work for that woman now, over there. He pointed to the tall woman standing next to Serghiana.

'Recognise her? You don't? You should. That's M.L.—Mary Lou Exner—she runs Central Pictures. I'm an EP with them now.'

I looked at him.

'Executive producer. And sometimes I even help those two liaise.'

'I heard Great-Aunt Serghiana had stepped away from that world.'

'You heard wrong. Although it looked that way at first, it's true: and we both thought it was curtains for her, didn't we, after that showdown, the last time we were together: but she's still got her interests—she's still a player. Always will be—it's in her nature. Ask him—I'm sure he knows the inside story.'

And he pointed to Professor Leo, who was making his way over to us.

'Young friend,' he said to me in an enthusiastic way: 'How tall you've grown: taller than me, though that's not saying anything: I heard you were going to join us—what news from your world?'

'It's spring break.'

'What's that?'

'A pagan festival,' said Lipsett.

'You told me you'd call and visit me in Zürich when you came this way,' Professor Leo said to me: 'You promised. You never do. Even so—what an experience: what drama we've been treated to! We're all in shock, I think: it's the first time any of us have seen those pictures—the impact's still sinking in.'

'Explain to him,' said Lipsett: 'He's only just arrived, he missed the screening, he always misses everything.'

'The evening's great event!' said Professor Leo, gesturing in expansive fashion: 'What we're all here for: it was pure horror: something to stop the heart: a documentary—from the States—the first on the fall of Saigon—the end of South Vietnam; the coming of the communists: tanks in the streets. That sent a shiver down my spine. But you'd have seen it all already, wouldn't you, at your school there?'

'Not really, no. I've been studying—my exams are coming up. Important ones. I'm not a natural scholar the way you are.'

'No, no, of course not,' said Professor Leo, proudly: 'But you must have seen some of it, surely—those haunting images that we just watched: the storming of the presidential palace, the lines of people begging to be evacuated, the helicopters on the aircraft carrier flight deck being pitched into the sea. I still can't quite believe what we were seeing. At last it's come—the end. The end of the war that seemed to go on forever. Another colonial domino tumbling down.'

'I'm not that torn up about it,' said Lipsett.

'Naturally not—you wouldn't have wanted to be sent there yourself and have to flee.'

'Actually I tend to think of you, professor,' said Lipsett, 'as the great expert on fleeing communist invaders.'

I looked at Lipsett, and then at Professor Leo: he seemed uneasy; he paused before answering.

'Yes,' he said. 'Worrying times, for those of us who chose to change camps. Exciting for you, though, Mr Lipsett—and for all the film people around us here, isn't that right?'

'Why do you say that?'

'Because it's the perfect movie. Fire in the East. The Indochina war—complete at last: the first war that was ever fought on television—for television, in fact: a war of appearances and images, a war decided by them: no? You could almost say a war designed for newsreel clips and propaganda films: staged with them in mind.'

'You really think that?' said Lipsett.

'I do.'

Lipsett glanced round. 'Well, then,' he said, 'I think I'll have to give M.L. a quick run-through of that idea.'

'What idea's that, Corey?' said Serghiana, who had come weaving through the room in our direction.

'Nothing, Madame Semyonova,' he began, but she had turned away from him.

'My child! How long since I've laid eyes on you! A year, more than a year. And you've arrived so late: did they tell you at the reception that we were waiting for you: the way I always wait for you? Were they helpful?'

'It was a five-star welcome.'

'I want to thank you for coming so far to see me,' she said then, and reached out towards me, and let the gesture die halfway.

'And I want to thank you for inviting me, Great-Aunt Serghiana,' I replied.

'So formal, so correct. You're here with me now. No need for blandness: for your American persona. Don't be circumspect and closed up like that. Go back to being what you are—and tell us: first impressions. What strikes you, now you're back here: how do I seem to you—after such long absence?'

'As magnificent as always.'

Serghiana stared at me for a second, and frowned. 'I suppose that's the right thing to say to some women—when you've been flown halfway round the world to see them. Not me, though: I don't want the well-trained surface—I want the core of you. And what were you three talking about, whispering away in your little splittist group? Why are you looking so anxious, Corey—and what's that guilty expression on your face—Leo—dear Lyova? Go on, tell me. What's the secret? I know there's something—I saw you watching me when I was with M.L. over on the far side of the room.'

'We were talking about the war, of course,' said Professor Leo: 'About the drama of the last few weeks. After what we just saw, everyone is.'

'And?'

'And saying how cinematic it's all become.'

'Borrowing my lines again, Lyova. Anyone would think I was the professor and you some novice without a thought or idea to call your own. I was just joking with M.L. and saying that she should have optioned General Giáp.'

'She will,' said Lipsett, laughing: 'You can count on it: she options everyone.'

'But it's not the right comparison, really, is it?' said Serghiana then: 'Not if you think the question through. The war was nothing like a well-made film. It might lend itself to another kind of artform, though. Some of the footage looks almost like the backdrop to a piece of modern dance: those plumes of fire exploding in the rice paddies and along the winding rivers—they could be from Merce Cunningham videos.'

'I'm sure they will be, in time,' said Lipsett.

'The truth is, Vietnam was always something else, wasn't it,' Serghiana went on, ignoring him: 'Something more classical. It was war as opera: it was Wagner—the purest of Wagnerian subjects: a perfect Twilight of the Gods!'

'Your favourite theme,' said a voice from behind her.

A tall man in a dark suit had joined us. Two women followed him: soon there was a new audience listening to Serghiana.

'Not at all,' she said: 'It's my nightmare. When empires begin to weaken, the costs rise high.'

'But that hasn't proved true of your country, has it, Serghiana Ismailovna?' said the tall man: 'Rather the opposite—revolution and the collapse of empire brought strength to the East: made the Soviet Union a superpower.'

Serghiana turned her eyes on him. 'My country?' she echoed.

'Forgive me—what a thoughtless thing to say. Let me cover myself in apologies—and try to be more diplomatic. We'll say instead a country that you used to think of as a homeland; one you still see more clearly than any of us.'

Lipsett and I had moved away from the centre of the room. 'Who's that man talking,' I whispered to him: 'I'm sure I've seen him somewhere before.'

'Unlikely,' said Lipsett: 'Unless you've got a thing for high technology. His company makes guidance systems. He's Austrian: very rich; he likes the arts, he's produced films, he's on boards, he sponsors festivals—he knows Semyonova—and M.L.'s got some project going with him.'

'But what's his name?'

'Amborn—Urs Amborn.'

'I have seen him before, then. In different company, a long time ago. He's very good at apologies—and when he says hello he bows and clicks his heels.'

'You jetsetter! That sounds like him. Quiet now.'

'So you believe we're at a turning point,' Amborn was saying: 'We've reached the end of the West's golden years?'

'Were they really so golden?' said Serghiana: 'Was that what we were living through—a golden age? And now the masters in the Kremlin have the upper hand, you think we're doomed to go through dark and fearful times? But that's not the way things are in our world. Nothing's so clear-cut, is it? It's never rise and fall in perfect balance. Empires are always growing and always faltering and changing into their successors, there's no noon and no midnight for them, their condition's always in between.'

'It wasn't clear-cut enough for you, Saigon collapsing—it wasn't absolute defeat?'

'Of course it was,' said Serghiana. 'For now: Moscow will take everything. They'll turn Vietnam into their client. All Indochina's lost. That's plain already. But it won't be that way forever.'

'A consoling thought,' said Amborn, and he gave a little laugh: 'But if I look from the western point of view, I see this as a reverse, a setback, and that's all: the end of a futile war we had to watch and live with for too long—much too long. It's a chapter's end, something we could all see coming long ago. We became impatient for it, we even wanted it.'

'And now what?' said Serghiana: 'You celebrate it—celebrate a disaster: because you made it your cause—defeat's your victory. Look around you—look at all of us—we're treating this as though it was some far-off contest staged for our amusement: nothing crucial, nothing that affects us: a game played on our television screens. Failure presents no problem. And that's the West in a single sentence, isn't it? Your modern civilisation: your permissive paradise. It goes from disaster to disaster—it survives by accident. The truth is, we're watching the last convulsions of our dark century. You see that, don't you? The years flow by: the era limps towards its close.'

'I understand you, Serghiana Ismailovna,' Amborn said: 'But I have to disagree with you.'

'A brave man,' murmured Lipsett.

'Indeed?' said Serghiana, and she looked at Amborn.

'I must. In fact I think the exact opposite. I think the West's at its strongest when it seems weakest. We can afford to be weak. We can afford to sell our enemies the rope they want to hang us with: that's what we always do. And still we prevail. Nothing does us any lasting damage: the only adversary we'd ever have to fear is one that steals our own beliefs—that imitates us so perfectly it becomes us in its turn.'

'And that enemy will appear at its appointed hour,' said Serghiana: 'You can count on it. I should have known you'd think this way. The paradoxes of a capitalist! I should have expected complexity and ambiguity from you: that's what Western Europe's become—the homeland of subtleties. And you're something like its crown prince,

Amborn—aren't you: the lord of contradictions: Wagnerian in your tastes—Wagnerian in your acts.'

'A compliment and a reproach at once.'

'And both intended—in the kindest sense.'

'But can you really think you stand apart from us?' said Amborn then, in a calm, poised way: 'Do you forget? You made a decision to join us. You chose to be part of us. You're much more a westerner than those of us who were born western. Once your world was Leningrad and Moscow: today—California and the valleys of the Engadine.'

'The choice I made is always with me,' said Serghiana: 'Can you doubt it? I have the taste of exile in my mouth. Every day and every night.'

'I think you were wise to choose as you did,' said Amborn: 'And brave, too, and principled. It was our great gain when you changed sides and left that world behind.'

Serghiana fell quiet and stared back at him. By now everyone in the room was listening to this exchange.

'Is that what you think?' she said, and she held up one hand and snapped her fingers: 'That it happened—just like that? A simple change of sides? It's not so easily done. Those of us who went from East to West can't go back. We're stranded here—but we haven't found a home. Nothing like it. We live in limbo; we're like flotsam—defined by a single act—defined forever.'

'But we don't think of you that way,' said Amborn: 'Not at all. We think of you as a friend—our dear friend. As if we'd always known you and been close to you.'

'Truthfully? Even though I don't see the world the way you see it—one side light and one side dark.'

'You don't believe you went from darkness into light,' said Amborn: 'From controlled to free? Why go over, then? Why? Why did you break with them?'

'It was a gesture,' she said: 'The moment needed it. It was asked of me: life demanded it: I gave it—but I already knew then what I know

now. East, West—at the deepest level there's no difference. They reflect each other, they summon up each other, they give each other life. It's the old interplay of opposites. You know that light's nothing without darkness; you know goodness needs its shadow.'

'And you think those are the forces that rule over us?'

'I do. I see them very clearly—as energies—distant, set high above us, far beyond our knowledge or capacity to frame and understand them—shifting, changing constantly, expressing themselves through us and our lives—and we, poor creatures, we have no awareness of them: we trace out our paths through time and experience, we make up our tales of love and hate—we play out our parts on a great chessboard where we can't even see the moves.'

'So sombre, Serghiana Ismailovna,' said Amborn: 'So bleak.'

'So abstract,' said Lipsett in a whisper into my ear.

'Another of these verbal jousts between her and Amborn,' said Professor Leo in a low voice: 'They never end well. Come with me, young friend—we should talk.'

'Should we?' I said to him: 'Why? What about? We never have before.'

'It's quieter over there, in the alcove.'

I followed him across the salon. We stood at a bay window, and looked out across the dark valley.

'Now,' he said, and looked at me in an earnest way: 'Tell me everything.'

'Why are you trying to be so friendly?'

'I'm concerned, of course,' he said: 'Madame Serghiana's concerned as well. That's why she brought you here: so you two could have a proper talk. She used to say you'd do well at all your schools, you'd be self-sufficient, she was sure of you—you'd live up to her expectations. But she gets reports. She worries. What's the way ahead for you now? She doesn't know. She doesn't even know if you have any idea yourself.'

I stood still beside him and stared out. 'She can ask me, then,' I said.

'It might be easier if you tell me: then I can explain your ideas to her beforehand. Prepare her. Give her a sense of how things stand with you: how you see the world.'

'I don't need a go-between,' I said. 'I'm not afraid of her.'

'Maybe you should be, at least a little. You think she's your flesh and blood? She's not. She supports you out of the goodness of her heart. Maybe you should have a story ready for her. Show her you have a goal to aim at. A program, a timetable, even. Have it all clear inside your head. What interests you. What fulfils you. Where you mean to live once you've reached adulthood.'

'Should I already know the answers to all those questions?'

'Of course you should. Can't you say where you feel most at home in the world? Don't you have a sense of where you belong?'

'What a thing to ask him!' said a voice from just behind us: 'No one worth knowing would be able to give you a straightforward answer to that.'

I turned. There, standing near me, was the man with the pensive face who had been at Professor Leo's side when I first came in. He looked me in the eye.

'Take what I'm saying to heart,' he said then: 'Be open to the whole world, not just one small corner of it. Don't chain yourself down. The free spirit, the individual without ties or shackles, the man who belongs everywhere and nowhere—that's the ideal for our time—that's what you should strive to be.'

'Is this talk we're having somehow your business?' said Professor Leo to him: 'Did Madame Serghiana ask you to interrupt us?'

'I'm sure she'd be intrigued to know what you were just saying about her,' said the stranger.

He smiled at Professor Leo, and the smile had an edge to it. He turned to me. 'I know Daru,' he said. 'He told me I'd see you here. And he sends his greetings.'

'Are you a diplomat?' I asked him.

'The opposite,' he said, and laughed.

'If you're wondering where you've seen his face,' said Professor Leo, 'that's because he's famous, in a secondary kind of way. You'd have watched his reports. You'd know his name: he's Delaunay.'

'The war correspondent Delaunay,' said the stranger firmly: 'But that time's gone. I write screenplays now—for your great-aunt. The one leads quite well into the other.'

'Some might say there's very little difference,' said Professor Leo.

'How come you know Stephane?' I asked him.

'You don't believe me? You want documentary proof? We grew up alongside each other, in Saigon: we were like brothers. We went to the same lycée. We played together every afternoon in the embassy grounds. We used to ride our bicycles down Rue Catinat, and explore all through the parks, and play hide-and-seek in the folds of the banyan trees.'

'A colonial idyll,' said Professor Leo.

'Didn't you ever have a childhood?' said Delaunay to him: 'Were you always old and grey and critical?'

'And you stayed there and became a correspondent?' I asked.

'No,' he said, his voice emphatic: 'No—I didn't stay. That's the whole point. That's why I'm telling you this. I was expelled from my paradise: I had to find my way back.'

'What happened?'

'I was sent off to France: to Paris—to university. It wasn't a home-coming for me. It was more like exile; unfamiliar faces, strange sights and sounds, a city that meant nothing to me. I was lost there. I missed the light I used to see when I was in the tropics—I missed the colours of the plants, the monsoon rain, the birdsong, the hum of insects—everything I used to love: I was suffocating, I couldn't thrive there. But in the end I found a way to be less lost. I had one gift no one could take from me: I was a child of Saigon. I spoke the language of an unhappy country. I knew that I could tell the world its stories. I went back.'

'Back to danger—and to fame on the frontline. An uplifting tale.'

It was Serghiana. She had found our secluded corner. She was watching us, a severe expression on her face.

'Why, then, am I so ill at ease?' she said: 'Why do I feel as though this is an indoctrination session?'

'What do you mean, Madame Semyonova—' began Delaunay.

'I know exactly what you're doing,' she said, and cut him off. 'What seed you're planting so tenderly: the dream of drifting freedom. I didn't school this child for him to end up as a correspondent working in the Third World; to throw away his life by living through the lives of others. I had a different aim in mind: for him to spend his days surrounded by art and beauty, not death and blood. Or would you like him to be just like you? Was your time reporting in the jungles so fulfilling?'

'It was a kind of heaven, actually,' said Delaunay.

'And that's why you abandoned it to come and work with us? Enough!'

Lipsett had come over, and the tall woman was with him.

'What's the drama now, princess,' she said to Serghiana: 'It's supposed to be a happy evening, remember? Peacetime; harmony.'

'Absolutely, M.L.,' said Serghiana: 'The collapse of all values, the carnival of emptiness.'

'But we've got something to celebrate, don't we? Tonight—tomorrow night as well. Corey, have you told them?'

'I was just getting round to it, Miss Exner,' said Lipsett.

'You're hopeless: what else was so important? Everyone here I haven't invited yet: come to us tomorrow—at sunset. My chalet, in St. Moritz; it's not far.'

'And what's the occasion?' asked Delaunay.

'You haven't heard? We've found what we were looking for: the ideal location—all thanks to our hostess tonight!'

She gave Serghiana a fervent hug. Serghiana extricated herself, looking both pleased and annoyed.

'It was nothing,' she said: 'Nothing at all.'

'Yes, it was,' said the American woman in an insistent voice. 'It was your suggestion—an inspired one.'

She turned to Delaunay: 'You'll laugh. We're making a vampire picture—but political—set in our day.'

'Heavy metaphor,' he replied.

'We were thinking we'd already found the perfect lead—but I've begun to hesitate—it occurred to me my favourite Polish émigré could both star and direct.'

'Where are you going to set it?' asked Delaunay: 'In this hotel?'

'Not bad—in fact, a good idea also,' said the woman, and she looked back to Serghiana: 'Your new screenplay writer? Maybe we should take him. Just kidding: I wouldn't do that to you—or if I did I wouldn't say before doing it. But we've already found the ideal haunted castle—you must have seen it: it's in this valley. That's why we're overnighting here. We went round it for the first time yesterday: Serghiana took us through and showed it to us: from the cellars to the eaves. And we'll go back tomorrow, won't we? It's a real find.'

'You mean Castle Tarasp?' asked Amborn, who was listening to this exchange: 'You do know the interiors aren't original—or even true to period: they're more like a fantasy of what a mediaeval castle ought to be.'

'Fantasy's my business—that only adds to the appeal.'

'And you know who owns the castle today?'

'Some German princely house,' said Serghiana.

'Spoken with real disdain,' said Amborn.

'I am the child of a revolutionary,' she answered: 'That's something I never let myself forget.'

They talked on; the evening drew to its end. I followed Lipsett out. Serghiana intercepted me.

'We'll resume tomorrow,' she said: 'Won't we? The way we always used to—at the hotel's breakfast table. Try for once not to be late.'

*

Morning came. I went downstairs and looked round for Serghiana and her entourage: no sign. I sank down into one of the lobby armchairs and waited. Minutes passed; a long half-hour. At last I felt someone standing over me. It was Lipsett.

'Do you do this on purpose?' he asked. 'Do you practise to be so good at it? You're late; they're all out on the garden terrace, waiting for you—again.'

I followed him. There was Serghiana, at the last table, two well-dressed men sitting to one side of her, the tall American woman on the other, while Professor Leo stood nearby, hovering, coffee cup in hand.

'You do this to vex me, don't you?' she said.

I started to explain.

She raised a hand to interrupt me. 'It's youth. Young people today. Everyone—forgive him. Come: sit with us. Sit facing me.'

'Like at an interview,' I said.

She paid this no attention. 'It's a good time for us to talk. The only time in the day, really: the mind's fresh, the heart's restored by sleep and dreams.'

She poured a cup of coffee from a silver beaker and handed it across to me.

'I don't really drink coffee very often,' I said.

'Impossible! Did you hear that, M.L.? Can you believe it? Coffee-drinking's a mark of character: of good cultural formation. Drink!'

I raised the cup to my lips.

'Pleasant to be staying here again?' she asked me: 'In the loveliest palace in all the Alps. Do you remember it well?'

'How could I?' I said: 'I've never been here before.'

'Of course you have: don't start suppressing your memories—rewriting history—that way madness lies.'

'I think that's more a Soviet specialty,' I said.

She gave me a measuring glance. 'So quick,' she said. 'And sharp. But you have stayed here—with me; when you were a little boy.'

'And we used to go on long walks together, on the forest paths—and you'd tell me all about your favourite books, the ones you used to read in your childhood.'

'You do remember!'

'No—but I can fill in the scene you like to paint.'

'I see,' she said: 'Or at least I begin to see: see what you're becoming.'

'What's that?'

'A young man of independent mind. And are you well rested, at least?'

'Well enough.'

'And your head's still full of that sweet French music from last night?'

I looked back at her.

'Delaunay's, I mean, of course,' she said: 'That siren song of his: the joys of the corresponding life?'

'I understood why he was telling me his story—and what he was trying to explain.'

Delaunay was standing off to one side of the table, beside Lipsett, and as I said this he gave a faint sardonic smile.

Serghiana shook her head in a grave way and made a quick gesture to the figures sitting at her side. 'You know everyone here, don't you?' she said to me: 'You met them all last night, didn't you? No? Not even these two here? My special helpers. They travel with me—location hunting. One's a designer—one's an architect.'

'Would I know the buildings?' I asked. 'Are they famous?'

The man beside Serghiana raised his eyes heavenwards.

'He's not that kind of architect,' she said: 'He's contemporary. He deals with flows of matter: movement through space. Structures, and how they interact with time. We've been scouting round: we were at the new dam on the border yesterday. It was a good trip. I think we found what we needed. That's what matters, isn't it, M.L.?'

'Absolutely,' came the answer.

Serghiana fixed her eyes on me once again. 'So,' she said: 'Lyova tells me you want to talk to me.'

I gave Professor Leo an even stare. He glanced away.

'Don't hold it against him,' she said: 'That's what he's here for—to filter people—to tell me what they want.'

She clapped her hands together. 'Everyone,' she called out: 'My nephew's deciding his future.'

'Am I?' I said: 'Does it have to be right now, this minute? With these two I've never met before sitting in like silent judges.'

'He's right,' said Serghiana: 'You two both—head off. It's not a trial—not exactly. We'll change the tribunal. Amborn—come, sit with me.'

She turned, and made a sign to Delaunay. 'You too, scriptwriter—the voice of freedom. Come over. Join us—listen in.'

She gave me a prompting look. 'Well,' she said: 'You were going over your ideas last night with Lyova—you were frank with him. You might want to tell me all about them too. Don't be embarrassed. You've been hanging back ever since you got here. In fact, you've been quiet and withdrawn for a long time now. I write you letters, full of questions: nothing comes back: you change schools—no effect. Have you even thought about what lies ahead for you? M.L.—help me: any advice for him?'

'You could ask him if he wants to go on to college.'

'It's what people seem to do in America,' I said.

'In Europe also,' said Serghiana sternly: 'With good reason. Will you even pass your examinations? Do I have to pull strings to make sure? Do you know what you're going to study?'

'Literature,' I answered: 'American, perhaps.'

Her manner changed. 'Seriously? You can't mean it. By your age any civilised person should be at home in literature. You don't need some professor telling you what to think about books. They're your birthright: the possession of all mankind. Choose a field that adds to what you know; to what you are. We'll talk about this later—just the two of us.'

This was said in a firm voice, with a quick glance around the table: everyone was watching.

'Why not now?' I said.

She looked back at me, surprise in her eyes. 'What?'

'Why not now—here?'

There was a pause—then she gave a quick clap of her hands and laughed. 'Your face—how determined you look. You want to resist me. Defy me. Really? Here? In front of everyone—people who are complete strangers to you.'

'Why should I care about them and what they think about anything?' I said: 'Who are they to me?'

Professor Leo had been edging nearer: he came up beside me. 'Young friend,' he said, and placed his hand on my shoulder: 'There's no need for this.'

'Let him go on,' said Serghiana, and she folded her arms and leaned back a little in her chair: 'Let him. I'd like to hear what he really thinks.'

'I know what you think,' I said: 'You think I should be grateful to you: give thanks to you, every single day: bow down here in front of everyone—be grateful for all of it—everything you've done for me.'

'But what I did was nothing, really, you mean.'

'That's not what I said!'

'I'll tell you what I did for you,' she went on: 'I looked after you, I cared for you and shaped you—I poured myself into you, I gave you more attention and regard than anyone would give a child. Without me, what would have become of you? What? You'd have knowledge, but not understanding; you'd see the surface and not the depths; and all the books we used to read together, those golden books you loved so much—yes, you might have come across them by now, it's possible, that's true, and even looked into them, maybe—but they wouldn't speak to you and live inside you. The writers we spent our days with— they'd be names to you, empty names, and nothing more. But they're not: you know them, and all their stories—they'll always be with you. And that's because I gave you the keys to them—I opened up your mind: I forced you to become what you are.'

She stopped, caught her breath and looked straight at me again, and there was a pleading quality in that look. I looked back.

'You know,' I said, 'I've always wondered what it is that drives you on. What makes you so unyielding—so harsh.'

'Have you, my child,' said Serghiana: her voice was low: 'Have you indeed? You've no idea?'

And then, without warning, she broke into a smile. 'You poor creature! You think I'm angry because of what you've just dared to say to me? I'm not. I'm overjoyed. I'm proud. It's the beginnings of a personality: you're stronger than all these hypocrites and hangers-on. I can see it in you now. You'd be quite prepared to break with me and go off into the wilderness. I thought the day would never come. I thought you were much too weak to stand up to me. Too mild and gentle—soft as milk. I thought we still had far to go. And I was wrong. We're almost on an equal footing now.'

She stood up; she looked around the table. Several strangers had come over and were listening: waiters too.

'Ladies—gentlemen,' she said then: 'I hope you enjoyed the scene. A little early-morning drama—spontaneous—the purest kind. But it's over now.' Her attention shifted to me. 'Gulp your coffee down, my child. I'll deal with things here—make my calls—and then we'll go.'

'Go where?' said Lipsett: 'I thought you were going to look through my screenplay notes. You promised you would.'

'Not today.'

'And there was something else as well: you said you'd keep the morning free for Miss Exner.'

'Cancelled too,' said Serghiana, in a triumphant voice.

And she gathered up the folders on the table before her, turned on her heel and strode back into the hotel. The group on the terrace dispersed. I walked over to the belvedere and looked out across the valley. Lipsett came up and stood beside me.

'Kiddo.'

'Corey.'

'That was something else, wasn't it?'

'Aren't you used to her by now?'

'No,' he said: 'I couldn't bear the constant sparring. It wore me down.'

'But you still talk to her, don't you?'

'All the time.'

'So you must know what she's working on: why she's here: why she made me come all this way?'

'Who could tell? Nostalgia, perhaps—she's got a sentimental streak. There's a script she's working on. We all know that. But it's still some kind of secret—from everyone.'

'Even you?'

'Especially me. It's something dramatic: historical. I know it's big-budget—that's what she's doing these days—and she's certainly not about to confide in EPs from other studios.'

'She wouldn't even tell the woman you're working for? They seem to always be together. As if they're collaborating—as if they're almost friends.'

'More like rivals. Each wants to know what the other's doing. They're spying on each other as much as actually helping each other.'

'So you really are well placed.'

'Between two fire-breathing dragons. And don't you dare repeat what I just said.'

'But you've landed on your feet—haven't you?'

'The only people you ever see along the way in life are the ones who land on their feet. You forget the others—they just fade from view.'

'Is that what you were afraid of? Is that why you stopped working for Great-Aunt Serghiana—after Sils Maria?'

'After the stand-off, you mean? What a movie that would have made! But you're wrong—I'm not a quitter—I didn't leave her then. I stayed. Right through: it was a strange time. You know she even kept up her Russian projects for a while: that's why she wanted me with her.'

'And did you ever finish that film you were just beginning when I was there?'

He laughed at this. 'The biopic—the Nietzsche? You've really got your finger on the pulse, haven't you? Are you still at that place in New Hampshire?'

'It didn't work out.'

'Why not?'

'Hard to say. It wasn't a good fit: they didn't seem to want outsiders there.'

'I'll tell you this for free—you're an outsider among outsiders if you don't go to the movies. The Nietzsche picture came out two years ago. It saved Semyonova. It won best foreign-language film. It made her what she is on the West Coast these days: she's on top of the pile.'

'Truthfully? I heard a different story.'

'Who from?'

'Maybe I shouldn't say.'

'Go on—who?'

'It was last year—things must have changed. I was staying with the Novogrodskys.'

'And that film went through as well. They fought like wildcats, but it was finished in the end—somehow. I was still with Semyonova for it. I did all the negotiations with her. Novogrodsky needed the publicity—for his orchestra—otherwise it never would have happened. I won't forget it—it was insane. Wild travelling in Eastern Europe—to places without streetlights or hotels. And then Vienna, for an age—and we had to film in Bratislava—and in Kiev. There was a young assistant working for Novogrodsky: she was something else.'

'You mean Elista?'

'I sure do: what a fox! I never met anyone quite that cool before. Didn't you think so? I'm still on the trail. I write to her. She likes philosophy.'

'Does she write back?'

'Look,' said Lipsett: 'Here's your amigo.'

Professor Leo had come up to us.

'I'll leave you two together to catch up—better go chase after M.L.'

'Professor?'

'Young man—I want to apologise to you—on behalf of Madame Serghiana.'

'What for?'

'She was harsh with you.'

'I'm used to it.'

'It was unkind.'

'I've heard her be harsh with you, too, professor.'

'That's her way. And she's on edge here—terribly on edge.'

'Because of what she's working on?'

'That never presents any problem. No—it's memory. The past. That's what she's here for. And I'm sure that's why she wanted you to come—to spend these days here—so you could bring some lightness to her.'

'I don't think I'm following you at all,' I said then.

'She's always sad when she comes back here: to Vulpera and Tarasp—it's this whole valley—all the Engadine, in fact.'

'Because of bad associations?'

'Good ones. She came here with her first husband, years ago. You've surely heard her speak about him?'

'Hardly ever.'

'But you know he was a man of science?'

'A geologist.'

'Exactly so—and prominent, and gifted. Well connected, too. He had the backing of high-ups. And he had his ideas—his ideas and special theories.'

'What kind of ideas?' I asked.

'Unusual ideas,' replied Professor Leo, and a new expression—part anxiety and part excitement—came across his face. 'Very unusual—I don't imagine they did him any good in the end.'

'Did you know him? Did you ever meet him?'

'No, no—this was in the days before eastern scientists could do much travelling. I know the outline of the story—but once he fell from grace, his name went underground. He was a Siberian. He had a true northern childhood: he grew up beyond the Urals. And he had a northern death as well. He vanished into Dalstroi.'

'Into what?'

'You've never heard of Dalstroi?' Professor Leo smiled, and shook his head: 'Once those two syllables were enough to strike fear into every heart. It's an abbreviation: Soviet-style. Far Northern Construction Trust. Dalstroi built the mines and labour camps—out in the arctic wastes: in the Kolyma—in the ranges beyond Magadan. Madame Serghiana never told you any of this? Nothing—no? Semyonov worked on its projects: he built dams for them, and power stations. That's why he was sent here—when the war was over—to study installations in the West. She travelled with him—it was a kind of honeymoon for them. They went to the Valais, to the high dam at Dixence: they saw it when it was still being built. They came here too—to the Graubünden. It was a golden time for her: she must be one of the only people in the world who finds dams and power stations romantic. That's the real reason why she comes here: she won't tell you, she keeps it as a secret, I've never heard her breathe a word about it—to any of these westerners—but it's true. Every summer, she goes back to the sites she saw with Semyonov all that time ago. Last year I took her to Sion and Dixence; only yesterday we all drove out to the reservoir at Punt dal Gall. She hides her feelings. Still, it's hard for her to be in those places. Time passing only seems to make it worse. I've said more than I should have. Please—don't let her know.'

'What kind of ideas, professor?'

'Semyonov's? He led prospecting expeditions in the taiga. For uranium. For gold. They were the first surveys: deep into Chukotka and the Verkhoyansk. But he was a dreamer: somehow he convinced himself he'd found rocks that came from asteroids: from space. It was a scandal in Soviet science. Enough! Say nothing now—here's Madame Serghiana coming over. She wouldn't want us talking about him.'

'Why not?'

'It's like a profanation for her to hear his name spoken by others—a sacrilege.'

Serghiana reached us. She leaned against the terrace railing next to me, and stared out. 'Such splendour,' she said: 'So inhuman. So heedless of us.'

She turned, and gave Professor Leo an inquisitorial look. 'Talking about me again, Lyova? That's not good.'

'But you're such an interesting subject,' he said.

'Is that the best you can come up with as an answer? You were much quicker when you were still living in the eastern paradise, and you used to follow me round in Prague and make reports on me. Your excuses were better then—your cover stories too. In fact I think I preferred you in those days.'

She gazed up at the sun and breathed in dramatically.

'Light,' she said: 'Pure, blazing light. I could walk all day with this pale sun shining down. Ready?' She glanced at me.

'I'm still in recovery from yesterday,' said Professor Leo.

'I wasn't inviting you, Lyova,' she said: 'Come, my child—just you and me. We'll take the path down through the forest. Our secret shortcut from before. Quickly. Let's make our escape.'

Rock steps, deep shade, sharp turns—the sound of the river far below us: Serghiana led the way. She made a gesture to me at one point to take her hand: I held back.

'No?' she said, and shrugged: then nothing.

I followed. Minutes passed. The path divided. She paused.

'Another of these silent excursions of yours,' I said to her: 'It's so exasperating when you do this. I don't know why you wanted me to come with you. I don't know why you wanted me here at all.'

'Is that so?' said Serghiana, quietly: 'It's such a mystery? Then let me tell you. It's because I need you to be here. Did you want to hear me say it? That I need you to come with me. That it's I who need you now—not the other way around. I think you already understand that. I think you know it very well.'

'But it's not the way it was,' I said to her, and she looked back at me. 'It's not?'

'How could it be? You sent me off to boarding school on another continent. It was like being banished. We're practically strangers now.'

'Strangers?'

'Yes, strangers. We hardly see each other anymore—and when we do, it's in some crumbling old hotel from the last century, and there's always a drama going on, always turmoil, never silence, never a moment's peace, never the slightest chance to talk. And it's like that on purpose: you want it to be that way. It's how you run your life: full of schemes and projects, endless people waiting to see you, queueing for a snatch of time with you: you at centre stage, and all your extras hanging round. We're not close, the way we were when I was spending every afternoon with you, when you took me with you travelling, from country to country, place to place, just the two of us together, for days, for weeks on end. It's nothing like that now: and I'm not what I used to be.'

'That's the full charge sheet?'

'Yes—for now.'

'Of course we're still close,' she said then: 'You don't know what closeness is. It's a bond, not a feeling. You just don't see it. You don't see yourself. You think like me, you speak like me, you even use my favourite words the way I use them, your eyes see like mine—you're made up from fragments, just the way I am—you're from nowhere—and you belong nowhere: you have nothing.'

'Concisely put,' I said.

'Nothing except for me—and what I give you—and I'm giving you everything I am. Now, come—we go down this way. Hear that—the ringing, clashing sound—rock on rock, stone on stone, water pulverising everything? Do you remember where we are now? We were all here together once, a long time ago. No? Being here on this path doesn't bring it back to you?'

'Not really.'

'It does to me. I can see the day. Clear morning: Indian summer—we were walking into town, we'd left the hotel terrace, we came this way then too: you were a little boy—with all the sweetness of a child. You asked me about the river: what happens to everything that's washed away. That question—it brought me a sudden stab of sadness. You could tell. You asked me why. You turned to your poor mother and you asked her. You said: "Why is Aunt Serghiana always so quiet and sad, and so alone?"—that's what you used to call me in those days, remember: both of you. And your mother said—"Because she knows what the world's like." "Doesn't everyone know that?" you asked her. "Very few people do," said your mother, in a serious voice: "But that's not the only reason," she went on. "Aunt Serghiana came here, once, years ago, with her husband, whom she lost—and being here reminds her of him." "I wish we could make her happy again," you said—and I found that very touching. I walked on ahead. The time I had here before came back to me in those moments: I saw myself and him.'

'Will you ever tell me about that time?' I said: 'Properly? You start to, but then you stop at once; you keep it as a mystery.'

We had come out at the riverbank. Pale blue water, foaming, flowing fast. She stopped. We stood side by side.

'The same river that washes things away,' she said: 'Your river.'

'I heard the first time you came here it was some official kind of journey you'd been sent on,' I said.

She laughed. 'Is that a question? No, it's not. I knew old Loewy would tell you something. I asked him not to—and I knew he would, and knew he'd try to swear you to secrecy—but you're not much of a secret-keeper, are you?'

'It's hard to keep things from you—don't tell him I said anything.'

'My child—I don't mind. How could I? It's not a secret for me—not at all. It's always in my thoughts—it's the memory of a time that's dear to me. And Lyova's right—he knows something of the story—from the outside at least. It was a scientific mission they sent us on—or that's what we thought, in our blindness, then. And I'd like to tell you about it all: those days; what led up to them. Why not? Before you're swept away from me—swept into life.'

She began: she spoke in a clipped way, as if describing someone else, someone remote from her: as if reciting facts from a dossier: the childhood she spent in the mountains, her wartime years, her father's fate, the memories she had of him; her first studies, what she'd hoped for, what her life turned into; then, and only then, at last—she smiled slightly—Semyonov: her first meeting with him.

She paused, and gave me an assessing look.

'Why wouldn't you ever tell me about those days when I was younger?' I asked her.

'Shall I say it didn't seem important for you to know these things then? Or that I knew everyone else would tell you their own versions of my life? All of them—Keleti, Daru, Palafay. But none of them saw me truly: they had no picture of the way I'd lived, what I'd seen before I joined their little world; and none of them knew Semyonov. I wish I could describe him to you: describe our time together here. Would you like that?'

'That would be wonderful,' I said.

'It would be wonderful, if we could bring back the ones we've lost: give them life again in words. But when I try, I find I'm describing scenes I barely remember: moments that escape me; events I don't understand: accidents, coincidences, patterns repeating.'

She broke off. She shook her head.

'Where did I get to,' she said then: 'What was I telling you last?'

'Science—geology—your first time at some institute: you didn't sound as if you liked it very much.'

'Of course: the institute. Of course: Moscow. I'll go on.'

'You don't have to.'

'Of course I do.'

Her husband's project; his team: their tasks. How she and he had travelled in the Alps all through one summer on their own: the sites they went to, everything they saw: high mountain barrages, the first ones being built, vast construction camps—ornate, ordered, beautiful.

'How majestic they were for him,' she said: 'He always meant to come back here—to see them finished: their high walls of curved concrete—their sheets of water underneath the sky. That's why I come to see them. That's why I make my visits every year: for him. Not because I like the country, or the old hotels—it's the knife of memory for me.'

'He never thought of staying: you never thought of it?'

She turned to face me; she looked shocked.

'Not going back? You mean defecting? Is that what you're asking me? Him? But he had his projects, his responsibilities, that was what he lived for—to build—to make the East. The bridges and the barrages you'd see if you went there today—all the dams that bear his imprint, on the Angara River; on the Amur and the Yenisei: he already knew the sites: every blueprint was drawn and perfected in his head.'

'And was he able to build them? Any of them?'

'Let's walk on,' she said. 'Climb a little—free the mind from its shackles—let it roam. We stayed here, in Vulpera, in the hotel where we're all staying now. It was a palace, to our poor eyes then, at least, our Soviet eyes—something unbelievable—it was grander to us than the Tauride or Peterhof—lovelier than the Hermitage. In those days, there were very few tourists left so late in the season, when we arrived. We had the forest paths and high valleys to ourselves. The hotel was just as it is today: the same wood-panelled walls, the frescoes everywhere in Jugendstil—and there was music in the salon, once darkness fell: they had a house pianist who played Chopin from memory—there was even a visiting string quartet. After the years we'd lived through of war and hunger, coming here was like being shown a glimpse of heaven. Every evening, Semyonov would write his reports at a desk in the reading room; and I'd sit near him, and make sketches in my notebook, and look out into the night—or we'd go walking on the terrace high above the river and stare up to the stars. He knew them all: he'd been a navigator in the war. I knew nothing, I thought at last my true life was beginning, it was a magic time—every day I spent with him was a day of discoveries.'

'Scientific ones?'

'Those, of course, up among the peaks and glaciers—above the tree line, where the rocks were open.'

'Open?'

'Where they were exposed, and bare—so they could be read. They were like books for him—books written in the stone.'

'And you went up there with him?'

'Naturally. Haven't you been listening to me? We were always together.'

'And that's why it was so difficult for you! I see it now—why you were so on edge, that day when we went up in the funicular—when we were alone on the summit—up on the rocks at Cassons Grat.'

'When was that, in fact?' she said, in a casual tone of voice: 'Was it the same summer that we read the *Princesse de Clèves* together?'

'The year after. The year of the Prague Spring—don't you remember? You must. You have to: it was the day that changed everything. For me. For both of us. It was that same day in August—the day the tanks went in.'

'My child, don't be so agitated. There's no need. All that was such a long time ago—an age ago—half your lifetime ago—and so much has happened since. What seemed important then seems like a little detail in the past's slipstream now.'

I stared at her. 'When you heard the news that day you said it was a great disaster, not a minor detail—I remember. I heard you, I was there.'

'Pit your memory against mine, by all means,' said Serghiana: 'But be precise. Don't make things up. I remember that day—much better than you: I said it was a tragedy, and entirely predictable. I understood at once that morning the way that things were going to be. It's the insignificance of what happened then that's the real horror.'

'But—'

She raised a hand in warning: she turned to face me: she cut me off. 'All these interruptions,' she said: 'You make it very plain: it's obvious what I'm telling you means nothing to you, it's a joke—it's without interest for you. We don't have to go on. It doesn't matter anyway—no one knows this story properly; there's no need for you to hear any more of it. Maybe one day I'll find someone else I want to tell it to.'

Her face was tense; she looked at me with bitter eyes. 'We'll go back now. Back to the pleasure palace: to the movie people; they'll dilute you. It'll make this easier to bear.'

'Please,' I said, and stopped.

'Yes? What? And think before you speak!'

'I'm not trying to fight with you, Great-Aunt Serghiana.'

'But you are,' she said, in a wondering way: 'Don't you see that? That's exactly what you're doing—it's all you've been doing since you got here: fighting me; defying me, betraying me. I told myself on the hotel terrace it was nothing, you were testing me—testing yourself, but now I look at you: I look into your eyes and I see they're dark, dark as night. You've closed yourself against me. As if you're doing everything that's in your power to devastate me—as if you have to do that to break free.'

'You know that's not true,' I said: 'That's not what I'm trying to do. Not at all. And I know everything that you've done for me: I'm full of gratitude.'

'Gratitude! I don't want your gratitude: gratitude's a weak, pulpy thing...'

'But what is it that you do want from me? Why am I here?'

At this, she smiled: it was a smile of pain. 'You ask me that? You? Isn't it clear to you? Hasn't it always been clear?'

As she spoke, she stretched out her hand towards me as if across a dreadful void. The expression on her face changed: it softened. 'It's not a thing to say aloud. There aren't the words for it. It should be understood between us. I want you to live truly—live well—be nearer to the truth and light than me. That's all: all I've ever wanted from you—for you.'

She looked at me, and said nothing more. The forest all around us suddenly seemed still. No rushing sound from the river far below; no wind in the air. I heard the noise of my own breathing. I could see Serghiana staring into my eyes, waiting for me to speak.

'Forgive me,' I whispered to her, and I mouthed the words a second time: 'Please.'

'Of course,' she said then: 'Of course—it's done. I'd forgive you anything the moment that you asked me to: everything! You already know that too. Whatever it is you do to me, I forgive you: you could stab me with a blade and I'd forgive it. Forgive at once.'

And she snapped her fingers in her most dramatic manner. 'Just like that. All the sadness, all regrets—let the wind blow them away.'

'But it was wrong of me,' I said: 'On the terrace, earlier. I shouldn't have spoken to you that way in front of everyone—I should have agreed with you: you were right. I am like you—and you did shape me. You made me what I am. I carry you with me in my mind—wherever I go. And what you remember me saying on this path—I still think that: I still want you to be happy again.'

She turned. 'My child,' she said: 'I know all that already. Such a declaration! You look as though you're about to dissolve in tears. You mustn't. Be strong. Ride emotion, don't give in to it. Of course we're close, of course we aren't at war with each other. There's nothing wrong between us—there never could be anything that's wrong.'

She beckoned. 'Come. And take my hand this time. What a duel we've just been having. We'll go together now, we'll walk up here—we'll look out across the valley and laugh at all the trials life brings. The joys of adulthood. What awaits you.'

I was about to say more.

She put a finger to her lips. 'No,' she said: 'Not a word. Don't speak. Let me.'

And she resumed her story. This time, though, she was vivid and immediate, her words came flowing out; I could see the scene unfolding as she spoke: see her and Semyonov climbing up the gorge track, he leading, she close behind. Bright sunshine. Pure silence. No birds calling; no sound of man. They paused at the midpoint of their climb. Serghiana looked around. There was a rock face reaching high above them. At that moment a trembling spread through it. A noise came from the heights—it echoed round them—it gained strength: like thunder, far off—but there was no cloud in the sky. Semyonov looked up. She held his hand, and whispered to him. Danger, she was saying, danger—then it was upon them. A boulder crashed down from the cliff above them, rebounded on the rock wall, struck the path before their feet and shattered: another fell, and then another: the whole rock face shook—it made a grinding, cracking sound: more stones came down—behind them; in front of them. Then all was still again. Semyonov looked at her: he held her close. You see, he said to her: we're safe—nature means us no harm. But she had felt the world's weight raining down on her in those moments—she was shaking, her heart was pounding, she was full of fear. She knew what had happened. It was an omen: a sign. It was the future made plain. She said nothing to him. She smiled. They even laughed. They climbed on. Their time in the mountains was almost at an end. The next day they set off on their journey back.

Serghiana fell quiet.

'A sign of what?' I asked.

'A sign that heaven's empty. A proof: that there's nothing you can do in this world to save yourself. Everything's arbitrary—the end's always the same. All we can do is sit and wait. I had no fear left in me after that: the rockfall showed me everything, it used up all my fear of life. I understood then. All must go. Youth, beauty, love—all this around us—everything. The world's strength is aimed at one goal—to unmake us, step by cunning step, to rain down blows upon us—to destroy.'

'Go on,' I said: 'Go on with the story.'

But at that moment a sound came floating up from far beneath us, from beside the riverbank—a voice: calling, shouting Serghiana's name. It drew nearer—it was Lipsett, hurrying, panting up the footpath.

'Why must this fool pursue me so constantly?' she said.

'He thinks he's close to you,' I whispered back.

'The sublime needs the ridiculous: that's how it is—he's saved us from the past—for now.'

He came up; he overhauled us; he stood there, breathing heavily. 'Miss Exner sent me,' he said: 'In pursuit. She insisted that I find you and bring you back. I told her I wouldn't fail—and here I am. She's still waiting for you.'

'Indeed—and why's that, Corey?'

'Don't you remember? You said last night you'd take her back to Tarasp castle; you said you'd go through with her again.'

'Did I?'

'You did: I was there.'

'She takes everything so literally: just like you, Corey—the American disease.'

'And then you could go on with her to the party, she said—talk on the drive.'

'What a thought!'

'But you're staying with her, aren't you—in their chalet?'

'Even the idea of it—no, impossible!'

We retraced our steps together. Lipsett spent the rest of the day with me in the hotel, and told me his latest batch of stories. The late light streaming through the windows softened; the reception was bathed in a gentle dark.

'I'll get ready,' he said: 'We'll go together.'

'I don't think I'm invited.'

'Nonsense. You heard her yesterday—everyone is. Think who you are. After all, you know me—you're my friend.'

A figure in uniform from the concierge's desk came up to us. 'For you,' he said, and handed me a note. I opened it. Lipsett watched.

'Who's it from?' he asked.

It was in Serghiana's hand, scrawled on a sheet of hotel notepaper, jumping from Russian to western lettering in her usual style.

'Get rid of Corey,' it read: 'Don't go to M.L.'s evening. Meet me on the hotel terrace at seven—be prompt.'

'What's it say?' said Lipsett.

'Nothing much.'

'Come on, kiddo—tell me.'

'It's from Serghiana,' I said.

'Of course it is—who else could it be from—but about what?'

'It's about a little problem that's come up,' I said, and heard the hint of hesitation in my voice.

'You really are all grown up now, aren't you?' said Lipsett: 'And taking after her and her kind.'

He looked at me for a moment, and left me there. The sun sank beneath the mountains. I went out to the terrace and waited. The air turned colder. Seven came and went. I paced up and down between the fountain and the alley of alpine trees. Half an hour more went by: no sign of Serghiana. No one. I was going through the double-entrance doorway back to the reception when I came face to face with her.

'I told you to wait for me in the terrace garden,' she said, and took my arm, and began to steer me back outside.

'Why?'

'I wanted to take you to the special lookout Semyonov and I had: a view over all the valley: our secret—our discovery. I wanted to live again in vanished time a moment—too late now.'

'Because you're late,' I said: 'Very, in fact.'

'That's true—but it's not for you to say so. You were never impolite or inconsiderate before. Another gift from American modernity.'

'Anything wrong?'

'Just thoughts. Come—we'll find a corner table in the dining room: no one will disturb us there—we'll sit and talk. Here: suitable surroundings, don't you think?'

A vast, high-ceilinged room: a gallery of sorts: Corinthian columns, chandeliers, mirrored walls, tall windows: a sea of tables, all set with white tablecloths, all empty: paintings in the lunettes atop the columns, stucco figures; a stuffed stag's head set above the entrance door.

'What a place!' I said.

'Once for the crowned heads of Europe—now for nostalgia seekers and the lost. Where was I in my story?'

'You were on the path up the gorge: and you'd used up all your fear of life.'

'I should have saved some. That was the last time we saw the mountains—we left from Zürich station; we travelled back by train: through the Germanies, through Poland, then home. His apartment. Within days it was clear to Semyonov: trouble lay ahead. He delivered his report and findings. He was called in: they interrogated him—they went on deep into the night: polite questioning, detailed: who, where, when. I told myself all this was normal—we were privileged; trusted to travel; there were always questions on return from the West: it had to be that way—it was that way for everyone. I was still convinced we were untouchable: we'd already come through all our darkness: he'd be safe.'

'Because of you—or your father's name?'

'Because of him—because of who he was. He was a hero of the Soviet Union; a god of science; he had his own institute. His work was vital—he had protectors at the highest level of the party. And he was a believer—a true believer, in his way.'

'In the revolution?'

'Absolutely—it was a cause—he'd fought for it. Don't give that ironic look.'

'You too?'

'I don't know. In those days, perhaps, still, yes—I believed in him.'

A waiter came by.

'A Kir—two, in fact—the drink of exiles,' said Serghiana in an off-hand way, not looking up.

She continued. Their return; its consequences; the mood among Semyonov's staff; the rumours circulating, the fears, the upheavals in the academies of science.

'I don't want to tell you every detail: how he was taken from me; how I let him go. It was all done by subterfuge: if I told you everything it would wring your heart.'

'But shouldn't you?' I said: 'Shouldn't I know properly? The real story—not a soft version, not a children's sketch.'

'Is that what you want?' said Serghiana: 'Am I turning into a case study for you? A piece of history? A tragic heroine? I'm not that.'

'Aren't we talking about the things that made you what you are?'

'The things I want you to be free of.'

'But free by knowing?'

'Maybe so,' she said then: 'Maybe that's the only way.'

'Then what?'

'They laid a perfect trap for him. Or for me, through him. I couldn't see it. I was blind to everything.'

'You were young.'

'I had experience. I'd lived through a war! I knew the party and the system. Once, I was near its heart. But I'd failed to learn the simplest lesson of them all: that the people you think nothing of in life are much more dangerous than those with power in their hands.'

'Why?'

'Because the ones without power are the takers: they have resentment on their side: resentment, the strongest force of all. If Loewy told you about my husband, he surely told you about his ideas as well: the pretext for his destruction.'

'He said hardly anything: minerals in asteroids: I don't think I understood.'

'You understood perfectly. That was Semyonov's theory: it explained what he'd found: it was current in those days—it had support. It brought him fresh prominence—before we went away—but then the landscape shifted, as it always does.'

'In science?'

'In politics. We'd been back three weeks, no longer: not long at all—all the time we had. How easy it became suddenly to make an attack on him—to pull him down. There was a power struggle underway: it spread everywhere. That was the autumn of the Doctors' Plot—the start of it. We heard the reports: Semyonov knew one of the first arrested: they were close—true friends. The purge began. Semyonov felt it would be prudent to be away: be out of sight—as if that could help. He wanted to send me to the Caucasus: he brought forward his trip to the dam site on the Angara: to Chukotka as well—the end of the earth—do you have it in your mind? It's where the Arctic and the Pacific meet: the region where he'd made those sample finds. He sent a letter to the presidium: he read it to me. He was proud of its precise phrasing. I listened to it in silence: I felt my bones go cold. Off it went—and another, to the ministry in Moscow. An official proposal. Can you imagine? How they must have laughed, the ones who wanted to destroy him. He made himself the architect of their plan: He asked them for permission—to enter Dalstroi! To go to Magadan. They didn't even need to drag him through the Lubyanka. His colleagues tried to warn him: I pleaded with him. He paid no attention: his mind was made up. He set out on that journey of his own free will.'

'And suspected nothing?' I asked her—but at that point the maître d'hôtel came up to our table and made a formal bow.

'Madame Semyonova,' he said.

Serghiana looked up at him with curiosity, and inclined her head.

'Permit me,' he went on, 'to welcome you here again.'

'You know me? You remember me?'

'I remember your visit years ago—how could I not? You made an impression, you and your husband.'

'In what way?'

'You were a striking couple—and you went everywhere hand in hand. We had very few guests in those days coming from the Soviet Union: you may have been the first. Every morning, at breakfast, your husband asked me for directions—for the walks you took; and he was always kind to the hotel waiters—he treated all of us as friends.'

'He was kind to everyone he met,' said Serghiana.

'And this is your son?'

'Of course,' said Serghiana, in a low voice.

'And may I bring you anything?'

'Whatever you think best. Being here again is feast enough.'

She smiled a little. The waiter retreated. She touched a finger to one eye, and then the other.

'If it was me on the verge of tears,' I said, 'you'd tell me not to be so weak and sentimental.'

'It's not you—and I'm not shedding tears for myself—it's you they're for, my poor child—you.'

'Why?'

'You have to ask? There's no need for me to lament my fate: it's always before me. I know it well. It was decided in those days: clear September days in Moscow. Semyonov left: he was excited to be going. We said goodbye at the Yaroslavsky station. You don't know it—it's a dreary place to leave one's heart. I went back to Tverskaya, to his apartment. I waited there. I expected the knock on the door. Nothing. Days went by. I tried to read: the words on the page were without meaning for me. When darkness fell I walked up and down the boulevard ring with all the night-time poets and the thieves, and gazed up at the dark windows of the buildings, and imagined all the raids and arrests they'd seen. I tried to picture my husband: where was he; had he been detained already: was he in Irkutsk, and safe: would they snatch him up from the Angara site instead, and tell everyone there he was a wrecker or a saboteur? Another week—then a letter came: it was in his hand—a perfect copy. It lacked our private signal; I knew he hadn't written it.'

'It was forged?'

She nodded.

'But why?'

'Why not? Who knows—the joy of the deception. I called at the institute. They had no news of him; they were terrified. Where to turn next? What to do? I couldn't bear the silence all around me. The next morning I went to the Leninka.'

'Where?'

'The state library: the best place in all the Soviet Union to be alone in a crowd. I took my place in the reading room for Russian literature. I used to go there often: it's quiet, and warm. The self dissolves—one can daydream, and feel anonymous and safe. Midway through the morning a man came up and sat in the seat next to mine. He had a thin, anguished face. "Permit me to join you for a moment, Serghiana Ismailovna," he said in a soft voice, almost a whisper. "Do I know you, comrade?" I asked. "We haven't met, but you know me well. You could say I'm an archetype." "In that case," I said, "I've been expecting you for some time. Where is he? Where have you taken him? What have you done with him?" The man looked at me steadily. "Engineer Semyonov? There's no need for you to feel concern. Your husband's undertaking his patriotic tasks. We protect him: he's about to set off on his expedition: he's perfectly well. And how are your studies at the film school progressing—may I enquire?" "I broke them off when we left for abroad—as I'm sure you know." "We feel you should resume them." "We?" "Please," he said: "Engineer Semyonov and you were away for several months: and on that journey, as you know well, he made foreign contacts—a number of them. So it may be some time before he's able to return to Moscow. I think you understand. And we also feel you should keep your views to yourself." With that, carefully, almost noiselessly, he pushed back his seat and slid away. And that was all. I looked down at the book open on the desk before me: it was *The Torrents of Spring*—a romance—a tale from the times of innocence. You spoke of lives changing: that was the day my life changed—forever.'

The maître d'hôtel had reappeared as she was telling me this story. He stood to one side of our table, a look of distress on his face.

'We're speaking of Semyonov,' said Serghiana to him: 'The man you remember. Sit here with us, if you'd like to. Listen in. There's no one else here—no need for you to stay in character.'

He hesitated, glanced around the dining room, then rested his hands on the back of the chair between us and leaned slightly forward, like a flanking angel in a painting from the Renaissance.

'No,' said Serghiana then: 'Sit down with us at the table. Be one with us.'

He did so.

'And then what?' I prompted.

'What always happens in these affairs. The little variations only underline the story's shape. Weeks passed. No news. I went back to the school of cinematography: no one there spoke a word to me about Semyonov. My friends were less friendly. My world quickly lost the contours that it used to have. I visited his closest colleagues—they turned me away. There was talk of moving the institute beyond the Urals—in the end they simply shut it down. I knew the name of Semyonov's great protector on the presidium: I tried to make an appointment to see him: I went to his office: that door was closed to me as well.

'And so, stage by stage, my hopes dwindled. I went back to the way I was living before I knew Semyonov: it felt as if my time with him had been a dream. I moved into a dormitory block. My studies ended. I began to work. I was in a pure limbo. I was under suspicion; I still had privileges. I was a red general's daughter, married to a man whose name had disappeared: a member of the special class and one of its victims at the same time. A year went by. Routine remade me. I was working on ethnographic film projects. I liked them; I became proficient. Stalin was gone by then—there was no more Doctors' Plot. People began to breathe more easily.

'One day I received a summons from the head of the central documentary studio: I went to see him. He received me with great formality. He sat me down at the long table reserved for dignitaries. His secretary fluttered round us, and served us little sweet delicacies and sugared tea. "I have a project for you," he told me: "A film about state goldmining operations. You'd have to travel far away." "That would be something welcome for me," I answered. "To the Sea of Okhotsk," he said then: "To Magadan." "Comrade director," I asked him: "Do you know anything of my circumstances?" "I know them precisely," he said: "I am authorised to make this offer to you." "Offer—not command?" He held up a typed document and read aloud from it: "I am also authorised to inform you that Engineer Semyonov, in the pursuit of his surveying duties, succumbed to illness during his journey to the district of Anadyr, Chukotka Okrug." I stayed motionless. I absorbed the blow in silence. "Did you understand me?" asked the director. "Perfectly well," I said: "I knew this information long ago—I knew it before it happened." "Serghiana Ismailovna," he said: "Your father would have been proud of you—of your spirit." And he made a little deferential movement of his head. "Comrade director," I said then: "My father and my husband lived in an entirely different world from you." I turned and left him. I didn't care what happened next in my life.'

She looked at us both, then around the empty salon.

'But what did?' I asked her: 'What did happen?'

'A week later I was travelling from Moscow to Irkutsk to join the ethnographic team. The harsh-weather season was close ahead: the trains we passed were full of men and women returning from the camps: they looked like a parade of skeletons. The crew I was with were from the army film-production unit. They were quiet, resigned people. They knew who I was: they were kind to me. We reached our destination. We were shown very little there: the buildings at the centre of the settlement; the apartment blocks, the grey coastline: wrecked hulks of abandoned ships offshore, half-lost in the mist in Nagayev Bay. Trucks brought us to the goldmine where we were to film: it was deep in the taiga, hours down a broken haul road. We drove through the night; we arrived as dawn was breaking—but I could see nothing that shone or glittered there: it was a pit, vast, jagged, gouged out from permafrost and rock—and that rock was dull green and pale lifeless brown. It had held precious metal; it had yielded it. Men had died there, by the hundred—but it was a natural landscape, it had neither charm nor menace, it belonged to itself alone—it was somewhere that had not been made for men's eyes to see and love.

'We set to work. We were ordered to work fast. No contact with the men we saw on labour gangs: that was forbidden from the outset: they waved in our direction—we were told not to wave back. Everything we were allowed to film was staged: we hid the harshness: no images of spoil or tailings; no images of the wooden barracks or prisoners toiling away. I'd seen the signs along the road we travelled, all celebrating Dalstroi: "Work is honourable, glorious, valiant and heroic." Those words reached into me. I thought to myself then: Dalstroi is where we're bound: all of us—it's everything—it's the fulfilment of our Soviet world. The sound recordist on our unit had been with a tank brigade on the drive towards Berlin. He told me he would take a year on the Red Army frontline over a week in the Djelgala valley goldmining camps.

'Before we left, we were ushered into to the headquarters block in Magadan. We filmed a meeting there with the Labour Force Administration chief. From his office you could look out and see the mountains in the distance and the pale light in the sky: like a world still coming into being. A silent man from State Security brought us in for the interview. He sat beside me. At the end of the meeting he followed me out and came up to me in the corridor. "Doubtless," he said, "esteemed Serghiana Ismailovna, you would like to know something of the fate of Engineer Semyonov." "Doubtless!" "I can tell you," he said, "that he performed heroic work." I said nothing. "He was here of his own free will." "I'm sure," I said. "He made scientific advances—advances of the greatest significance." "I believe you fully," I replied. Then the man came up closer, and whispered this to me: "He was looking for special structures—you must have heard them mentioned: structures in the rocks. Rare materials: he found them. He was certain of it. It was a triumph. A discovery of something magical and wonderful: but at high cost. He and his prospecting team had gone deep into the Koryak Mountains— where there's no one, and nothing. It's a remote place." "Unlike here, you mean?" I said. "Remote even by these standards. He fell ill: it was impossible to evacuate him." "Where from?" "Anadyr." "I should like to visit that place one day," I said. "Inconceivable," he answered: "It lies within a military zone. It's an area of strategic significance." "Am I not a soldier?" I asked him: I was wearing an army uniform. "Even telling you this is telling you too much," he said: "I do it because of my regard for you, and for your name. I myself have been there: often. As a location, it has a beauty all its own. You can imagine the soul setting out from there on a voyage to distant worlds." "An unusual thing for a man with your function in life to say!" "I was a prisoner here once," he answered: "Many things happened here before my eyes: nothing affected me as deeply as Engineer Semyonov's death." "Why's that?" I said: "One man's life is like another's. All deaths have equal value." "I was on the prospecting expedition," he replied." "You knew him?" I asked then: "You were with him?" He nodded his head, and in that moment looked away from me. "You sent back reports on him, I imagine?" "He was a mystic—a stargazer. There was nothing that could be done for him. He wanted what came to him to come." "Who are you, comrade?" I asked him then: "May I know your name?" "Names in this world come and go," he answered, and left me there.

'We returned to Moscow with our footage. We made our little propaganda film. I've already told you about my life in the years that came afterwards, haven't I? Endlessly, in fact, I'm sure.'

'Not really,' I said.

'You know the essence—the details hardly matter: you know when the first changes came. There was a new faction at the helm: they relaxed their hold: there was a horizon for us, then: suddenly, there was a hint of space. My work became more straightforward: escapism, fantasy. I wrote scripts: I made sure there was funding for them: I made sure they followed the prevailing winds. The time came round to mark the *Chelyuskin* expedition: the exploring vessel trapped in arctic pack ice. A great chapter in the Soviet story—or a failure gilded and made into one. It was the anniversary year. We prepared the outline; we received approval; we found our director. I told him that we had to see the sites; nothing else would do—it was necessary for us to be real documentarists, to be relentless in our pursuit of accuracy: to bring back truth. And so he made the request to film where the drama had unfolded; out at the furthest edge of Soviet land—and beyond— in the old Dalstroi kingdom. Word came back: impossible! But I had a high-up ally of my own by this stage: that man you've heard Loewy and me speak about. I pressed him. It was arranged for us. We asked for special transport: it was given to us—an Ilyushin to fly our crew and equipment. We asked for access to the north-eastern coastline: they provided it.

'They brought us to a missile base in Chukotka, on the Bering Sea. It was still under construction: everything gleaming, everything new. Across the bay was a settlement—and that was Anadyr. Silent, like an abandoned stage-set. A few blocks of housing, a port, storage tanks. Grey sky, grey water—the place where the world runs out. You could see it all in half an hour; we spent days there, weeks on end. I explored it, I knew it from every angle: the foreshore, the road up to the light-house, the empty docks. At night the northern lights were in the sky, and you could watch them, shifting, pulsing in a gentle rhythm, casting their lovely glow. By day there were seabirds, gulls and terns, hovering in the air above you, almost motionless—and that was all: that was everything.'

She fell quiet, and looked up.

The maître d'hôtel had been sitting throughout this story, silent and solemn. He leaned forward now. 'You found no trace of your husband, Madame Semyonova?' he asked: 'No grave, no memorial?'

'I went to the little clinic hospital: they had no record of him. I knew there'd be nothing: I had no reason to believe a word of what I'd been told in Magadan. I'm sure he met his end soon after he left me. I'm sure he died in the mines—somewhere bleak and frozen, some-where fearful like Elgen or Yagodnoe. They made a legend for me; they thought it would be enough for me, they thought I was the kind who needed stories to believe.'

'A legend, madame?'

'They gave him a heroic, tragic death: you know the idea: a death to live with, a death with significance: he'd been the leader of a scientific expedition, he was a martyr for the cause of knowledge, he'd found rarities—wonders, treasures, deep in the arctic wilds. And that's why they eased my path. They wanted me to go in search of him, go on my quest—go to the ends of the earth, and grieve there, and imagine that I'd seen through all their duplicities; believe I'd found fulfilment: compose myself. It was a charade—a piece of theatre.'

'But why, then,' I asked her: 'Why did you go?'

'For the horror of it—to be in that red heaven; that emptiness. To see it; feel it. I asked myself if places could preserve the memory of people: I asked myself if I could sense anything of him at all in those northern wastes—if I could dream him into memory there.'

'I hope you did,' said the maître d'hôtel: 'I hope that very much.'

'I found something else,' she answered: 'It was calm all through the time we spent at Anadyr. Not a breath of wind in the air; a sea like glass—but it was a calm with an undertone. I was uneasy after a few days there. I had the sense that the stillness all around me was the stillness of exhaustion—the calm wasn't peace—it was the aftermath of pain and suffering; of all the violence and the fury that had rained down on that far-off corner of the world.'

She placed her hands on the table. 'Enough, now,' she said: 'Enough sentiment. In every life a time comes when you've reached your goal. The point when truth is shown to you—and everything after that is epilogue. I looked out across the dark sea at Anadyr and knew that time had come for me. It's pleasant enough, of course, to be here with you, to sit in this dining room, to see this place again, this valley, this building that was the scene of such happiness for me—pleasant enough to live this life, read books, have knowledge—but the shadows stay.'

There was a noise from the front of the hotel as she said this: from the reception—laughter, voices.

'Madame Semyonova,' said the maître d'hôtel, and he stood up, and rested his hands on the back of the chair: 'With your permission...'

'Of course.'

He retreated. She glanced at her watch.

'Past midnight. Can they be back from their evening already? So soon—it's not possible. I can't bear the thought of seeing all of them. Now go, my child, sleep soundly—think of what I've told you, and leave me with my thoughts.'

*

Years passed. I entered adulthood. Her story stayed with me—its light and dark, its details. But a time came when there were no new messages from Serghiana, she had fallen from the headlines, I could find no trace of her—so it was something startling for me when, one winter morning, chance intervened in my life in its imperious way, and I heard her name again.

I had just stepped off a Swissair flight: I was at Geneva airport. It was early in 1990: the last of the eastern regimes had fallen; my months of travelling with photographers and camera crews were over. I made my way into the arrivals hall: As I fetched my case I was conscious of a woman with blond hair looking at me. She was staring at me. The face was striking: familiar, in a far-off way.

'Hello,' the woman said then, and came closer: 'Hello, my little someone.'

It was Josette—older, slightly faded, immaculately dressed, a look of amusement in her eyes. She tilted her head slightly away from me, and held the pose. 'Kiss me on both cheeks, you poor creature,' she commanded: 'You shouldn't forget your manners—always remember who you are.'

'Josette—it's you?'

'You look dreadful,' she said then: 'Worn out: half-starved. Where have you been? Where are you flying in from?'

'Bucharest.'

She gave knowing smile. 'So that's what you became—a journalist—a correspondent. What a choice! Self-effacement incarnate.'

I took a step back from her, and tried to read her expression. 'Why do you say that?'

'You know very well: it's the simplest way to cancel out yourself: tell other people's stories, not live inside your own. And they were always talking about that for you, weren't they? They all thought writing was the key to power. Pure delusion: that was a dream from long ago. I used to imagine that you'd end up doing something else with your life: that you'd rebel against them, just a little. Make a little revolution of your own.'

'And is this your part of the world now?' I asked her.

'Is that so unexpected?'

'No more Paris? No more Malzahn?'

'Ancient history! I got rid of him. There was a scandal. Perhaps you heard about it? Nothing? No? I live here now, with my current husband, and his daughters. We're across the lake—at Cologny, up high. He's a banker, or he has a bank, I should say, maybe—but I suppose you'd already figured that out, hadn't you?'

She drew close again, and reached out her hand towards me. 'Don't flinch like that—I'm not going to hurt you. Let me see you properly: see your face. You still have that guarded look. I remember it, from the first time I met you, from when you were just a boy; when I took you up to visit Nietzsche's chicken bone. How I felt for you in those days. I thought you needed protecting.'

'There were people looking after me,' I said.

'Protection from them, exactly. Such deranged guardians you had: storytellers, fantasists: the empresses of exile—rulers of their own resort hotels. And what attentions they lavished on you: room service, boarding schools, hauteur, neglect.'

She glanced round in a restless way. 'I should go,' she said: 'Not dwell on past time. It's never a good idea.' She waved her hand in a quick farewell, and turned away—then turned abruptly back. 'And will you see your great-aunt?'

'Who do you mean?'

'Why, Serghiana, of course. Who else could I mean? She lives on the lake. Didn't you know that?' And she tilted her head in a questioning way.

'I've rather lost contact with her,' I said.

'Truthfully? I thought you two were inseparable—like two particles bound together by the strong nuclear force—infrared freedom, ultraviolet slavery, that kind of thing.'

'What?'

'Nothing—pay it no attention. We had a dinner for the physicists at CERN the other night: we help in raising funds for them. It was fascinating—the things they told me. All quite bizarre—but that's modernity for you, isn't it? The rate of change overhauling us more and more, the faster we run? We poor mortal beings always losing the race.'

'You were talking about Great-Aunt Serghiana. I thought she'd disappeared from the face of the earth.'

'I won't tell her you said that! She's at Vevey. She has a suite in the Hotel Miramar—she has for years. It's the one that looks like an Italian palazzo, with a row of linden trees in front of it. Very restful, I imagine. Near the marina—it's hard to miss.'

I hesitated.

'Just go—and see her,' said Josette. 'Go tomorrow—it would be a welcome visit—and a well-timed one. Don't call first: surprise her. Bring her joy.'

All through this exchange a man in dark suit and peaked cap had been standing to one side, waiting, the expression on his face fixed. Josette made a sign to him. 'Here, Ruggiero—let's be off.' She handed him her little case.

'*Bizous*,' she called out to me, and waved again as they vanished in the crowd.

*

Two days later, my work tasks done, I took the lake steamer for Vevey and the mountains. The morning was cold and crisp, the peaks stood out like silhouettes against the sky, the landscape was as clear as a high-resolution photograph. There was the marina, and the promenade; there was the hotel behind its barrier of trees. Inside, in the reception, all was quiet. A young woman was sitting behind a scroll-top desk, reading. She looked up at me with a faint air of curiosity and went back to her book. She turned a page, and frowned, and gave a little laugh.

'What are you reading?' I said eventually.

She held up the book: a thick, parchment-coloured old paperback.

'Céline,' she said: 'You know him?'

'An inspired choice,' I answered.

'Were you looking for someone?'

'Do you have a Russian guest staying here? The name is Semyonova. She lives in the hotel, I think, for much of the year.'

The young woman gave a sigh. 'Serghiana's been waiting for you—for some time. She's in the Persian chamber—along the corridor.'

I took a few steps.

'Here—in here, my child.'

It was the austere, familiar voice. And there she was, as angular and aquiline as ever, seated in a darkened salon full of draperies in dark-patterned fabrics, a samovar before her on a glass and metal tabletop. She had a wry expression on her face. Her hands were tightly clasped. I looked at her intently. I took her in. She turned away after a few moments, as if it hurt her to be seen.

'Great-Aunt Serghiana,' I said.

'I've been expecting you—for two days—two whole days,' she said in an accusing way: 'And I hear you thought I was gone from the world: perhaps you even hoped it.'

'Josette promised me she wouldn't tell you that.'

'Surprise! She broke her promise. I'd have thought you might have worked her out by now—you can see how high she's flown. She said you'd been in Romania. Much shooting?'

'It was chaos. It still is.'

'I can believe it. Romanians have a penchant for drama—and for revenge. It's nothing compared to what you'll see when the Soviet Union breaks apart.'

'Is that likely?'

'It's a certainty: give it a year or two. Then we'll have old Russia back again—the dark, panting beast that prowls at Europe's gate. Sit now—sit with me, there, across from me. Tell me everything. Sink into the sofa. Sink into dreams.'

'But why are you here, beside the lake?' I asked her: 'It doesn't seem like you. I thought you preferred the mountains. That's where I'd go to look for you.'

'If you'd been looking. But the mountains aren't what they once were. Think of Vulpera.'

'What about Vulpera?'

'Were you so cocooned in your world of revolutions that you didn't hear? There was a fire at the Waldhaus—almost a year ago, in springtime, at the end of May. Nothing's left there but a shell. It was in all the Swiss and German newspapers—long reports, very detailed, but saying nothing. It was arson, of course: it always is with grand hotels. The blaze burned through the night—it made for striking images—sheets of flames consuming everything: fires in the great reception hall, roof beams splintering and cracking, balconies and towers tumbling down. A pleasingly symbolic event.'

'In what way?'

'Hundreds of ways. A cleansing of memories. The old order's summer palace burning to the ground. Goodbye to nostalgia. Goodbye to that enchanted world of loss. New griefs for new times now.'

'You must have been heartbroken when you heard.'

'Not at all. Buildings are just backdrops for us—stage-sets, nothing more. I was pleased—even happy; happy that that the last traces of the days and weeks I lived through there have gone. No one can walk through those reception rooms that I remember so well anymore:

they've passed into unreality. And I'll never make the journey to those mountains and the valley and Tarasp castle again: I can only see them in my mind. You might like to go back, though: go back and see what's left. It should be your ideal landscape—you were always fond of ruins.'

'I was? I don't remember that.'

'I promise you it's true. I know you better than you know yourself. Émigrés and exiles have a love of ruins. It's natural, it's almost diagnostic of them—ruins are their home.'

'Is that what you think I am?' I asked her.

'Fencing with me? Still? It's not necessary. Surely you can tell. You're free from me now. Free to reinvent yourself. And I can see you've already made a start.'

She raised her eyes to mine, and looked straight into them, and smiled her most inward smile.

'That's an ambiguous look,' I said.

'How hard it is! You can't imagine: it's the hardest thing in life—letting your creations go.'

I was about to make an answer. I paused: I took in the room around us: the winding patterns in the carpet, the hanging tapestries, a gilt-framed mirror reflecting shadows, heavy curtains, half-faded, their hems of golden thread. It was a cage—an ornate cage: and at its centre, hands still clasped together, frail, determined—her.

'Why are you staring at me that way,' she said: 'Assessing me—weighing me up—as if you've never had the chance before?'

'Is that it?' I said then: 'Is that why you vanished from my life—why you stopped writing those long letters to me; stopped calling; left me in the hands of others?'

'It had to be,' she said, in a hard voice: 'You had to make your way. It was time to cut you off. Of course I could dream up some soft pretence for you: a pleasant tale, and send you away with a happy feeling in your heart. I could tell you there were other reasons: many of them—I was producing films, it was California, the West Coast, demanding people and demanding times. I could tell you it was just life, the way of things—random life that takes people away from each other, events, chance, the ebb and flow. But I'd be lying. It was done on purpose. I'm sure you knew that already. It had to be that way.'

'And you've come to rest here now? It's nothing at all like the West Coast: there's no resemblance.'

'You don't like it? You don't find it suitable?'

'Isn't it rather a bourgeois place for a red general's daughter to end up?'

'A stab! So let me parry. This isn't just a riviera full of plutocrats.'

'No? I can guess what you're going to tell me—that it's the lakeside of tranquillity, the misty shore where dreams begin.'

'Along those lines—though not in quite such florid terms. Adjectives are a weakness: at least remember that!'

'You use them,' I said.

'What an insult! I never use them: I despise people who use adjectives.'

'I'll take it on board,' I said.

She gave me one of her measuring looks. 'So casual—so at ease in your chosen life. I'm glad.'

'You sound the opposite. You sound critical.'

'I can be both at the same time.'

'The important thing,' I said, 'is that you're at ease here: you've found a place that suits you well. How did you find it? And why did you choose it?'

'Don't you know? Isn't it plain to you? After all your years of schooling and study? After a childhood spent at my feet?'

I shrugged. 'I give up. Tell me.'

'The lakeside's always been a sanctuary—a paradise of exiles. Musicians, artists, dancers, writers—they all flocked here. Everyone who mattered in the nineteenth century came to Vevey: Gogol, Byron, Shelley, Lamartine.'

'Anyone more recently?'

'Eminescu, Sienkiewicz, Adorno, Kafka.'

'You're making that up!'

'Well, the last name, perhaps—but still—it's a distinguished parade of ghosts, don't you think? And that's even without counting the old white Russian chloroforming his poor butterflies up at the palace in Montreux: not that I'd ever count a soft-voiced reactionary like him.'

'And that's why you came here: to join the list?'

'No: I came to make a film: about someone else. Someone much more significant. No idea? Where's your history? We were going to make a film of *The Confessions*—Rousseau.'

'Of course,' I said: 'Because it would lend itself to cinema so wonderfully well.'

'There's no call for sarcasm: another bad habit you've picked up. I think I still had poor Corey back with me then. All the financing was in place. We set up here, in this hotel. But there was a problem with the actors: the way there always is: the project fell apart.'

'You could still make it. He's almost in fashion these days—the me generation, self above all else—that's a tune people want to sing.'

'It'll never happen now. The time for dreams like that has gone.'

'You were going to set it in his time?'

'That would have been much too easy. The book's like a screenplay for a costume drama. That's what Rousseau did with his life: change scenes, sketch characters, try out attitudes. And the stage-sets are all still standing: you can walk down the promenade here and find the lodgings where he lived: there's a little plaque to tell you he was there. What fame! But I had something different in mind: reveries: screen meditations, a series of them, meanders: in his style; true to him; set in the places where he found refuge. Do you know any of them?'

I shook my head.

'No? The retreat at Ermenonville? The house near Chambéry? The island where he was so blissfully happy, on the Lac de Bienne?'

'Afraid not,' I said: 'There hasn't been much time for cultural excursions—you can see life's been taking me down different paths.'

'You should change course. The years to come would be well spent if you made a pilgrimage in the footsteps of Jean-Jacques.'

'You think so highly of him?'

'He was a monster—but he freed himself from life's chains. I've never come across a writer whose presence lingers quite so strongly in the places that he loved.'

'Your tastes have changed since the days when we used to read the *Princesse de Clèves* to each other in the mountains.'

'Not at all,' she said, her voice triumphant: 'You're wrong: quite wrong! Jean-Jacques admired Madame de Lafayette greatly—he wanted his books to be like hers.'

'I'm glad I've been able to give you a moment's satisfaction,' I said.

She looked back at me. Her expression broke. 'My child, don't you understand anything? I was happy then—I was happy, reading to you. When you were a boy—your eyes so wide. I was giving you the world. Those days were everything for me. I never wanted them to end.'

'But they did. Abruptly.'

'How cold you sound. I taught you well. You learned from the Princess, didn't you?'

'Learned what?'

'You know what the lesson was: to be circumspect in everything. To keep your feelings locked up in the fortress of your heart.'

'And that's why it was the first book we read together, after all those little mediaeval tales you dragged me through?'

'I was trying to show you something else as well by choosing it. Something even more important.'

She gave me a stare of challenge.

'Show me what, exactly? Should I guess?'

'That there are magic books for us to turn to—a handful of them: books to heal the wounds of life.'

'As they did for you?'

She looked uncertain. She paused, and clasped her hands together more tightly. 'Do you regret those days, when we used to sit together so peacefully all afternoon long? Do you think that time was poorly spent? From the tone in your voice it almost sounds that way.'

I was about to make some answer when a concierge from the hotel appeared at the entrance to the salon.

'Madame Semyonova-Terek,' he began: 'Something for you and your guest?'

'Leave us,' she said: 'We're talking.'

'Terek?' I repeated: 'You've added a name?'

'It was my father's nom de guerre. Appropriate, don't you think? Made up—or borrowed, if you like. It's the name of the river that runs through the mountains of his homeland: pale blue and cold and pure.'

'Like all your favourite rivers.'

'The names we choose aren't immutable. I use them to remember. To bring things back. It's a trick that works, much better than madeleines.'

'Madame?' It was another concierge, looking even more flustered. 'Forgive me, please.'

'What?'

'The banker from Zürich.'

'Tell him to wait.'

'He's already been waiting for some while. You gave him a time for his appointment with you. Such people generally don't like being made to wait.'

'This one will wait, I assure you,' said Serghiana. 'It's his role in life to wait.' She gave a quick, dark laugh and waved the concierge away. 'Go on,' she said to me: 'More talk.'

'I was in Zürich last month,' I said: 'After Prague—before Romania. I hadn't been there since I was a boy.'

'Really,' said Serghiana, in an abstracted voice.

'I saw Ady there. Can you believe it, after so long?'

She turned to face me. 'My child,' she said: 'Either your imagination's running away with you—which isn't that unlikely, in fact, is it—or

335

you've lost your sense of time. Not a good thing in your chosen profession, I'd think, on balance.'

'Why do you say that?'

'Didn't you hear? Palafay's dead. She took her own life: in Vienna—in that mansion; not long after her husband died. She was true to herself—deceptive to the end: stealing across life's last frontier without papers like the refugee she was. At least she remembered to have those two outlandish dogs of hers put down the day before. I thought that was an elegant touch.'

'I had no idea,' I said.

'You must have been mistaken, then, in thinking that you saw her,' said Serghiana, firmly.

I took in this news.

'Why so quiet? Do you feel the loss? Do you miss her, now you know she's left us? Would you miss me the same way?'

'Please,' I said: 'Don't even think such things.'

'How trite and conventional you sound! How tamed and soft. Why shouldn't I think them? Don't you see how it is here for me? Look around you: all this pointless splendour. Jasmine and tiger lilies in every vase; blue rugs from Isfahan; Fortuny damask on the walls. Everything pleasing: everything in perfect taste. Through the windows the sun on the peaks each morning, dazzling the eye; the women with their lap-dogs, strolling on the promenade; the lake steamers from Lausanne and Montreux calling at the jetty, always exactly on time. It's like Svidrigailov's eternity in *Crime and Punishment*.'

'Remind me.'

'All there will be forever is a little room. A tiny room, like a cabin in a bath-house, with black dust and grime on the walls and spiders skulking in the corners—that's all, forever. Changelessness. I never guessed it could be so hard to bear. I thank my stars I've got the exit visa in my passport.'

Those words spoken sharply: almost spat out.

'What on earth do you mean?' I said: 'What are you talking about?'

'You do a good impression of understanding nothing. You want me to show you X-rays?'

She saw my face. She stopped.

'Please,' she said then: 'Don't be agitated. Compose yourself: for me. Just look at me, and tell me. Can you see the signs of it in my face? Is it there? How do I seem to you?'

'You always seemed majestic.'

At this, she smiled faintly, and even gave a little laugh. 'A telling choice of the past tense. Your mouth is for speaking truth, not lying. Your eyes are for seeing truth, not illusion. Use them. Avoid pretence. Can't you say what you see in front of you? Silence? You can't say anything? Then I'll tell you. I'll tell you what I see in the mirror. There's no light left in me—my skin is pale like ash, my breathing's like a whisper, my heart barely stirs. And see these—my hands?'

She held them up, and flinched again. 'How twisted they are. How bent out of true. They revolt me.'

I got up from my seat to go across to her.

'Stay where you are! No scenes. I don't want you coming over here and kneeling at my feet.' She glared.

'What do you want?' I asked then.

Her manner changed. Her face became gentler. 'You remember how I tried to teach you everything I knew, don't you?'

'I do,' I said.

'I tried to show you all the secrets of the world when you were with me. All the wonders I'd seen rushing past me in the journey I took through life.'

'A wild life,' I said.

'It was a fiasco. In exile from exile. At home in homelessness. That's why you were so perfect for me. As I always told you: you belonged nowhere—you had no home.'

'Weren't you that for me?' I asked.

She paid those words no attention. She looked upwards and frowned. 'My child—you must know this is our last meeting.'

'Then I'll carry you in my thoughts,' I said.

'That's your affair. Make your own way now. All my life I lived with scorn for others: scorn for their weakness. Now I'm weak in my turn. Before the nothing—before the grandest, most romantic path of them all. Tell yourself I'll watch over you—always. Now leave me be. Go on your way through life. Live for me, see for me, breathe for me. Send in the banker. Go.'

VII

Envoi: Bodensee

YEARS WENT BY before I saw the alpine peaks again. I travelled; I lived in different countries. I saw conflicts, I moved between them, I described them, I steeped myself in them until I was settled in this system of impermanence: it suited me; I scarcely felt the beat of passing time. Then, one autumn, after long negotiations, an East–West summit was announced: to be held in Davos, in the shadow of the Schatzalp. The usual piece of theatre. I was sent to it. I attended. I watched. Motorcades, leaders and their teams of diplomats; banquets, speeches, words of prudence, a communique, success. Such concord, so precisely scripted: I was glad when at last the time came to escape. I went back to the press hotel, and looked round for my photographer to say goodbye to him. We had worked together before, often, in the Middle East, in South-East Asia: we used to know each other well. I found him on the terrace promenade, his expression serious.

'I was just thinking about you,' he said.

'Time for me to take off, Bruno,' I told him.

'Really? You don't sound very sure. You don't look very sure. In fact you look as though you're in two minds. Lost. Nothing new, of course.'

'Your laser judgement,' I said: 'And your intuition. Still in place.'

'What would I be without them? Just a man with a camera. To make a picture you have to know what lies behind it. The image is the easy part.'

'I remember.'

'So?' he asked me: 'What's the shadow—what's the trouble? You can tell me. Aren't we still friends? Aren't we like brothers? Feeling uneasy—is that it? Being back here, with your paradise of childhood so close by?'

'Did I ever talk about that time with you?'

'You used to speak of little else.'

'Don't exaggerate,' I said.

'I'm not. You don't see yourself that clearly: word people never seem to. You think you have a perfect front: a disguise against the world. You think it works so well that no one knows you; but all it does is stop you from knowing anyone. That's why you're better when you're part of a team; you need someone else around, someone to look out for you.'

'Is that right?' I said: 'You don't think you're reaching a little—extending your analysis too far?'

'No. Anyway—you were just getting going. Telling me your problems. Don't stop now. Keep on: although you don't actually need to. I can see the trap you're in: your precious past—it's too close up, and too far away.'

He looked at me. His smile had sympathy in it—an edge of amusement too. He had read me to perfection; he knew he had.

'Go on,' he prompted: 'I'd like to hear. I'll keep your secrets; you can trust me on that. I always have.'

And so, haltingly, I told him, or tried to tell him: how I still remembered those days of summer in the mountains and the figures I'd first known then; how there were times when they seemed close by me, almost present to me, when I could hear the sound of their voices in my head: and what he'd said was true—I did feel a longing to see those peaks and valleys, and the skies of my childhood: to walk the forest paths again.

'But you haven't gone back,' he broke in: 'And you won't. I can tell. It would have been easy for you—at any time. The simplest thing. The truth is you're careful to keep away. You'd rather stay safe in your nostalgia: you're afraid of disappointment: afraid you might destroy your imagined heaven. Nothing's changed in you. You want to keep the past intact; you don't see preserving it destroys the present: you hang on to an ideal: it makes you happy and sad at the same time—you're its hostage—you don't really live your life.'

'Strangely I've heard something like that before. But that doesn't make any of it true.'

'From your profound great-aunt.'

'Did I speak to you about her? Surely not!'

'Your fake great-aunt, to be exact. The Red Princess. Don't you remember anything? Or do you just block things out? When we first went off on assignment together she'd only just died. You were full of grief then: I'd almost want to say you were heartbroken.'

'I don't remember it that way.'

'It's true. You told me all about her. Long stories, every evening. Out in the desert, with the oilfields burning in the distance and lighting up the sky. Don't give me that look of disbelief: you did. And it was a normal thing to do. People share their stories; that's how they know each other. That's why they get along. That's why we get along.'

'And here I was thinking it was the charm of your nature and your propensity for passing judgement on your friends!'

'Ease up, brother,' he said then: 'Sarcasm's not your thing. So: what's the call?'

'Meaning?'

'Where to next for you? Where are you actually supposed to be headed next?'

'Back to Zürich. Three days free, then an onward flight.'

'You could come with me,' he said: 'Give me a ride.'

'Where to?'

'Not far—two hours, no more, the way you drive: a place called Mainau. It's near Konstanz: on the shore of the Bodensee. I've got a commission there.'

I laughed.

'Don't tell me you know it.'

'The flower island! I used to. I had another great-aunt—she liked to drive me out there when she collected me from boarding school on weekends.'

'Another one! How many were there?'

'Just two.'

'Both equally controlling?'

'In their different ways.'

'And which of them did you prefer?'

'What kind of question is that to ask me? What would you expect me to say? It was long ago: I look back now and I can see they went together. They were perfect opposites. One without the other would have been unbearable. I think they knew that themselves.'

'You mean they worked in tandem.'

'I mean they served as counters to each other.'

'Fire and water,' said Bruno, firmly: 'The way the world works. You were lucky to have that shown to you so young. Let's drive.'

We did: the road wound its way towards the lake. He told me stories from his most recent journeys—wild exploits. Then he began to reminisce; his youth in São Paulo; how he escaped; the teacher who gave him his first camera; what happened to it; how he found it again; the dreams he still had of going home—dreams unfulfilled.

'You too,' I said.

'Of course. Why else would I be so interested in your story—if it wasn't my own? That's why we're on the road together—that's why we always used to end up working together. You know that: we both live in transit, always moving, we're airport people—we've both been made to realise there's no way of going back.'

I took this in: I let the thought sit with me, and said nothing in reply.

'You don't agree?'

'I think I always have,' I said.

We had made good time; we were across the border now, past Konstanz. I turned off the motorway.

'How easy the journey's been,' I said to him. 'And look how far we've come. Here's the road to Mainau, up ahead. I wanted to keep you talking a while longer. I wanted to hear your ayahuasca story, about the jaguars with diamond eyes—the one you began telling me when we were together last.'

'Yes,' he said, 'that's a real saga. Too late: a shame. But I'm happy that we've seen each other again: it makes me think our lives have a shape—a symmetry—if only we can read it: find the code.'

'And you're convinced of that?'

'It's a working hypothesis. Maybe one day we'll know for sure.'

I pulled up. He jumped out and shouldered his camera bag. We walked along the causeway to the island slowly, side by side.

'I could wait for you,' I said: 'If you're not too long. What is it that you're actually doing here?'

He gave me an enigmatic smile. 'See the glow on the lake from the sun through the clouds: what an image: how full of mystery. We'll never really know what makes beauty, will we? See you.'

'That's a sad-sounding goodbye,' I said.

'Beauty always makes me sad,' he answered: 'That's what it's for.'

And he strode off down the avenue of tall trees toward the buildings in the distance, his gait even, his bearing self-assured. I watched until he was no longer in sight, and wondered if I would ever see him again, and realised the same thought had occurred to him. I turned away.

I was about to retrace my steps when I saw a narrow path that ran beside the shoreline: winding, shaded, half-overgrown: and in that instant I knew it was the same zigzag path I used to take with Ady, so many years before. I followed it, trying to picture her and my young self beside her, memories of the days we spent together coming back to me, each image leading to another, each more vivid than the one preceding it: I was caught up in them: summoning them up, receiving them—it was almost a surprise when the path curved round to its end. I was at the entrance to the island's little harbour. Halfway along the jetty was a man in an overcoat, facing towards the far shoreline, taking in the view. He turned and watched my approach.

'Hello, friend,' he called out to me.

I stared back at him. He was in his middle years; his features were soft and pleasant; the red scarf at his neck was loose in the breeze.

He tossed it back over his shoulder, then raised up his hands, palms open, as though to prove peaceful intent.

'That's not a very friendly look,' he said.

'Am I your friend?' I answered: 'What makes me that?'

'Why the pensive air?'

'It's reflective—not pensive.'

'What are you reflecting on, then?'

'Memories: from here; elsewhere: people; what they were—the usual things.'

'Time in its passage,' he said. 'The past—unmastered, constantly receding from us—it's hard to bear, isn't it—the way we're so estranged from what we once were?'

'I think I'll keep on moving,' I said.

'Wait. Maybe you need to talk to someone: maybe me.'

'And maybe not.'

'Don't be in such a hurry. Conversation with a stranger can be liberating.'

'Is that right? Are you a priest or something, looking for a confession to hear: a conscience to ease?'

'I might be. And you might benefit.'

'I'll pass, and take my chances,' I said.

'Or I could even be an angel. One of the thirty angels sent to save the world.'

'Thirty-six,' I said.

'What?'

'Thirty-six, not thirty—and they're not angels, they're the hidden figures of humility. If you're going to quote the Talmud, it's probably best to get it right.'

'Theology's not my strong point, to be truthful with you. And I'm not really an angel, I'm an ecological investigator.'

'Almost the same thing, these days,' I said.

He made a little bow, and we shook hands.

'And you look after this place?'

'Not in a formal capacity,' he said: 'Though I study it. For the most part the rarer botanical specimens, of course.'

'It must lift up your spirits, spending time in such surrounds.'

'You mean it's peaceful—harmonious—all the elements in communion with each other: nature in its lush profusion, the great bowl of the sky, the shining water, the whole framed, completed by the graceful works of man.'

'I might have put it more succinctly,' I said. 'But yes.'

'It seems so, on the surface, doesn't it? The opposite is the truth. When I come here I fight the darkness every day.'

I looked back at him.

'You don't know the history—what happened here?'

'I remember it used to be a Swedish possession—isn't that right?'

'It is. It was: then wartime came. Shall I go on?'

'I can guess the general drift.'

'But you need the details. What's history without the fine particulars: the specifics that give us the truth of life?'

And he launched into a recitation that had a rehearsed, perfected quality about it: it had wit; it had pace; it had surprises and twists in the telling.

'A new chapter now,' he said, and his voice dropped down in sombre fashion: 'After all the early battles—once the war had begun in earnest—it was the time of Speer.'

He paused. 'Normally, at this point, people ask me if I mean the architect.'

'I already know about his plan to build villas along the lake shore for the men who ran his weapons factories.'

'You do?' he said, sounding rather crestfallen: 'I imagine it would have been something like those grand projects they're building on artificial islands in Dubai today. But I'm sure you don't know about the French connection to Mainau, do you?'

'Why should I?' I said: 'I'm not French.'

'I didn't think you were. It's a story for all civilised people to know:

no matter where they come from—even if they don't have any nationality, even if they're homeless in the world.'

'So—tell me.'

'Let's sit, then. Here, on the bench beside the barrier, looking out: why not? We'll sit together: spend a few minutes—perhaps longer. We can watch the light as it changes: it's majestic here—we'll let it lift our spirits up.'

And he resumed, his eyes on my expression as he spoke: Mainau as the headquarters of French collaborators when the war was in its dying days, Mainau in the French occupation zone, Mainau as reception camp for French survivors brought from Dachau after the liberation of the camps, as their burial place. He paused again.

'Well?' he asked me: 'Now what do you think?'

'What anyone would: that the stain of that time seems to reach everywhere. That it's spread out over every part of this poor continent.'

'That stain is history,' he said then, in a triumphant voice: 'The history that sweeps us all up. And the shadow never goes: we're always in the shadow—even if we try to hide from it or quarantine it, even if we pretend that it's not there, polluting everything, defiling everything the way a dust cloud discolours the whole sky. And so we put our trust in ignorance. Like you. Look at you: you know this place, you thought you knew its past—you know the standard version—but you didn't know what I just told you—you had no idea.'

'How could I have?' I said: 'I was eight or nine years old the last time I came here. My great-aunt used to bring me with her on days out from school.'

'Because she felt the shadow! And wanted to expiate it.'

'Not at all—she loved coming here, it made her happy: she always said Mainau was beautiful. It was convenient—it was nearby. And she thought coming here was good for my cultural education as well.'

'Why?'

'She said Wagner found the inspiration for *Parsifal* here beside the lake, when he looked out at the peaks after the first falls of winter snow.'

'Pure mythology. Like all those Wagner stories: I've even heard people say the inspiration for the *Rheingold* theme came to him when he was sailing down the Italian coast from Genoa to La Spezia. People say anything they want about art. At least she was a Wagnerian, though, your great-aunt: that counts for something.'

'But she wasn't. She was the exact opposite. She couldn't stand Wagner—she thought he was responsible for all the formlessness in modern art: music, painting, everything. She thought he was a monster—a manipulator of emotions—the composer who made sensation and sentiment respectable: she said if she listened to him for too long she felt as though she was about to dissolve.'

'Why listen to his music at all then?'

'She didn't have much choice—she was married to a conductor—a Wagner specialist.'

'Indeed: and who was that?'

'Novogrodsky.'

The man's face lit up. 'The Maestro—how wonderful: this is wonderful!' He jumped up from his seat, he reached out as if to clasp me by the shoulders, then checked himself: he paced about, he swung back and looked at me with earnest eyes.

'I knew it,' he said in an exultant voice: 'I knew there was a reason behind it—it wasn't just coincidence, my running into you here, my being here today. I wish I could tell you what I feel now—how much Novo meant to me: he was like a hero in my mind, a god in music: I had all his recordings, I went through every interview he gave: I made up something like a private cult of him: how lucky you are to have known such a genius!'

'I didn't, really,' I began to say; he spoke over me, his voice rising.

'I saw him conduct, several times, in fact—in Zürich, in Salzburg, of course, and Munich and Vienna, even at the festival at Bregenz on the far side of the lake: and those were always red-letter days for me. I used to watch him on the podium, follow his movements, study him—see him reaching up as if he was touching the hidden texture of the music—and no performance of a piece was ever the same as the one before, or the one that came after—each time he built a new world of sound—from air—from nothing: I came to think he fed on his musicians; even on the audience and their energies: as if we were all cocooned together in the auditorium, our minds joined in a single task. I treasured those evenings I spent watching him, listening. I had the feeling he was giving me a brief escape from life: raising me up towards the stars.'

'I've heard things like that said about Novogrodsky before,' I said then: 'Often, actually: his stage presence, his majestic air.'

'But that's not how he was in person. I met him once. We spoke: as equals: he was warm; he was charming; he was modest: he told me he was gripped by fear each time he went out on stage to conduct: and that was the reason he gave up studio recording—because the anguish that built up in him was too much to bear. Fear was the royal road to purity in art, he said. Whoever fears is on the pathway to be followed: whoever knows true fear can breach the limits of the self. He told me this in all seriousness: as if he was imparting a great secret to me— something for me alone.'

'And it's a treasured memory for you?'

'Naturally. It was at the end of an evening I won't forget: a recital: a private gathering. You know how much Novo hated those kinds of events: he'd somehow held on to the idea he was an artist for the people: but my uncle persuaded him: he was a sponsor of that orchestra of young musicians the Maestro was setting up just then. We all were there: at the villa, on the lake shore: a perfect setting: a glass conservatory with majestic views. Novo was late; we waited patiently, all in our seats: an hour—longer, even. The weather changed: a storm came up: thunder rolling between the mountains: lightning stabbing down. At last he made his grand entrance, entourage behind him. He strode to the piano: no introduction—nothing—not a word. I don't know what we'd been expecting him to play: Bartók, maybe, Chopin, even Janáček—music from that hinterland, that tradition. What he chose that night was quite different. He launched in: it was like a military attack. Scarlatti sonatas, one after the other, virtuoso pieces, swift, cascading, violent, no breaks between them, no score to read from—just a man and his powers, calling up the elements, challenging the storm: it strengthened—the rain poured down on us, it drummed on the conservatory's glass roof—he played on. It was a sublime half-hour—I was transfixed: I could scarcely breathe. When it all was over he stood, gave an amiable, compact bow and stepped away into the throng. At once, as if on cue, the rain slackened; the storm was past. The audience clapped politely: they were the usual businessmen and culture brokers and minor Austrian nobility—they had no idea what they'd just been witness to. I waited. I could see the dignitaries, and the Maestro, surrounded; caught. I don't believe his wife was with him, in point of fact: I don't think I saw her.'

He looked across at me.

'You wouldn't have missed her if she'd been there that night,' I said: 'She stood out. Tranquil face, lovely clothes, golden hair.'

'No—no one like that. A secretary of some kind, dark and bent and gloomy—and an assistant who was always standing with Novo, close beside him—a young woman, Central Asian, I think, very striking, black hair, hard eyes. I edged my way through towards them. I made a sign to my uncle: he liked me: he beckoned to me to come up. "Make a little space for my favourite nephew," he said: "He has an artistic streak." "Uncle Urs," I said—'

I broke in. 'Wait: what was your uncle's name—family name, I mean?'

He gave a sad smile: he inclined his head. 'Yes,' he said: 'I can see you've worked it out. It was inevitable. You're right, of course. He was Amborn—that famous, notorious, unfortunate Amborn—whose name's remembered now for one thing only.'

'I have no idea what you're talking about,' I said.

'Really not?' He gave me a suspicious stare.

I shrugged. 'None at all.'

'So—where were you in the late nineteen-eighties? Taking a long vacation on a different planet?'

'In a way: I was working in the Soviet Union and the Eastern Bloc. Not much news from outside reached us back then.'

'But the scandal was all about the East! You do know my uncle Urs was an arms dealer, don't you?'

'Precision guidance systems, I thought. And medical equipment.'

'Among other things.'

'And he had a foundation.'

'Among other things: like export-import companies in Sofia, and a Kazakh goldmine and ties to Moscow and a private militia in the Middle East. There was a problem with one of his subsidiaries: minor—financial. It became public: an investigation began. All this not long after the recital at the villa on the lake. My uncle loved that place; he designed it himself. He called it the Villa Sorgenfrei—a bad choice—God knows where he got the name.'

'I can't imagine,' I said.

'And all this passed you by? There were front-page stories everywhere: Zürich, Munich; I think even the United States. It was a witch-hunt; it gathered strength. He tried to defend himself: he insisted he was innocent, wholly innocent: he'd been made a scapegoat; he was working for the West, and governments knew it; foreign ministries knew it: they could vouch for him; they could clear his name.'

'And what happened then?'

'What always happens. There were inquiries, reports—no clear evidence against him, no charges, just rumours and vague stories of misdeeds and the sense of murk persisting, deepening. He lost his board seats: his friends and business partners pledged their loyalty and drifted away. I know the rest from his daughter: we were close at that time. He tried to salvage what he could; his contracts ran out; he had large fines and legal costs to meet: he sold off what was saleable: he stayed away from Konstanz, and spent his time at the villa, always on his own. Early one morning, before daybreak, he went down to the conservatory. He opened the double doors that looked out across the Bodensee so he could see the first sunlight on the water: then he shot himself through the head.'

He fell silent.

'A bleak ending to your story,' I said.

'But it's not the end—it wasn't the end at all: at least not for me. My uncle left something behind him: a letter, for his daughter. Handwritten—it was lying on the desk in his study, the pen he wrote it with still open. She showed it to me a while later, after she'd been alone with it long enough. She felt it was also meant for me; that I should read it—it would speak to me. I told her she should have it published: along with the essays her father wrote from time to time: for art exhibitions, for the feuilletons. He had a strength of intellect: but he believed in reticence: he used to say there were things he'd lived through he never wished to tell.'

'But what was in the letter?'

'He wrote about his love for her: his wish for her to lead a happy life.'

'And did she?'

'She's not with us anymore. Please—let me continue.'

I made a sign: he did.

'He said nothing about his troubles. He set out his beliefs for her: he was convinced life had meaning, nobility and purpose—both in the living, and at its end. And if there was a force greater than us, set above us, that force showed itself in symmetry and pattern, in the forms of nature, in art too, art that clarifies our picture of the world. He wrote about his life: how he wished he'd told her more about his childhood: in Vienna; in dark years. The people who shaped him and made him what he was when he was growing up were all easterners, from Europe's furthest edge. Ever since that time it had been his aim to bring East and West together: the people he felt closest to all came from that other Europe, and only lived a life of exile here.'

'Hence Novogrodsky.'

'And others, too. Then he drew to a close. He asked her forgiveness. He knew how fragile she was. He feared for her. She had been his greatest joy; the purest joy on earth was a parent's love. When she was a child, and they lived in Basel and he was building up his empire, she'd asked him what he most valued in life—and he'd told her: not possessions, but ideas—ideas that give us the eyes to see beyond ourselves and our surrounds, that let us seek truth in the chaos of the world. But now, he wrote, he'd changed his mind: it was words that were the magic gift in life: each word was a wonder, each word was a crystal gleaming in the light of language: where he was bound, though, there would be no need of them any longer, world and individual would be joined as one. He ended on that: it wasn't a sacrifice for him to leave this earth: he would see the sun shine on the water and feel reborn.'

'And that was it?'

'That was it.'

'A disturbing kind of farewell letter.'

'Beautiful and disturbing: that's what gave it such special force. My version just then was nothing like the original—what he wrote was plain and majestic at once. The only thing I've ever come across that made the faintest sense of suicide.'

'It must have affected you,' I said: 'You would have been quite young then.'

'I could think for myself. I had an engineering degree—a good one. I'd started down that track: I was already doing site work in Africa: it was in the air that I'd end up working for the Amborn group; that door closed when the scandal hit. I changed course. In part because of my uncle, and what he'd written, and what I took from it. It seemed like a summons: I felt he was commanding me—don't waste your life; don't put your faith in power; live for truth.'

'And did you?'

'That depends on your perspective. I look back now and find I don't see that time clearly; it's as if it was lived through on my behalf by someone else. I had to leave: get away—that was obvious. I knew the curator who'd looked after my uncle's art: we spoke often in those days: I confided in him. He was well-connected; he pulled strings for me—he helped me into a place at the art school in Düsseldorf—the academy, the famous one, where Beuys and all the other sacred monsters used to prowl around. That seemed the right idea. Answer a death with new beginnings. I'd wanted to see the world in new ways. Free myself from everything unexamined that I'd learned: reject the passions of mankind. I travelled north: to my new home. I was out of luck! It was that time when the two Germanies were coming together. The academy was a madhouse of politics. The students there all knew my story. They treated me as though I came from tainted stock: either I was an eastern spy or an agent of western capital—or both at once.'

'And you stayed on there, despite that?'

'I kept to myself: I studied in art the way I used to study in the sciences. I made my artworks the way I used to run experiments. I was my own experiment: a project in self revision. No one among the professors there found anything I did of interest. But one good thing came from it. A wondrous thing. It opened up a new world for me. I was able to see Hombroich.' He gave me a questioning look.

'I don't think I've ever heard the name,' I said.

'When I found my way there it seemed like the garden of delights—and I needed something to light up my world. I was lost in the academy. The only people I was at ease with were the technicians. One of them told me about a collector who'd bought an estate outside the city to house his art. Nothing special, I thought: that's what all rich Germans do. Soon the whole of reunited Germany will be an archipelago of museums set up by millionaires who want to be remembered for something other than what they were. Just like the courts of baroque times: tiny kingdoms devoted to their own prestige and nothing else. "Remember who you're talking to," I told the technician: "I'm from the world of capital. I know the syndrome." "Go and see before you write it off," he said: "There's nowhere like it. It's called Hombroich. It's still being developed: it has a purity about it. There are secrets there, if you have eyes to see them. Go."

'One weekend I did. It was January: ice on the roads; that ghastly yellow-grey sky you see in the depths of winter there. I found the site:

surrounded by open fields; down narrow back roads—quiet. It was unattended—at least I saw no one there. I found a way in—steep metal steps down: a green expanse, a valley, sheltered, a stream flowing through it, meadows, trees, mist swirling everywhere, and rising up in that mist the shapes of buildings, strange shapes, a handful of them, like temples, each one geometric, each one with open doorways and wide windows that seemed to draw the landscape in. They were empty—the first few I saw—then I found others: a gallery that held abstract works, large canvases, all laid out on the concrete floor like stepping stones—and nearby another pavilion, high up, set apart: it was dank, and ill-lit—when I first went in it felt like a shrine or some freshly excavated ancient tomb. My eyes adjusted. I made out etchings and prints and paintings on its walls—hung in an odd way—in disorder—in mockery of order. New work by East German artists; old blurred photographs; Dutch treasures from the Golden Age. Was that what I was meant to see? Was that the secret my technician friend had been hinting at? An end to all hierarchies—art shown without context: art judged on its form alone. The logic of the place sank in on me: I stayed for hours, meandering, exploring, making new discoveries, losing my way. There were footbridges that led nowhere; forking paths that doubled back onto themselves—there was a portico that held Asian statues, a line of figures, staring out; they seemed at home, perfectly so: and beyond them, in the open, wooden sculptures, grouped together: suggestive, monumental—they looked like shapes found in nature: they may have been. And who was the collector, I asked myself: what scheme had guided him. Later, of course, I found the answers to my questions—but by then the questions hardly mattered. I knew what I'd seen there: it was a theory brought to life; it was the negative of Versailles and all the lovely gardens of the West. A garden where nature itself was the art form, and human art its frame.'

As he was telling me this, one of the ferry boats from the far shore came into view. It was some way off; its course changed; it drew towards us. I followed it with my eyes.

He continued speaking. His voice became insistent. 'That's when it came to me. When I understood the message in the note my uncle left. It was time for me to forget my own ambitions; let the four winds scatter them. The finest artwork I could ever make would be in nature. That was what lay ahead for me. That's why I redesigned my life.'

'All this from a single visit?'

'It was an epiphany: it changed me, it struck through to my heart— to the centre of my being. It was given to me only when I was ready to receive it: I saw that nature's patterns exceed ours: that's the mystery at our beginning—and our end.'

We could hear the ferry now: it slowed, and drifted in towards the pier: its engine made a grinding noise. My companion turned.

'And here it is. The lake steamer from Meersburg: always without passengers—always perfectly on time. Ready to bear me away. See where it came from—over there—the haze, the clouds—there'll be a storm this evening.'

'Like the night Novogrodsky played,' I said to him: 'I'm sorry I brought out such sad memories in you.'

'You're wrong: Those were the golden times for me. The memories I treasure most. I'm grateful to you. Stories told to strangers are the best and richest.'

I was about to speak: he held up his hand.

'No farewells. Never farewells. We'll say au revoir instead. Once you've come across someone you see them again and again. It's pattern, not coincidence.'

'That's what you find?'

'Always—people keep coming back to you—you can count on it.'

And he climbed on board with light steps, looked round in my direction, then waved as the ferry made its slow turn from the pier and began to glide away. I drove to Konstanz down the coast road, my mind full: Bruno; Ady; the stranger, his tale, its music, the rhythms in his story: sounds, vistas, voices, little details—how much past we carry inside ourselves, I thought: that's what memory really is: it's weight, it pulls and pulls—and what would death be but that moment when the weight becomes too much, the self gasps and gives way. The sun was low by now, the light soft: here was the Rhine Bridge, rail and road together, the inner town ahead, the monastery hotel: how familiar it all was—I still knew the streets and one-way system, I even knew the short-cuts and the turns to make.

I pulled up outside the hotel, took the last space in a row of Mercedes sedans and went in. A young man in a fine suit eyed me from behind the reception desk, and welcomed me in an unwelcoming way. I glanced around: the counter made from choir-stall wood, the arched windows, the cloister walk that led towards the guest rooms—I remembered them as well.

'Here for the council, sir?' he asked me, sounding sceptical.

'The council?'

'The council of European private banks.'

'Actually no,' I said, and thought I might have done well to say yes and go from there.

'Reservation?'

'No again.'

'Your name?'

I told him.

'Unusual. Have you stayed with us before? It should be easy to find your details.'

'A long time ago.'

'Our record keeping's excellent.'

'I have no trouble believing that,' I answered.

He looked at his screen, typed, and made a slight whistling sound as he scrolled through. Then he stopped, a look of triumph on his face.

'It was a while ago, for sure. Booked by a Madame Novogrodsky.'

'That sounds right.'

'On the account of her husband. *The* Novogrodsky—the conductor—can it be?'

I nodded.

His manner changed perceptibly. 'How wonderful,' he said: 'We have a suite for you—with views across the lake. We're happy you've come back to us. If there's anything...'

And so it went. A porter with dramatic features and long black hair appeared.

'Raimundo will show you up—and even tell you something of the history of the building on the way, won't you, Raimundo?'

We walked along: down corridors, through the old cloister, past the high-vaulted breakfast room with frescoes on the walls. The porter began his narrative.

'No need to worry about all that, Raimundo,' I said to him.

'It's Ramun,' he said, 'if you want to be kind and human to me.'

'A Romansh name?'

He nodded his head: we had reached the room. The balcony's French windows were open on the lake: it was almost sunset: the light had turned the water shades of gold and dazzling red.

'How magnificent,' I said, trying to sound appreciative.

'You get used to it, I find,' the porter said. 'It's like that almost every evening: a scene of blood and violence on the lake. Shall I turn the television on for you?'

Without waiting for an answer he clicked the remote control and a vast screen sprang to life: a Swiss newsreader was staring intently out at us, his expression at once disarming and grave.

'And now, if you don't need anything else.'

'Wait,' I said: 'Please: Ramun. Is there a news broadcast in Romansh?'

He gave me a look of surprise. 'Yes. Just for a few minutes every evening—round about now, as it happens—but it's on another channel.'

'Could you switch to it?'

'You know Romansh?'

'Not at all: I wish I did. I used to hear it being spoken, when I was young. In hotels, for the most part, in the Engadine: and I heard people singing in it, praying in it—I loved listening to its sound; someone once told me it was the most beautiful of all languages, and if everyone spoke it there'd be no more wars in the world.'

He smiled on hearing that. He clicked through the channels on the remote, then stopped: there was a picture of an arctic mountain range on the screen, and the soft sound of a man's voice: blurry syllables, spoken fast.

'Shall I translate for you?' he asked.

'I'd like that.'

He stood beside me, his manner serious, one hand to his chin, and began to whisper in my ear.

'It's a strange story: it's about science. Scientists looking for rocks—in the Russian far east.'

'Go on,' I said, and in that moment distinctly heard the newsreader pronounce two place names that I knew: Magadan and Anadyr. 'What's he saying?'

'It's complicated. I'm trying to understand.'

Images appeared on the screen: a group of figures lined up in hiking clothes; a tracked vehicle plunging into a river; more mountains, again snow-covered; a sea coast; a piece of rock in close-up.

'I think I see now,' Ramun said: 'Why are you interested in this?'

'Tell me—before you forget.'

'So: long ago, in Soviet times, explorers went out into the Koryak Mountains: to a river called Khatyrka—a remote place: deep in the wilderness.'

'Yes—near Anadyr. And?'

'They collected rock samples there: one in particular was something strange: something that seemed completely new. The rock was sold abroad: it was in a collection, in Italy, in a museum. There was a special kind of crystal in it—they call it quasicrystal now. They were a dream of science. No one thought they could be formed on earth. I'll listen more.'

There were interviews, brief, with voiceover, more narration, the sounds soft, elusive, running into each other—a further set of images, then, abruptly, the newsreader smiled and brought his hands together in front of him, a theme tune played: the program was at its end.

'They're saying the rock came from a meteorite: a rare kind: older than the earth and all the other planets. At first it was a great mystery, a problem: where did the sample come from; how was it found. Then it turned into a detective story: a hunt: they traced the first prospector: he was in Moscow: he knew the site: he led an expedition back there: to the same Khatyrka river—western scientists—they were talking to them on the bulletin, about what they experienced: hard conditions; mosquitoes biting; bears prowling round—they dug and dug; they found more samples: everything confirmed the first ideas. It's just been announced in scientific journals. Crystals of a new kind, that came from space; that date from the time before the earth was made.'

He broke off.

'That's all they said?'

'It's not enough? Are you a scientist: a geologist?'

'No,' I answered: 'Not at all. It's just that story was like an echo of something that I heard once—a long while ago—and never thought I'd hear about again.'

'I have to go back,' he said: 'I'm glad to have spoken to you.'

'I'm glad to have heard you,' I said: 'Glad to have heard that news in such a perfect language.'

He went. I looked out: the lake's surface was deep grey now, the slate grey of an undeveloped film. I could make out a faint pulse of motion on the water—unending variations in a monotone. I watched until the dark had become absolute before surrendering to sleep.

It was a bad night: broken, memory-laden dreams. Dawn approached: I watched the sun come up: after a decent interval I went downstairs and found a corner alcove in the breakfast room, drank coffee, and gazed up at the painted saints and bishops on the walls. There was a long table beneath the high window: a group of men, grey-haired, were occupying it, speaking softly to each other, making expressive gestures, their manner relaxed and elegant, their voices rising and falling in a rhythmic, pleasant hum. I glanced across at them: the private bankers—in their element: I was about to look away. I stopped. Could it be?

I looked more closely: it was—my old friend David Blaize was there among them, seated at the head of the table, saying little, watching the movements of his companions, hands joined together as if in prayer. How long since I'd last been in touch with him? A year—more? The two of us had shared our schooldays, and our student life: there had never been a rift between us, or a slackening in our friendship, despite the different paths we followed: we saw each other often, on his travels or mine, but the meetings that seemed warmest were the handful that came about by pure chance. I smiled to myself as I watched him there—at which point he saw me, tilted his head back in a silent laugh, rose from the table, said something to the man beside him and made his way across.

'I won't say I'm astonished to see you here,' he began: 'Although any time you're seen in Europe, any time you're in a western city should be cause for amazement, shouldn't it? You here—in the lost and drifting west, the home you won't return to—but I'm not that surprised: I caught sight of you for a moment just the other day, at least I think I did—in Davos—at the summit.'

'You were there? I didn't see you—and I'm supposed to be a trained observer.'

'Supposed being the operative word. I was keeping a low profile. I was advising the US delegation.'

'You're not American.'

'Not in the strict sense of the term, no—but I am a financier; that seems to count as honorary citizenship in some circles over there.'

'I see,' I said.

'I doubt that, on the whole—but no matter. How relieved I am to see you again.'

'You always say that—you even sound relieved—it's as if you think we're survivors of some dreadful conflict raging all around us: some nightmarish guerrilla war.'

'But we are: surely you know that: our war against time. The invisible war. The war we'll have to lose one day. Plans—for the morning?'

'Of course.'

'Cancel them: I've got something better for you. An adventure.'

'Your track record in that area hasn't been that great in recent years, though, has it—if you think back? The car crash in Canyonlands; you losing our passports in Bogotá; and then there was the unfortunate episode in Yellowknife.'

'Those were false adventures: what we used to think of as adventures—indulgent games, efforts at self-escape—not activities of self-fulfilment, not projects tied to what we need to experience: need to see and take in to ourselves. I mean a true adventure: a proper one; one fitting for you. You won't regret it.'

'This activity wouldn't have any tie to art collecting, would it, by some strange chance?'

'It might. You know it's my religion, it's what gives me the greatest joy I find in life.'

'There's no end to it—you don't feel you've gone down that road far enough?'

'There's been a change. I've been rethinking things. Twombly died a year ago: I'm sure you heard. He meant a great deal to me. When that happened I couldn't bear to have his paintings up: I realised that after death there has to be a period of eclipse: for the art as well. I looked around the rooms at home in Cologny: it was like being in a mausoleum: a shrine to the glorious dead. I decided on recalibration. I began giving my attention to a different kind of work. Precision, not expression: the modest and the grounded, not the wild sublime. A trend in keeping with the present. Art of rigour. Art that measures what we see of our world—that's what I'm collecting now.'

'Almost like starting again?'

He agreed, but at that moment a tall figure wearing a bright red scarf came in, made his way over to the bankers at their table and joined them. He glanced around the room, spotted us and inclined his head in greeting. It was the man I had spoken with on the pier at Mainau: I looked across again: it was him.

'Who's that—the man with the scarf who just came in?'

'Schoenfeld? He's the chairman of our little group. Do you know him?'

I explained. Blaize laughed.

'And he said he was an ecologist? That's amusing. He's a good story-teller—and technically it's true, in a distant kind of way: he runs an investment fund. It's called Deep Chlorophyll. It makes money, that's for sure.'

'And did he have some connection to Amborn: Urs Amborn and his bank?'

'That rings a bell.'

'They were related.'

'Most people are related to each other in some fashion in this milieu: it's like a family—only with incest.'

'And there was a scandal—and Amborn and his empire fell apart. You must know about it.'

'No need to be quite so quick to judge: there was a re-engineering of assets. Amborn cut a few corners dealing with the East, that's all. It was a long time ago. Scandals come along in banking; they serve their purpose, and then they go—into oblivion. It's the norm. No one here's completely innocent of financial sin.'

'How reassuring,' I said.

Blaize ignored this. His expression changed. 'I want to tell you something.'

He fixed his eyes on me.

'You sound serious.'

'I am. Each time I've seen you in the last few years, I've thought the same thing. I've never told you—I've been a bad friend to you that way—but now I have the feeling the right time's come.'

'Go on.'

'You live like a nomad: still. Whenever I hear from you and hear where you are I can't help thinking it shouldn't be that way: with you always moving, always a stranger among strangers, taking hotels for your home.'

'Why tell me now? You know it goes with the terrain: with what I do. And I seem to remember you living in a hotel once—it was a very extended stay.'

'Three months in the Carlyle during a divorce isn't the same thing as years at a stretch in Bangkok or Beirut.'

'Your point?'

'I don't believe it's chance when our paths cross, like this morning. I've never really believed in chance. Materialists don't.'

'Fate instead?'

'I've come to think the pieces of a life join up as you live on—they start to make sense. You can read them.'

'And mine say what?'

'Listen to me. Take what I'm telling you to heart. I'm the only friend you have who knows what your life was like when we were at school together. Who it was that brought you up, and how. Those two old twisted gargoyles!'

I looked up at him in surprise.

'How strange,' I said: 'Strange you say this now.'

'Why's that?'

'They've been in my thoughts—for the first time in ages. Because of where we are.'

'I'm sure they're always in your head: that's exactly what they wanted. Remember: I saw you with them when they were in their glory—in full flight. They treated you as if you were clay for them to refashion in their own image. I know what they were—monsters of vanity and pride. Mesmerising ones, it's true, with a glamour of a kind about them—but monsters just the same.'

'You're talking about the two people I loved most in the world.'

'I'm afraid I know that too. I've always known it—I wish I didn't have to say all this to you. I wish I didn't have to bring them up at all.

Are you actually going to disagree with my description of them?'

'They were émigrés. Exiles: adrift in the world. They had the features of the breed. I can see what you're building up to; what you're going to tell me next: that I'm repeating the pattern of their lives; that I live like them; it's years since they died—and I'm still under their spell. But it's not true. They didn't like the path I chose—they did everything they could to stop me. There were showdowns: dreadful scenes. I almost had to break with them—in a sense I did. Nothing was ever quite the same afterwards. You didn't hear about any of that when it was happening. You were living in Hong Kong—remember?'

'I remember what it cost you. You think you won that struggle: I think they did. They live on in you. You're a bird of passage, just the way they were. That's their legacy to you—your inheritance. I'm right about them, and you know it.'

'I certainly can't fault you for lack of candour, Blaize,' I said.

'That's a sad smile. I know you so well—but when we talk like this I realise you don't want to know yourself.'

'It's not the task of a storyteller to know himself—but to see and describe others.'

'In seeing other people you reflect yourself.'

'You undo yourself.'

At this he laughed his silent laugh again, and shook his head.

'No comeback to that! What an exchange. Down to bedrock. Let's make tracks.'

He led the way outdoors.

'Where to?'

'Jump in,' he said.

'Into this? Seriously?'

He was standing by a sleek sports car. Its top was down: he rested one hand on the steering wheel, swung his legs over the low door into the driver's seat and eased himself in.

'Plenty of room. Like it? I had a gull-wing for a while last year, but it was just impossible: everywhere I drove I was afraid of damaging it—it was like owning a Fabergé egg and taking it out on the road. This one's another story: spare parts are easy: you can drive as you like—do what you want.'

'Has it been in many accidents?'

'Nothing major—not as yet.'

He reversed back, twirled the wheel, sped out onto the main road, just missed a truck coming in the opposite direction and eased into the far lane.

'See—handles well. I bought it for my new wife, actually, as a wedding present; just for when we're at the summer house at Annecy. But she didn't like it: she thought it was too small, too petite: she said she was afraid her long hair would get caught up in the wheels and she'd be strangled, like Isadora Duncan: involuntary suicide.'

'A joke?'

'In bad taste—but that's one of her special charms. You'll take to her: she's intoxicating. She's lovely.'

'What happened to the last one?'

'You know these kinds of marriages aren't meant to be permanent. They're more like chapters in a life. Friendships are what stay; loves and passions, they go. Each new marriage comes from a shift in sensibility.'

'It's that clear-cut with you?'

'Absolutely—they point to a prevailing cast of mind: a philosophy, even. You see that all the time with artists: new wife, new style. Marriages work for a period, then they don't—the mist of the initial strangeness starts to rise—the flaws in the compact become clear.'

We were in open country now: he accelerated past a line of trucks.

'So wonderful—pure sensation—the wind of life. Don't you find that? Or are you still annoyed because of what I said?'

He turned in his seat to look at me.

'I'd watch the traffic,' I replied: 'Where are we going, anyway? We're on the slow road along the shore. It'll take us to St. Gallen in the end: no mysteries or surprises for us there.'

'Relax. We're headed into an image: I'll explain when we arrive. For now—take a look.'

He handed me his mobile.

'See. That's it. Check it out. Right there—yes—you're looking at it: it's my screensaver.'

'A square of grey and white: a horizontal line. Not much to respond to.'

'Look properly: examine it, look into its texture—don't pretend to be a philistine. We'll be there soon. I promise you: the journey's worth it. It's a journey into depth. I was going to bring Sylvie here to see—but she decided at the last minute to stay behind. I like that—having space: having a wife who gives one space.'

'That's why you married her?'

'No—I married her because she looked so much like Proust's Odette.'

'Truthfully? She reminded you of a fictional character?'

'Odette was real to me: and I know what she looked like.'

'Real enough to me, too: but a thousand readers could have a thousand different images of her: otherwise what's the point in fiction? You might as well give up and go to arthouse movies instead.'

'But you're wrong! Completely—Odette's described: it's specific—there's no room left for the imagination—none. The second time Swann calls on her at home she's unwell, she receives him in a gown of crepe de chine, she looks at him with those great eyes of hers that seem so tired and sullen when there's nothing new around to light them up, and he's struck by her resemblance to Botticelli's Zipporah in the Sistine Chapel—and in that moment he falls in love with her: he's lost. Hold on!'

He braked hard, and swung the car into a sharp turn onto a side road. 'We're close now. You'll see what I'm talking about with your own eyes. It began in Luzern, of all places: three years ago: I was at a meeting of prime lenders: it was a wasted day—problems kept piling up. I turned it over to my number two, and walked out: along the waterfront, across the bridge towards the station. The sun was down below the mountains—it was almost dark, but the modern-art museum was still open: it gleamed in the murk, it looked inviting. I went up: there was a retrospective of an artist I'd heard of, but never given much attention—a Japanese artist: Sugimoto—Hiroshi Sugimoto—you probably know all about him.'

'Just the name.'

'That was how it was for me too until that day. The galleries were empty. I wandered in, thinking to myself: More photographic art, I can't bear this kind of thing, its limits and its archness and artifice— and that mood stayed with me for the first few minutes I was there. I went striding through, my thoughts and prejudices all in place, my eyes casual, my mind judging and rejecting everything I saw—then I came to a corner gallery with a single framed photograph on the wall facing me: black and white; a large square, bisected by a line dividing two fields of different greys, the image blurred—or so I thought. It held me: I looked and looked—from near—from far away. I realised then it was in focus: perfect focus—it was an image of indistinctness, of mist and blur, of optical effects. Yes, yes, I told myself as I was looking, staring: it's clear—I understand it, it's a depiction of the uncertainties in image-making, it's a reflection of the viewing eye: the elements are clear enough—light and dark, distance and nearness, the now and the eternal, clarity and delusion—every trite dichotomy the experts of the art world could list for you at a moment's notice. Those were my thoughts— but what I felt then was quite different. Horizon, line, the pale, shining light—it was our movement through time: our trajectory. The mystery: in a single diagram. Beyond me; familiar—as if I'd seen it in my dreams a million times. I looked at the wall text beside the work. I thought that might anchor it somehow; explain away its impact. The image dated from years earlier: it was a view of the sea taken in Cassis, of all places.

'I stepped back: tears were running down my cheeks. I tried to dab them away. "Is something wrong, sir," said a voice from close beside me: "Some misfortune?" It was a gallery attendant: a young woman in uniform, looking up at me. "Forgive me," I said: "I thought I was alone here." "Nothing to be forgiven for." I took a step away, and tried to compose myself. She followed me, and stood at my shoulder again. "We're closing soon," she said, almost whispering: "I have to escort you out." "Leave me in here," I said: "Please." "I don't think that would be a good idea," she answered: "The management wouldn't like that very much. You understand, don't you?" "Maybe I could buy the work," I said then, and realised how ridiculous that sounded. She smiled. "Maybe you could," she replied: "But not this evening." We walked out together through the galleries, and down in the elevator: out into the cold. "I too find it an image that stirs up deep feelings," she said then: "None of our visitors seem to notice it or pay any attention to it. I spend hours in that corner space alone." I went on my way along the darkened street. It was raining: I walked back to the hotel, unsure of quite what had happened to me. I'd never had that kind of reaction to a work of art before. Can you believe it? Me: the man of confidence and certainty: me—the king of arbitrage—the empire builder: subjugated—lost for words before a photograph of nothing—on my knees before an image a child could have made.'

'Easily enough,' I said.

'You know the question was rhetorical.'

'And did you—buy it?'

'That image in the evening gallery? Of course not, no—but it was the starting point for something: a new enthusiasm for me: a quest. Do you want to hear?'

'You're my oldest friend,' I said to him: 'I'm interested in everything you do. You know that. Tell me.'

'I was methodical. I made my enquiries. I spoke to the usual curators and consultants; contacted galleries. I was more seized by art in those first months than I had been since the days when we were wide-eyed and impressionable and Manhattan graffiti was coming up. Those golden days.'

'You believe that—and you were actually there!'

'So cynical! I studied Sugimoto's output. How he'd started out: his different phases, how each one led on to the next. The work I'd seen was part of a series: a sequence of seascapes, made all round the world, over a stretch of years: the schema identical in each one, only the sheen of the water and the light in the sky differing.'

'A set of variations?'

'Exactly: like music made visible. They were from remote coast-lines, almost all of them: in the South Pacific, on the Black Sea, the Great Lakes, the wildest seaboards of Japan. I began collecting them: I made a pact with myself that I'd visit all the places where those images had been made.'

'And did you?'

'It wasn't easy. I went first to Cape Breton Island; then Hok-kaido, the north coast of Norway, Lake Superior, Rügen on the Baltic, Crete: I became a traveller to places I'd never thought of seeing: empty beaches, barren headlands, cliffs without names. I prided myself on getting to the exact spot where Sugimoto went to make his images: and when I reached my goal I'd feel a great serenity, as if I'd brought the world into alignment with an ideal. And it was that way for me every time—except in a single case.'

Blaize had sped up as he was talking; he frowned, and gripped the steering wheel. We clattered over a level crossing; turned; turned again.

'You're going quite fast,' I said to him: 'Very, in fact.'

'You're not worried, are you? Ease back—enjoy it—we've been on much more alarming drives together. And there's a reason: I want to time my little story and the reveal at the end properly. It has to be like this. It so happens that the very last of the seascapes I bought was an image of the Bodensee—the lake seen from an Uttwil pier—it was the loveliest and strangest of them all—the one that gave least away—and here we are!'

He braked: the car lurched and screeched to a halt in front of a barrier: the pier and the lake were spread out in front of us: the water looked like plate glass, the far shore was shrouded in haze.

'That was really crazy,' I said.

He laughed. 'But beautiful, too! Aren't you proud to know someone who can make a quick burn down Swiss backroads into art—kinetic art.'

'I'm proud I've survived the friendship so far: I'd like to keep it that way.'

'And we shall. Let's walk out—along the pier. All the way into the emptiness. Not that pier, not that broken-down old one: this one—the long jetty with those hooked steel posts at its end and that steel arch that looks like the way down into hell. Ready? Coming with?'

'Can't wait.'

We walked out slowly, side by side. There was a shimmer on the lake's surface: the boundary between sea and sky began to blur.

'Storms come up when the air's damp like this,' Blaize said, then fell silent.

That silence stretched out. I began telling him an involved Pacific island story: the sequel to a journey we'd once made. He cut me off.

'Let me,' he said: 'Let me at least try: try to tell you what I brought you here to tell you. We've been here together before: you won't remember. With my father, when we were at the Lyceum Alpinum: he kept a boat then on the lake. We cruised all the way to Kreuzlingen and back, and put in here. A happy day.'

'You're right: I don't remember. And you don't often bring him up.'

'But I still feel a kind of sympathy for him. I made sure to lead the kind of life he couldn't. I learned from his example. That's what he did for me.'

'Are you going back into your past now—reliving it, resurrecting it: doing what you were just complaining about me doing?'

'Not at all: I don't revisit what's been before. On the contrary. I acknowledge it, then leave it in my wake. It's not the repository of truth and meaning for me the way it is with you. I accept what's been—and that's all. I leave a space in my thoughts for events, for people. Like a little memorial: a plaque.'

'Nothing more than that—ever?'

'No: nothing more. I see the past in a clear light. I also see there's a dangerous aspect to it, like a mirage: like a lost love—all it has to offer is nostalgia, and longing for what was, or even worse, what might have been. I don't give house room in my mind to hopes and dreams that didn't become real.'

'That's because you don't have any of those,' I said to him: 'Your life's what you dreamed it should be.'

'Is that what you think? Really?'

'Well—it's true you did want to write novels in the style of Dos Passos at one point: on the whole I think it's a good thing that didn't happen—and there was the verse-tragedy phase that went nowhere as well.'

'When you jump off the springboard into life you have to be committed to your choices: stay with them; keep to them always. I did—you've watched me, you know it's true—I live with that knowledge: and with the consequences. We both see what's happened to me: you see it—very clearly, even if you pretend not to out of kindness: my path to art's turned into a dead end: all I do now is buy it. I have to laugh: that's what's left to me—money buys the fuel for the pyre of my hopes.'

'You used to say you were as creative in collecting as any artist: only you were working with ideas and affinities, not technique, not form.'

'The kind of consoling lie I liked to tell myself. How bitter to hear it recited back to me.'

We were close to the pier's end. He stopped. He looked me in the eye again.

'I came here a week ago: before Davos. Alone. It was early in the morning: rainy weather: scudding clouds, their shadows moving on the lake. I walked out almost to the jetty's end, to just a few steps in front of where we're standing now. Something happened. The light changed: the contrasts between dark and bright strengthened: the far shore was blotted out; there was a pulse in the water, and at the same time a sound: I could scarcely hear it: a hiss, a constant whisper—I shielded my eyes to see—I gazed out—I glanced behind me: I was in the image; the near shore was gone too—no buildings, no cars, nothing, just the pier vanishing into a shining haze.'

He turned away from me, then back. He tried to smile.

'Go on,' I said.

'I listened: I strained to hear: the pulsing strengthened: there was an echo in it now, a voice hidden in it: it was coming from the water: it knew me—it was for me—it was speaking, the same thing over and over—it was saying to me: "Dissolve: return—come." How dark it was in those moments: everything dark; everything gone. I don't know how it ended: I pulled away—it was so close to me—it was claiming me. It was frightful: death won't be that dark.'

'That's not what you were seeing?'

'It wasn't an end—it wasn't emptiness; not at all: it was something else—more like a sentence being passed: a judgement.'

He put his hands to his eyes, and bowed his head.

'I'm sorry,' he said softly—I could barely hear him: 'Forgive me.'

And he sank down on one of the wooden benches beside the ferry landing stage. I sat beside him, and reached my arm over his shoulder.

'Be still,' I said: 'Let your feelings leave you. Let them go.'

He began to breathe more evenly. There was silence—then he lifted up his head: a look of relief came over his face. He turned towards me and began to laugh.

'How strange it is! I am calmer now. I am. It's gone. What I couldn't do for myself you did for me.'

'I'm glad,' I said.

'I have a theory—of course.'

'Of course.'

'About what I was seeing, hearing. It was like seeing behind the face of things; seeing for an instant past their surface; listening to the secret at the heart of life. I was overwhelmed at first: swept off balance.

It took me a while to work it out: be sure it wasn't just my own demons chasing me down.'

'And?'

'It was something outside me: I know it. There's a resonance all around us here. It's far beyond our compass: it comes weighing down on our shoulders: that's the darkness—that's the burden. And I know you feel it too. You've always felt it: all through this landscape. That's why you stay so guardedly, so pointedly away. Why I was amazed to see you here.'

He swung round to check my reaction: he was himself again: he sprang up, paced over to the far railing, leaned against it, then turned back to me. 'I'm right, aren't I? That's the reason.'

'There's a hundred reasons,' I said: 'We should move. See the storm coming—from the far side?'

'Of course I see it. That's why we should stay. Storms sweep down onto us to intensify our feelings; to confirm them—they don't come for nothing. And this one's well-timed. There's something else I have to tell you. It came to me when we were talking earlier: something simple: about the way you see the world and your place in it.'

'Is that so? You've told me how I ought to change my life—now you want to tell me how to think as well?'

'Don't be defensive like that—not with me. You keep your ramparts up so high, you're still so aloof: so self-contained—or at least you think you are—but the moment I came over and sat with you in the hotel dining room I realised—I could tell; I could see it in your face.'

'See what?'

'How caught you are; how lost. You're at the midpoint of your life. You should be master of yourself—it's the time for control, for clarity: but they aren't with you. The past's fading from you, it can't guide you anymore, and the future's veiled, you can't see its shape, you're not even sure it's there.'

'To me that sounds very much like you,' I said to him: 'You on this pier—a week ago. You're projecting.'

'Am I? Really? Yet here you are, like me: circling back to your beginnings.'

'It's pure chance I'm here. A chain of accidents. Nothing more meaningful than that.'

'Always an answer for everything. Words for everything. You've known so much, you've spent so long searching, looking, watching—reading every clue and pattern you can find around you—but your eyes look out, not in. It's just the way you said it: you don't see the simplest things about yourself.'

'You always go too far, don't you, Blaize,' I said: 'You always have.'

I turned to leave him. He held me back.

'Let me,' he said: 'Let me reach you. There were times when you reached me, before—by being a friend to me, by not judging me. You helped me—more than you could ever know. Don't be proud and hard—not with me—not now. Let me give you something: just this once.'

'So give, then. Give, if you can—go ahead.'

'Remember when we first met?'

'The nostalgia card. You've got nothing else?'

'Do you? Do you even know where it was?'

'It was in prehistory: why should I? I suppose it was at school in Zuoz.'

'You're wrong. It was before that—it was at the Rosenberg in St. Gallen. And Serghiana Ismailovna was with you: she brought you. You didn't want her to leave you there. She knew my father somehow: she spoke to us—she took me aside; she told me to look after you. "Keep an eye on him," she said to me: "Keep him on an even keel: stop him from running away." I'd never met a grown-up quite that fearsome and commanding. "I'll try," I said. "Don't try," she snapped at me: "Succeed—promise it." And off she swept.'

'And you failed. On both counts: spectacularly!'

'I'm still trying now.'

'And the point of your excursion into childhood memories?'

'The point is that this morning when I was sitting with you I brought up your great-aunts: at once your face contorted: it was as if I'd stabbed you. And suddenly I saw how much you still miss them: both of them: what an ocean of sadness there is inside you.'

'Of course I miss them: and there are other figures I miss just as much—as you know well—more. I'd be inhuman if I didn't feel that way. But you think they're with me, in my mind, haunting me constantly. That's not the way it is—they're not.'

Back he leaned against the railings, silhouetted by the storm clouds, and gave me a long look, as if weighing me on some unseen balance scale. I waited for a fresh blow to parry. None came. His face became gentler.

'My poor friend,' he said: 'You really don't see what I'm leading up to, do you?'

'Enlighten me, then. And skip the lesson: jump through to what you're trying to say.'

'You write constantly—you probably do it in your sleep. You spend your life travelling to torn, dark places and describing them. You write whole books about the lives of others; you waste your time imagining new worlds and new dramas—you make them up to hide what's there inside you: your golden grief, your secret story of the ones you've lost. Serghiana; Palafay; the death closest to you we won't speak of. But everyone suffers like you. Everyone has to lose the people they most love. Those before us die to lead us on: that's the way of things. It's ordinary.'

'Did I ever suggest otherwise to you?'

'You never said or suggested anything at all—about any of this.'

I gave a theatrical sigh.

'You're not on stage,' he said then: 'The pen you hold; the words you write; the mind that makes them—what good are they to you the way you use them? What's the point to them when there's a silence inside you that rules everything? What? Tell me.'

I raised my eyes to him. He returned my look.

'You glare back at me like a trapped animal, run to ground—cornered and trying to get away. Like one of those wild dogs in the desert that gnaws off its leg to break free from a trap.'

'Quite an image for a banker to come up with!' I said to him.

His face was calm. 'Not one of your finer efforts. You can hurt me more than that and still not make me flinch!'

'Are you really saying what I think you are?'

'I am,' he answered: 'And you know I am. I'm saying that the moment's come. The key to that trap's in your hands. Tell the story that's burned into you, the one that means the most to you. Don't be a writer who writes everything except the thing that matters. Leave fiction behind you. Give breath to the ghosts inside you. Tell the story you know best.'